**RAGS**

At the end of the year, the old assistant at the Hampstead shop contracted pneumonia and had to stop working. Leo leaped at the opportunity to take his place, preferably in a slightly more managerial capacity. Nathan discussed it with his brother-in-law, who couldn't understand the dilemma.

'But you've been telling us for six months how good he's been – how the business has improved. You're lucky, he's a real asset to you. I mean, look at Bernard's boy!' said the brother-in-law.

'But you don't understand,' said Nathan. 'He's so independent. He's not good to please me, he's good because he wants to be. He seems to be wanting to prove himself all the time.'

'So what's wrong with that? To be ambitious, that's healthy. He works hard, he causes you no trouble. So he wants to run the Hampstead shop – let him,' said his relation.

'But he's only sixteen still,' protested Nathan.

'But he's bright, he's very bright. These types of boys are always old for their age.'

Nathan shook his head. 'I'm not so sure,' he frowned. 'I'm not so sure . . .'

But of course he knew he would give in to Leo.

**About the Author**

Peter Burden was born in 1948 and educated by the Jesuits at Beaumont College which he left at the age of 16. After various jobs ranging from ICI to West End Interior Decorators, he entered the rag-trade, buying and selling ethnic fashions. This led, in 1975, to the founding of Midnight Blue, a chain of shops and a brand of jeans. The original shop still flourishes in the Fulham Road.

Peter Burden lives in London with his wife and young son. RAGS is his first novel.

'A racy tale of the swinging sixties boutique trade, *Rags* is an effortless but by no means inelegant read'

*Company*

# Rags

Peter Burden

**NEW ENGLISH LIBRARY**
Hodder and Stoughton

**British Library C.I.P.**

Burden, Peter
  Rags.
  I. Title
  823'.914 [F]    PR6052.U/

  ISBN 0-450-42398-0

TO THE MEMORY OF
LAWRENCE KLONARIS
AND
EDWARD BROTHERTON-RATCLIFFE
TWO FRIENDS I SHALL MISS

# Acknowledgements

A host of thoughtful and tolerant men and women provided help, hospitality and encouragement in the writing of this first novel, among them Gill Coleridge, Victoria Petrie-Hay, Mark Daniel, Stanley Myers, Mark Sykes, Harvey Sambrook, Damian Russell, Diana and Anthony Mackay, Michael Pearson, Derek Armandias, Charles Sawyer-Hoare, Crescent Giffard, Beryl Williams, John Scott-Lewis of El Tesorillo, the Neilsons of Catton, the Dyotts of Freeford, the Percevals of Pillaton, and my wife, Didi.

My thanks to them and all the others who helped.

# 1984

'How long does a body last in a thing like that?'

It was a casual enquiry, uncompromisingly Yorkshire.

The detective from the Murder Squad stood beside his boss in the main security office at Heathrow's Terminal 3. He was in his late twenties, wearing well-faded jeans and a Wrangler jacket. The two men were silhouetted against the grey March morning that feebly penetrated a full-length window. They gloomily contemplated the activity on the concrete apron sixty feet below.

An oblong, aluminium container, like a giant professional photographer's kit-box, was being gingerly offered up to the rear underside of an Air India 747. Two loaders tentatively, and needlessly, fingered the container as a fork-lift truck began to raise it high into the bowels of the plane.

The senior man turned, and looked with disapproval at his sergeant's appearance.

'That container is constructed along the lines of a thermos flask. Even if there isn't sufficient refrigeration in the cargo hold, it'll keep quite happily till the ceremony in Varanasi.' His clipped London accent matched his small trim moustache, grey covert coat and dark suede brogues. As he spoke he pulled a small aluminium tube from an inside pocket of his coat. He studied it for a moment, unscrewed the cap at one end, and slid out a firmly rolled Montecristo No. 4. With his canine tooth, he carefully nicked the rounded end of the cigar and surreptitiously spat a small piece of tobacco leaf into a wastepaper bin. He spoke between puffs as he lit it.

1

'This is one of the few perks of investigating the murder of a very rich man.' He crumpled up the tube and threw it into the bin.

His assistant was looking at the spot where the large aluminium container had disappeared from sight. Now the other passengers' baggage was being fed into the same opening.

'Sir, why couldn't they cremate him here?' He rubbed his unshaven chin. 'I mean, it wasn't as though he was particularly religious. He didn't even come from India.'

'I'm not so sure that he wasn't religious.' The detective inspector continued to suck his cigar vigorously. 'Anyway, he's obviously not taking any chances. I'm told that Hindu funeral rites require that the body is washed in yoghurt, then placed on a pyre. More wood is stacked over the body, then the whole thing is lit and left to burn for three days. After this, the family crack the skull to release the spirit, gather up the ashes, and chuck them in the Ganges.' The little moustache twitched up on one side. 'This is hard to achieve in East Finchley, so if you're a half-way committed Hindu, and rich, your family sends your body to India.'

His sergeant looked doubtful.

'I don't know how committed Kalianji was. Nobody seems to have known the man. No one I interviewed really seemed to miss him; people don't miss people they don't know.'

On this case he had done far more interviewing than his boss. Normally he would have had a pretty good idea of the dead man's personality by now; but in the case of Raju Kalianji, there were constant anomalies and conflicts among the impressions that he had been given. The press-cuttings' file had been even more confusing. One week Kalianji would be partying with the hyper-rich in Gstaad, and the next he would be opening a centre for Hindu studies in Birmingham. He had left a fortune approaching fifty million, but his widow seemed neither happy nor sad – she had just kept on quietly saying: 'He didn't deserve to be shot.'

The senior detective broke into his thoughts.

'Any sign of the mourning party yet?'

'Oh, yes, Sir – I should have said. They're all gathered. They're in the security VIP lounge.' He nodded towards an internal window at the side of the office. 'We can see them through that two-way mirror.'

'Right, let's take a look.'

They walked over and gazed, frustrated, into a room furnished with a small bar, a number of low tables, sofas and chairs, designed to impress, not for comfort.

There were six people there. A small Indian boy of six or seven was sitting, tearful and dazed, on a sofa between a sari-clad woman of considerable beauty, evidently his mother, and a small, attractive English woman in her late thirties.

On either side of a round coffee-table were a tall, blond man, about forty, well-dressed and self-assured, and his tastefully presented wife. They were talking to each other in quiet, considerate voices, trying to avoid the bleak eyes of an old wrinkled Indian woman, who was wedged into an uncomfortable armchair, and weeping without restraint.

The detective inspector sighed and shook his head slowly.

For all he knew, any one of these people, except, he supposed, the small boy, might have arranged to have had Raju Kalianji shot. But he had been unable to present any case for restricting their movements.

'I suppose if one of that lot doesn't come back, that could give us a lead,' suggested the DS.

'Thank you, Sergeant, very helpful. Now get your notes and let's run through these people again.'

The younger man pulled a dog-eared notebook from a pocket of his jacket.

'Right. Reading from left to right: the good-looking Indian lady; Reena Kalianji – Raj's widow. Married in 1975 by arrangement between their parents. Born in Uganda; came to England with her family in 1969. The lad next to her is Paul Kalianji, only child of Raj and Reena; aged seven.'

As he talked, the aluminium container in the hold of the 747 was unceremoniously nudged along by one of the handlers. Inside it, the blue-grey corpse rolled for a moment from side to side, then settled back on the tightly confining padded lining. There was a full complement of passengers and a lot of excess baggage on the ten o'clock flight to Delhi. A pair of elegant Italian suitcases tumbled down and nestled beside the metal casket.

The lugubrious Leeds tones of the detective sergeant continued.

'The blond English bloke: Simon Riley MP, Junior Minister at the Home Office, and expected to go on to even greater things.' He glanced at his boss. 'I thought it was going to be very awkward dealing with him, but he was really helpful. Of all the people I saw, he was the one who seemed most keen for us to get a result – I mean, I think he wanted it from a personal point of view, not just political.'

'Don't you believe it, Sergeant. Politicians always tell you that they want things for deeply held personal reasons. That's their charm. But carry on.'

'Right, Sir. The dark-haired lady with Mr Riley is Claire Riley, American, née Calloway, from Virginia. Married Riley in '73. Claims to have known Kalianji quite well. Confirms that he and her husband had known each other for years – denies that they had any business dealings.' He paused and turned over a few pages of his notebook. 'Ah, yes, the old Indian lady in the red sari: Kalianji's mother. Born in Uganda – arrived here in '72 with her family, husband died two years ago. Didn't get much from her – hardly speaks a word of English. She's about sixty and doesn't seem to realise that her son was murdered.'

He shifted his gaze to the white woman who sat on one side of the small brown boy. A mass of well-organised loose curls of shiny dark brown hair enveloped the woman's small, utterly appealing face. Her features suggested both vulnerability and determination. Her dark brown eyes moved slowly and thoughtfully above a small, straight nose and a mouth, not quite too large, that seemed

4

to offer comfort and excitement. She was in her late thirties, the DS knew, though she looked younger and was dressed with a plain elegance in a trench coat that would certainly never see a trench, and short, squashy-ankled boots.

'That is Sarah Freeman, highest-flying designer of clothes for the girl in the street. Very tasty, wouldn't you say? But tough. She was managing director of Kalianji's rag-trade operations. She wasn't much help though. She answered all my questions okay, but she offered no theories of her own. Said she was as mystified as anyone – and she didn't seem too put out.'

The detective inspector was still nodding thoughtfully when the door of the VIP lounge was opened and another man joined the party.

He was about five feet ten, lean and carrying himself with easy energy. His strong, sensual features were deeply tanned and framed by thick, dark wavy hair, grey at the temples. Deep lines were etched in his forehead and between his eyebrows. He was wearing Gucci shoes and a well-cut suit of pale beige, light-weight cloth.

He walked into the room, giving only a hint of the discomfort he was feeling.

'I'm not coming with you.' His voice echoed through relay speakers. 'I've just come here to give Reena and Paul my condolences.'

He shook hands with everyone and patted the boy on the head. He poured himself a whisky at the bar and stood for a while without saying anything, looking at each of the mourners.

Behind the mirror, the DS's little moustache twitched slightly.

'Now, there's one man I didn't expect to see here; not now he's come back and taken over the whole show. Mind you, he was the man that started Rags.'

'I haven't seen him before. Who is he?' asked the DS, who was too young to remember the big names from the Swinging Sixties.

'That's Leo Freeman.'

5

# 1959

The army surplus store stood at the bottom of Hampstead Road, just before it reaches Euston Road. Nine o'clock on a Saturday morning, and the owner had just come down from his flat above and opened the front door of the shop from the inside. He shuffled down the narrow space between the metal racking shelves, glancing either side of him at the piles of military paraphernalia – Primus stoves, greatcoats, bayonets, horses' nose-bags, webbing gaiters and gas masks – all obsolete – all the result of over-ordering by pessimistic quartermasters. Now, in 1959, he was one of the few people still making money out of the Second World War.

He knew his stock intimately. He could recall every Ministry of Defence auction that he had ever attended and he remembered the prices that he had paid for everything in his shop, down to the last pair of Royal Marines' long johns. In his little glass-windowed cubicle in the back corner of the shop, he lit a cigarette and a Primus stove to boil a kettle for his first pot of tea. He sat on an old metal cantilevered chair and put his feet on a gap among the jumble of papers on his open roll-top desk. He rubbed his unshaven chin and opened the *Daily Sketch*.

The shop door clicked open with a rattle. Someone rummaged. He carried on reading – his clientele derived a lot of satisfaction in finding what they wanted without any help from him. After a while, he heard the potential customer approaching his little cubicle. A boy with curly, dark hair and bright, deep brown eyes watched him defiantly through the open door.

The owner of the shop was amused; he had seen many avid young bargain hunters, fanatical to increase their collection within the limitations of their pocket-money; though this boy, maybe fourteen, looked more determined than most. In his left hand, he held a small, square satchel made of khaki webbing. It was a standard dispatch satchel, with a broad webbing shoulder strap and a single brass buckle. He pointed at it with his free hand.

'How much is this?' he asked in a husky, north London voice.

The shopkeeper nodded towards it. 'There's a price tag on it. You look old enough to read.'

'I'm old enough to read, and I'm too old for fairy stories.' He fingered the dangling tag. 'This says five bob.'

'That's right,' said the shopkeeper. 'If you want it, give me five bob. If you don't, put it back,' and he turned back to his *Daily Sketch*.

The boy looked slightly surprised.

'Sir,' he said, with a broad, winsome smile spreading across his face, 'I really want it badly, but I've only got a shilling.'

'Oh, have you?' The man sighed. He knew every bargaining ploy in the book, but still wasn't immune to some of them. 'Well, if you promise to stop pestering me, you can have it for half a crown.'

The boy looked fiercely disappointed.

'Come on, here's a shilling,' he said, pulling a coin from his trousers pocket. He offered it to the shopkeeper, who started to shake his head. The boy came into the glass cubbyhole and slapped the shilling piece down onto the desk.

'Go on. Take it,' he said, urgently persuasive.

The man gave in. His eyeballs rolled up.

'Blimey. All right, all right.' He reached over and took the shilling. 'You're a bit young to be pushing so hard. What's your name?'

'Leo. Leo Freeman.'

'Well, Leo, you've got yourself a bargain there. I paid more than a shilling for those bags.'

Leo was sceptical.

'I bet you didn't,' he said. 'You wouldn't have taken my shilling if you had.'

The shopkeeper studied the boy. It was quite true – he had paid £22.10s.0d. for a parcel of fifty dozen satchels – nine pence apiece. As he looked at the boy he thought how he had always wanted a son like him; clever, and with that special determination which marked the ambitious man from an early age. And this was a likeable kid, in a cheeky sort of way.

'Anyway, son, there it is. You got your bag for a bob, so let me get on and read the paper.'

But Leo wasn't going.

'Sir,' he said, 'how many more of those satchels have you got?'

'Oh, I dunno, thirty, forty maybe.'

'I counted seventy on the rack out there,' said Leo. 'Have you got some more in your storeroom?'

'Why do you want to know?'

'I might have some friends who'd want them. I'll come back at half-ten to see how many you've got – all right?' Leo turned to make his way out through the cluttered shop.

'Hang on!' said the scruffy trader. 'How many do you want?'

'A hundred. At a shilling a bag that's a fiver – right?'

The man was resigned. 'All right. I'll get you out a hundred, and make sure you're back in an hour.'

Leo's father, Nathan, owned two small, old-fashioned tailors' shops, one in Whitechapel and one in Haverstock Hill, Hampstead. Nathan's chief cutter had a son of nineteen called Charlie, who drove the shop van, a gleaming grey Austin A35 with 'N. FREEMAN, BESPOKE TAILORS' painted on it. Leo had persuaded Charlie to help him this Saturday morning. He hadn't told him why.

The older boy was waiting in the van for Leo outside the Hampstead shop. He was annoyed with himself for letting this pipsqueak son of his father's boss talk him into wasting a Saturday morning and, maybe, getting into trouble. He wasn't supposed to use the van for personal journeys. But it was hard to say no to Leo.

Leo leaped into the passenger seat.

'Hello, Charlie, glad you're here. We've got to be down the bottom of Hampstead Road at half past ten.'

'What are we doing there?' asked Charlie.

'Oh, we're picking up a bit of stock I've bought,' said Leo vaguely.

'Stock? What for? For the shops?'

'No, no, for a bit of private trading I'm doing.'

'How can you do trading?' laughed Charlie. 'You're still at school doing your GCEs.'

'Yeah, well, there's a lot of potential customers at Highgate Grammar, and I can't survive on the pocket-money my dad gives me.' He paused and decided to confide a little. 'You know that old client, Mr Whittaker? I was in the Hampstead shop just before Christmas, and he came in to pick up a suit. He saw me and gave me a fiver and said, "See what you can make out of that." Dad tried to make me give it back, but I reckon Mr Whittaker knows how tight he is with me and said, "If your son gives me back that fiver, Mr Freeman, I'll feel very insulted and won't get my suits made here any more." Well, that was it – no argument after that.'

Leo pulled the large, important-looking banknote from his pocket and waved it triumphantly.

'Anyway – I've bought a bit of stock and I've got to get it back home.'

He folded his arms and put his feet on the windscreen ledge. He was tasting for the first time the excitement of making a really good buy.

For three weeks, since he had been given the five-pound note, he had been pondering what to do with it. He didn't want to buy anything for himself. Ever since he had been at the grammar school, he had been so ashamed of getting only sixpence a week pocket-money, that he had made up for it by boasting about the size of his father's business. He exaggerated a lot and said that when he was older, he would own it all. Meanwhile, he said, he was saving all his pocket-money to start his own business, and that was why he didn't spend any money now. He was confident and convincing – the other boys believed him.

Before making a decision about this unexpected piece of capital, he had waited to find out what was the most coveted of Christmas presents that any of his school mates had received.

Playing at soldiers was as popular a boyhood pastime as ever. There was a constant demand for any piece of equipment with which to authenticate military games. One of the boys had been given an ex-WD dispatch rider's satchel. When it appeared at school as a substitute for the standard leather satchel, it had been admired for its ruggedness and soldierly connections. Leo had quickly decided that this would be an easy item to sell, and doggedly had set about looking for a source.

They pulled up outside the surplus store.

'This is it,' Leo said. 'Open up the back doors and hang on there till I tell you.'

He clambered out of the van and dashed into the shop. At the back, he found the owner, who looked up without surprise.

'You back then?' said the shopkeeper. 'I thought you were just boasting.'

'Never mind that,' said Leo. 'Have you got a hundred of those bags?'

'Matter of fact I have. There's two cartons of four dozen each, and four loose ones, just out there.' He pointed to two cardboard boxes just outside the door of his office. 'But look, son, you can't have 'em at a shilling each. I only gave you one at that price because you said you wanted it for yourself. You can't want a hundred for yourself.'

A look of disbelief and disappointment clouded Leo's eyes.

'I'm sorry, son, but they'll have to be one and six.'

Leo was furious.

'But you agreed! You sold me one for a shilling. I know you made a profit on that, now you'll make a hundred times that profit – and I want those hundred bags a hundred times more than I wanted the single one.' He changed his tactics slightly. 'Go on,' with a broad grin and sparkling eyes, 'if I do all right with these, I'll be back for more. I could be your best customer!'

The man gave a snort of friendly laughter. He had known all along he was going to accept Leo's fiver but he had wanted to see him work for it, just a bit. 'All right, you horrible little rogue, give us the fiver – but don't expect me to help you carry out the goods.'

With relief, Leo thrust over the five-pound note, and ran out of the shop to fetch Charlie.

'Come on, it's only two cartons.'

Charlie picked up one box, Leo put the loose satchels on top of it, and picked up the other box himself. They put them in the back of the van, got in the front and turned back towards where Leo lived.

After a while, Charlie remarked, 'I don't know why you needed the van for those two little cartons.'

'I thought a hundred of those bags would take up more room,' said Leo. He stopped talking suddenly and turned round to look at the cartons. 'Good God,' he said. 'I hope there are forty-eight in each box.' His face paled – he might have been taken for a ride! 'Stop the van. I want to go and count them.' With his heart pounding, he leaped out and ran round to the back. Why, he thought, *why* didn't I check them at the shop? The old bastard's robbed me! He'll never admit it – and I didn't get a receipt.

He opened the back of the van and pulled one of the cartons towards him. It was sealed as if it had never been opened. On the side of the box was stencilled: 'Purse, Dispatch, Khaki, 48. WD 1944.' He felt a little relieved, but tore open the box and pulled out the contents. A minute later, a surge of relief flooded through him. There were forty-eight, tightly folded and packed. He put them back in the box, shut the doors of the van, and rejoined Charlie in the front.

'All right?' asked Charlie.

Leo nodded.

'What d'you want with all them bags anyway?'

Leo looked at him pityingly. 'I told you, Charlie, for some private trading.'

'But who's gonna want them?' asked his driver persistently.

'I'll worry about that, Charlie, and when they're all sold, I'll give you ten bob for helping me pick them up.'

When they reached Leo's home in Salmon Street, he was relieved to see that his parents' car wasn't outside. His father would have taken the bus into Hampstead, and his mother must be out shopping. Leo and Charlie carried the boxes round the side of the house, through the back door and up to Leo's bedroom.

'Thanks, Charlie,' Leo winked and patted his helper on the back. 'I'll have that ten bob for you in a couple of weeks.'

Charlie, puzzled by the whole notion of Leo buying and selling things, left, glad to get back to the normality of his own company.

Leo started to unpack the boxes, and stuff the satchels under his bed. The door opened quietly behind him. He looked round. His sister, Sarah, stared at him with wide brown eyes. She was just thirteen, still small for her age, dressed in a plain shift that her mother had made. Her wild brown hair was caught up into two unruly bunches. She was fascinated by her older brother, by everything that he did. She loved to hear him explaining things to her. He seemed to know so much more about everyday things than her parents did. And in return for the eager audience she provided, Leo confided in her. He had told her all about his hopes and plans: how he wanted one day to make 'N. FREEMAN, BESPOKE TAILORS' into a huge business, like Marks & Spencer, how he hated sitting in school studying languages he would never speak and a past in which he had no interest.

Sarah worshipped him and fiercely, loyally, respected these confidences. Now she asked, 'What are you going to do with those funny bags?'

12

'I'm going to sell them at school. They all want them instead of their old leather satchels.' He threw one over to her. 'Here, what d'you think? They'll never wear out. This stuff was made for soldiers crawling around through jungles and mountains and what have you. It's very tough.' He tried to pull one apart to demonstrate. Sarah was impressed, but doubtful.

'But they're not very smart,' she said.

'That's why people want them,' Leo said confidently. 'It's the only thing they can wear that isn't uniform. Don't worry. I only paid a bob each for them, and I'll sell 'em for half a crown, maybe three and six.'

Sarah was reassured. 'Can I have one?' she asked.

'Yeah, 'course – if you give me three and six.' He laughed. 'I'll tell you what. When there's only one left, I'll do you a special price.'

After lunch, Leo met some friends for a game of flip-football in the back of a café in the High Street. When he returned at six for his tea, he was met in the hall by his father. Nathan looked furious. He thrust one of the webbing bags beneath Leo's nose.

'What's this, Leo?'

Leo shrugged defiantly. 'What do you think, Dad? It's an army pouch.'

'Don't be so cheeky with me, Leo. I know what it is. But what are you doing with it and hundreds more like it? Where did you get them? *How* did you get them?'

'I bought them in an army surplus shop with that five pounds Mr Whittaker gave me,' said Leo expressionlessly.

'What – hundreds of them?' His father waved expansively.

'Only a hundred; they were a shilling each – that's five pounds.'

'I can add up, Leo. Don't try and be smart. What are you going to do with them?'

'That's my business,' said Leo.

'You're my son – my only son – so it's my business, too. You're a schoolboy. Why are you hoarding army bags?'

'When I said it's my business, Dad, I meant it's my trading business. I'm going to sell them at school.'

'You're what? My son, my bright, clever son is going to hawk old rubbish round the grammar school! My God, is this what me and your mother have worked so hard for, to give you a nice home, a position – and now you want to be a street trader.' He spread his hands in despair, and then took his son by the shoulders. 'Leo – I forbid it. We'll take the bags back to the shop and you ask for your money back.'

'You can't do that, Dad!' yelled Leo. 'I spent ages bargaining with him. You can't blame me for wanting to make some extra money. You only give me sixpence a week pocket-money. You won't let me help in the shop on Saturdays or in the holidays, so I can earn a bit. You won't let me get a bicycle. All the other boys have bikes and money to spend. I can't even go to the pictures – some of them go three times a week. It was my money! I haven't done anything wrong, and there's a lot of boys who want these satchels, so I'm helping them – doing them a favour. I'll only ask three and six, and the shops charge five bob. What's wrong with that? Anyway, I won't tell you where the shop is – and you can't confiscate them. They're not doing any harm. If you want to blame someone, blame yourself for giving me so little money.' He shook his shoulders free from his father's grasp, lowered his head and stormed to his bedroom.

On a wet Sunday morning, Miriam Freeman came back from the Whitechapel Hospital with her first child. Nathan had somehow persuaded the tricky old pawnbroker, whose premises adjoined his little tailor's shop in Commercial Street, to lend his old Austin for the short journey.

It was May 1944. Londoners had completely forgotten what peacetime was like. Shortages, waiting and inconvenience were endemic to every activity. Business was terrible, but then it had never been good since, in 1932, Nathan and Miriam, in their early twenties and eager, had taken over his father's shop. Through the charity

14

of Miriam's relations, they had re-established the little business but, in spite of Nathan's skill and diligence, they could barely scrape a living from four or five suits a month. Then, when the V1s were beginning to drop all over London and Miriam announced her pregnancy, Nathan didn't know whether to be terrified or excited about the prospect of a child.

When a healthy son was born, he decided to be excited. The son, a good eight pounds, was named Lionel, and soon became known as 'Little Leo'. Little Leo had thick black hair and bright brown eyes, which even then Nathan found disturbingly alert and restless. The child was paraded around all the relations with great pride, and shown to Rabbi Salaman from the Whitechapel Synagogue; arrangements were made for his circumcision. There was no doubt, the family all said so, that he was an exceptional little fellow. He hardly cried, he looked at everything, and he smiled a lot. Meanwhile, as the European war was ending, Nathan felt a surge of optimism – now he had a son to work for. With a smile on his face, and a joke for everyone he met, he found more and more people coming to spend what they could on new suits for their demobilised sons. Good cloth was hard to find, but somehow he always managed to wheedle something, only slightly illicitly, out of his friends among the textile merchants. Some of London's leading black marketeers were proud to tell their friends that they were wearing a 'Natty Freeman' suit.

Leo learnt to walk and speak, and became a great favourite with the customers. Someone taught him to wink one eye, and he discovered that he could count on an approving or affectionate response whenever his father said, 'Come on, Leo, give the gentleman a smile and a wink,' and he obliged. When he was five, his father proudly saw him down to the primary school off Plumbers Row, a new cap bouncing on top of his curly black hair.

Eighteen months after Leo was born, Miriam gave birth to a daughter, Sarah. She became a pretty, clever girl. Because she never knew any different, she accepted as normal the family's adulation of Leo.

Nathan's business had grown substantially. He was no spendthrift and had carefully built up his trade. He had successfully trained two young cutters to cope with the increase and the shop, always neat and freshly clean, had that pleasing air of quiet bustle that is peculiar to the successful tailor. For nearly twenty years, Nathan and Miriam lived in the small flat above the shop, but now there was enough money to buy a house, somewhere away from the noise and busy streets of Whitechapel. They decided to move, like many of their friends and relations, out to Highgate, where it bordered with Golders Green.

Salmon Street was a wide avenue of detached villas. Leo made full use of the garden and space. He was now a well-developed nine-year-old, and loved the chance to climb trees and to run about in the open. He quickly sensed that they had gone up in the world. At his new school lots of the children's parents had cars and lived in similar houses to his. Most of the families around them were Jewish, and the influence of the Rabbi prevailed among many of them, as it did in his. Miriam and Nathan weren't fanatical about their religion, but it was an important part of being Jewish, alongside the traditional cultural values of thrift, hard work, honesty and respect for the family. They enjoyed their increasingly high standard of living, but they weren't flamboyant. They kept their expectations within realistic limits.

The plan for Leo was that, after a good, practical education, he would join his father in the business and eventually take it over when Nathan retired. So far, Leo's performance had been encouraging. He was fit, healthy, eager to know the answers. Sometimes, though, he showed a disturbing lack of respect for the status quo.

When they had all gone down to The Mall to join the vast crowd watching the Coronation procession, Leo had been intrigued by the importance of the Queen. Why did she have Buckingham Palace? Why did hundreds of colourful soldiers ride beside her? Why was everyone cheering for her? Why was that ordinary-looking boy in the carriage behind her?

Leo wondered what these people had done to deserve such adulation. Miriam told him: 'But she's the Queen, and one day the little boy will be King.'

'Why? Are they very clever?'

'They're a very important family,' said Nathan solemnly. 'They've ruled England for hundreds of years.'

'But Dad, what do they do?' Leo persisted.

Miriam often became annoyed with Leo's constant questioning and frustrated by her inability to give satisfactory answers.

'Now look, Leo. She's the Queen and she's the head of the country and that's that,' she said.

Leo decided then and there that if these people could be so important, then one day he would be too. He looked forward to riding down The Mall in a carriage, with a million people cheering him.

'How much does a golden coach cost?' he asked. 'Are the horses expensive?'

Nathan sighed. 'A lot of money, Leo. More money than you'll ever have.' Leo didn't think so, but he thought he'd better not say so.

He took the eleven-plus exam, the 'Scholarship' his parents called it, when he was ten. He passed. The following autumn he started at Highgate Grammar School. His mother pressed his flannel shorts to a fine crease, and his father taught him to knot his tie neatly.

He found the work easy and without trying he consistently came top of his class. He was a little younger than the others in his form, and didn't make himself popular by pointing this out to them.

Neither did he make himself popular by selling the army satchels. Leo's instincts had been right; all his classmates wanted one, and they grudgingly paid up the three and six he demanded. They knew he was profiteering and resented him for it. But Leo forced himself not to care, and saw his five pounds turn into seventeen pounds ten shillings.

The girl had long, light brown hair that hung smoothly to her shoulders then flicked up and outward in a neat wave.

Leo could see that she was looking at him with interest. Her blue eyes had a humorous naughtiness in them as she gazed through the shop window of 'N. FREEMAN, BESPOKE TAILORS', at the top of Haverstock Hill.

Leo was sitting behind the counter at the end of a quiet January Saturday. His father and the cutter had gone home at lunch-time, but Leo liked to stay on the off-chance that a serious customer might call in if they saw the shop still open.

He looked back at the girl, smiled and winked at her. She grinned, and he beckoned her to come in. The 'ting' of the bell as the shop door swung open coincided with the tingle of excitement that suddenly pervaded Leo's young body. The girl shut the door behind her and stood for a moment, looking around at the dark wooden panelling, the pin-striped cloth draped over a felt torso and the bolts of suitings neatly shelved behind him.

'Can I help you, madam?' Leo was ironically servile. 'A nice tweed for the country? Something dark for the more formal occasion? If you wouldn't mind stepping over here, I'll just take a few measurements.' He draped a tape-measure round his neck and walked round from behind the counter.

'I was really looking for underwear,' the girl giggled. 'I've broken my suspender belt. Perhaps you could repair it for me.'

'Well, corsetry's not really our line,' replied Leo, whose body was telling him that a fantasy might just be coming true, 'but we like to think we'll turn our hands to anything to oblige a customer.' He stood close to her now, nervously pulling the tape-measure back and forth behind his neck. He guessed that she must be nineteen or twenty, three or four years older than him – and experienced. And she watched him greedily – his fit, eager body, laughing eyes and full, smiling lips.

Leo remembered that a client had left a bottle of whisky as a present, and that it was still unopened on a shelf in the stock-room.

'We usually entertain our more valued customers with

a drink in the private salon, while we discuss their requirements in detail,' he said, putting one arm round her waist and indicating the door at the back of the shop with the other.

'Oh, thank you,' said the girl primly, then giggled and walked slowly towards the stock-room. Leo quickly shot the bolt on the front door and flicked the 'open' sign to 'closed'. He followed the girl into the back room, shut the door and invited her to sit on the only, rickety bent-wood chair.

'Madam, would you like a whisky?' he asked, reaching to the back of the shelf for the bottle of Johnny Walker. The girl nodded. He poured two large measures into thick, white teacups.

As she sat sipping, Leo pulled a dozen assorted bolts of cashmeres, wools and tweeds to the floor, to create a sort of divan.

'Perhaps madam would be a bit more comfortable here?' He reached over, took her hand and pulled her down beside him. She shut her eyes and lay back. Warm, confident lips kissed the lobes of her ears, then moved slowly round her chin until they landed, strongly, hungrily on her own responsive lips. She opened her mouth and caressed the boy's clenched teeth with her tongue, trying to find a way into his mouth. She wondered vaguely if he was a virgin. Suddenly he seemed to understand, and their tongues were twining around each other. She felt an exploratory hand on her knee, moving, first tentatively then boldly, up the inside of her thigh. As she felt a tug at one of her suspender straps, a husky voice whispered, 'Is this the offending article, madam?'

'Mmmm,' she nodded, and felt her suspender clips being undone, one by one, a pause between each. Slowly she felt her stockings being rolled down, so she pushed her shoes off with her feet, and lifted her heels to let the boy pull the stockings away. Once more the hands made their way, gently, triumphantly, up to her thighs. She felt his fingers slip under the elastic of her knickers, and probe gently towards where she was ready and waiting.

Leo heard her gasp a little as he played his fingers over the soft lips. He couldn't believe the excitement of it. This is what it was all about! He was oblivious now to everything but the warm smells, noises and sensations of sexual encounter. He thought his fly-buttons would burst as he felt her grappling with his belt buckle. She couldn't undo it with one hand so he had to help her; then she quickly undid his fly, and pulled him, shining-headed, from his underpants. She looked down, eyes glittering.

'That looks healthy!' she murmured. Leo felt her lift her buttocks so that he could slip her knickers off. She kicked them across the room, and started to help Leo to pull his trousers and pants off.

Leo drew her skirt up to her waist. He lay for a moment between her splayed legs. She put her hand down and guided him gently, firmly into the waiting, wet warmness.

He was astounded by the sensation. It was as if he had entered a soft, hot sea-anemone, wrapping round him, gently sucking. Slowly, instinctively, he started to move back and forth on her. She responded, lifted her hips to meet each thrust, started to gasp, loudly, ecstatically, in time to the motion.

After two or three minutes, when he came, he felt as if he had pumped a gallon of sperm into her. He felt her shudder, and wrap both her arms tightly around him, and they lay still, locked into one another, sweating and exhausted. She wriggled a little, and pushed his torso back so that she could see his face.

'That was quick – but powerful,' she said, looking at him appreciatively. 'What do you do for an encore?'

Leo looked down at her and winked knowingly. 'Wait and see,' he said. He slowly unwrapped himself from her, then stood up coyly, not used to being looked at naked from the waist down. But he managed to walk across the room with his dignity intact and pour two more whiskies into the teacups.

They sat up together on the bolts of cloth and sipped their drinks. Leo glanced at her every few moments, and smiled uncertainly. Her mascara had run. Maybe she was a bit more than twenty, maybe twenty-five. She didn't look quite so crisp and neat as when she'd come into the shop – in fact, rather raddled.

No, she wasn't beautiful, but she did have those naughty eyes that always seemed to be looking at you sideways. And anyway, she didn't hold back like all the other girls he'd tried it with. Before this, he had never got further than kissing and feeling nipples through a blouse. Bloody hell, he thought, if fucking's always like that, I don't know why anybody ever does anything else. And slowly he felt himself reviving, growing bigger. He gulped down the rest of his whisky, and turned towards her. She lay back ready, and this time he was in her for twenty minutes.

Afterwards they lay side by side, comfortably on the crumpled suitings, caressing each other, sometimes kissing. For a while, Leo even slept. When he touched her he could feel her bubbling with anticipation – and he enjoyed the sense of control that this gave him. To think that he – until two hours ago a virgin – could arouse such excitement in a woman.

He sat up and leant on one elbow and studied the half-naked body beside him. He couldn't take his eyes away from the mound of curly black hair, the slightly damp thighs below. Then he looked at her face; the eyes, submissive below drooping lids, confirmed, he thought, his dominance of her sensual fulfilment.

He was a little disappointed by the ordinariness of her face, but, he thought, she's a good fuck. Then he thought again: maybe it's me that's good. Yes, that was it – any woman would be good if she were being made love to by him.

The girl at last sheepishly pulled on her knickers and stockings and left the shop reluctantly. Leo had said that he had to clear up. He kissed her briefly on the mouth, didn't ask her name, wouldn't tell her his.

He tried to straighten out the rolls of cloth, dabbing at them with a sponge to remove any marks. He replaced them on the shelves, rinsed out the teacups and hid the

21

half-empty whisky bottle where he thought it wouldn't be found for years.

He chose to walk home and as he walked, he reflected on this significant watershed in his life. He had known that it would happen. For the last year, indeed, it seemed that he had been preparing for it.

It was only a year since he had argued with his father about the army-surplus stock. His father had given in – not that he had had any real choice, Leo thought, because he had had nothing with which to bargain. There had been nothing which he had been able to take away from Leo in retribution for his disobedience. Leo loved his father, but he didn't admire him; he even felt rather protective towards him.

Since that argument, Leo had gone on to do several more deals with the surplus-store owner. He sold the stock he bought to other boys at the grammar school and to his cousins and friends from neighbouring streets. Each deal was bigger and more profitable than the last. His techniques for buying and selling were becoming more sophisticated, and he learnt some fundamental ground rules of trading – he never bought anything unless he was absolutely certain of a market, and he never sold anything that wasn't exactly what he said it was. He carefully hoarded the money he made. And when his father, remorsefully, had offered to buy him a bicycle for passing seven O levels, he had declined it and asked for the money instead. Leo didn't want a bike now; he wanted a car – a Triumph TR3A, he had decided.

During the previous summer holidays, he had persuaded his father to let him help in the Hampstead shop and now he continued to work there on Saturdays. His school work suffered, but he didn't care any more. He could see no point in learning for its own sake. His mother and father wanted him to stay on and take his A levels, then aim at going to university. But that would mean another eighteen months, and Leo was determined to leave as soon as he could, that summer. Especially now that he was a man – after this afternoon.

On the following Monday evening, Sarah found Leo lying sulkily on his bed staring at the ceiling. His lips were pouting, his eyes damp. Sarah didn't believe he could have been crying, but she knew he was upset. She ran over and sat on the bed beside him. 'What's the matter, Leo? You look really sad.'

Leo rolled away from her, onto his side. 'I want to tell you, but you're not old enough to understand.' He turned back towards her, 'But I will tell you when you are. You're the only one who doesn't try to put me down and criticise me. Dad and Mum do; those brainless jerks at school do. When I used to come top of the class they called me a greasy swot; when I sell them all that army stuff cheap, they call me the Jewish merchant, and there's dozens of other Jews at school – though they don't stand up for me. And now they're jeering at me just because I've done something they all wished they had – stupid bastards.' He rolled back and faced the wall again.

Sarah was mystified. She had never seen Leo upset like this. She put her hand on his shoulder and squeezed it, full of affection. 'I won't let you down, Leo. Tell me what it was. I'll understand. I promise,' she pleaded.

'I can't tell you. Go away.' His voice was muffled by the pillow.

Tears sprang in Sarah's eyes as she left the bedroom quietly. She was going to find out what they had said to upset her brother, and she was going to make them regret it.

She didn't have to wait long to find out. Next morning Leo had, as usual, left for school before her, but there was still a small group of grammar school boys at her bus-stop. Guiltily, they stopped talking and laughing as they saw her approach. She saw quite clearly that they must have been talking about her, or, more likely, about Leo.

'What's the secret?' she demanded.

'You're too young to know,' said one of the boys.

'Just ask Leo about the Hampstead Harlot,' said another, giggling.

'The Hampstead what?' asked Sarah, puzzled.

'Harlot – don't you know what that is? Look it up in the Old Testament,' said the first boy.

'Will she be able to look up "Phantom Cradle-Snatcher"?' asked the other, laughing unpleasantly and loudly at his own joke.

Sarah didn't know what they were talking about. 'Just because you're jealous of Leo. Just because he's cleverer than you,' she said defiantly, and turned away.

But the words haunted her all day. She asked some of the other girls, but they could not help her. So she decided to ask the English teacher what a harlot was. The mistress drew herself up primly and asked why Sarah wanted to know.

'Oh, I read it in the Old Testament,' said Sarah.

'I see. Well . . . er . . . it means a woman of easy virtue,' the teacher told her.

'You mean she finds it easy to be good?' asked Sarah.

'Well, no – just the opposite really. It's a woman who makes herself available to men, for money or favours usually.'

Sarah wanted more clarification, but the English teacher offered no more details, and it seemed risky to ask about phantom cradle-snatchers. However, the combination of men, women and cradles seemed to suggest the making of babies. And she was aware that this involved a mysterious, taboo process between parents. She couldn't see a connection with Leo, but was excited at the thought of him being associated with this very adult activity.

When he left school that summer, Leo agreed, as a concession to his parents, to go and work in Whitechapel with Nathan's most experienced old cutter. Leo enjoyed the *bonhomie* in the little shop in Commercial Street. Some of the customers, and most of their names, he already knew and the cutter, the shop assistant and the other staff had worked for his father for years. They did not resent Leo, and took it for granted that they might, one day, be working for him. And Leo reciprocated. He preferred talking to adults about adult things; they enjoyed his quick wit and appreciated his natural street-wisdom.

There was no doubt that his parents and his vociferous relations were bitterly disappointed that he had refused to take advantage of his academic ability, but Leo had been adamant that he would not stay at the grammar school. He insisted that, as he was now earning a regular wage, he would contribute to his keep at home. His mother, tenderly and tearfully, told him how much it would hurt her to take his money, but he insisted. Each week he left two pound notes wedged in front of the clock in the sitting-room, and as they accumulated, Miriam showed her cousins. They were more practical – this showed healthy parental respect, they said, and an appreciation that you can't get much for nothing in this life.

Eventually, the wad of notes disappeared, and the arrangement continued, unreferred to. Meanwhile, Leo carried on dealing in his army-surplus goods. He had been to several auctions, and had bought some joint lots with the owner of the Euston shop. A number of smaller shops from out of town bought stock from him in bulk, and he had been allowed to take over half the storage space behind the Hampstead shop.

His father, reluctantly, admired his meticulous method of trading. Leo was an outstanding salesman, too, without ever being ingratiating or servile. For years Nathan had called his customers 'sir'. Leo called them by their Christian name, or even 'mate' or 'chum'. Nathan couldn't object; there was a perceptible uplift in business – customers buying two suits at a time, when before they would only have bought one.

The cutter, whose son, Charlie, had helped Leo with his first load of stock, had taught Leo as much as he knew about making a suit and Leo had learned quickly, always eager to know the reasons for everything. Within six months he had quite satisfactorily made up patterns and cut some suits without the customers finding fault.

At the end of the year, the old assistant at the Hampstead shop contracted pneumonia and had to stop working. Leo leaped at the opportunity to take his place, preferably in a slightly more managerial capacity. Nathan discussed it with his brother-in-law, who couldn't understand the dilemma.

'But you've been telling us for six months how good he's been – how the business has improved. You're lucky, he's a real asset to you. I mean, look at Bernard's boy!' said the brother-in-law.

'But you don't understand,' said Nathan. 'He's so independent. He's not good to please me, he's good because he wants to be. He seems to be wanting to prove himself all the time.'

'So what's wrong with that? To be ambitious, that's healthy. He works hard, he causes you no trouble. So he wants to run the Hampstead shop – let him,' said his relation.

'But he's only sixteen still,' protested Nathan.

'But he's bright, he's very bright. These types of boys are always old for their age.'

Nathan shook his head. 'I'm not so sure,' he frowned. 'I'm not so sure . . .'

But of course he knew he would give in to Leo.

The first thing Leo did when he arrived to run the shop at Haverstock Hill was to take out the sombre oak panelling that projected half-way up the back of the window display and have the panelling inside painted white. This immediately made the shop lighter, airier, and more inviting. To his father's horror, he ordered two plaster models, and put them in the window wearing finished suits.

But it worked. He soon had customers asking to buy the suits in the window, so he had more made up in a range of sizes and colours. Bit by bit he replaced the bolts of cloth on the shelves with shirts, ties, sweaters and dressing gowns. The traffic of customers through the shop increased. A lot of these new customers ordered bespoke suits, so Nathan couldn't complain, though he grumbled to Miriam that their shop was meant to be a tailors', not a hosiers' and gents' outfitters. The other staff in the shop

26

didn't complain. The place was busier and livelier now than it had ever been. The cutters and boys in the work-room were earning a lot of overtime keeping up with the increasing orders and Leo's need for ready-to-wear stock.

Leo himself was aware of the impact that he had made on the business in such a short time. When he occasionally saw his ex-schoolmates passing the shop, or in the street, he knew that they envied him his freedom, and his success.

Since his encounter with the girl in the stock-room, and the subsequent pillorying he had received, he had been careful and discreet in choosing girls to take out. He looked at the pictures of models in *Vogue* and these became his ideals. Nobody would laugh at him if he took out girls like that. When he spotted any girls who seemed to fall into this category, he wasted no time in trying to get to know them. Quite often he was successful, though as yet he had not had the opportunity to repeat his first experience. At home, he lay in bed fantasising, placing the head of his current fantasy on the body of the Phantom Cradle-snatcher. But he wasn't too concerned; when he took girls out he wanted to do it properly, and that cost money – and he wasn't prepared to start spending money, yet.

A year or so later, in the spring of 1961, Leo saw a group of his old classmates sitting huddled around a table in a pub by Hampstead Heath. Between bouts of laughter and loud buying of drinks, they were obviously discussing some scheme. Leo had arranged to meet one of his army-surplus customers, who was late. He was sitting on his own at the bar, pretending to read his paper, but really trying to hear what his old antagonists were planning. When they noticed him, they glanced over and nodded amiably. One of them, a good-looking boy of eighteen called Trevor, got up and sauntered over to him. Leo braced himself.

'Hello, Leo, how are you doing? I hear you're making a pile, running your old man's shop in Hampstead.' He was smiling and seemed perfectly friendly, but Leo kept his guard up.

'Yeah,' he said. 'It's doing pretty well. Dad's sort of left me to get on with it.'

'You still selling that surplus gear?'

'Yeah. Why?' asked Leo.

'Well, nothing really. We were just thinking that you've always been pretty good at business, and me and those other poor idiots could do with a bit of help.'

Leo was surprised. 'You're going into business.'

'No, no. We've formed a group. You know, a rock 'n' roll group – three guitars, piano and drums. Do you remember how we used to do that stuff at school shows? Well, we play rock 'n' roll now and a bit of rhythm and blues, that kind of thing. Come on over and talk about it. We reckon we need a bit of management,' said Trevor.

Leo hesitated. 'Well, I'm waiting for a customer. He's late but he'll show up soon.'

'That's all right – you'll see him from over there. Come on.'

Leo nodded and made his way over to the table. The others made room and drew up a chair for him.

'Well,' started Leo, 'if this is going to be a long business discussion, we'd better get some more to drink. If somebody gets 'em, I'll pay for 'em.' He looked around.

'God, still the same old Leo,' sang Nick, a small, dark boy of Cypriot origins. 'Don't worry,' he said quickly, seeing Leo's eyes darken. 'Give me the money and I'll get them.'

'Okay then,' said Leo, 'let's get down to business. How good are you?'

After a lot of laughter and jeering about each other's lack of talent, they agreed they were good – more than competent; and they had a huge repertoire – Buddy Holly, Little Richard, Eddy Cochrane, Elvis, Chuck Berry, Cliff Richard, The Shadows, Billy Fury . . .

Leo wasn't surprised. They had all been known at school for their enthusiasm for pop music, were often seen carrying around battered old guitars and copies of *Melody Maker*.

Leo remembered the shows they had done at the grammar school. He had felt the excitement and the immediacy of the rock and roll they had played. And he had been reluctantly impressed and envious of the standing it gave them among their schoolmates and their sisters.

'What sort of places have you played in?' he asked.

'Oh, youth clubs mainly. Some church halls. And we're doing a party at Hornsea Art College.'

'How often do you do them, and how much do you get paid?' Leo pulled out a silver ballpoint and clicked it.

'Once, maybe twice a week. Sometimes we do it for a share of the door-money, sometimes we get a tenner. We're getting twenty quid for the Hornsea dance. You see, that's why we need a manager. We love playing, and we'll do it for nothing if someone asks. But I reckon if somebody who wasn't one of us looked after the business arrangements, we'd get more dates and more money.'

'Yeah, well,' mused Leo, 'you're asking me from a business point of view. There doesn't seem to be a lot of money in it.' The others started protesting, but Leo held up his hand impatiently. 'But that doesn't mean to say there couldn't be. I'll have to hear how good you are, see what you look like and try to see what you've got that's special – if anything. I mean, there are groups popping up all over the place and hardly any of them are going to get anywhere, so you've got to have some magic ingredient. By the way, what are you called?'

'The Heathmen,' said Trevor.

'Oh dear,' Leo groaned, 'we'll have to do better than that.' He spotted his customer peering round the bar. 'Look, my punter's arrived. I'll have to go and talk to him. Give me a ring and tell me when you're next playing so I can see you in action.' He handed Trevor a card, having crossed out the 'N' and 'Bespoke Tailor' and scribbled 'Leo' above 'Freeman'. He stood up, nodded round the table at them all and walked over to see his anxious-looking customer.

Two weeks later, Leo was contacted by Trevor. During that time he had become excited about the idea of managing a group, though he knew that he had to contain his enthusiasm until he had heard them. He spent hours talking to Sarah about it. She was fifteen now and, like Leo, was proving very scholastically able. She had passed all her O levels and was in the sixth form studying English and Art. She was becoming startlingly attractive, too, and like all girls her age, was preoccupied by boys, clothes and music. She eagerly accompanied Leo when he first went to see the group playing at a youth club in Willesden.

They weren't disappointed. The boys played their instruments and sang well and Trevor, the lead singer, achieved a natural rapport with his audience. Leo was pleased to overhear a lot of the kids asking each other where they could next hear the group. He was less pleased about their appearance, though. Wearing black trousers, white shirts and their hair in greasy curls and duck's-arses, they looked very ordinary. If he was going to manage them, they would have to take his instruction over all aspects of their presentation.

At the end of the final set, Leo and Sarah joined the group in a cramped little locker-room where they were swigging bottles of pale ale.

'That was pretty good,' said Leo. 'Better than I'd hoped, but there's a lot of room for improvement. I've got loads of ideas for you, so if you're interested in hearing them come up to the Hampstead shop Monday evening and we'll try to sort out a deal. You all look knackered and half-pissed so we won't talk about it now.'

'Thanks, Leo,' said Trevor. 'Yeah, it was a good gig – the audience really loved it. Christ, did you see that bird up the front? I thought she was going to tear her knickers off and throw them at me.' They laughed and drank, brimming with the satisfaction of having given a good performance.

Meanwhile, they had been eyeing Sarah, wondering, until Nick, the little Greek drummer, asked, 'Aren't you going to introduce your bird, Leo?'

'What're you talking about? You know my sister, Sarah, don't you?'

'Oh, yeah. Hi,' they all said appreciatively.

'My sister, remember,' said Leo, 'so hands off.' He put his arm around her shoulder in mock protection. 'Anyway, it's time we went. See you on Monday.'

'Tommy and the Tigers?' exclaimed Trevor.

Leo nodded.

'But it sounds like something out of a comic,' said Mick, the pianist.

Leo nodded again.

The group sat sprawled around the back room of the shop, some on chairs, some on the floor. Leo himself sat at a small desk. In front of him was a pad of paper covered in notes and lists.

'Look,' he said, 'you've got to have a name that leaves some kind of impression, some definite image that the memory can hook on to. Being successful in this game isn't just, or even, about being good. It's about promotion. And the main part of promotion is presentation. The initial impact you make.'

'But if we're going to be Tommy and the Tigers,' said Nick, 'one of us has got to be Tommy.'

'Yeah, sure.' Leo nodded towards Trevor. 'Him.'

Trevor looked pleased but embarrassed. 'But we're all equal in the group,' he said.

'Of course you are,' Leo smiled, 'but you're the lead singer and a natural front man – so let's use that to the benefit of all of you.'

He had known that this suggestion would cause dissension, and had decided to open the meeting with it. Once he had their agreement on this, the rest would be easy. After ten minutes' discussion, and some truculence, it was agreed. In fact, they began to get excited about this simple but critical change in their act.

'Right, next,' Leo said briskly. 'We need one extra member of the group.'

Again there was an outburst.

'What the hell for? We've got all we need. Why split it six ways?'

When they had quietened down, Leo spoke. 'What we want is a girl, playing a guitar.'

'What for?'

'Because no other group has a girl member, and it would be a talking point. Don't you see? The more you're talked about, the more people will want to see you.' He paused. 'And buy your records. I promise it'll make a difference, and having one-sixth of a success is better than having a fifth of nothing.'

The group thought about this for a moment.

'My sister plays the guitar,' Mick nervously volunteered. 'She's not great, but she's not bad-looking, is she?' He looked around for confirmation. The others nodded.

'Well, why don't you try her in a practice?' said Leo. 'She only needs to be a second rhythm guitar – or Trevor could stop playing at the gigs and just sing.'

They agreed to try that and, once again, realised that what Leo was saying made sense.

'Right, clothing – my speciality,' Leo went on. He pulled a roll of cloth from behind his chair. 'I found this great tiger-print dress cloth. We can make up shirts and trousers from this, and Trevor can wear a white safari suit. Maybe he could even come on wearing a topee – you know, one of those big-game hunter's hats.'

They loved it. Leo knew that he had convinced them, and for another hour they sat and talked details of percentages. By the time the meeting was over, it was agreed that Leo would finance everything. This would be paid back to him from their earnings. Leo would take thirty per cent of all income, after expenses had been covered. He would arrange and negotiate all bookings and pay for a session in a recording studio to make a demo-disc.

The group left, satisfied that they were better off like this than they had been before, in spite of vehement arguments to the contrary put forward by Nick. But in the end, even he had accepted the logic of Leo's proposals.

Afterwards, on his own in the stuffy little room, Leo sat back, very satisfied. He had spent all the time he could down in Denmark Street, the music world's 'Tin Pan Alley'. He talked to people in management companies, studio engineers, publishers, anyone who was prepared to gossip to an eager young man who said that he wanted to get into the business.

He was pleased with the cohesiveness of his plan, and he was pleased that he had applied his principle of only dealing in quality products: these boys really could play well, and Trevor was a great, strong singer. He was certain that with correct handling, they, and he, could make a lot of money.

He had grown up with the sound of Tommy Steele, Lonnie Donnegan and Elvis Presley in the background, never particularly aware of it. Now he listened avidly, all the time, to Radio Luxembourg and the Light Programme. Cliff Richard and Adam Faith were still the teenagers' heart-throbs, but Leo bought dozens of other records in an attempt to analyse what made a singer successful, what made a hit song. Humming to himself, with complete conviction, 'What do you want if you don't want money,' he rejected the Larry Parnes approach, and the notion of surly young men with implausibly angry names. He was aware of the dominance of the Americans in the music charts, but there was so much talent around in England that he was sure that this must change. Cliff Richard looked as though he might break into the States, and Presley's reputation was definitely flagging.

Meanwhile, the shop was doing well and his wholesale business was providing regular, overhead-free profits. Now was the time to invest some money on creating a bit of front for himself. He was aware that the cheapest, most effective way of projecting a high profile was by driving a flashy car. He had been taking driving lessons and practising in the shop van, and one day he came home proudly flourishing his new driving licence.

Ignoring his father's horrific stories of high-speed crashes, and his mother's worried face, he visited every Standard-Triumph dealer in London. When he was certain that he had identified and negotiated the best cash discount available, he drove back to Hampstead in a state of great excitement, and a brand-new, white TR4.

By the end of 1962, Tommy and the Tigers had played a string of major venues; they had been back-up group in a Shadows' tour, Decca had signed a record contract with them, and they had appeared twice on *Ready Steady Go* as their first record nudged into the Top Twenty. Other groups approached Leo and asked him to manage them, but he resisted the temptation as he didn't think they were good enough. He went to look at dozens of performers who he knew were either badly managed or unmanaged, but none had any outstanding potential.

Then, of course, the Beatles burst on the scene with 'Love Me Do'. Leo was full of admiration for what Brian Epstein had done for them, but he was envious of Epstein's Liverpool background and the large stable of other Liverpudlian groups and singers that he had been able to accumulate.

No one could really claim to have predicted the colossal revolution of which these were the harbingers. Parents all over the western world looked on, astonished, alarmed and powerless against the impact of the Beatles and shortly after, by way of a *coup de grâce*, the Rolling Stones. Everything about them was new and unfamiliar: their clothes, their hair, their utter disregard for any accepted conventions.

The newsreel shots of thousands of girls in concert halls screaming so loudly that scarcely a note or a word of 'Please, Please Me' or 'I Wanna Hold Your Hand' could be heard were totally incomprehensible to a generation who had last been turned on by Glen Miller.

Leo's own parents were appalled as his hair grew longer, his shirts and ties more flamboyant, frilled and flowered, and the heels of his elastic-sided boots higher. But he was reacting not only to the mood of the time; also to a vast new market.

A side-effect of the appearance of the Beatles was that groups and their managements became very much more

34

clothes conscious. As Leo had been so successful in kitting out his own group, a lot of others had come to him, and he now had a thriving business making bespoke stage-gear. And he knew this could go on indefinitely, and without risk of investment, whereas there was no doubt that eventually the Tigers' popularity, having peaked, would diminish rapidly. He had to make a decision. If he was going to develop his management activities, he had to find other acts. But record and management companies were scouring the country for new, undiscovered talent and Leo was up against formidable opposition. He was not prepared to risk the profits he had made on the Tigers in trying to promote any second-rate group that he might be able to sign. He had no illusions about the fickleness of the record-buying public, and decided to sell the remaining three and a half years of his management contract with Tommy and the Tigers while they were still on the way up.

When he announced that he had negotiated the sale of his contract to the James Richard organisation, the group was devastated.

'But Leo,' said Trevor, 'without you, we all know we'd never have made it. You've been very fair with us. We know you've made a lot of money out of us, but we've done well, too. Why do you want to sell?'

'Look, it was always a business arrangement. I'm glad it's been successful, and with JR Music you'll have a lot more behind you. I couldn't afford to promote you properly in the States; they can. And also, to be honest with you, if I were going to continue in this management business, I'd have to find other acts, and I can't find one that's any good. But the stage-gear business is booming, so I want to concentrate on that. Listen,' Leo coaxed, 'you'll be all right, I've sorted you out a better deal with a bigger company.'

'But, Leo, we're all friends. Sure, I like Bill at JR Music, but you've been right behind us since we were nothing. Can't you stay on as a personal manager or something?'

Leo shook his head, but was eventually persuaded to continue as a kind of informal consultant.

They held a farewell party in a Hampstead bistro. Leo was amazed by their warmth and affection: he had only taken on the group because he had seen it as a good business proposition; he would not have touched it unless he had known they could make it. He had made a lot of money out of them, and had sold his contract for seven thousand, five hundred pounds. They seemed to think that he had done them a favour – and he thought he understood what motivated people!

After this, Leo was determined to restrict his activities to the rag-trade, at least for a few years. He continued to cast around for opportunities. Surprisingly, it was Charlie's father, still working as a cutter in the Whitechapel shop, who whetted Leo's appetite for what promised to be a very interesting deal.

Leo had mentioned that he wished they were able to make up accurate copies of army dress tunics, the bright red and blue ones with epaulettes and brass buttons. He had seen a couple hanging in a shop in Carnaby Street and noticed that they had sold immediately.

'I don't know why you want to make new ones,' said the old tailor. 'There's still loads of the real McCoy lying around.'

'There aren't,' said Leo wearily. 'I've been to dozens of surplus sales. There's never any there. None of the dealers have them.'

'Oh, well, they wouldn't have, would they?' continued the cutter. 'They didn't used to belong to the army. They were the officers' private possessions. They used to get them made to measure at those military tailors up the West End. Well, you think what 'appens; they order a tunic and then go off and get killed in the war. No one tells the tailor. 'E finishes the job, and then it 'angs around for ever waiting to be picked up. I know they've got 'undreds of 'em in the storeroom at Turnberrys.'

Leo's heart leaped. This could be one hell of a deal.

'Are you sure about that?'

'Oh, yeah. S'matter of fact, I was only talking about it

36

the other day to old Tommy – 'e's one of the storemen there, lives out our way in Finchley. Can't remember how we got on to it, but 'e was swearing about the space they take up.'

Leo drove straight to Covent Garden, parked his car amidst the debris of the vegetable market, and walked casually into Turnberrys. He found Tom, the storeman, and mentioned the conversation he had had with Charlie's father about military tunics. He didn't suppose that anyone would be interested in selling some of this old stuff, would they? Tom looked dubious, but led Leo to the small office where the stores manager ruled his basement domain. Leo explained to this sponge-bag-trousered grandee that he worked for a small firm of bespoke tailors. As they had some military clients, they might just be able to use some of the old military mess jackets.

The stores manager looked sniffily down his nose. 'I don't see how. All regiments, sometimes even battalions, have different uniform details. It would be extraordinary if they were the right size *and* the right design.' He glanced at Leo's card. 'You have military clientele in Hampstead and Whitechapel?' he asked, disbelieving.

'Oh, yes, through recommendations,' Leo answered blithely. 'But I appreciate what you're saying about the sizes and design. Perhaps if I bought half a dozen from you, I could see whether it would be worth trying a larger quantity later.'

'Well,' the stores manager said, 'it would be injudicious and undesirable for us to sell them upstairs, and it has always been one of our terms of business that we reserve the right to dispose of any bespoke orders that have not been collected within ten years of completion. So, yes, we are at liberty to sell them.' He stroked his chin thoughtfully. 'Yes,' he said, 'there are some tunics that have been here since 1915. Perhaps we'd better start with those.' He turned to Tom. 'Take Mr Freeman to the oldest stock and select six for him.' And, turning to Leo, 'Come back here when you've finished and I'll make you out a bill. How will you be paying?'

'Oh, cash, for a small deal like this.'

'Good, good,' said the manager.

When Leo and Tom returned with six beautifully made and perfectly preserved jackets, the stores manager had been on the phone to his immediate superior, who had in turn contacted one of his directors. Word had come back down the line that, as the items had been written off the company's stock years before, they could be sold at five pounds for a single piece or two pounds apiece for a bulk sale.

Leo could hardly believe his luck. He had been prepared to pay five pounds apiece for every mess tunic that they possessed. He expressed his amazement that they should ask so much, but finally agreed to pay two pounds apiece for this first half-dozen, on the understanding that they would negotiate a better price if he bought a substantial quantity. He handed over a tenner and two grubby pound notes and could hardly stop himself from running up the stairs. Outside the shop, he didn't stop himself: he ran, dodging the cabbage boxes and old potato sacks, to his car and drove as hard as he could up to Haverstock Hill. He rushed into the shop, and immediately started to pull the suits off the models in the window and replaced them with one red and one navy blue tunic. As he did this, he called to his assistant to write up a sign: 'All Genuine World War I Mess Tunics – Unused – £12'.

By lunch-time the following day, he had sold the last of the six and rang the stores manager at Turnberrys to say he would like to come down and buy all the remaining tunics they had. He also telephoned the Whitechapel shop to tell them that he wanted Charlie and the van ready and waiting for him in a quarter of an hour.

Tom had told him that there were about two thousand assorted mess uniforms. Leo called in at his bank and withdrew four thousand pounds in cash so there would be no delay in getting the stock back to Hampstead. Even if he had to pay two pounds apiece, he reckoned that he could wholesale a thousand at six pounds, probably within the week. Then he would be two grand ahead with another thousand tunics left to retail, perhaps over six months! At twelve pounds each – a total profit of fourteen thousand pounds. A whole lot easier than managing Tommy and the Tigers for another six months.

He drove down to Commercial Street in his white TR4 and sat, fuming, for twenty minutes.

Where the hell was Charlie?

Leo was just getting out of his car to go into the shop to find out what was happening, when the van appeared, slowly weaving its way down the street. It pulled up at last. Charlie fumbled with the door handle, jerkily opened the door, and stumbled out of the driver's seat.

'Oh, Christ,' Leo moaned. 'He's pissed as a rat.'

He ran over and grabbed Charlie by the lapels of his jacket. The driver, five years older, six inches taller, reeked of whisky. He didn't resist as Leo shook him and pushed him back over the bonnet of his van.

'You stupid, drunken, fucking prat,' Leo snarled. His face was a few inches above the other's. 'Here I've been waiting for you for half an hour so that you can help me pick up the best bloody deal I've ever had – and you turn up pissed and no fucking use to anyone. You're fired, you bum!' He pushed Charlie off the van. 'Give me the keys, I'll have to do it on my own.'

Charlie had sunk to the ground like a stringless puppet, sobbing and muttering. 'Sorry, Leo, sorry, Leo – I had a bet. Bloody dog. They told me it'ud piss it. A month's bloody wages – you can't sack me, please,' he blubbered.

Leo winced. He looked round and saw Charlie's father watching from the front door of the shop.

'Get him inside,' he yelled. 'We'll talk about it later. I've gotta go.'

He climbed into the van and roared off down the street. His whole body was still throbbing with fury when he pulled up in the delivery bay at Turnberrys. He sat for a moment, breathing deeply, forcing himself to calm down. Then he ran a comb through his hair, straightened his pink and white flowered tie and went down to confront the pompous stores manager. He was met with a polite smile, even a little deference. He didn't know that his offer to clear out all the accumulated uniforms had solved a long-standing problem.

'There are 1,877 tunics, a few with mess uniform trousers,' he was told.

'I see,' said Leo. 'As many as that?' And I'm going to count every one of them, he thought. 'Well, if I'm going to take the lot, what are you asking?'

'As I told you before, I've been instructed to sell them at two pounds apiece in bulk, though we won't charge you for the trousers,' was the reply.

'Two quid each for nineteen hundred pieces! That's nearly four grand for stock that's been written off. I can't pay that, I'm sorry.' Leo shook his head. 'I've brought cash and I can give you a pound apiece.'

The stores manager drew himself up. 'Mr Freeman, I am not at liberty to bargain with you. I have my instructions. You telephoned to say that you wished to buy them all, and they are all ready for you. I've made out an invoice for 1,877 garments at two pounds, that's £3,754. So if you'd care to let me have that sum, I'll make you out a receipt, and instruct the storemen to help you remove the goods.'

Leo held his breath a moment, turned and took a few paces towards the door, then looked back. 'Look. When I took the first half-dozen, we agreed that if I took the rest, you'd negotiate on the price. I'm prepared to take the rest, but not at two quid. So, if you want to clear them out, you'd better get new instructions.'

He leant against the door post and challengingly faced the self-important manager, who said, after a pause: 'Would you mind leaving my office while I speak on the telephone to my superior?'

Leo nodded affably. 'Of course not.' He went out, closing the door behind him.

Two minutes later the stores manager came to the door, and beckoned Leo in. 'I have been instructed,' he announced, 'that I may sell these garments at one pound ten, and no less.'

Leo smiled to himself. Five minutes' work, he thought, and I've saved nearly a grand.

'All right, I'll go for that,' he said curtly. 'You'd better make out a new invoice and I'll start checking the quantities.'

'As you wish, Mr Freeman, though I assure you it's not necessary.'

'For £2,805.10s. in cash, it is necessary,' replied Leo.


He drove back triumphantly to Hampstead, parked the van outside the shop, opened the back doors and carried in the first box himself. He pushed through to the stock-room at the back and dropped it down, shouting happily at one of the lads to go and unload the rest. Then he noticed his father, sitting behind the desk looking furiously at him.

'Leo,' Nathan's voice quavered. 'What have you done to Willy's boy? My old friend, my most loyal worker – and you have to beat up his son. It's disgraceful – my own boy attacking the staff – and who do you think you are to be firing people? Nobody's sacked unless I say so. May I remind you that I'm the boss, not you.' Nathan was close to tears and his face was white with anger.

Leo was appalled that his father could be so shockingly upset – that his own actions could be so grossly misreported. He walked around the desk and laid his hand on his father's shoulder. 'Dad, for God's sake, calm down; please. It's not as bad as that.'

Nathan tensed. He tried to shake off Leo's hand. 'Don't start that soft soap with me. You only do it when you think you won't get your own way by yelling.'

'It's not true, Dad.' Leo withdrew the hand and stepped back. 'I hate to see you so upset. I know how important Willy is to you. But I didn't beat up Charlie. He was so drunk, he fell over on his own. He could hardly stand.'

'Drunk? What do you mean Charlie was drunk?'

'I mean he was drunk, pissed. He'd had too much to drink – an excess of alcohol in the bloodstream – what do you think I mean by drunk?' Leo closed his eyes and inhaled deeply, then, 'Sorry, Dad, but he was. Didn't Willy tell you?'

Nathan shook his head. 'But Charlie's so reliable. Why would he be drunk in the middle of the day?'

41

'He said he'd lost money on a dog. I don't know how or why – I didn't have time to discuss it. I'd arranged to pick up this stock from Turnberrys,' said Leo.

'That's another thing, Leo, what is all this old rubbish? I heard you had fancy dress on the models in the window yesterday. I've given you too much freedom with this shop, Leo. You're not even twenty, and you go round like you own Harrods. You've got a lot to learn, you know.'

'I know, Dad, I know,' said his son, 'you've often told me before, and I'm doing my best. And don't worry about this stock, Dad, I bought it with my own money.'

'Never mind that, what am I going to do about Willy? You'll have to apologise to him,' said Nathan.

'What are you talking about? I didn't even speak to him! It wasn't my fault Charlie was drunk. Of course I'm not going to apologise.'

Nathan sighed. 'In that case, you'd better not go to Whitechapel again. I'm not having my staff there intimidated by you. And I've already told Willy that Charlie can stay on – so you'd just better keep away from him.'

Leo turned away, biting his lip, trying to keep the anger from his voice. 'Don't be ridiculous, Dad. They like me down there, and anyway, how can I run this shop without going to the Whitechapel workroom? I can't set up a new one here, there's no space – and it'd be a waste of money.'

But Nathan had decided. He shook his head firmly. 'I think, Leo, that the time has come for a parting of the ways. I know you've done well here, in your own way, but it's not my way. All these pop groups and flowery shirts. Your mother and I and your uncles have agreed that you can take over this shop. You must pay for the stock and fittings, and you must pay the rent and rates, and all the other bills. And you will then be fully responsible for it. Just remember not to disgrace the good name we've built up here over fifteen years.'

He looked at his son mournfully.

Leo looked back. Sadness and elation vied for dominance in his dark eyes; sad at this severing of an umbilical cord; thrilled at the prospect of controlling his own destiny.

42

# 1966 – Uganda

Raju Kalianji watched a flock of flamingos – flaming pink in the late sun – drop down to the gently rippling surface of Lake Victoria. The coffee plantation through which he calmly steered his horse was on a promontory on the northern shores of the great lake which stretched southward for a hundred and fifty miles.

Looking away from the sun, he could see his father's acres spreading over the flat landscape as far as the horizon, with occasional trees standing isolated in a sea of serried coffee bushes. There were signs of both uncertainty and excitement in the soft dark eyes, for, that day, his father had agreed that he could take the place that he had been offered on a post-graduate course at the London School of Economics.

When he reached the stables at the plantation house, he slid his slightly gangling, youthful body off the overgrown polo pony that was one of his special possessions.

'All right, Effendi?' asked the groom, his black face shining.

Raju smiled and patted the horse's rump. 'Oh, yes. You do him very well.' He walked round to where his father waited in his gleaming Mercedes.

As the car bucked and jerked along the dirt track towards the main Kampala–Jinja road, Raju contemplated the father that soon he must leave. A good-looking man like himself, he wore his wealth comfortably. Vishnu Kalianji was no visionary, commercially or politically, but he was well-liked among the other Indians in Uganda and had sufficient charm and tact always to have had the ear of the prevailing government – the British up until 1962 and then, since Independence, the mildly socialist regime of Milton Obote.

He was well aware that both the white and then the black governments treated the Asian population of Uganda as a necessary nuisance. Brought over at the turn of the century as railway builders, engineers, skilled labourers and clerks, the original Indian immigrants had been followed by trading families. As early as the 1920s, Indians were growing as well as dealing in cotton, and building big spinning and weaving factories. Some, like the Mehtas and Mahdvanis, had established major sugar plantations and refineries. Now, in the sixties, the population of eighty thousand or so Asians ran eighty per cent of Ugandan business. This not unnaturally wounded the pride of the newly independent Africans and generated their resentment.

Vishnu's family, originally fairly modest shopkeepers, or 'dukawallahs', had become important middle-men in the coffee trade. Vishnu himself, through hard work and astute opportunism, had acquired his own plantation shortly after the end of the Second World War.

By Independence, when most of the Europeans had left, the Kalianjis were among the wealthiest families in Uganda and Vishnu had become a principal spokesman for the Indian community, even enjoying a small degree of confidence with Obote's government for whom, on occasions, he acted as a commercial advisor.

Inevitably, his business had continued to grow. He had spread his activity to include trading in all Uganda's major commodities, as well as the very profitable importation of European tractors and agricultural machinery. This wide sphere of activity, and his influence with the government, meant that it was in the interests of most Asian businessmen to give Vishnu favourable terms and the first bite of any profitable-looking cherry. Sooner or later, any successful trader, dealer or man-with-a-plan found his way to Vishnu's Kampala offices.

Raju was his parents' only child. He had been brought

up sheltered by his father's wealth and the family's strict Hinduism. The Asians in Africa adhered closely to their traditional culture and religion; this very aloofness and disinclination to integrate was one of their great commercial strengths, though perhaps a political weakness. Relationships crossed many national borders. A Ugandan trader might have one cousin who was a Customs officer in Mombasa and another who was a senior clerk in the Kenya railways. When anyone, black or white, needed something in a hurry and was not too insistent that it should arrive through strictly legitimate channels, they would turn to one of the Indians.

Raju had attended the leading Asian school in Kampala, run like a caricature of an English public school. He had excelled in the classroom, on the cricket field and the tennis court. He was admired by, but not close to, many of his school fellows. During his teens, he had spent all his school holidays on the plantation near Lugazi, or up in West Nile, where his father had a house in Arua. Here he would choose one of his father's polo ponies and ride round by himself, planning and daydreaming, and in the evenings he read avidly everything from Dickens to *Time* magazine. Thus he had become an aloof, solitary young man, and it was only now, since he had been at Makerere College in Kampala, that he was beginning to enjoy other people's reactions to his ideas.

Raju had arranged to meet some friends at his tennis club that evening. After two energetic sets, the four young Indian men sat on wicker chairs on a white-painted veranda, drinking cool beers brought to them by a silently polite black servant. They were discussing what they would do once they had got their degrees. Raj was reading economics, and the others engineering.

There was, Raj said, so much scope in Uganda. There was a booming world market for their sugar, coffee, cotton and tobacco. If the government's plans for a comprehensive development of manufacturing industries were successful, they were surrounded by markets for agricultural machinery, chemicals, communications equipment. The neighbouring countries were desperate to establish themselves in the twentieth century before it was too late and they sank beneath the mass of their own exploding populations.

In Uganda they, the Asians, were the commercial elite. Though the Minister of Finance and the Minister for Trade and Development nominally held the power of decision-making, the Asians controlled the outlets, the channels of import and export. In a country so rich in resources and so fecund, this was an enviable position. But Raju's views on how this position could be used differed greatly from the conventional Indian attitude and he had gained a reputation as an enlightened, even a revolutionary, thinker – at least among his fellow students.

One of his beliefs was that employees and workers should have significant shareholdings in all enterprises; new industrial plants should provide full social services and amenities to the workforce, and this practice should be applied to the country's existing mining and agricultural holdings. Asians should become more involved in politics and work with the Ugandans to this end to secure the country's future.

These notions were anathema to the other Indians in the community. Many had taken British nationality at independence, and for them Uganda was simply a place to live, a place to trade. They were unconcerned about the nation's political aspirations. Raju's ideas, based on what he called shared capitalism, seemed to them rank socialism.

But Raju's companions on the club veranda nodded their agreement and enthusiasm. They knew that they would never have the will or the skill to put this philosophy into practice, but they were confident that Raju would. They knew it was better to be a member of an elite in the best-run, most prosperous country in East Africa than to be eking out a living in a degenerating economy run by governments of uncertain longevity. Political stability rising above the indigenous tribalism was vital to the well-being of all of them – and it was their duty to involve themselves.

Raju's own motivations were more altruistic than this, but he had learned to sell his ideas on his listeners' terms.

The conversation drifted into envious speculation about Raju's forthcoming trip to England. His companions offered advice from their scanty knowledge as to what he should see and do, where he should go, which people he should meet. Everything was there: night-clubs, Buckingham Palace, the Tower of London, the Houses of Parliament, the Queen, Mr Harold Wilson.

'And the girls, Raju!' one of them enthused. 'There are so many beautiful girls – and they will all do what a man wants. The Europeans are not at all strict.'

Raju shook his head. 'I'm going there to work, not to engage in a great orgy,' he smiled. 'And anyway, my mother's cousins in London will be telling my parents everything I get up to.'

'Have your parents fixed you a bride yet?' Raju was asked.

'I don't think so. Well they haven't told me, but I expect they've started discussions. But I'm sure my parents will choose someone very nice and very suitable.'

'And very sexy, I hope,' added one of his friends, grinning broadly.

Privately, Raju was perplexed by his parents' insistence on what he considered an archaic custom in this matter of his marriage, but he wouldn't dream of telling them so. And his parents, after all, had come together in the same way; they seemed perfectly matched, so he guessed it would work for him.

The question was raised again on the very day that he flew from Entebbe to London. His parents came to see him off. His mother tried not to weep and pressed an embarrassing little parcel of Indian delicacies on him to supplement the airline meal. His father quietly lectured him about financial arrangements and about upholding the family's good name, then, with an embarrassed glance over his shoulder, 'Be very careful of diseases you can catch from European girls. I know that you're a man now, but restrain your urges. And remember, by the time you return, we will have arranged your marriage.'

Then they were at the flight gate and Raju's father solemnly shook hands with him. His mother hugged him. And as he walked towards the plane, he glanced back and knew that he was entering a very different world.

# 1964

'Rags? *Rags!*' Nathan Freeman yelled and shook his head.
His eyes protruded in puzzled astonishment. 'Why? How
can you call a shop "Rags" and expect people to come in
and buy clothes?'

Leo sat opposite him in the front room of Nathan's
house. 'Well, Dad,' he said evenly, 'at least I won't be
spoiling your good name.'

His father stood and paced back and forth on the 'Empire'
design Axminster. He clenched and unclenched his fists in
frustration, then stopped and gazed bleakly at Leo across the
chasm of his lack of understanding. 'Leo, since you moved out
of home it's like you've moved to another planet. Sometimes
I wonder if we're both talking the same language. I know
you're doing well in the shop but maybe it's gone to your head
– and all this mixing with pop music people and those Carnaby
Street hooligans selling all that rubbish.'

'Dad, I don't mix with them. I just do business with
them.' Leo held his hand up as he saw his father about to
continue. 'And I'm doing a lot of business with them. In
the six months since I took over Hampstead, I've turned
over more money than both shops did in the two years
before – and that's not including my wholesale business. I
don't know what you're so upset about.' He spoke faster
now, and less calmly. 'You know, Dad, things do change;
tastes change, fashions change. I mean you wouldn't have
done too well if you'd stuck to selling frock coats and spats.
People are fed up with gloomy, boring old clothes. They
want a lot of colour . . . to express themselves. And kids
have got money to spend now. Look at the record business,

they know it – they aim all their sales at the teenagers. It's a big market and I can't ignore it.'

Nathan looked lost. 'But why do you have to call the shop "Rags"?' he asked. 'It sounds so dirty and rubbishy.'

'Dad, people are a bit more sophisticated these days. They're sick of advertisers trying to con them with fancy names. If I call the shop "Rags", they're going to think – he's not trying to pull the wool over our eyes, let's see what he's got. And, they'll remember the name. I mean, "N. Freeman, Bespoke Tailors" doesn't say anything except "we can make you a suit." Well, ninety-nine per cent of the small number of people who still want a suit get one off the peg at Burton's or Hepworth's.'

Leo stood up and looked fondly at his father. He had known that this conversation was going to be tricky. He had known that his father would be upset. He even admired him for trying to defend what he thought of as his business standards. He could have gone ahead and changed the name without mentioning it, but that would have hurt Nathan a great deal more than this token consultation. 'Look,' he said deferentially, 'I've got to get back to the workshop. I'll show you the drawings for the signboard before it goes up, all right?'

'Don't bother, Leo; whatever it looks like, I'll hate it. Just go and talk to your mother before you leave.'

His mother was laying the table in the dining-room. She smiled at him warmly. 'I hope you haven't left your father all over-excited. He worries so much about you.'

Leo kissed her on both cheeks. 'I try not to upset him, Mum, but I don't know why he should worry about me.'

'You do really, Leo. You know he doesn't trust things that happen too quickly, or too easily.' She went on, anticipating Leo's reply. 'Yes, yes. I know you've worked hard and I know you're a clever boy. For myself, I've forgiven you for leaving school early. You've made a success of your business and you've caused us no trouble. But you see, your father doesn't understand. He had very different hopes for you. But he's not against you. You must know that.'

'Well, what can I do about it?' shrugged Leo. 'Whenever I talk to him he wants a row.'

'Oh, he'll be all right,' said Miriam. 'Give him time. Just try and show some respect for him. Don't lecture him and talk down to him. You're only twenty, and he thinks he should still be teaching you.'

Leo nodded slowly, smiled and winked. 'I know, I know. I'll try. I want him to be proud of me, but I'm not going to do business his way. It's too slow; I'd get left behind, and you know I wouldn't like that.' He leaned over to kiss her again. 'I've got to go. Sarah's coming round to the workshop with some friends from her college. They think they're going to sell me some designs.' He laughed. 'They haven't even finished their first year and already they're Courrèges!' He gave a small wave as he left the room and went out to his white Triumph.

When first Nathan had barred him from going to the Whitechapel workshop, Leo had considered eating humble pie and apologising to Willy and Charlie. To lose the use of the workshop and the staff who knew his stage-gear business so well was potentially catastrophic. But as he had been handed an opportunity to run the shop entirely on his own, he was determined to eliminate any further reliance on his father's business. Just off Hampstead High Street, in Flask Walk, he found a derelict flat on three floors above a second-hand bookshop. It had its own entrance on one side of the shop window and two large rooms on the first floor. He was supposed to get permission from the landlords and the council planning department to use these rooms as a workshop, but he felt that if he occupied the top two floors himself, he would get away with it without asking.

As soon as he had agreed a rent that reflected the filthy condition of the long-uninhabited rooms, he moved in two out-of-work school friends with several gallons of white paint, an electric sander and a couple of cans of varnish. Within a week he had bought and installed all the machines he needed. A series of advertisements in the *Draper's*

*Record* offering well above average wages produced a good crop of enthusiastic Greek, Turkish, and even English applicants for the cutting and machining jobs he had to offer. By the time the new workshops were ready he had hired four of the best of them. He had all the work-in-hand, special cloths, patterns and orders relating to his Hampstead shop brought over from Whitechapel and delivered to Flask Walk. Surprisingly, Charlie was driving the van and helped unload. He grinned sheepishly at Leo, who ignored him until he was about to drive back to Whitechapel and then leaned through the window with a pound note in his hand.

'Thank you, Charlie,' he said. 'Buy yourself a drink.'

Leo worked on his new premises for a fortnight without a break. His new team, though keen and as competent as he had hoped, had to learn about his particular kind of business. He slept in a room on the top floor on a huge brand-new bed which he had had delivered by Heal's, and washed and shaved with the help of an ancient gas geyser.

So, within three weeks of losing the use of the East End workshop, he had established his own and caught up with the backlog of orders. Of the people that he had taken on, one girl, Min Cooper, was a natural organiser. She was only twenty, but had several years' experience working in her parents' small dress factory in Nottingham. Like Leo, she had a natural sense of independence and had come to London to prove to herself and to her family that she could make her own career – and, of course, London was synonymous with excitement and glamour, money and adventure.

Leo quickly recognised her inherent authority and the skill with which she encouraged people to do precisely what she wanted. Her constant laughter and banter made the other two machinists and Jerszy, the cutter, eager to please her, and Leo realised with relief that under her guidance the workshop would soon become an autonomous, self-motivating team, so that he could concentrate on buying, selling and promoting.

During those first few weeks, when he had been working

flat out and sleeping on the premises, he had come to enjoy the freedom of living on his own. When he told his parents that he intended to move to Flask Walk full-time, they accepted it with resignation. They both came to see it, and though Nathan grumbled about the shortcomings of living over a workshop, and neither of them approved of the Conran furniture and art deco wallpaper, they could see that he was living in clean and civilised conditions. Miriam insisted that he brought his laundry home every week and would call in regularly to make sure that the kitchen was stocked with wholesome food. Leo didn't mind that at all; it was one less thing to think about. 'But remember, Mum,' he implored, 'give us a call before you come over, okay?'

Sarah had left school the previous summer with a good crop of A levels and a place at the fashion design school at Regent Street Polytechnic. She had developed a strong, idiosyncratic sense of shape and colour and had been very happy when Leo asked her to help him decorate his new home. As a result, she felt very comfortable there and would drop in several times a week for a chat with Leo. She enjoyed her design course and was lucky to have two very able lecturers who strongly encouraged her individual view of fashion.

She was still close enough to Leo to criticise him without annoying him. She acknowledged that commercially he knew exactly what he was doing and that it was right for the times. 'But the trouble is,' she said, 'what you're selling are innovations and outrageousness for their own sakes, without much concession to the aesthetics of line and colour. Right now, any fashion idea that's new, or that shocks, is what people want, but sooner or later girls are going to look around for beautiful, feminine clothes, and men will want a kind of elegant casualness. I mean, there's a limit to the visual effect you can achieve by dressing simply to shock.'

Leo liked listening to her ideas and enthusiasm. He also liked her bringing her friends round from college.

Especially Sammy.

Sammy had mysterious origins. An English mother and an American father, long since separated, had played a kind of malicious hand-ball with her across the Atlantic since she was six. She spoke with an American accent interspersed with inappropriate English vowel sounds, and was convinced that each of her parents either loved her or hated her, depending on which she had seen most recently.

She had contrived, with no little guile, to obtain a place at the fashion school and now lived with her mother in Kensington. This caused her mother a great deal of inconvenience in the pursuit of her complicated love-life, and Sammy felt that she was resented for being an ever-present source of guilt. Her interest in clothes lay far more in the wearing than in the creating of them, and her spectacularly slender body, short blond hair and sharp boyish features, made her an unusual and exciting clothes-horse.

Leo had first seen her modelling in the college's Christmas show and had persuaded Sarah to bring her to his flat one evening. The three of them had dined in a dark little Italian restaurant in Hampstead High Street, and Sammy had seen Leo at his most relaxed and best. His acceptance of Sarah's teasing gave him an uncharacteristically gentle air. The wit and pace of their conversation enthralled her, and she was flattered by Leo's extravagant attentions.

After she had been round to Flask Walk with Sarah a few more times, Leo asked her out on her own.

He picked her up from her mother's large house in Argyll Road, took her out to dinner at San Frediano in Fulham Road, then to Blazes, a club in the basement of a large, dirty-white stucco Victorian terrace in Queen's Gate. Members of rock groups pushed their way happily among the tightly packed crowd of property whizz-kids and young aristocrats.

Leo found Trevor – Tommy of the Tigers – and Roger Daltrey sitting at a table surrounded by bored and boring-looking girls. The men's eyes lit up when they saw Sammy and everyone squeezed up to make room for her and Leo. Introductions were made over the pounding, sliding sound of the Stones' 'Route 66'. Large drinks were poured for them from the bottle of vodka on the table, and Sammy was whisked off to the tiny dance floor, where there was only room to stand and wiggle in time to the music.

Leo didn't mind. He knew she would be back, and he knew she was a winner. He flirted with the other girls around the table, talked music business with Trevor, and, after a while, drifted over to the black-jack table. There were no other punters around so he sat and played two boxes against Gina, the dealer. He was only playing a pound a box and didn't much care if he won or lost as he bantered suggestively with the girl. She, in turn, dealt him a string of winning hands. Leo was confident that Gina was interested in him and decided to play her along – for some future rainy day.

After a quarter of an hour, he felt the back of his neck being caressed possessively. He turned, smiling, to receive a kiss on the lips from Sammy. 'Come back to find a real man, have you?' He slung an arm around her shoulder. She grinned and nodded slowly.

Leo turned back to the table, divided his pile of chips into two and placed one pile on each of his two boxes. 'Come on, Gina. One nice hit before I go home,' he said. His first box showed twenty-one; on his second were two low cards. He drew two more to seventeen. The dealer's card was a picture. Leo nodded and Gina gave him an ace, then drew herself a seven. She pushed two large piles of chips towards Leo, who shook his head. 'Change 'em for cash. I'm off. But thank you, darling, you played beautifully.' He winked, and Gina counted out a pile of fivers and pushed them over to him with a flutter of her long false eye-lashes.

Leo and Sammy went out into the fresh spring night, found the Triumph and drove back to Hampstead through the empty streets. Leo hadn't had to ask where she wanted to go. Her whole demeanour made it clear. Her bare arm clung to his neck. Her head lay on his shoulder. A hand squeezed gently on his thigh. Every time that he changed gear, the hand squeezed a little harder. At every red light, his mouth was met by hers with warm, eager abandon.

When they reached Flask Walk, an uncompromising erection made clambering out of the low driver's seat a difficult business. 'Look what you've done, you randy little thing. I'm never going to get out from under this steering wheel.'

'You'd better,' Sammy said, 'I want to go to bed.'

Upstairs, she was suddenly and surprisingly coy. 'Turn the lights out. I don't want you to see my tiny tits yet.'

Leo laughed and did as she asked. They sat on the bed, groping each other's clothes in the dark. When they were both naked they lay stretched out, experiencing the excitement of a first encounter with a new body. They kissed, stroked, caressed and clutched each other.

Leo's lips found her nipples. 'Your tits aren't small,' he mumbled, 'they're non-existent, but these nipples are delicious.'

Sammy giggled. 'Shut up, and don't talk with your mouth full.'

Eventually, gently, they coupled. Leo felt just a moment's tension, hesitation in her slender body, before it relaxed, acquiescent, cooperatively rhythmic. 'Oh, Leo, don't stop, don't ever stop,' she murmured as slowly, higher and higher, they found themselves reach a sudden and explosive climax. Leo lay long in her, exhausted, in love with her for a while. And they had no sleep that night.

In the morning, Sammy sang as she showered, and brewed coffee. Leo felt he was bursting with energy as he flung the windows open to let in the bright morning sun and the spring birdsong. Sammy left at eight to face her mother. She wouldn't let Leo take her but telephoned for a minicab.

'Don't leave it too long before you call again,' she said, and ran down the stairs before he could reply.

When the girls arrived in the workshop, Leo was already there, going through the dockets and looking at the previous day's work. His elation was obvious, though he didn't realise it until Min Cooper asked, 'Well, have you won the pools or something? You look like the cat that got the cream.'

Leo surprised himself by flushing. 'I'm not always an angry bastard,' he said, 'but, yep, you could say that, if I were a cat, I had got the cream.'

Sammy gave up the fashion school that term, and by the following autumn she was rapidly becoming one of the most popular models in London. Terry Standing, a club-owning photographer in his fifties and now at the back end of his career, had spotted her when she was at his club with Leo, introduced himself and become her mentor. His years of dealing with magazines and other photographers made him very adept at creating a career for a new young model of such an unconventional type. By refusing a lot more jobs than he accepted on her behalf, he had quickly made her much sought-after.

Sammy took it in her stride. She had no difficulty in remaining detached from all the fuss that was being made of her. Leo wasn't sure whether to be pleased or annoyed. On the one hand he found her passivity irksome, too contrary to his own positive dynamism; on the other, she was becoming very famous, everyone knew who she was, and it was very satisfying to be seen out with her. And he knew a lot of people envied her obvious loyalty to him.

They had seen each other two or three times a week during that summer. When Leo wasn't seeing her, he was working and she was being taken out by an endless variety of men who thought that they had a chance with her. They soon found that they hadn't. Leo put this down to Sammy's deep underlying need for a constant and secure relation-ship, and to her laziness – she just didn't want the hassle of dealing with unknown quantities.

Sarah was puzzled that they lasted at all; she thought that they were temperamentally too unalike. But it seemed to be making Leo more tolerant and approachable, so she happily condoned it, and, in fact, actually used it in order to persuade Leo to take her work seriously. Although Sammy had left the college, she and Sarah met often and together they conspired to arouse Leo's interest in Sarah's designs. Four or five times in succession, when Leo took Sammy out, she wore a different dress that Sarah had designed and made. There was a very pronounced 'hand-writing' to Sarah's designs, and it was evident to anyone in the business that all the outfits had come from the same source. The unusual soft, dark colours and slightly Edwardian, romantic styling didn't particularly suit Sammy, but were none the less striking and effective enough for Leo eventually to remark on them.

'Who's been giving you a free wardrobe? You must've been wearing clothes from the same designer the last half-dozen times I've seen you.'

'Do you like the look?' asked Sammy.

'Yeah, I do, though I don't think it's right for you. You're too fair and skinny. Whose is it?'

'It's Sarah's collection for the end-of-term show at college,' said Sammy triumphantly.

Leo laughed aloud. He knew he'd been set up, but he was very impressed. 'So this is what she keeps trying to show me! I had no idea she'd developed such a strong look. I mean, she's been at design school for not much more than a year.' He began to get excited. 'Fancy my little sister having such a talent. Obviously, she's got a lot to learn, but she's certainly gone in her own direction.' He looked down at his watch. It was 11.30. 'Shit, it's too late to ring her now. Look, tomorrow's Saturday. I know I wasn't going to see you, but do you think you could come back in the morning with all the frocks and I'll get Sarah round with her drawings?'

Sammy said yes, sure she could, then listened quietly as Leo started to plan his sister's future.

When he saw the whole collection – there were twelve outfits in all – Leo was stunned. He had been concerned by the number of other shops which had sprung up all over London and had copied his Hampstead Rags. The look he had pioneered was well established now and easy to imitate. He had plans to expand the retail side of his business, but didn't want to do it without the benefit of a strong, promotable identity.

And here, under his nose, in his own family, was a designer of indisputable originality. This was a look that in many ways ran counter to the prevailing fashion for hard lines and stark colours – and in a year or so, it could be just the alternative that girls would be looking for.

Sarah had designed no men's clothes, but Leo didn't think this a disadvantage. He had slowly increased the emphasis on women's clothes at Rags and he wouldn't be sorry to move over entirely to female fashions. It moved a lot faster than men's, and gave far more scope for the visionary fashion entrepreneur. When he had studied all the designs and drawings, Leo stood up and began pacing around the room.

'Right, Sarah – you're a little genius! From now on, any time you want to use this workroom, or the girls here, help yourself. Any extra sampling, alterations to the patterns, ask Min; I'll tell her to give you all the help she can. But you can't show this collection at college. It'll be ripped off, watered down and into the crappy little multiples before next autumn. Keep the whole collection under wraps, improve it, increase it, get it perfect, and we'll launch it in a new shop this time next year.'

Sarah's eyes, bright with excitement, darkened for a moment with doubt. 'Leo, that's great, but I don't think my collection will go with what's in your shop.'

'No, no, of course it won't. You've got to design or select everything in the shop, down to the last belt buckle and pair of stockings. I'm talking about a complete look, right through to the shop fittings, the logo, everything. And I'll change the Hampstead shop at the same time. We won't tell the press until a month before. We'll give them a high-security preview so they can give it a build up, but we won't give too much away. And once it's open, it'll be too late for anyone to copy us, and by the time they do, we'll have your next collection out.'

He paused, looking with amazement at the clothes and drawings strewn across the cutting table. 'It's brilliant,' he

said, 'we're going to make a lot of money, me and you.'
He turned to Sammy, 'Thanks, you Yankee shrimp. You
did your bit well, and, Sarah, little sister, I'm really sorry
you had to set me up like that before I'd take you seriously.'
He took her in his arms and squeezed her. 'Let's go out
and drink a bottle of champagne to celebrate.'

Before Christmas of that year, 1964, Leo organised the
opening of a small showroom for his stage-clothes business.
He decided to incorporate it as a separate company, called
Showbiz Clothing Ltd, and look for a manager to run the
sales end of the business. If he was to make a success of
Sarah's collection, he must have no distractions. Anyway,
he was bored with being amiable to self-important rock
musicians, and it was clear that if he was going to retain
his share of that market, he should have premises in that
part of London where most of the music business was done.

Nick, who had been drummer with Tommy and the Tigers,
had had a raging argument with his new management
during a recording session that summer. The quality of his
drumming had been questioned, and an outside sessions
man had been brought in to play on one of the tracks. His
Greek sense of pride had overridden his undeveloped
sense of prudence. He had walked out of the studios and
refused to return.

Leo met him by chance soon afterwards and commiserated. If he wasn't going to go back to the group, or join
another one, he said Nick should let him know if he wanted
a job.

Leo wasn't particularly surprised when he didn't hear
from him, but he was disappointed. Nick's family owned
a small chain of restaurants and a lot of property, so Nick
himself had been brought up with a healthy understanding
of how business worked. Leo also knew that he was ambitious, acquisitive, determined and intelligent. So after a
couple of months, he rang Nick at his parents' home,
where he was still living. They arranged to meet in a Soho
restaurant for lunch next day.

Leo arrived first. Nick was ten minutes late. Leo knew that this was an affirmation of independence. He also knew what course their discussion must take.

They shook hands warmly and sat down to a typical London Italian meal of pasta, scallopine and Barolo.

'Well, Nick,' Leo snapped a grisini, 'what's new? Have you got anything going yet?'

Nick looked wary, but despondent. 'My dad's trying to persuade me to take over one of the restaurants. I do a couple of nights a week there at the moment. But I tell you, Leo, arguing with drunk customers about kebabs and broken plates, with my uncle hovering in the background, that isn't my idea of how to spend my life.' He took a long drink of the strong red wine. 'I've thought of staying in the music business, but everyone's heard about what happened in the studio. Maybe I shouldn't have lost my cool, but you know me. I wasn't going to be told I was okay to play live when nobody can hear anything, but not good enough to play on recording sessions. Anyway, I'm not going round begging to join up with some new group that nobody's heard of.'

Leo nodded. 'Any money left?'

'Oh, yeah. A few grand.'

'Do you want to go into business with me?' asked Leo quietly.

Nick looked up, pleased. He had thought he was going to be offered a job, not a partnership. 'But you don't need a few grand invested in your business, do you?' he asked.

'No, no, I don't. But I'm hiving off the stage gear business as a separate company. It needs someone to run it. I know you wouldn't work for just a wage – so – do you want to buy it?'

Nick put his knife down and extended his hand across the table. 'Provided we sort out a fair deal, Leo, you're on.'

They shook hands and spent the rest of lunch discussing that Nick would lend Showbiz Clothing Ltd five thousand pounds and own thirty per cent of the company, with an option to buy a further nineteen per cent after the first year. The company would own the lease on the showroom, pay a proportion of the rent at Flask Walk, and pay the workroom staff by the hours they worked for it. Nick also agreed to contact his old management company, who were big clients, and make his peace with them.

Leo drove back to Hampstead, secure in the knowledge that between Nick and Min Cooper, Showbiz Clothing would soon be able to run itself without him. Nick had a natural feel for the business, and was quite prepared to sit down with Min to learn all he had to about measuring and styling. Young designers were always dropping in with drawings of outrageous fantasy, and there would be no shortage of fresh ideas.

By Christmas, Nick was in total control and loving it. He was already asking Leo about exercising his option. At the Christmas party which Leo gave for all his staff from Soho, Haverstock Hill and Flask Walk, there were ten of them besides Nick and himself. He looked round, pleased with the little group that was the nucleus of the retail empire he was determined to build. He arrived home alone at two-thirty, adrenalin still stirring in his blood. The real prospect of achieving what he had dreamt of since he was fourteen had never shown itself more clearly than in the enthusiasm and the loyalty of the people who worked with him and were at his party that night.

As he climbed up the stairs towards his bedroom, he was surprised to hear the sound of Booker T's Hammond organ seeping from under the door. He was half-glad, half-annoyed to find Sammy in bed with a bottle of champagne open on a bedside table; annoyed because this dispelled the flow of his private, excited reverie; glad because the excitement and the drink had made him very randy.

'What the hell are you doing here, Sammy? How did you get in?'

'Sarah lent me her key. I was feeling sad because you didn't ask me to the party tonight. Anyway, aren't you glad to see me now?'

'The party was for people who worked for me. Why the hell should I have asked you? I didn't even ask Sarah for Christ's sake! And I'm not married to you, so don't go getting ideas like that.' He stopped, and poured himself a glass of champagne. More gently, unbuttoning his shirt, he said, 'But since you're here now, I am glad to see you.'

All through the following spring, Sarah worked on her collection. She went to all the lectures she was supposed to and turned in consistently good work at the college. But she managed to disguise her plans with Leo from everyone but two of her close friends – also keen young students. They would often come back to Flask Walk in the evenings and at weekends to help to perfect the huge range.

Sarah had known from the start that Leo's proposal was in earnest and was determined to produce garments that could not be faulted. Min Cooper, sworn to secrecy, stayed on for many extra hours each week to lend the benefit of her pattern-cutting experience. As the collection grew, so did Leo's excitement. He knew that he shouldn't crowd Sarah, but he couldn't stop himself from exerting some influence over her.

The results were good. Brother and sister had always been close, and as they pondered over every new design, every fresh sample, they grew closer still. Often they had no need even to speak to one another. This intimacy affected Leo's attitude towards Sammy. Compared to Sarah, she seemed to know and understand so little.

And Sammy, in turn, became increasingly jealous of Leo's closeness to Sarah. Without any decision on either part, they saw less of each other. Leo didn't really notice. He was so absorbed in his plans for the new shop and the new collection. He had posed himself a number of questions, and now wanted to be confident that he had satisfactorily answered them before he started looking in earnest for a site.

What, precisely, was the market at which he was aiming with this new look? How big was the market? What size should the shop be and how should it look? Where should it be? What should it cost?

He saw his typical customer as a girl between eighteen and thirty, whose mother might buy clothes in Bond Street or Knightsbridge, or, perhaps, a girl who was making a career for herself, from a somewhat less affluent background. She would be an individualist, independent but romantic. The price of the clothes would be higher than the average high street multiple, but the collection was distinctive enough to justify this premium. The whole shop, including the façade, would have an art nouveau/art deco feel – wooden floor, wooden hat-stands, pools of light, huge wood-framed mirrors. Black, maroon and gold would be the basic colours.

Leo decided to look in Kensington for a shop three or four times the size of the average 'boutique' that was appearing all over London: minimum two thousand square feet; at least thirty feet of frontage. After several weeks of telephoning, visiting and cajoling estate agents, he heard that an old-established grocer's shop in Kensington Church Street was closing down. The premises were a little smaller than his ideal requirements, but they were near enough. A new lease on the property was offered at a bullish rent of five thousand pounds a year. The shop front was in its original Edwardian condition and lent itself well to Leo's ideas. He immediately made an offer of ten per cent less than the asking price, conditional on being accepted, with a contract, within fourteen days. Contracts were exchanged on the thirteenth day. In June Leo took possession of his new shop.

Over the next three months, preparations occupied every waking hour of every day. Leo, Sarah and Min went to Nottingham to persuade Min's parents to take on the making up of the clothes at their factory. Mr Cooper and his wife responded to the enthusiasm of the three young rag-traders. They were prepared to accept that their optimism was well-founded, but Min's father took Leo aside and led him to his office, where he asked bluntly about the financing for all this production. Leo was ready for that.

From the large Gladstone bag that served as his brief-case, he pulled several fat folders. These contained his projections and cash-flow forecasts for the first two years' trading in Kensington Church Street and three further shops he planned to open during 1966.

'By God, son,' observed Mr Cooper, 'you can't be planning on more shops when the first one hasn't even opened. And these sales projections – it'd be a bloody miracle if you achieved that. Of course, we'd be very happy to produce the kind of quantities you're talking about, but we'd need cast-iron guarantees of your payment.' He looked doubtfully into Leo's calm, hard eyes. 'It isn't fairyland out there, you know, and I'm not going to be your fairy godfather.'

Leo said nothing for a moment. He opened a second file in which were the audited accounts for the first full trading year after he had taken over the running of the Hampstead shop. These had been drawn up to show the relative performance of the three activities: the shop in Hampstead, the stage-clothes business and the wholesale side. Beside these, he placed the accounts for the preceding five years.

'Mr Cooper, I'm twenty-one now. I was sixteen when I left school to start in my father's business, and I'd been buying and selling for a couple of years before that. If you go through these accounts with me now, I can show you when and how I contributed to the growth of the business. In the autumn of '63 I took over my father's Hampstead shop, and started a new company to do it. Last year, I split up each of my main activities into different companies, and sold thirty per cent of Showbiz Clothing to the managing director. I've also got here the half-year figures for each of these companies. Now, if I leave you alone for twenty minutes, you can read through all the figures, and I can talk to your wife about your production. When I come back, tell me what you think.'

He didn't even wait for Mr Cooper's concurrence. He went to the office door, saying, 'I'll see you in twenty minutes, then,' and left the older man staring after him with disbelief.

Min had told her parents a lot about Leo, but they had been inclined to discount her descriptions of his business success and acumen as naïve, youthful adulation. As Mr Cooper read through the accounts, however, it became clear that Min had not exaggerated. It was not only the dramatic increase in sales that impressed him, it was also the obvious and complete control that Leo had over his resources. He was curious to know the source of the substantial loans that Leo had made personally to the company but was encouraged to see that he had recently capitalised the loans by converting them to share equity. This meant that he wasn't using the shield of a limited liability to protect his investment if the company went bankrupt; a clear indication of confidence.

By extrapolating the sales in Leo's existing outlet to the larger, better-sited Kensington shop, the projected figures were perfectly realistic.

When Leo reappeared in his office, he was ready to talk. 'All right, young man,' he said, 'we'll work for you. But you know we'll want seven-day payments. I can see that you'll be all right for the first stock order, but what about after that? Has your bank agreed to the facility that your cash flow requires?'

'Well, Mr Cooper, I don't need to discuss my banking arrangements with you, but you can see the maximum credit I could build up with you over, say, four weeks, so why not put in for a bank reference for double that and see what comes back?'

Mr Cooper nodded. 'Right. Well, if the girls are getting on all right, let's have a drink to a fruitful relationship.'

With production organised, Sarah turned her attention to the buying of accessories and some additional clothing stock. In the first year, she had decided they would buy in knitwear, coats and hats. In spite of the pressure put on her by Leo to include these in her exclusive Rags range, she absolutely refused on the grounds that she had neither the time nor the experience to do it properly. As it turned out, she was able to find two knitting factories – one in Leicester and one in Hawick – who would work very closely to her colour and styling specifications and were quite prepared to put in Rags labels.

Leo allowed Sammy to help her with the selection of accessories as there were simply too many to see on her own. But, on her own, with Leo's critical encouragement, she produced all the working drawings for the shop front and the interior. The effect of this was to create, as Leo had envisaged, a relationship between the clothes and the surroundings in which they were to be sold.

One day in June, Leo burst into Sarah's workroom, very excited and rather drunk. He had just returned from the preview of a new Quant collection.

'I told you you should have come,' he slurred at Sarah. 'We may be the best, but we're not the only people with new ideas.'

'Oh, Leo, you're plastered.' She held up a conciliatory hand. 'All right, what have you seen that's so great?'

'Pussy-level hem-lines!' Leo groaned and grasped his head in both hands and shook it in mock trauma. 'Skirt lengths have been going up – but they've taken them all the way – on dresses too.'

'Doesn't sound too elegant.'

'Listen, I wasn't worried about elegance. When those models came on, there wasn't a man in the place that didn't get an instant hard-on – except the poofs of course. It's the horniest thing I've ever seen. I think it's the little glimpse of flesh above the stocking top that does it; and the suspender clips, just asking to be popped.'

At that moment, Sammy poked her head round the door, and came in carrying her portfolio.

Leo grabbed her, and a simple sleeveless *crêpe de Chine* dress from a rail. 'Dump the snaps, Angel, and put this on a moment.'

'Hang on, Leo.' Sarah tried to grab the frock. 'I'm still working on that.'

'S'all right – just wait, I want to show you.'

Sammy obligingly discarded the blouse and skirt she was wearing and stood in her bra and tiny knickers for a moment. Leo made a playful lunge for the trim little body, slipped his hand into the unresistant underwear.

'For God's sake,' Sarah was annoyed. 'Make up your mind – do you want an orgy or do you want to look at this dress?'

Leo retreated reluctantly and Sammy slipped the flimsy garment over her head. It hung quite closely off the hips to a point three inches above her knees.

Leo picked up a box of pins and knelt down in front of her. He tucked the hem up inside itself until it was level with Sammy's crotch, then pinned it. He got to his feet and stood back shaking his head in wonderment.

'For God's sake, Leo – I can see her knickers,' Sarah said.

'What's wrong with that?'

'That's just too much. That's not sexy or provocative, it's just obscene. Here.'

Now she knelt, unpinned the hem and dropped it an inch. 'That's a bit more subtle, don't you think?'

Leo laughed and nodded. 'It's delicious – you've got to do it.'

Sarah smiled. 'Yes, I suppose so. It had to come.'

Leo decided against having a major press conference. Instead he invited just one journalist, Suzi Clifton from the *Sunday Times*, to lunch and gave her an exclusive presentation of the new Rags. Suitably impressed, she agreed to make the new shop her lead story. Her photographer was sworn to absolute discretion, and Sammy modelled the clothes. Sarah's sketches of the shop front and interior were also used to illustrate the article.

They opened on the following Wednesday. On Tuesday, they invited all the models from Lucie Clayton's and Askew's to a private preview, with a fifty per cent discount on anything that they bought; nearly all of them bought something.

By the weekend, a combination of word of mouth and the *Sunday Times* article had generated a relentless flood of interest in the new Rags.

It was an extraordinary sight. Excited girls and young women could be seen scurrying from all directions, up and down Church Street, eager to be part of this new look right at the start. They entered the shop breathless, and looked around, not knowing where to begin this feast of self-indulgence. Then, clothes were yanked off hangers and held against posed bodies. Hats were grabbed and tried on a dozen ways, scarves were wound and unwound round long white necks. The changing rooms resembled a battlefield. Frantically scribbled cheques were proffered to harassed cashiers at constantly ringing tills. It was a retailer's heaven.

Leo and Sarah scarcely left the shop from the moment that the doors were flung open until the last customer left on Saturday evening. But by then, there was no question. They had created a major success. As the tills were checked and the items sold were totalled, Leo could hardly believe that the reality had outstripped even his most optimistic projections.

He was still only twenty-one, and nothing could stop him now. He had made it.

Within a year, two more Rags were opened, one at the Sloane Square end of the King's Road and one in Beauchamp Place, by the junction with the Brompton Road. The shop in Haverstock Hill had been converted when Kensington had opened and its turnover had more than doubled. The Rags look was completely established and, as Leo had anticipated, the imitators had already shown themselves. But they couldn't keep up. Sarah's imagination and her capacity for work seemed inexhaustible. By the second autumn, every single item in the shop had either been designed by or exclusively for her.

The fashion press would not leave them alone. No issue of any women's magazine was without at least one reference to them. Sarah was persistently and eagerly sought for interviews, but she hated giving them and gladly let Leo speak for them both. He performed well, both in print and on television, where he was often invited to appear as a spokesman for young British fashion.

It was with supreme confidence that in spring '66, a fifth Rags was opened in Bond Street. What Leo's advertising agents called the 'demograph' of their typical customer had, it appeared, widened simultaneously both up and down the market. It would not be unusual if a young countess from the shires and an aspiring audio-typist from Dagenham both bought, and were delighted with, an identical dress. This had as much to do with the mood of the moment as it had with Sarah's designs, but Rags's success lay in the skills and the acumen that had anticipated and interpreted that mood.

Leo was very much in control, but he found an unforeseen problem. What he hadn't expected, or even thought about, was the loneliness of success. Paradoxically, his adolescent insecurities, which had fired his ambition, were not diminished by a surfeit of the approval which he had so eagerly sought. Nick, Min, even Sarah, grew away, rather than closer, as his fame and success increased.

And Sammy provided no solace. Her own preoccupations did not allow her to see Leo might have any problems of his own. Leo didn't rationalise this, he simply knew that she had nothing more to offer him. She bored him. Punctuated by intermittent minor tantrums on her part, their relationship just faded away.

The last time he saw her was in a television advertisement for shampoo, and then his attention was riveted by the other girl in the ad. Her wonderful dark auburn hair set off a pair of bright, mischievous blue eyes that showed great independence and an unchallengeable knowingness; he made a mental note to find out who she was.

With the diminution of Sammy's never very strong claims on his attention, Leo had not been reluctant to use his increasing wealth and fame in the pursuit of sexual adventure. He told himself, with more truth than he realised, that he would have made most of his many conquests without the aid of his money. His energy and spontaneous wit and his arrogant self-confidence were a powerfully attractive combination. He was not a handsome man in the classical sense, but his dark features exuded promise of great sensuality. He seldom had difficulty in running his chosen quarry to bed.

Now that the Pill had allowed promiscuity to become a practical option for most girls, Leo was amazed by the depth and breadth of choice on offer. He was fascinated by the diversity of female sexual tastes; could not resist the promise of a new, and possibly unexpected, variation. Inevitably, the more he loved and left, the more the women responded – as much to the rumours and the aura of energy and power that he brought to his lovemaking as to the skill and enthusiasm with which he performed.

This success scored him great notoriety, and some envy, among other men whose paths he crossed in his pursuits. He became much in demand for any fashionable gathering and spent his evenings with the rock aristocracy and emergent young film stars. He could compete on more than equal terms with them; and, for him, this was the cream on the sexual cake.

After the Bond Street shop was successfully launched, Leo bought the freehold on a double mews house in Adam and Eve Mews, off Kensington High Street, and threw himself into the business of creating a penthouse flat, a suite of offices for himself, with design studios and a head office below. The purposes of this lavish but tastefully refurbished building were twofold. First was the gratification of his own desire to be surrounded by obvious and daunting opulence; second there was the more pragmatic commercial purpose – to present a front that affirmed both the design strength and the financial security of his company. It had taken only two years since the launch of the new Rags to reach a position of substantial market influence and consistent profitability. Leo wanted those cynics among the people with whom he did business to know: Rags was solid; Rags was here to stay.

# Autumn 1966

Raju Kalianji arrived in London four days before the academic year began at the London School of Economics.

He was met at Heathrow by Paul Paintal, one of his mother's many relations. Paul had come with his family to England, after having moved to India from Uganda some fifteen years before. He was an intelligent and able accountant, working at Her Majesty's Customs and Excise in the Central London Purchase Tax office. Raj's parents had insisted, in spite of his protests, that he was met by someone who could show him around a little, and help to familiarise him with London.

Raj was agreeably surprised to find that Paul Paintal treated him as an adult and an equal. He had been slightly nervous about leaving his family for the first time in his life and arriving in an environment that was so foreign. Although he had read dozens of books about Britain, her culture and her politics, he had not been prepared for some aspects of England that the books had not mentioned: the smell and crispness of the air; the opaqueness of the light; the confident, affable briskness of the people; the sense of orderliness in the streets and houses. And as Paul, interested and well-informed, talked to him about Uganda and seemed to take his views seriously, Raj began to feel comfortable, to feel that he was moving into a new and exciting phase of his life.

Paul had arranged to take time off work so that he could show his young relation around London. He had decided to present to Raj a cross-section of the cultural history of the great city, and as they drove between the Tower of

London and the Tate Gallery, the British Museum and Westminster Abbey, he tried to summarise his views of life in Britain for an Asian.

'The British attitude to us is very ambivalent. On the whole, they are generous and kind people, provided you don't trespass too far onto their privacy. Those whom you've met in East Africa are mostly the remnants of colonial Britain, and they aren't typical. Of course, there is a great deal of ignorance. English people tend to assume that all Indians and Pakistanis are the same, and not much allowance is made for individual variations, despite the far wider cultural and religious influences in our history.'

'But they seem very polite, and helpful,' Raj protested. 'I'd read about an English politician, Enoch Powell, who seems to have spoken very aggressively about all colonial immigrants, and the article suggested that he has a following here. I was a bit afraid that I might encounter some of his animosity, but I haven't.'

Paul looked over at him and smiled. 'You will,' he said, 'but don't let it depress you. It's not hard to see the reasons for it, but just remind yourself that they're bad reasons, born out of a very irrational fear, and try to ignore them.'

Paul and his wife had no children. In the time they had lived in England, they had concerned themselves with the local Hindu community and were liked and respected within it. They lived in a neat 1930s semi-detached villa in South Harrow. The tree-lined street was about fifty per cent occupied by Asians. So far as Raj could see, the immigrant community existed quite harmoniously with their indigenous neighbours.

'It's true,' Paul agreed, 'but we're fortunate. By local standards, I'm well paid and respectable. I drive a new car, live in a neat, tidy house, and wear English suits. These are visible outward signs that they can relate to, and the same applies to other Indians in this street. As long as we're not pinching their jobs, we'll be tolerated. But some communities, for example the Pathans in Bradford, appear so very different that the gap between the two cultures is harder to bridge.'

Raj was depressed by four days of this morbid and negative attitude. He came from the commercial elite of his country, and had been readily granted a place in one of Britain's most prestigious universities. He could not reconcile this with the second-class citizenship which, his cousin seemed to imply, was the best that he could hope for.

A few days in the hall of residence in Malet Street and the induction course at the LSE gave him another perspective. Here there was no hint of resentment of his colour. Indeed, at least a quarter of the students seemed to be non-European, and the English students met him on more than friendly terms. He was aware of a conscious effort on their part to avoid any reference to his race save where occasional, over-stated jokes about curry and the Kharma Sutra would be made, accompanied by deprecating little smiles just to show that any apparent differences between their races were entirely superficial.

But everyone was prepared to talk politics. Nearly all the English students were strongly socialist, some to the point of Trotskyism. The Establishment was universally disliked, mistrusted and castigated. British Toryism was considered an anachronistic joke, and the right-wing Conservatives like Enoch Powell were loudly vilified.

Early in the term, Raj found himself sitting in the students' bar with a group of altruistic young Englishmen. Here, it was not his colour but his political viewpoint that put him in the minority.

Dave Traps was the most vociferous member of the group. He was a second-year student; a noted and uncompromising debater. He had come from one of the premier public schools and his father was a leading and very rich QC.

'Look Raj, all the independent African states have adopted some version of European democracy – and it's a flop. God knows, the system doesn't even work here. This country's always been run by a tiny elite Establishment. The people have got no say at all.'

Raj was puzzled. 'But you have free elections. The people are presented with options, and may choose.'

'Ah, but the options are very limited. Harold Wilson and his chums may have conned the working classes into believing they're on their side, but in the end, a government can only do as much as its civil servants allow it. And quite apart from that, socialist politicians are no exception to the "power corrupts" syndrome. Once they've enjoyed swanning around in big black cars and guzzling brandy, they're quite prepared to make compromises to remain in comfort.'

'But I've always believed that your parliamentary democracy was the fairest system yet devised. The problem with the African nations has always been tribalism. After all, Britain used to be a nation of tribes, but over the centuries it has worked itself out.'

The English students laughed patronisingly.

'That's a myth. The Scots, the Welsh, even the Cornish are all screaming for devolution. They're not interested in being exploited by a bunch of bowler-hatted folk in Whitehall.'

'Well, what alternative are you proposing?' asked Raj.

'Revolution, of course. Constant revolution – like the Chinese, where leadership can never get complacent.'

'But Mao's been in charge for years,' protested Raj.

'Yes – but he's not complacent.'

'All right, but revolution is totally destabilising to an economy.'

'Great – it's only the fat cats that benefit from a stable economy.'

'But really, Dave,' Raj persisted, 'that's rubbish. Look at living standards here, under your own noses. They have been soaring for everyone, not just your fat cats. After all, you're not starving: but then, of course, you're not from the working classes. So why do you care so passionately about them? What right have you to impose your views on people with whom you have so little in common? Surely, if the workers wanted revolution, they would have set about it before now.'

The others smiled indulgently.

'Raj, you've got a lot to learn.'

'True – but that's hardly an argument to support your theories.'

At first, in the hall of residence, he had not allowed himself to get drawn into any particular friendships. He merely wanted to work as hard as possible and to establish an academic standing that would justify admiration rather than tolerant indulgence from the other students. He did, however, slowly develop a rapport with a Sikh student from Delhi, called Jay Singh.

Jay was more idealistic and less able than Raj, but he came from a cultural minority with more than its fair share of influence in India, and this inequity concerned him deeply. He found Raj a useful sparring partner, and the strength of his views effectively complemented his lesser academic abilities.

In other ways, Jay was more worldly. He had made a number of friends among the English students, particularly the women. One evening, he persuaded Raj to join him for a cheap dinner in a Charlotte Street restaurant with two girls in their first year at LSE.

Apart from knowing that his parents, if they had not done so already, would select and expect him to marry a bride of their choosing, and occasional strangely stimulating sessions of dirty talk in the tennis club in Kampala, Raj had given very little thought to girls. They were irrelevant to his main aims in life and he had not started worrying about self-propagation, but once having agreed with Jay that he would go, he found himself looking forward to this dinner with an unfamiliar excitement.

They all met in the students' bar at Malet Street; Jay introduced Sue Hardcastle and Diana Quinn. It was clear that he considered Diana to be his date for the evening. Raj was supposed to do his best with Sue.

At first, Raj found himself reluctant to communicate at all, and only answered questions when urged by one or other of the girls. The girls, however, did not seem put out, and continued to include him in the conversation.

They walked to the Spaghetti House and Jay ordered a large straw-covered flask of Chianti. Slowly, Raj found himself being drawn and fascinated by Diana. Sue was solid, sensible and sincere, but Diana was controversial and daring in her views and had the wit to support them. Every opinion that she managed to extract from Raj, she disagreed with, not aggressively, but objectively, almost indifferently. And, sitting opposite him, as she talked to him her bright blue eyes gazed straight into his, and she smiled, lightly challenging him as she spoke.

Raj could feel Jay's resentment, but relaxed and smiled back at Diana, laughing at himself, apologising for his political innocence. Slowly, the conversation moved on through music, films, art and theatre. Raj was intrigued and impressed by the breadth of her knowledge. She led the conversation, provoking Sue, encouraging the two Indians. It was the first time that Raj had spent any time talking about the arts. He had had little interest in them, a conventional general knowledge of them, and no strong views. But he proposed that they were not very relevant to the world's problems and was met with a forceful lecture from Diana on how, throughout history, the arts had influenced politics.

And during this conversation, he felt, beneath the narrow table, the inside of his knee touch hers. He decorously moved it away, but somehow, contact was re-established, and sustained. As they talked, his attention kept returning to the spot where, through her woollen skirt and his flannel trousers, some violent fusion seemed to be taking place. When Diana talked of the tradition of erotic art in India, approving this healthy recognition of the role of sexual activity in human experience, he felt his blood rising, his pulse quicken. He wanted to touch her, feel her body against his, feel her lips caressing his skin. The awkward hardness in his groin was unmistakable in its purpose.

Somehow, he managed to stop himself from jabbering and panting and making his thoughts too obvious. Instinct told him to pursue his urges neither too fast, nor too crudely. He forced himself to concentrate on the conversation, but found that he had little to contribute.

Jay seemed to have accepted that Diana was more interested in Raj than himself, and directed his suggestive attention towards the other girl. Sue was quite unable to disguise her pleasure at this. Men usually found her openness and idealism disquieting and she had been disappointed by her lack of success with them. She was more than ready to take advantage of the situation that had developed as the meal had progressed.

Jay's blood was up, he was slightly drunk, and Sue was an uncomplicated, comfortable person. After a while he stood up suddenly, put some money on the table and announced that he and Sue were going back to his room for a nightcap. Sue said nothing, but got up self-consciously and half smiled goodbye to Diana.

For a moment, Raj and Diana sat looking at one another, not speaking.

Then he said: 'What an unanticipated pleasure.'

'What a ghastly expression.'

They laughed. Raj leant forward, and put his hand gently on hers. 'Diana, I don't want you to think I'm only interested in your intellect – and your impressive knowledge of the arts.' He squeezed her hand gently, and felt an increase of pressure on his knee. 'But,' he continued, 'I'm not asking you back to my room for a nightcap.'

'Well – I'd have turned you down anyway, beautiful and mysterious though you are. But, look on the positive side. The longer it takes to unwrap a present, the more exciting it becomes.'

Raj did not see her for a week. He had looked out for her, rung her digs, left a note – which was collected – on the *poste restante* and puzzled over why she had seemed to make her intentions so clear, then failed to respond. But on the next Saturday morning, he found a note which had been slipped under his door.

'*If you want to increase your knowledge of western culture and British customs, meet me in the students' union bar at 7.30 this evening.'*

Raj found Jay and told him he would not be seeing him that evening, as he wanted to put in some extra work on an essay he was writing.

For once, that afternoon, he found he could not concentrate on his books. Disgusted with himself, he walked up to Regent's Park and followed the Outer Circle the whole way round, trying to come to terms with this new, extraordinary sensation. He went back to the university library and looked up Indian cultural history books. He gazed at photographs of the great relief sculptures on the temples of Khajuraho, where hundreds of beautiful men and women are carved in stone, in startlingly varied postures of sensual love-making. These were celebrating Hindu gods, his gods; and how unashamed and glorious they looked. He felt his excitement grow, as he imagined himself with Diana, exploring the infinite, intimate ways of bodily contact.

Eventually, he bought a copy of the *Economist*, went to the bar, and tried to read as he waited, but the words on the page danced beneath his eyes and reformed themselves into voluptuous, beckoning women, firm, round-breasted, with wide, inviting apertures.

A soft voice in his ear made him start.

'Raj,' she said, 'not still working?'

Diana had struggled all week not to respond to Raj's messages and invitations. She had wanted to rationalise her undeniable physical attraction to him. She was interested in him intellectually, although she knew men more academically sophisticated and visionary. She found his determination to understand and justify modern western democracy impressive, though naïve.

And she did want him to make love to her, to swallow her up in those big brown eyes, to wrap her round with those strong brown limbs.

As she had entered the bar, she had seen Raj leaning over a magazine, reading intently. She had stood for a moment, watching his long black eyelashes flickering over the page, his straight, jet-black hair falling in a shining curtain over his forehead, the innocent calmness of his fine, classic features. When she walked over and spoke to him, he looked up quickly, guiltily, then relaxed with a wide smile of greeting.

They walked up Kingsway to a small bistro near the Museum. This was the first time Raj had ever taken a woman out alone, but Diana's easy naturalness made him feel as if he had been doing it for years. In the week that had passed since their first meeting, he had developed an avid interest in the arts. He had eagerly read and re-read reviews in the papers, had attended a recital in the Wigmore Hall, and had gone back to take a more critical look at the Tate. Already he found that he had something to say as they strolled – she with her arm through his – to the restaurant.

Diana was impressed that he had made this effort for her, and that he showed such a quick understanding of the aims and methods of the artists they discussed. He confidently challenged her view of Mozart as a frivolous courtier: the sonatas that he had heard at the recital seemed to him to demonstrate a great depth of feeling, without which such heights of melodic beauty could not have been achieved.

They sat down to eat off a red and white checked table-cloth, with a guttering candle stuck into the top of a wine bottle between them.

'You've a clever woman,' Raj told her over the soupe à l'oignon. 'You know a lot about a lot of things. What are you going to do with all this knowledge?'

She looked awkward and despondent. 'I don't know. It's very depressing, but I don't. I don't know what my politics are, what my role in life is, what I want to see achieved. I feel strongly about everything and nothing. I think I'm one of life's natural journalists. I want to watch, report and analyse – but I don't want the responsibility of actually doing anything.'

'Why – why not? You seemed to have such strong views last week, and so much logic and enthusiasm to back them up. You've had a life surrounded by all the great cultural traditions of your country – and you seem to know about them and to approve of them, and at the same time you seem to want to reject them.'

'That's just it. Sometimes I want to attack, sometimes defend the environment I grew up in. I'm a privileged person, you know,' she smiled sardonically. 'My parents are wealthy. They're kind, but they're also unbendingly conservative. I went to a private school, and I was good at everything, even lacrosse.' She paused, laughing. 'Coming to LSE was a deliberate decision to let people know that I didn't want to follow the obvious route for a clever middle-class girl. That's a pretty negative reason, wouldn't you say?'

'I don't know,' Raj shook his head. 'My father wanted me to do my postgrad course at Oxford, but there really wasn't a suitable one. I chose LSE because it's supposed to be the world's leading school of politics and economics. Maybe your decision was partly based on that fact?'

'Well, maybe,' she said.

'Tell me about your parents,' said Raj, 'and where they live.'

'You should come and meet them. My father's a retired brigadier, formal but jolly, though I don't think he's ever learned to show his true feelings. When he disagrees with me, he just looks hurt and grunts. My mother's gentle and considerate, though without knowing why. They live in a very pretty Queen Anne house near Sherborne. That's in Dorset, in the west of England. When I came to university they bought a little house for me to live in, in Cleaver Square, just over the river from Vauxhall Bridge. I asked them not to, but I suppose they felt they weren't losing me if I lived in their house. Actually, I don't mind – it's a lovely little cottage. But there you are – another contradiction. I'll argue all night long against bourgeois ethics, but I love my parents, who more or less epitomise them.'

The main course, boeuf bourguignon, arrived. 'My problem is different,' said Raj, when the waiter had gone. 'I think, essentially, my father and I want the same thing.

But my aims are more far-reaching. My father's a wise chap, but I'm better educated. And anyway, he's reached the age where his main concern is for his family. Also, of course, we Indians in East Africa may have a lot of problems over the next few years. I think we're all right for the moment with Obote in power, but that could change overnight, and I don't think my father's interested in looking beyond that possibility. Also, to be truthful, I have doubts about my role, as an Indian in an African nation. After all, my ancestors came to trade along the East African coast simply because there was more chance of doing business there than in Gujarat.'

Diana looked at him intently, fascinated but puzzled. 'You seem to be a real hotch-potch of conflicting aims,' she said. 'Totally mercenary on the one hand, and concerned about the validity of your status on the other. Tell me, how do you find it, being an Indian in England – I don't mean here at the university, but out and about, in the streets?'

'I have encountered a few, really crass examples of prejudice, and even when people are being polite, I sense a sort of restrained disapproval. Maybe I'm getting over-sensitive, but I don't think so. I must admit, it has slightly tempered my admiration of the British. Not all of them, of course,' he laughed, looking into Diana's eyes.

'Well,' she said, 'I don't know whether to admire your aspirations or not, but you've got lovely eyes. Do you have many girlfriends back in Uganda?'

Raj shook his head. 'No. We really don't mix much. There were practically no Indian girls at the university. And my parents are traditional Hindus. They will expect me to marry a girl they choose – so courting, as you call it here, is not expected. At the tennis club, all my friends were men, and of course, playing cricket is a male activity.'

'No wonder you seemed so shy last week. Well, you're in London now, so, as St Ambrose said to St Augustine – "When in Rome . . ."'

'When in Rome . . . what?'

'Do as the Romans. Do you want to come back to

82

Cleaver Square and have coffee when we've finished?'

Raj nodded.

When they left the restaurant, Raj, with guilty extravagance, hailed a taxi and Diana gave the cabby her address.

They talked about the buildings and the monuments as they drove through the Saturday-night crowds; until, gently, Raj put his arm around her shoulder and drew her to him; her cheek on his shoulder; her face, framed by her short, curly brown hair, below him; eyes expectant, anxious, eager; her mouth, a little open, emitting short, deep breaths. And for the first time in his life, he kissed – and felt as if he had been administered some magic drug. So soft, this special contact between two pairs of lips, two probing tongues. And hungrily, they kissed their way from Trafalgar Square to Stockwell.

In the little house, all pine and posters, potted plants and abstract prints, they lit a single lamp and the small gas fire. Diana poured Raj a brandy from a dusty bottle and made them cups of coffee. She put on a Bob Dylan album, and lay on a rug in front of the fire, her head resting in his lap, where he sat on the floor, legs outstretched, his back against a solid, ancient armchair.

They talked, relaxed, very happy at their mutual discovery. Raj looked down, caressed her face, slid down onto the rug beside her. All the time kissing her neck, her ears, her eyelids, he moved to lie on her, felt her legs part to accommodate the bulging hardness in his trousers.

And then she said, 'Raj, I want to feel you all naked next to me. Let's undress.' And slowly with fervid, trembling hands, they did. Then, when she guided him to her, their love-making was slow and gentle. Sensuality blocked out all other thoughts; their whole universe was concentrated in the sensations that they triggered in each other, until they lay hot, sweating, spent, content, still in each other's arms, gently touching.

They slept, later, in Diana's little bed.

Autumn morning sun beamed fully through the windows. Raj was surprised and charmed by the chintzy little room, tried to reconcile it to his lover's fiercely-spoken ideas, and began to understand her more. She walked into the bedroom with cups of coffee and placed them beside the bed. Then Raj watched as her dressing-gown slid to the ground to reveal her fair and perfect body; small, round, firm bottom, little waist, tiny tummy.

They stayed in bed till midday, then went to the pub at the end of the square for lunch. They drank and read the Sunday papers together. The afternoon was so fine that they chose to walk back over the river, through Sunday London to Bloomsbury.

That evening, when Diana had gone, Raj could hardly believe his happiness and sense of fulfilment. He turned to his neglected essay with his mind sharp, alert and positive. How wonderful that sensations so intense could still allow him to focus his mind on other things – even if, every so often he found himself thinking of her, her ideas, her eagerness, her quandaries, her generosity and her soft, willing body.

Raj was not looking forward to the Christmas vacation. He was not going back to Uganda. It was not worth it. And he could do a lot of work, staying at the Paintals'. But he was going to miss Diana. They had seen each other at least every few days over that autumn term, sometimes at her suggestion, sometimes at his. He told her that he was not going to let his work suffer, and, in a way, she was glad that she did not see him as often as she wanted. Her other boyfriends had given up trying. They still took her out for her wit and provocative company, but her relationship with Raj had become an accepted fact and she was respected by the men, envied by the women for it.

Diana did wonder, though she tried not to, what Raj would do when he returned to Africa the following summer. Would he stay there? Would he conform with his parents' wishes and marry their chosen bride? He would not speak of it. He gave no sign of changing his originally stated plans. But he had learned so much and understood so much since she had met him that she believed he would have to modify these plans. For now she loved him, fiercely and possessively. She had come to admire his great capacity to absorb and analyse information, and his determination to extract, intellectually, all that he could from the course he was on and the people around him. And when they slept together, his strong gentleness and passionate inventiveness convinced her that he must love her too, but he certainly never said so, and she was not going to ask.

Two weeks before Christmas, she asked him if he would like to come and stay at her parents for a few days over the New Year. Raj willingly accepted the invitation. He could afford to lose a week's study and guessed that a whole month with the Paintals could be depressing. Anyway, he wanted to see Diana, to see her background and meet her family.

Most of the students had gone by the time Raj carried his suitcase up to Euston Station to take the tube to Harrow. As the train rattled mournfully westwards, he tried to prepare himself for the change in culture. Already he felt sure he knew a great deal more about the world than Paul Paintal, and expected to be bored and frustrated by the smallness of his cousin's horizons.

When he arrived, he spent most of his time in his bedroom, working, and aching for the thrust and parry of Diana's argument and the giving softness of her body. Paul did his best to amuse him. Over large, traditional Indian meals, he explained the history and customs of the western Christmas; explained that, as with many of their Hindu feasts, original Christian motives had been amalgamated with the rites of older deities, and modern social mores.

Paul explained well, but always as an outsider, an observer. Raj asked him why he did not become more involved, since he now lived in Britain. After all, the basic tenets of Christianity were not so very different from those of their own religion, and maybe it was this cultural aloofness that prevented a satisfactory integration.

Paul smiled with irritating condescension. 'There are innumerable factions among Christians who refuse to see eye to eye. And the Jews have maintained their religious independence, but now could be said to be thoroughly integrated in British society.'

'No,' interrupted Raj, 'they're still not quite there, although they've been here for four hundred years!'

He felt that his point was proved, but Paul just shook his head and resolved that next time he wrote to Vishnu Kalianji he would mention his worries about Raj's attitude and lack of respect for traditional Hindu values.

Raj set off with relief to catch the early afternoon train from Waterloo to Sherborne. It was not crowded, and he found an empty, pleasantly musty compartment. He sat by the window, looking forward to his first view of rural England. A woman in her mid-forties, with two children, slid open the door, saw Raj sitting there, and closed it again to find another, empty compartment. Raj shrugged to himself. He'd have done the same, but it was frustrating not to know if this woman had done it because he was just a person, or a brown person.

When the train pulled out of the vast iron-girder cavern, he was fascinated by the changes in the streets and houses as they moved from the inner city, through the increasingly wealthy-looking suburbs, which seemed to stretch for twenty miles. After Woking, he was enchanted by the neat old farms, the small lush fields between the little woods and sunken lanes. In Hampshire, the weak winter sun lit huge rolling expanses of sown plough, discoloured by uneven blotches of chemical fertiliser and broken by long lines of iron pylons, strung out to the horizon.

When the land had changed to small hills, pastures full of grazing cows and orchards of naked trees, the train arrived at Sherborne. Diana was waiting, her nose a little red, wearing a huge multi-coloured scarf, with a knitted hat to match.

She threw her arms around him, laughing. 'Oh, Raju – it's great to see you. How was the train? Not too cold and smelly, I hope?'

Raj kissed her forehead and gave her a decorous hug. 'It was fine,' he answered. 'I enjoyed it, but I'm glad I've arrived. It's good to see you, too. You look different somehow, as if you've changed your personality to suit the surroundings.' He smiled. 'You look less militant than usual.'

'Yes.' She shrugged. 'I suppose I am, down here. There's no one to have an intelligent argument with, so – I don't. Anyway, don't forget your case. I've got my mother's car just outside the station.'

As Raj carried his suitcase through the barrier and handed in his ticket, Diana hung on to his arm, grinning and relaxed. The back of the green Morris Traveller was full of Wellington boots, dog blankets and a dirty, amiable springer spaniel.

They got into the car. Diana shivered and turned on the engine and the heater, and soon, warm air was blowing up from below the dashboard. They set off through Sherborne, making a detour so Raj could see something of the old town and the Abbey, then headed south for ten miles or so into the Blackmore Vale.

It was almost dark now, and when Diana drove the car between two old red-brick gate-posts and up a short hedge-lined drive, the squares of muted light shone warmly from the large house. They stopped in a stableyard, and Diana led Raj across to a dark back door. They went in and brushed past a row of old coats and mackintoshes, walking-sticks and more boots. Cartridge belts and odd bits of bridle hung from hooks, and in the gaps between them, dusty sporting prints and sepia photographs.

'I'll take you up the back stairs to your room, and you can unpack and wash or change if you want to, and I'll tell my parents you're here. My mother wants us to have tea in the drawing-room so I'll come up and find you in ten minutes.'

She showed Raj to the end of a corridor on the first floor, and opened the door to a small, warm bedroom. An electric fire glowed in the fireplace, and the bedside lamp threw shadows on the long, chintz curtains. When Diana had gone down again, after giving him another, slightly self-conscious kiss, he put his clothes in a huge mahogany wardrobe and washed at an ancient basin in a corner of the room. Raj was impressed by the solidness of it all. It looked as though little had been changed for fifty years. It was somehow very reassuring. The quiet, confident atmosphere of the place was completely new to him, but all his instincts approved. He smiled to himself as he straightened his tie and combed his neat black hair.

When Diana came to fetch him, she laughed at his tweed jacket and flannel trousers. 'My God, you look more English than a Savile Row shopwindow. Oh, well, at least my father'll be able to relate to that. Come on, they're waiting to meet you.'

In the drawing-room downstairs, a log fire burned. On a low table between two large sofas, the apparatus for serving tea was laid: silver gleaming, not too brightly, fine bone china with a slightly worn, delicate floral pattern.

Brigadier Quinn was a tall, solid man in his mid-sixties. Clean-shaven and with thick grey hair, he was not an ex-military stereotype. He looked more alert and observant than Raj had imagined, and he could find no fault with the warmth of the old man's greeting. Mrs Quinn, perhaps ten years younger, had features typical of her class, supported by the predictable, neat, slightly waved hairstyle, tweed skirt and cardigan. Her face was open and kind.

'We've heard a lot about you, Mr Kalianji. I'm so glad you could come,' she said. 'This is the first time Diana's asked anyone down from the university. We were beginning to wonder why she hadn't.' She smiled tentatively.

Her husband joined the conversation. 'We can't call you Mr Kalianji for the next five days. Do you prefer to be called Raju?'

'Oh, please call me Raj. It's easy to remember. Just think of the British Raj.'

Diana sat next to Raj on a sofa. Her parents, opposite, asked him where he came from and expressed surprise when he told them. 'Oh, you're from Africa? One quite forgets there are so many Indians there too. Have you been to India as well?' Diana's father asked.

Raj shook his head. 'No. My family have been in East Africa for several generations. But I would like to see Gujarat, where they came from. And I've recently become more interested in Indian cultural history, partly thanks to Diana.'

'Good Lord,' said the Brigadier, 'what does she know about it?'

'Not much,' Raj answered amiably, 'But you don't have to know a lot about a particular culture to know that it's important. And I had rather neglected it. Of course, I've been learning a lot about western arts, and comparisons can be very interesting.'

'How do you mean?' asked Mrs Quinn, genuinely. 'I mean, you can't really compare Indian music with, say, Beethoven.'

'Well . . .' Raj paused. 'Yehudi Menhuin seems to have found some common ground. He's considered quite good, isn't he?'

'Oh, of course. I didn't know he played Indian music,' said Mrs Quinn, embarrassed.

Later, the Brigadier offered Raj a drink. Diana was helping her mother prepare dinner, and the two men stood in front of the fire drinking whisky.

'I understand you're on a one-year post-graduate course at Diana's college. Will you be going back to Uganda after that?' the older man asked.

'Yes. My father wishes me to join him in his business. He feels, I hope rightly, that my training in international economics will be useful. There are also broader, political activities in which I'm interested.'

'I see. You mean Ugandan politics?'

'Yes, and East African generally. We Indians have tended to stand aside from these things. First the British were there, and now the Africans have formed governments. But we are important to the economy and I think we should become more involved in the politics.'

'Well, those African governments certainly seem to need a bit of help, though I'm not sure that Ian Smith has taken the right course in Rhodesia. I can't see him ever getting what he wants.'

They talked on politely. Diana's father expressing views that were predictable, though not without well-informed consideration. He wasn't used to young men and he found Raj's confident opinions disconcerting, but he couldn't deny that they were rationally and respectfully presented.

At one point, Raj wanted to go to the lavatory and the Brigadier directed him to one at the end of the back corridor. Passing quietly by the kitchen door on his return, he overheard her mother talking to Diana.

'He seems very polite and intelligent, dear, and rather good-looking, and he speaks awfully good English, but don't you find him very different from your other friends?'

'Not really. And the ways in which I do are distinct improvements on the others. He's much more mature and self-sufficient than the English students – and he's got a lot more to work for.'

'Oh yes, I'm sure he works hard and everything . . . but what about religion?'

'Oh, really, Mummy, what's your religion to you apart from keeping in with the vicar and worrying about the church roof? A good Hindu isn't much different than a good Christian.'

'Well, I daresay you're right, just as long as you know what you're doing. After all, you're only nineteen.' A moment's silence. 'By the way, what does he normally eat. Will he be able to have this beef casserole?'

Diana laughed. 'Of course he will. He's not a holy man from half-way up the Himalayas. He's a perfectly normal man who plays cricket and tennis and drinks wine and has girlfriends. Just forget he's not the same colour as you and behave accordingly.' Raj carried on back to the drawing-room where a second whisky was waiting for him.

Conversation over dinner was slow, and Raj was not sorry when it was over. Diana suggested that he and she have coffee in the study where the gramophone was. Her parents agreed. They wanted to go to bed.

'I'm sorry they're a bit sticky,' said Diana when they

were alone together. 'They're like that with anyone from London.'

'Or Uganda,' added Raj. 'It doesn't matter. They couldn't have been more polite – and I don't think I horrified them, do you?'

'God, no. I think they really like you.'

They settled into an old armchair, listening to an *MJQ* record, and held each other warmly.

'You can't sleep with me here,' Diana whispered, 'not with my parents in the house – so don't get me too excited, or yourself.'

When later, with pounding hearts, they had kissed goodnight outside Raj's room, Diana saw the light in her parent's room go out as she opened her bedroom door.

The next day was New Year's Eve. After breakfast, Diana showed Raj all round her parent's property. The house was a classically symmetrical Queen Anne manor-house, in warm and mellowed red brick with window arches and decorations in Purbeck stone. The stable block, built at the same time, had not been altered, apart from the coach-house, which had been adapted for cars rather than coaches. In front of the house, a formal eighteenth-century garden was surrounded by a yew hedge eight feet high and five feet thick. In the corners were Italian renaissance statues of two muses.

'Those,' Diana pointed, 'are my father's only tangible concession to aesthetics. He bought them in Italy at the end of the war, but I'm afraid their influence on him hasn't been too noticeable.' Behind the house, to the north, neat paddocks sloped up a small hill to a wooded ridge. Two horses in green canvas rugs grazed, then looked up, elegantly quizzical, as Raj and Diana approached.

'Do you ride them?' Raj asked.

'Sometimes. I used to a lot – I loved it really. But hunting seems pretty fatuous now. I don't mind about the foxes – if there wasn't any hunting there'd probably be no foxes – but a lot of the people who go out are rotten riders and know nothing about hunting. They just think it's smart. You told me you rode in Uganda, didn't you?'

'Yes, but not for sport. Relaxation rather, and it's the quickest way to get round a big plantation. I used to find it helped me think, and get things in perspective.'

'We'll take these two out tomorrow, if you like. It might help clear the New Year's Day hangover.'

Diana's mother wasn't hunting the next day, and, pleasantly surprised when asked, she offered no objection to Raj using her horse.

That night, they went to a New Year's Eve party given by the son of old family friends near Sturminster Newton. They arrived quite late at the old stone-built manor-house, and in the huge galleried hall a group of young, public-school musicians incompetently hammered out current rock and roll hits.

The hundred or so guests, mostly young and dinner-jacketed, laughed and shouted and clumsily danced. There was no chance to talk, so Diana and Raj danced a little, and when Diana was grabbed by an enthusiastic young blood who would not take a refusal, Raj stood quietly in a corner with a glass of champagne. A couple of people spoke to him, but lost interest when, in answer to their enquiries, he said he knew neither 'Bubbles' Jaipur, nor the Maharajah of Jodhpur.

The rock band stopped playing after a while, and a hearty voice shouted.

'Right everyone, we're going to do a bit of reeling.'

This was answered with enthusiastic whoops and guffaws.

'Let's have an eightsome!'

The floor cleared, and then refilled, people pulling one another into a series of loose circles. Raj was grabbed by a heavily-built girl wearing a shapeless long dress of cotton chiffon printed with large, stark orange and green flora.

'Do you know how to do this?' she asked.

Raj shook his head apologetically. 'I'm afraid not.'

'I thought not. Don't worry, you hang on to me and I'll show you what to do.'

The opening chord, on accordion and fiddle, announced the first dance.

Suddenly there was a whirl of activity. A man and a woman leapt into the centre of each circle, and started prancing erratically, whirling their hands and shrieking hideously.

Raj was completely unprepared when he found himself being forced to skip round sideways in a hand-holding ring. The large girl opposite him smiled encouragingly and yelled, 'Get ready, we're next!'

Raj was thrust into the centre and collided with his partner, who laughed and pushed him off. He stood, dazed, then jumped up and down with both feet.

'That's no bloody good,' yelled one of the men in his team. 'You're supposed to jig.'

Raj desperately tried to do what the previous dancers had done, and, feeling utterly foolish, lifted a hand above his head. Meanwhile, his partner pranced energetically and inaccurately, eventually barging into him, catching him off-balance. He was sent sprawling across the circle.

He lay on the polished old oak boards for a few moments, winded and breathless. Then he looked up to a ring of white faces leering down at him.

'Silly wog's buggered up our reel. Thought you chaps were supposed to have a sense of rhythm,' said a flabby, pale-eyed man of around twenty, a bland sneer on his face.

Raj clambered slowly to his feet; no one helped him. He confronted his taunter. His eyes burned below half-closed lids. His face paled to a light yellow-brown.

'How dare you!' – an articulated whisper. 'My sense of rhythm is quite adequate. My partner's sense of space appears to be deficient, as does your sense of anything. You are impertinent, offensive, and not a gentleman.'

The flabby young man recoiled from the vehemence, from the danger he saw lurking in the Indian's eyes.

'Okay, okay,' he prattled in embarrassment. 'I'm sorry. There's no need to get uppity.'

'With people like you – none at all.' Raj spat the words,

turned on his heel, and walked to the other end of the hall.

Diana looked bored and resigned in her hooting eight-some. She had not seen the incident. The relief that Raj felt helped the quick recovery of his composure, before he walked through to another room full of less energetic revellers.

At midnight there was the customary raucous rendering of 'Auld Lang Syne' and much kissing and mutual wishing of good luck.

Diana nudged Raj. 'Let's get out of this kindergarten. If another hearty thumps me on the back or tries to kiss me, I think I'll throw up.' They drove back through the little lanes in the Morris Traveller, and stopped for a while on the way. But soon, even the heat of their excitement was not enough to protect them from the freezing night air seeping into the car.

It was a crisp, clear morning, with little wind. The horses were fresh and keen, and as they cantered along the low ridges and through the leafless woods, Raj and Diana experienced a new closeness. She admired the unaffected lightness of his hands on the reins, and his natural balance in the saddle. When they came across fallen logs and hunt tiger-traps, she watched him collect his horse's stride and flow smoothly over.

Before turning back, they stopped and leaned towards each other laughing, trying to kiss each other's frozen noses as the horses danced impatiently about.

Over lunch, Raj enthused about the horses.

'You must come again and ride in the spring,' Diana's mother said hesitantly. 'It's lovely then.'

'How kind of you. I should like that very much.'

But the following evening, Raj's last, the Brigadier turned the conversation towards the problems of immigration. 'It's a shame you know, these poor people turning up from Pakistan and the West Indies, thinking they can make a living here. There aren't enough jobs to go round for the

English work force. But these chaps turn up, prepared to work all hours for practically nothing . . . I suppose they're used to a much lower standard of living and it doesn't matter to them. But then, of course, our own people lose their jobs. What do you think about this problem, Raj?'

'It doesn't affect me, so I haven't thought about it,' said Raj, anxious to avoid an argument.

'Come now, surely you sense some resentment from the man in the street. After all, he doesn't know that you're only here temporarily.'

'Since you ask, I have some experience of idiotic bigotry – but usually from such uneducated people, that I ignore it.'

'Well, you can't blame them. This country's already over-crowded without inviting in tens of thousands of foreigners.'

'As I understand it, those people who have migrated here were certainly not invited – far from it. But they were exercising rights granted them by the British as a result of their country's inclusion in the British Empire. It seems to me unreasonable when things are going well for the British Government to say, "Well, you chaps are all subjects of Her Majesty Queen Victoria" and then, when Empire management becomes more tricky, to say, "Well, actually, we didn't really mean it – you're not British any more." This would be dishonourable, un-British, and, after all, many of these people, or their parents or grandparents, fought for the British Crown in several wars – and they didn't do it just for the money. It is up to the British to choose whether or not they go back on their word. Other nations have done it.'

The Brigadier appeared to struggle a moment before saying: 'As you say, though, it doesn't affect you. At least you're going back to Uganda.'

'Daddy!' Diana exclaimed. 'What a bloody rude thing to say to a guest in your house.'

'He's your guest, Diana.'

'And it's your house. I'm not going to sit here and listen to you insulting my friend. Come on, Raj, let's go.'

Raj shook his head. 'I would rather finish my dinner. I'm not insulted. As I told you, I don't take it seriously.'

Diana rose from her chair and left the room, banging the door behind her. Dinner was finished in silence.

When at last, the Brigadier left the room, Mrs Quinn turned to Raj with tears in her eyes, confused and embarrassed. 'Mr Kalianji, I am sorry. I'm sure my husband didn't mean anything against you personally.'

'I'm afraid, Mrs Quinn, that I'm less sure of that than you; but, please don't worry, you have been most hospitable and I've enjoyed staying in your house very much.'

Raj left the dining-room and found Diana in her bedroom, crying. Wordlessly, she put her arms round him, and clung to him. He stroked her curly hair. 'Don't worry, beautiful little goddess. See, I'm the one who's supposed to have been insulted – and I'm all right.'

She looked up at him angrily. 'Why should you take that from a bigoted old stuffed shirt like him? He's so bloody smug. And everything you said was perfectly true and he was too damned prejudiced to admit it – or even answer it!'

'Look, Diana, it really isn't that serious. He didn't call me names. He's been a generous host to me. Your parents live down here, miles from reality. You can't be too hard on them for not understanding things they're not used to. Anyway, I have no intention of losing my dignity over it.'

Diana kissed his eyelids, his cheek, his mouth. 'You're so bloody strong, aren't you? So bloody self-sufficient. You're pretty smug yourself, you know.' She laughed, 'He's probably hurt himself more than you.'

Raj continued to stroke her hair. 'That's better. You should go to bed now. It'll all seem much less serious in the morning.'

Diana stood on the platform waving until Raj's train curved away and she was lost from his sight. For a while he looked out at the grey day and the little patches of damp mist resting in the land's hollows. He felt very sad – the closer

Diana got to him, the wider the gulf between them seemed. He could never be part of that warm, secure existence. He wouldn't have chosen it for himself, but he would have liked the option.

He pondered over his relationship with the other students. He felt that he was beginning to understand them – their preoccupation with revolution, or at least radical change. They devoted far more time and energy to demonstrating and politicking than they did to their studies, but he supposed that for them, this was part of education. They found his notions of progressive capitalism quaintly old-fashioned, but he had a very different world to go back to and deal with. In the end Diana was one of them, but he admired her for trying so hard to see his point of view. He knew that she would do anything for him and, occasionally, imagined her with him in Uganda – but ultimately he knew it was unthinkable. His parents would be horrified, and though he might boast a little to his friends, he certainly wouldn't tell them about everything that he had learned and done in London.

Maybe one day, when he had achieved things of significance in his own country, he would visit England again and show his fellow students how right he was.

But, he reflected, in the end, he didn't really care what they thought.

And Diana? Well, she was providing a very happy incident in his life. He was grateful – but she would never really understand either.

It was mid-September and Paris wore its high, striated sky. Raj sat reading a *Herald Tribune*, outside the cavernous art nouveau brasserie opposite the Gare du Nord. A calf-length camel-hair coat, with its wide collar turned up, protected him from the sharp north-easterly wind.

He had told Diana to meet him at this place, but it was easy to miss people in the vast interior. So he sat outside, and every so often he looked up, over at the crowds surging in and out of the great station: students, tourists, businessmen, all mingled as they do at any capital terminal, but here the variety of human types and attitudes was startling.

And between glances at the crowd and glances at his newspaper, he thought of the six weeks he had just spent, on his own, travelling round Europe. To Diana's dismay, he had insisted that he go alone, and he had been right. He had set his own pace, varied it when he felt like it and tried to approach each new place, building or work of art with his own objective attitudes.

He sat where Hippocrates had sat when he had been planning the world's first hospital. He had walked the ancient streets of Delos, looked at the Minoan temples of Thera and gazed at modern Athens through a smoggy haze from the Parthenon. In Rome, he had sat in the Colosseum, trying to conjure up the noise, excitement and smells of the crowds urging on the gladiators. In Florence he had stood awestruck below Michelangelo's David. In Venice he had walked the quiet, trafficless alleys, and admired the horses of San Marco while sipping frothy cappuccino. He had known that he would never again have the chance to do or to see these things, and had convinced his father that it was a good idea to let him stay on in Europe before returning to London to collect his degree. Then it would be back to Kampala and a desk in his father's office.

Diana had persuaded him to let her at least see Paris with him, and now, he was glad that she had. On his travels around classical and renaissance Europe, the only women he had looked at were made of marble or painted in oils, and his fit young body yearned for the realness of Diana's gentle caresses.

But even so, he was surprised at the strength of his reactions when at last he saw her wandering vaguely across the forecourt of the vast station. And when she saw him, she ran, oblivious of taxi-drivers' abuse and frenetic horns, across the wide, cobbled street. Her long scarf trailed out behind her, with a knitted Peruvian bag, its strap looped round her shoulder. She held a small, battered suitcase that pounded against her knees as she ran. When she reached Raj, luckily unscathed, she flung it down and threw herself at him. She wrapped the loose ends of her scarf around the back of his neck and pulled them tight.

'Oh, Raju – I've missed you. I'm going to tie you to me so you can't escape again. God, you look well – aren't you suffering from cultural indigestion?'

'If I was, I'm not now. It's wonderful to see you.' He kissed her lightly but definitely on her lips, then extricated himself from her arms and scarf and picked up her case. 'One of the more cultural aspects of France is the food. I suggest we start right here.'

They entered the noisy, busy brasserie and were shown to a table in the corner, where they sat, surrounded by art nouveau splendour, and talked. Diana wanted to know of everything that Raj had seen, every impression that he had received, every experience that he had encountered. They ate and drank their way through Fine Clair oysters and Chablis, calves' liver and Burgundy, tarte tatin and cognac. They left the restaurant, still talking, and hailed a taxi.

Weaving in and out of the evening traffic, hurtling along the cobbled embankment, they reached the little hotel in Rue Saint Simon, in the seventh arrondissement. A somnolent porter handed them a key and they clattered up to the room which Raj had taken the day before. They flung themselves on the wide, hard bed, laughing, pleased to be alone at last.

They were memorable, those few days, for both of them. Each away from their own world, they shared Paris on equal terms. Together they looked, walked, marvelled, laughed through the elegant vibrant city. No one noticed them or bothered them as they listened to jazz in Saint Germain, played chess in Montmartre, gazed at the Mona Lisa, or drank coffee in the Dôme. They spent hours walking through the autumn parks, and each evening they went back early to their hotel and fell into each other's arms.

Back in London, though, the spell cast by Paris soon

wore off. Even as Raj took Diana and her luggage to Cleaver Square, he sensed her awkwardness. He had a drink with her there, then declined to stay for some supper. He had, he said, a lot of organising to do before leaving for Uganda.

At the Paintals', he lay on his bed and tried to get used to the idea of returning home. It was almost a year since he had left Africa, and it felt as though it had been a dozen. He knew that he could only communicate with his parents on their terms and that all that he had learned and experienced in Europe would be at least meaningless, if not heretical, to them.

He and Diana had arranged to meet the following day. Raj walked out of Sloane Square tube station, and walked a few hundred yards down the King's Road to the Kardomah, where Diana sat waiting for him. He sat down opposite her and they looked at one another sadly.

'Do you have to leave straight after the degree ceremony?' Diana asked plaintively.

'I do – yes. It's the best flight of the week and my parents will certainly be there to meet it.'

'When are you coming back to England, Raju? Aren't you going to miss it here?'

Raj reached over and took her hand, squeezing it briefly. 'Of course I'll miss it – and you, but I live in Uganda. I don't know when I'll come here again. I really have no cause to. But perhaps sometime I may find a reason.'

'Maybe I could come out and see you in Uganda,' Diana suggested hopefully.

'Oh, no,' he replied quickly, 'it wouldn't work. You wouldn't like it.'

'But you said it's so beautiful, out in the reserves and on the plantations,' she persisted. 'I'm sure I'd find it beautiful too.'

'It's not that,' said Raj. 'It's just that society's very different there – you wouldn't understand.'

He put his hand on hers again, gently, to stop her. 'Look,' he said, 'before I go I want to buy you a present.

Not jewellery – something beautiful but useful. What would you like? Diana, look at me.'

She shook her head. Her lip quivered as she said, 'Oh Raj – I don't want a present. I want you.'

'Well, you'll have me in spirit if not in body – so why not let me get you something tangible, that you might have with you every day, to remind you of me? Please let me get you something. I'll be miserable if I leave you with nothing.'

Diana looked back at him and then smiled. 'I suppose it would be very selfish of me to refuse to take anything.' She paused and thought. 'Well, if you really want to get me something beautiful and practical, they've got some fantastic leather coats in Rags – and they've got a branch just down the road here.'

Raj was pleased. 'I'd be very happy to get you a coat. When it's wrapped around you, keeping you warm, you can pretend it's me. Come on, let's go and get it.'

He stood up and helped her from the seat. Walking in the street, in the fresh wind, she took Raj's arm and held it tight. In the large, warm shop, they found the coat Diana had seen. They had to find an assistant to unlock the padlocked chain that ran in and out of the arms of the long leather coats.

Diana took one and held it up against her, then looked at the price tag. 'My God, Raj, they're very expensive. Are you sure you want to get me one?'

He nodded. 'Oh yes, quite sure – try it on.'

It was a very particular shade of maroon, very dark, slightly blue, a stunning colour for Diana. She unbuttoned it eagerly and put it on, then looked in the mirror, disappointed.

'Oh – it's far too big. I know these shoulders are meant to be full but I look like an American football player. Is there a smaller size?' she asked the sales girl.

'What's that – a twelve? Then you need a ten. I don't think we've got any left,' the girl told them as she looked along the rail. 'Oh, look, here's a ten in chocolate brown,' she announced triumphantly.

Raj said coldly: 'No, we don't want chocolate brown – we want this colour.'

A man with dark curly hair, five feet ten or so, with deep, still, brown eyes had approached and stood on the other side of the rail. He looked hard at Raj, then said to the sales girl, 'Don't try and sell customers colours they don't want – find a maroon ten. Now!'

'But . . . but, Leo,' said the girl nervously, 'there isn't one.'

'What the hell are you talking about?' the man barked. 'There may not be one here, but we've got five branches. Have you asked if they've got one?'

The girl said nothing.

'Well, have you?' the man demanded again. He sighed, and turned back to Raj and Diana. 'I'm sorry. These girls are so bloody dumb sometimes. I'll get the manager to ring round the branches.' He turned and strode towards an office at the back of the shop.

The sales girl stood awkwardly looking after him, on the brink of tears. 'I . . . I've only been here a week,' she sniffed. 'I can't know everything at once.'

Diana put her arm around her shoulder. 'Don't worry, I'm sure you'd have thought of it without that horrible man yelling at you. Anyway, we'll make sure it's your sale.' She smiled encouragingly.

A moment later, the dark-haired man reappeared, beaming. He winked at Raj. 'It's all right. They're sending one down from Beauchamp Place right away.' He turned to the sales girl. 'As for you, the manager will see you in his office – now.'

The girl walked away dejectedly. Raj looked at the other man a moment. Then very precisely, he said, 'There's absolutely no reason to reprimand that girl. She'd only just started looking, and no doubt she'd have tried the other branches.'

'There's plenty of doubt she would. However, we have found what you want, and I don't need lectures in how to run my business from . . .' he paused. 'Foreigners.'

'May I remind you,' said Raj quietly, 'that, though a

102

foreigner, I am, or at least was, a potential customer. Perhaps you need lectures in how to run your business more than you realise.'

As Raj turned and walked towards the front door of the shop, Diana joined him, fuming. 'Oh God, Raj. What a bloody scene to have on your last day in England. Oh, well, at least you don't have to get me that expensive coat.'

Raj waved down a cab. As they climbed in he said, 'Of course I do. You don't think I'm going to be put off having what I want by an ill-mannered little shopkeeper.' He opened the partition to talk to the cabby. 'Beauchamp Place, please.'

As the taxi rolled off, they looked back. The dark-haired man stormed out of the shop, climbed into a puce-coloured sports car and drove off westward down the King's Road.

Leo put his foot down hard as he pulled away from the King's Road shop. He just managed to reach the correct side of the road in front of an irate, hooting taxi.

Why are people so difficult? he wondered. All he had tried to do was to find them what they wanted. They should be grateful; most other shops down here would have tried to fob them off with another colour, another garment. Arrogant bloody Paki.

Mostly Leo was annoyed because he had been put down so calmly. Usually he found that people had to lose their tempers before they contradicted him. He knew that he had got the worst of this confrontation by losing his temper in the face of the other man's self-control.

He was to meet Tony Scott, an estate agent, for lunch at the Roebuck. He wanted to persuade him that it would make sense to buy up the leases of the two large shops adjoining the King's Road branch of Rags and create one very large unit. He needed Tony's cooperation in order to get the bank funding required, but Tony thought he was mad. The prices asked for the leases were a lot more than they were worth. Leo didn't care. Normally, Tony wouldn't have cared either – agents always get their fees – but he wasn't going to put his name and reputation to a gross over-valuation. The banks very soon get to know which agents indulge in creative valuations, and discount them accordingly.

The two young men confronted one another over their steaks and burgundy. They were well-matched. Leo had been an important client to Tony Scott, but he wasn't his only client – and Tony wasn't going to foul up a very promising future in commercial property just to accommodate Leo.

Leo tried cajoling, persuasion, promises of back-handers and threats to dispense with Tony's services. And then he finally lost his temper.

As his voice rose, the quality of abuse sank. Conversation at adjoining tables and at the bar slowly died. Tony Scott remained silent and continued to eat his steak, but when he tried to drink some wine Leo grabbed his glass. 'Don't you sit there getting pissed while I'm trying to help you make money. Who the fuck do you think you are – telling me what a property's worth? I've done my figures and it's worth it to me, so it's worth what they're asking and you know they won't take less.'

'Look, Leo,' Tony said. 'You know bloody well the reason they're asking fifty grand more than they should is because they don't particularly want to sell those leases – and because you came on so strong when we first went to see them. They're not idiots; they know you want the sites desperately, and they're not interested in doing you any favours. If you think it's worth it to you to pay fifty grand more than you should that's your business, but I'm not going to recommend it.'

'You little berk,' yelled Leo, rising to his feet. 'I'll find another agent who understands how retailing works, and isn't obsessed with poxy little valuation charts. And you – you've just done yourself a lot of damage.'

He turned and stalked out of the bar, leaving his steak barely touched, congealing on the plate. Outside, in Beaufort Street, a traffic warden had just finished writing a ticket. As she reached over to tuck it under a wiper-blade, Leo grabbed it from her, screwed it up and threw it in her face.

'You fascist, ignorant bitch, you can stuff that!' he snapped. He climbed into his car, started it and roared off, wheels spinning furiously.

Leo glanced at the black and gold art deco clock on the mantelpiece in his drawing-room. It was 8.30. After the row at lunch-time with Tony Scott, he had gone back to his office and yelled at everyone within earshot. He felt as though his company was entirely staffed by incompetents, choosing to forget that most of them had been approached with tempting offers from some of the increasing number of his competitors.

At the end of the afternoon he had mellowed, and given himself four large Black Label whiskies to deaden the effects of the adrenaline which raced round his body. After going up to the penthouse and lying in the bath, he had rolled a joint, put 'Sergeant Pepper' on the stereo, and fallen asleep.

Little Nicci Brown was giving a party that evening. How the hell Nicci had got so established so quickly, Leo could not think. Since *Vogue* had used him for a couple of shots, everyone wanted him – but on the face of it, Nicci's talent was solely that of creating a mess of hair that looked like nothing on earth. Certainly his style did not suit the romantic, stylish chic of Rags, and Leo would not dream of using him. But then Nicci was giving a party, and Leo was asked, and he would go and be friendly with him and talk about the girls they knew, and they would pretend they liked each other.

Leo went into his bedroom and pulled a pair of tight, bright yellow satin trousers from his wardrobe. He squeezed into them and put on a matching frilly, high-collared shirt. Over these, he wore a thigh-length royal blue brocade jacket. He put his feet into a pair of royal blue patent leather pumps with stacked heels. His dark hair fell in long curls to his shoulders. He looked at himself through dark, angry eyes, smiled ruefully at his reflection and went down to get his car from the garage.

He eyed the pale puce drop-head E-type with distaste. It was time that it went; the joke had worn a bit thin. An art deco Cadillac – that would make a bolder, rarer statement. Maybe one of Dave Davis's young art students had a way with an airbrush and an understanding of Lalique.

The party was in a large house at the south end of Royal Avenue. Leo wondered whose it was. It couldn't be Nicci's – not so soon! He found a gap just around the corner in St Leonard's Terrace and walked casually to the house, avoiding eye-contact with the other guests arriving. He liked to be hailed first, and even then only responded if the hailer was a potentially useful man or a good-looking woman.

The whole house vibrated with the psychedelic sounds of a new band – Pink Floyd. There was a small ballroom at the back of the ground floor which smelled strongly of incense and hashish. Leo found some whisky and poured himself a large one, nodding at familiar faces as he did so. He was rather surprised, though pleased, to see the manager of his new King's Road shop. 'Hi, man, who let you in?' he asked.

'I knew Nicci when he was working for Leonard. He's been in the shop a few times. He bought one of those crocodile coats,' Chris said confidently. He was tall and blond and not at all in awe of Leo.

'Where is the little crimper then?'

'I last saw him rolling a joint with some nice black Lebanese hash upstairs in some kind of library. That old slag Lady Mountross is with him. I think this is her pad.'

'Christ, has she got her claws into him?'

Leo drifted off. He thought he would go up later – he could use some good strong dope; he was still feeling very uptight from the frustrations of the day. Around him there was a great party going on. Everyone was talking, laughing and shouting. No great ideas were being discussed. Actors uttered obscenities out of keeping with their public images; artists said that other, more famous artists were talentless phonies; models stood about, looking meaningfully sexy; young businessmen pretended to be turned on and loosened up.

Leo spotted a Eurasian girl whom he had used recently on a new poster. She was dumb but decorative, so he made his way through to her where she was talking rather half-heartedly to two photographers. At once they made room for Leo to join them, nodding deferentially to him. He ignored them, put his arm around the girl and kissed her on the forehead. 'How are you, you sexy brown thing?' He had forgotten her name. She grinned at him self-consciously. She had found, like a lot of other women, that it was difficult to say anything to Leo without sounding foolish. He never appeared to listen, and he never answered a question. Still, he was the man who owned Rags. That meant that you had to try.

'They've written some horrible graffiti on the posters in the tube at Ken High Street. I wish you hadn't made me cling to the palm tree like that,' she said.

'Don't worry, Angel; that was a lucky palm tree. Anyway, the more graffiti, the more the punters see the poster.'

He was about to suggest that she should come and look for the joints with him, when over her shoulder he saw a very beautiful dark-haired young girl who looked vaguely familiar. She sat on her own with her feet up on a chaise longue reading *Interview*. She took no notice of anyone else, in spite of the crush and noise all around.

Leo took his arm from the brown model. 'You look after the demi-luca,' he said to one of the photographers who was still lurking and strolled over to the chaise longue. He looked down at the girl, who had not even glanced at him. He lifted her legs off the end of the sofa and sat down. She looked up from *Interview*, said, 'Fuck off, pushy,' in a soft, low, public-school voice, crossed her legs in front of her and carried on reading.

Leo blinked. That was one of the most exciting things that anyone had ever said to him. He had only caught the bright blue eyes for a second, and his insides were in a turmoil. She wore a short, red silk dress over very dark stockings – he could just see the bump of the suspender clips through the thin cloth. Her beautiful legs stretched arrogantly in front of her. Her lips pouted slightly, as if she disapproved of what she was reading.

'You're bloody rude, even for an educated girl,' he said. 'What's your name?'

'Riley. What's yours?' She glanced at him quickly.

'Guess,' he said.

'Something-Stein, I should think.'

'Ah, old-fashioned English anti-Semiticism,' Leo laughed.

'I'm not English and I'm not anti-Semitic. You asked me to guess your name. You look Jewish so you've probably got a Jewish name. Okay?'

'All right. I'm Leo Freeman – Rags.'

'Rags?'

'I own Rags.'

'I suppose someone's got to.'

Leo was getting nervous. This girl was a new experience for him, but he could not let that show. He leaned over and took the paper from her, and noticed that she did not have a glass.

'What does a rare and lovely creature like you have to drink? Tell me and I'll find you one,' he said.

She looked up at him thoughtfully. 'I was in the American Bar at the Connaught yesterday, and that little ginger-haired barman made me a delicious cocktail from champagne and peach juice, with a few dashes of God knows what else. I'd love one of those.' She looked at him and smiled challengingly.

'Fine,' said Leo. 'I'll see what I can do.'

The girl watched him push his way impatiently through the crowd and disappear into the hall. She picked up the discarded copy of *Interview* and tried to carry on reading where she had left off.

Leo walked quickly out of the house and round the corner to his car. He made it to the Connaught in six minutes, parked the car outside the front entrance between two waiting Rolls-Royce Phantoms, told the doorman that he wouldn't be long and not to move it, and dashed into the American Bar.

He interrupted the barman in the middle of shaking an order for two distinguished-looking Americans. 'Barry,' he said breathlessly, 'you had a beautiful dark-haired chick in here yesterday and made her something with champagne and peach juice. Can you make me another now, quick?'

Barry looked at him reproachfully. 'Mr Freeman, you know I can't stop in mid-cocktail,' he said, 'and, anyway, I haven't any fresh peaches here today.'

'What do you mean, you haven't got any fresh peaches?' said Leo, incredulous. 'This is meant to be one of London's best hotels – you must have peaches.'

Barry's whole torso moved rhythmically as he continued to waggle the cocktail shaker over his right shoulder. 'I didn't say there weren't any in the hotel. I just don't have any at the bar. Usually they send them up; today they didn't.' He managed to shrug his shoulders through the shaking. 'But if you hang on, I'll see what I can do.'

Leo headed for the door. 'Don't worry,' he said, 'I'll find the peaches.'

He went into the restaurant, which was full. He found the maître d', who reluctantly recognised him, standing guard in a corner by the kitchen door. Leo put his hand on his shoulder. 'Alphonso,' he said, 'do me a favour. I must have a couple of fresh peaches, right now, for a cocktail for a very beautiful woman.'

Alphonso was going to say no – he was too busy; but the pressure of Leo's hand on his shoulder, and the apparent urgency of the request changed his mind. 'Arright, sir, I find you a couple myself; all the boys are busy.' He ducked out of Leo's grip and pushed through the swing doors towards the kitchens.

After two minutes he reappeared with two large peaches on a plate, a silver fruit-knife beside them.

'I don't want all the bloody crockery,' said Leo, grabbing the peaches off the plate, one in each hand, 'but thanks,

Alphonso – you're a good boy.' He winked and grinned before returning to the bar almost at a run.

Barry was gathering up glasses from a table that had just been vacated. 'Never mind that,' Leo said impatiently. 'Here are the peaches, so get squeezing.'

Barry returned to the bar and started putting the ingredients into a shaker.

'Where are you going to drink this?' he asked. 'I put the peach juice mixture into the glass from the shaker, and then pour on the champagne after.'

'That's okay. Make enough for two and I'll take the whole shaker and a bottle of champagne with me. Oh, yeah, and you'd better give me a couple of the right glasses.' He saw Barry's misgivings. 'Don't worry about it – if you don't get them back, send me the bill, all right?' He looked at his watch. 'Now get on with it. The chick's probably died of thirst by now.'

A minute and a half later he was running down the front steps of the Connaught, clutching a bottle of Krug, two glasses and a cocktail shaker. He put them on the passenger seat of the E-type, spun round the triangle of pavement in Carlos Place, and headed back towards Park Lane. Twenty minutes after he had left her, the mysterious Miss Riley looked up to see Leo, laden, pushing his way towards her. He placed the champagne, the two glasses and the cocktail shaker on the side arm of the chaise longue. Carefully he poured half the contents of the shaker into each glass, then topped them up with the champagne. He handed a glass to the girl, took the other himself and said, 'Cheers, Angel.'

He took a drink and smiled. 'What a clever girl; what an amazing drink!'

The girl smiled back and raised her glass. 'Cheers to you, Batman, and thanks.'

Leo sat beside her. When they had finished their drinks, he stood up and put out his hand. 'Let's go and find a joint.'

'I don't want any dope, but you deserve a little prize so I'll come and help you sniff it out.'

She let him take her by the arm and led her across the room. As they squeezed their way up the crowded stairs, Leo bumped into Chris, who said, 'Happy hunting, Boss.'

Leo noticed men noticing Riley (if that was her name), and the more their bodies came into contact, the more excited he became.

On the first floor, there was a high-ceilinged, panelled room with deep, red leather chairs and sofas around low mahogany tables. Nicci was sitting with his head lolling against the wing of a tall chair, passing a fat, pungent joint to an overdressed, overpainted woman in her late forties.

'Hello Leo,' said Nicci. 'God, where do you find such ugly women? Here Norma, pass Leo the joint. Do you know Leo? He's East Finchley's answer to Courrèges – well, his sister is.'

Leo took a long drag and offered the joint to the girl who shook her head. 'This pad's a bit tasteful for you, Nicci, whose is it?' He slumped into one of the club chairs and pulled the girl with him.

'It's lovely old Norma's.' Nicci waved his hand towards the extravagant lady on the sofa.

'Why do you let him do this to you?' Leo asked her.

'Oh, he's such a sweet little chap,' Norma said, leaning over and patting Nicci's hand.

The girl in Leo's lap turned her face towards his and said quietly, 'Do you think there's a room in this house with fewer creeps in it?'

Leo nodded and pushed her up. 'I'm taking these instruments of pleasure somewhere peaceful,' he said, putting his arm round the girl and waving the joint vaguely in the air. He led Riley out on to the landing and up the next flight of stairs. There was a small Chinese sofa with large ebony lamps on either side in a corner of the next landing. He led her to it and indicated that she should sit. She did and he joined her. 'God, you were right. All that slagging. You're much too beautiful, too original to waste bullshit on. Here, have a toke.' She took the smouldering remains of the tightly packed joint, inhaled from it deeply and

111

stubbed it out in a plant pot beside her. She looked at Leo thoughtfully, smiling slightly:

'I don't think you're as big a shit as you look. Do you?'

'Oh bigger. I want it that way. I don't like to give people the benefit of doubting it. You know, it's much easier dealing with people if you know they all dislike you. That way you can't be caught out. And anyway, it's easy to be nice if you want to be.' He looked at her and shook his head. 'With you I think I want to be.'

'Well don't look so depressed about it, and anyway, I don't suppose you'll manage it. Niceness is in the eye of the beholder and there doesn't seem to be anything contrived about your frantic arrogance.'

Leo laughed. 'So you're a student of psychology . . . as a matter of fact, what are you?'

'What am I, what do I aspire to be, or what do I expect to be?'

'All, in that order.'

'Well, what I am is what my genes and my environment made me. My parents are Irish, real Irish. My mother's beautiful, my father's brilliant.'

'So much for the genes,' said Leo.

'I went to a convent when I was little so most of my education came from nuns; mostly bloody repressive nuns – though they meant well. I really think they thought we'd lead happier lives if we never had sex, and that the only remotely good thing about it was that we would provide future generations of little girls for them to influence. They must have been good at teaching, though. I got my A levels.'

'What ones? When?'

'Art and English, last summer.'

'Christ, you're a real nipper. How old are you?'

'If it's relevant to anything, I'm eighteen.'

'No, it's not relevant. What are you doing now?'

'Nothing I'm very proud of so I don't think I'll tell you. Though I am trying to get to art school.'

'There's nothing to be proud of in going to art school.

You can only start being proud when you've done something that people want to see and have.'

As he had been talking, Leo had put one arm around her. 'Matter of fact, you've already got something I want to see and have.'

He gently put his hand to her jaw and drew her face towards his. He felt her mouth open as his lips touched hers. He dropped his hand to her thighs; his fingers crept gently over her stockings below the silk dress, up to where stocking-top gave way to warm, soft, slightly damp flesh. Her legs parted a little. His fingers met the scalloped edge of silk panties and silky little curls below them.

After a few moments he drew his head back from hers and asked, 'What's your name, Angel?'

'Alison,' she murmured. 'Leo, let's find somewhere more private.'

He nodded, pulled her to her feet and led her across the landing to where a door was ajar. He pushed it open. It was a bedroom. The enormous bed was piled with coats. He swept them off, laid her on the bed and fell down beside her. She kicked her shoes away, eased off his brocade jacket and started to undo the buttons on his frilly shirt. Slowly, between kisses, they undressed and pulled the heavy Casa Pupo cover over themselves. As they were caressing each other, the door to the room was pushed open. A couple stood silhouetted against the landing light. Alison giggled and so did the intruders, who backed out and shut the door behind them.

'Christ,' said Leo, 'it'd be more private in the bar at the Aretusa.'

'Never mind,' Alison said. 'We'll ignore anyone else.' Leo got off the bed, took all the coats to the door and flung them out on to the landing. He fixed a chair under the door handle, and came back into Alison's waiting arms.

She had only slept with two other men before. She had tried, unsuccessfully, to love both of them. And her experiences of love-making had been brief and disappointing. Her instincts told her, though, that with Leo it would be good.

113

He kissed her everywhere, his tongue searching out little areas of magical stimulation, and, just when she was ready for him, she felt him, full and warm, slip gently into her. The slow deep thrusting, the lips searching round her nipples, brought her through a mounting crescendo of dizzy, tingling release. And when she felt Leo pump his last deep into her, they lay back sweating, exhausted, kissing and whispering. So they slept and made love until the noises of the party faded and ceased.

They dressed and went downstairs, stepping over two male figures slumped against the banisters. There were a few people still in the library where Nicci was playing cards with a bald, very drunk old man. In the ballroom on the ground floor, Norma Mountross was flopped on the chaise longue fast asleep.

Out in Royal Avenue, the birds were anticipating the dawn.

'Where do you want to go?' Leo asked.

'Home – Hampstead.'

'Okay, I'll drive you.'

They walked round the corner. Leo opened the door of the E-type for Alison. She got in and curled up in the bucket seat. Sloane Street was empty as Leo opened the Jaguar up to ninety m.p.h. and shot the red lights by the Cadogan Hotel. When they reached the bottom of Haverstock Hill, he reached over and caressed the sleeping girl awake. 'Where in Hampstead?'

'Spaniard's Lane,' she replied.

At the top of the hill, Leo slowed down and pointed.

'That's where I started Rags,' he said.

'I know all that – I read it in *Honey*.'

'So you knew who I was all the time,' he laughed. 'Listen, that article was rubbish. Those bloody girls have got too much imagination.'

'Don't worry,' she laughed. 'I think I've found out more about you in eight hours than any journalist would in eight weeks.'

Up at the pond, the dawn was beginning an unequal struggle with the damp grey night. Alison directed Leo to her parents' house, a large, detached mock Tudor mansion among a garden of pine trees and rhododendrons. She opened the door of the car, got out, leaned back in and kissed him on the mouth, then strode up the drive. After a few paces, she turned and whispered, 'See you soon.'

Leo watched the morning breeze ripple her red silk dress and felt his whole body go limp. With this girl, he knew, he wasn't in control.

'Don't think I'm complaining Leo,' Sarah said to her brother a week later, 'but you've been very quiet for the last few days. If you don't start running around yelling again soon, people are going to think you're ill.'

Leo looked up from his desk and smiled slightly. 'Don't worry, it's only temporary. I've had a couple of things on my mind. I really want to do this King's Road deal, but I'm getting no help from anyone over it. They're all so cautious – I mean, it's not as though things aren't going great. We've done our targets in all the shops and the bank thinks I'm the Boy Wonder, but they won't cough up any more bread unless they've got three hundred per cent security. But I'm going to get those bloody shops – one way or another.'

Sarah looked at him quizzically. 'Leo, these sorts of problems don't make you go quiet – so what else is on your mind?'

Leo shook his head. 'No, there's nothing else really.'

Sarah saw him glance at a magazine on his desk, which was open at a full-page advertisement for a new herbal shampoo. Two girls, one fair, one dark haired and very blue-eyed, gazed from the page. Casually, Leo indicated the dark one with the end of his pen and turned the magazine towards Sarah. 'I think we might use her for some poster shots. What do you think?'

'Since when did you care what I think about the chicks we use?' She studied the page. 'I'd have been surprised if you wanted to use the blond one. That's Sammy isn't it?'

'Yes, yes,' said Leo irritated. 'That's not the point. Look at the dark girl.'

'She looks familiar. Who is she?'

'She's um, Alison . . . Riley. They were running a telly version of the same ad. You've probably seen her in that.'

'Yeah, she looks okay.' Sarah shrugged, then, understanding, 'Ah, I see. You know her, I suppose?'

Leo didn't look up.

'Christ,' said Sarah, 'don't tell me you've finally found someone fascinating enough to merit your attention. This must be the first time since poor old Sammy was sent away whimpering.'

'What do you mean?' asked Leo, 'Sammy's all right. I bumped into her a couple of weeks ago. Even if I did give her a hard time, she was too thick to notice. And anyway, I've taken out loads of chicks since her.'

'Yeah, but you usually can't even remember their names next day, let alone their faces. So, what about this Alison?'

'I met her at Nicci's party last week.'

'And I suppose she's offering services in return for some modelling work. What's new? Or won't she come across until you've signed on the dotted line?'

'Sarah, you're getting a bit cynical for someone whose hardly old enough to vote. Maybe it's time somebody tangled with your underwear. As a matter of fact, I didn't even know this chick was a model. She said she was an art student, and I can't get hold of her anyway. I've already left three or four messages with her mum – I suppose it was her mum – and I've found out her agency, and left more messages there, but she hasn't called back. She's not your standard hustling tart – but she's bloody tasty, and I think we should use her.'

'Well, well, I think you're in love, Leo. That explains the peace and quiet round here. Great! If she has this effect on you, I'm all for her. I hope you find her again.'

When Sarah had gone, Leo stared across his office. Almost every moment since he'd watched Alison walk up the drive of her parents' home, he had been aware of her, recalling her smell, her touch, her deep, private eyes.

He sat there longing to undress her, stroke her, gently penetrate her.

Four or five days later, Leo was at his desk, staring furiously at the telephone which he'd just slammed down. For six months he had been talking about those two sites in Chelsea, and now, just when he thought he was going to be able to do the deal without borrowing, they had been sold separately, a Mary Quant look-alike on one side, a Carnaby Street cowboy on the other. Tony Scott had done both deals, and had just rung to let him know – the bastard. Leo stood up and walked about the room, his fingers knotted into angry fists, hating the man, wanting to do anything to let him know that he hadn't beaten him. He punched the wall, surprising himself with the pain, then stared out of the window thinking of revenge.

'Leo?' The word was said in a woman's soft voice. He hadn't heard the office door open. He turned sharply.

'You don't look very pleased to see me,' said Alison. Her long dark-stockinged legs emerged from a short black leather skirt, above which she wore a voluminous Aran sweater. A Mexican plaid bag hung on a long strap from her shoulder. She stood, one hand on her hip, her head to one side, and looked at Leo with large eyes and a small smile.

'Er, hi,' said Leo. His body was already tense with anger and somehow this tension now increased and joined with the elation and relief which he experienced on seeing Alison. He had almost forgotten that she was real, so vivid had his fantasies about her been. For a moment he could hardly speak. He turned back to the window and tried to compose himself. When he looked at Alison again, she was sitting on his table, her legs crossed, lighting a cigarette.

'Did you get my messages?' Leo asked, trying to sound casual.

'Yeah, all of them. No wonder you've done so well in business. You really try hard, don't you?'

'Well,' said Leo, 'when I saw that you were a model, I thought you'd be great for some shots we're doing for the spring collection. You know we do all these things six months ahead.'

'Is that the only reason you wanted me to get in touch?'

'Er, yeah – I'm glad you came.'

'Well, I'm afraid I'd better go. I'm not a model. I told you, I'm going to art school. I just did a few jobs because I got talked into them and needed the money to go ski-ing.' She paused, and slid off the desk. 'So, I'll see you around.'

'Hang on,' said Leo. 'I'll buy you lunch before you go. At least give me a reasonable chance to talk you into doing this job for me.'

Alison grinned. 'Okay, but you won't succeed. Modelling's about as exciting as being a steak and kidney pudding in an illustration for a glossy cookery book, and it takes a lot longer.'

'Come on then,' said Leo laughing. 'Just looking at you makes me hungry.' He had completely forgotten about Tony Scott.

They drove to Alvaro's in the King's Road, where the manager greeted Leo with unconvincing Italian warmth and seated them at the most visible table in the restaurant so the other customers could have the pleasure of seeing the best-looking woman to have walked in that lunch-time.

Leo and Alison chatted like old friends over soglio and Frascati and lingered with coffee and sambucca until well into the afternoon before driving back, rather drunk, to Adam and Eve Mews.

As they walked into the office, Leo's secretary looked up, surprised and censorious.

'Leo,' she said, 'the architect with the drawings for King's Road has been here since two o'clock. You had an appointment with him.'

Leo felt a sharp twinge of annoyance and guilt. He prided himself in never being late for a date, let alone missing it completely. 'Oh, shit,' he groaned. 'Tell him I'm sorry. I don't need to see him. That bastard Tony Scott's sold the bloody sites off under my nose – just to prove to everyone what a prat he is.' He realised he still had his arm around Alison and said, 'Look, I'm going to discuss

118

some poster shots in my office, and I don't want any interruptions – no visitors, no phone calls.'

Once in his office, Leo drew the blinds and turned to face Alison. He put his arms around her and felt her hands reach up behind his back to fondle his neck. For the first time since the night they had met, he kissed her. Two weeks of aching longing were transmitted through his mouth and, without a word, they greedily kissed and fiercely caressed each other. Then Leo, with one arm under her shoulders and the other beneath her buttocks, lifted her off the ground, held her horizontal then dropped to one knee, and laid her on the carpet in front of his desk. In a trance of eager, unquenchable sensual passion, he undressed her until she lay naked except for her tiny knickers. He knelt over her. Slowly she helped him to discard all of his clothes until his eager organ sprang magnificently from constricting underpants, rigid and ready.

Gently, he turned her on to her stomach and gazed, awe-struck at the perfect little buttocks only partly covered by the small triangle of delicate cotton. He bent over and found the thin elastic waistband with his teeth, bit through it, and triumphantly tore the tiny garment away from the two mounds of unblemished flesh. Kneeling behind her, he pulled her buttocks up and towards him. While she kept her elbows on the ground and spread her knees apart, he gently brushed from side to side across her bottom, while his hand felt round to the front of her thighs and fingers gently sought the ready opening.

Then he plunged, deep and firm, and felt, as he slowly, almost completely, withdrew, like King Arthur with Excalibur. Then gradually he gathered speed, but without loss of power. Alison gave a short stifled 'Oh, yes,' and he felt her legs almost give way beneath her. Without leaving her, he spun her round to face him and continued with her beneath him until they climaxed hugely and seemed to fuse into one another. Breathing slowly, they lay together, he on her, unaware of time or place. What seemed like hours later, Alison whispered:

'Leo, you may be a bastard, but you fuck with great affection.'

She didn't want a lift anywhere.

'I'm an independent girl,' she said. 'See you. 'Bye.'

Before Leo was aware of it, she'd left. He heard the outer door of the building bang shut, echoing through the empty offices. Going to the window, he looked down and watched her swing away, across the shiny wet cobblestones. Wearing only a pair of trousers, he surveyed his scattered clothing and displaced furniture. Already he felt achingly lonely. He looked at his watch – seven o'clock, and the rest of the evening seemed to stretch before him like a hundred miles of desert.

Leo never rang Alison after that. She would arrive unannounced, sometimes at his office in the daytime, sometimes in the early evening at his flat. She wouldn't arrange anything in advance; sometimes she didn't appear for a week. Leo didn't know if she ever came while he was out – no one ever gave him any messages that she might have left. And the powerful, surreal magic of their meetings did not diminish. Leo lost his previous, perfunctory interest in other girls. In the gaps between Alison, he worked hard and well in the glowing anticipation of their next encounter.

He was more fascinated than frustrated by the fact that he seemed to have no control over the frequency of their meetings, and anyway, he was aware that surprise contributed to the quality of passion. It occurred to him that Alison didn't have the benefit of this extra ingredient, except in that, when she set off to see him, she could never be certain that he would be there. Leo wondered why he never saw her at weekends, but he did not ask about it. He tended to spend Saturday around his six London shops, talking to the managers, looking at the customers and noting their reactions to the stock. On Sundays he saw his parents or Sarah, or spent long lunches with new-found famous faces.

One Thursday shortly before Christmas, Alison turned up late in the afternoon. She carried a huge shopping-bag, with various Mediterranean vegetables visible at the top.

'I hope you weren't planning to go out to dinner tonight, because I'm going to cook for you,' she announced.

'Yes. I'm supposed to be giving dinner to a new PR we're taking on,' said Leo. 'A chick called Liz Macintosh and her boyfriend.'

'Well, tell them to come to dinner here, and sling them out early. Chuck me a key and I'll go up and get started.'

Leo obeyed, and told his secretary to ring Liz and change the venue for dinner.

Alison had prepared a beef ragout and ratatouille, and Leo found some bottles of burgundy. It was a delicious and well-presented dinner. As they ate, Alison spoke about fashions and PR as if she'd been involved for years. Leo had never had the chance to see her with any of his friends or associates, as he always seemed to be alone with her. For once, he found that he wasn't dominating the conversation, that Alison was making the jokes and relaxing his guests. He had only met Liz a couple of times, and hadn't really assessed her cynically humorous Glaswegian character – but she was young, clever and very keen. He was confident that if he gave her a start now and the right brief she would serve him very well. Chuck, her Canadian boyfriend, was one of those designers of male fashion whose clothes were much photographed by fashion magazines, but not much worn by the paying public. Leo knew him even less, and wondered what Liz saw in him. He didn't think their relationship could be very physical.

At half past ten Alison took charge. 'Leo's got an early start tomorrow, so we're going to push you out now.'

Leo was torn between annoyance at her interference and pleasure at her eagerness to be alone with him. 'Yeah, 'fraid so,' he mumbled.

When the others had left, he turned to Alison and put his arm around her. 'You beautiful, wicked little angel.'

She smiled and kissed him. 'I saw your male pride struggling for recognition; I'm afraid it failed.' She kissed him again and said, 'What are you doing tomorrow? Do you have an early start?'

'Yes, as it happens, I have,' he replied. 'I'm going to Brighton to look at a pitch. I've decided to move into the sticks as there aren't any interesting London sites around at the moment. Do you think provincial England is ready for Rags yet?'

'Yeah, sure. Why don't I come with you and we could stay down there?'

Leo's heart leapt – a whole weekend with Alison! 'Only if you stay down there with me till Sunday,' he said as firmly as he could.

'Okay,' she said simply.

Two days and nights alone with Alison in Brighton left Leo in no doubt. He was uncontrollably in love with her. Everything she did, everything she said, every gesture and expression delighted him. He had felt some anxiety, in the early part of the relationship, that he did not and could not dominate her. But that no longer seemed to matter. She certainly seemed to love being with him, and wanted to know about his family, his business, his ambitions. She seemed puzzled by the fact that all he wanted to do was own a multi-national retailing empire.

'But, Leo,' she protested, 'with your capacity for work and understanding of people's needs, you could do much more important things.'

'Making Rags the biggest fashion retailer in the world is as high as I seem to be able to aim at the moment. What other more important things do you suggest I should do?'

'Well,' Alison said, 'I believe that if you're lucky enough to be exceptional, outstanding in some way, you have a moral obligation to give other people some benefit from those gifts.'

Leo laughed. 'The influence of the nuns lingers on. Listen, by opening up Rags all over the world, I'll make lots of people happy – okay?'

Alison shook her head, but said no more about it.

Absorbed in one another, they walked around Brighton, bought each other presents from the little shops in the Lanes, ate, went to the movies, talked, made love – the better they knew each other, the sweeter the love.

Leo suggested, a little hesitantly, that they might go away again together, perhaps for more than a weekend.

'Yes,' Alison said quickly. 'Come ski-ing. You'll like that. My brother and two friends from Oxford have taken a chalet in Méribel for a week in January. I'm going, and there'll be plenty of space for you in my room.'

Leo was taken aback. 'I meant, just you and me, alone together.'

'That's okay, we can be alone,' she paused, 'and I'd like you to meet some of my family.'

That was what Leo was dreading – that, and the fact that he had never skied. He mentioned the second of these objections.

'Oh, don't worry about that,' Alison replied. 'With your physique and a bit of guts, you shouldn't have any trouble.'

After their weekend in Brighton, Leo still saw Alison only intermittently, but now it was by arrangement. He took her to all the pre-Christmas parties, but he hardly noticed the looks of appreciation on other men's faces. He didn't care what anyone else thought about her – now he was with a lover, not a fashion accessory. And Alison took Leo to Ronnie Scott's and the Tate, and introduced him to her art school friends, who didn't trust him and certainly didn't understand him.

Sarah met Alison at the Rags staff party. Leo had taken over the Factotum Club for the night, and the two women sat either side of him at dinner. As Leo wandered around, talking to and dancing with various members of his surprisingly devoted staff, his sister and his lover got to know one another.

Alison, from what Leo had told her of Sarah, had been worried that Sarah would be jealous, and Sarah herself was surprised and relieved to find that this wasn't so. They seemed to understand each other's affection for Leo. Sarah was glad to discover Alison's perceptiveness and obvious independence, while Alison had expected a hard-headed, hard-bitten female version of Leo, not this sensitive, thoughtful and almost delicately pretty woman.

Leo, looking at them for a moment across the room, felt a great relief, then annoyance as he realised how much his sister's approval still meant to him.

That night, their increasing closeness amplified the excitement of their diverse sexual experiments. The pleasure, the joy of it, was better than anything either had known before. Lying fulfilled in each other's arms in the dark, Leo whispered huskily, for the first time in his life, 'I love you.'

After a moment that seemed like an hour to Leo, Alison murmured, 'Me too, Leo, I love you too.'

They said no more and slept with their bodies still entwined.


Alison had been buying Christmas presents in Hampstead, and had arranged to meet her brother, Simon, in a coffee bar in the High Street. She saw him through the window, reading the *Spectator*, and watched him fondly for a moment, reassured by the reliable, clever features, the rather aquiline nose, loose straight hair, and eyes as blue as hers, keenly concentrating. She swung through the door. He saw her and stood up.

'Hello, Ali – my, God, you're f-far too beautiful to be my sister.' They kissed each other's cheeks warmly and Simon ordered cappuccino in his deep, resonant voice, which suffered no loss of authority from his slight stammer.

Simon, aged twenty, and in his second year at Balliol, had that uncomplicated confidence peculiar to most young men produced by English public schools. In addition to this, he had proved himself outstanding academically and was the subject of a private, ante-post bet by his tutor that he would get a first in his finals in eighteen months' time. He wore an old tweed jacket, elbows patched, his college eight tie and loose cord trousers, but this outward conformity to type belied an individual and open mind. Not particularly handsome, his humorous eyes and relaxed charm made him a popular man, and Alison loved him, loved to ask and receive his advice.

They had not seen one another since the previous September, and as Alison asked all his news, she wondered how he would react to hers. When he asked her if she was going ski-ing with him and his friends, she said, 'Yes, and I want to bring a man with me.'

'Oh. Who is he?'

'He's a man I've seen a lot of recently called Leo Freeman.'

'I haven't come across him, have I? Do you mean to tell me after all your talk of independence you've got a regular boyfriend? What's he like?'

'Don't worry, I haven't sacrificed my independence, quite. But it seemed silly to stick to a principle simply for its own sake. Anyway, this man's a bit unusual.' She paused. 'He's probably not quite what you expect.'

'I wouldn't expect anyone too ordinary, that's for sure,' said her brother.

'He's Jewish. His father's a small-time tailor. Leo left Highgate Grammar when he was sixteen to work for him, then branched out on his own and has built up a chain of shops called Rags – you may have seen them.'

'Oh, yes. There's one in Haverstock Hill, and isn't there one in Kensington Church Street?'

'Yes, and King's Road, Bond Street, all over the place. He's very successful, and his sister's a fantastic designer. But he comes across as being rather aggressive – well, bloody rude really. And in spite of being in such a visual business, he's a real philistine. But . . . there's something very creative and exciting about his tremendous dynamism. He seems to be able to make things happen incredibly fast and people are mesmerised by him and nearly always do what he wants.' She laughed. 'He gets confused when they don't, and loses his temper because he can't understand why anyone should disagree with him.'

Her brother was looking at her pensively. 'I can see you find that attractive, but isn't it rather boring if he never listens?'

125

'Oh, he does – to me. And all his confidence and aggression are just a cover for some deep insecurity – though I haven't got to the bottom of that yet – and you know how we love a good cause.' She laughed. 'It must be deep-seated, inescapable Catholicism which makes me justify a relationship with a man like Leo by thinking that somehow I'm going to help him, but – maybe I can.' She stopped and looked anxiously at her brother, 'Anyway, I love him, and I hope you're going to be able to see why.'

'And you've asked him to come ski-ing with us?'

Alison nodded. 'He's never been before, and he's going to find you and your Oxford chums pretty incomprehensible. I'll only ask him if you promise to be nice to him.'

'Ali, I trust your judgement. You don't need my approval, and anyway, it doesn't seem as though this chap needs us to be nice to him. Of course we will be and let's hope he's nice back.'


Alison and Leo flew to Geneva, where Leo rented a large Mercedes. The others were driving over from England with all their skis, but Alison had agreed that she would rather fly. They stayed for a night at the Beau Rivage, where they could see Mont Blanc over the cold grey Lac Leman. The next day, they set off for Méribel, stopping for lunch at the calmly grand Palace Hotel on the Lac D'Annecy. After an extravagant lunch they strolled along the lake shore in the crisp, bright air.

They continued their journey in the dying light, through the deep valleys and half-way up a mountainside to the pretty, sophisticated ski resort. Simon and his friends had reached the little chalet before them and they all went out for an early dinner. There was a lot of banter between the Oxford undergraduates, slightly drunkenly arguing about their prospects with the chalet girl, who was evidently to be strongly competed for.

Leo took a while to adjust to being treated on affable, equal terms and to the disadvantage of not being able to ski. He understood few of the references to literature, philosophy and Oxford politics. But, relaxing, he joined in with appropriate anecdotes and jokes, his sharp London accent contrasting with the drawling public-school voices of the others. They began to ask him about himself and Rags, and became perceptibly more respectful as he answered. By the end of dinner, over Montecristo No. 2s, which he had insisted on buying for them, he regaled them with outrageous and slightly embellished stories about the rag-trade and his rise within it.

The next day Alison took him to the hire shop and helped to sort out skis and boots, then took a button-lift with him to the junior slopes. After a very short while, Leo said, 'Look, you go on up with the others, and leave me to it.'

She nodded gratefully and he watched her *schuss* elegantly and swiftly to the bottom of the lift.

He had discussed the principles of ski-ing with Simon at breakfast, and Simon had explained well, giving the basic techniques and ergonomic reasons for them. So Leo doggedly put them into practice. For hours he descended and ascended the nursery slope until he felt that he had developed some rhythm and feel for the sport. That evening, Simon asked him how he had progressed, Leo said that he thought that he could handle a tougher slope.

They agreed that they would go together to one of the higher pistes. The next day, and for the subsequent four days, Simon spent an hour with Leo each morning, encouraging and criticising. Simon himself had skied since he was eight and now possessed a calm and fluid style, which Leo could not help admiring; it was so unflamboyant and understated. You could see that he skied for pleasure, not for show.

After ten days' hard work, Leo had skied, albeit fairly slowly, from the top of the mountain. He had enjoyed the lunches at the little log restaurants perched improbably on the steep mountain side. He even felt almost at home with Alison's brother and his friends. And each night, buried under a huge duvet, he and Alison pursued an extravagant and unrelentingly passionate love-life of their own.

It was nevertheless with relief that he entered the office on his first day back in London. This was territory that he knew and commanded, where he was the final arbiter and decision-maker. Justifications for his words and actions were neither sought, nor expected here.

His campaign to spread Rags to the provinces of Britain had engendered an enormous amount of work. In quick succession, he visited Oxford, Manchester, Nottingham, Cheltenham, Edinburgh – all the cities and towns where his instincts told him that Rags would be well received. Sites were found, surveyed, planned and financed. Projections were made and stock orders increased to cater for a doubling of the size of the business over the next year.

He now saw Alison every few days and, at Easter time, he made the decision to introduce her to his parents.

Miriam and Nathan had carried on living much as before. They had long ago realised that they had no effective influence over their son, but they loved him as much as ever and tried, with no great subtlety, to reach him through Sarah. Sarah's relationship with her mother was warm, and with her father, respectful. She still lived at home because she knew how distraught her parents would be if she moved out as well. But her loyalty to Leo meant that she spent many hours defending him to her father – though when Leo himself came to see them, his father forebore to criticise him to his face.

Nathan continued to run his little shop in Whitechapel, and somehow there were still faithful old customers, though few new ones. He still maintained that his way of doing business was the right way, and that Leo's success was just a flash in the pan. His relations and his wife put this stubbornness down to sour grapes and were very proud of Leo's success. Miriam's only concern now was that Leo should marry a suitable, competent, Jewish girl.

It was Sarah who suggested the slight subterfuge of introducing Alison to the family as her friend rather than Leo's. This way Alison could be assessed objectively and without the prejudice that would be inevitable if she was known to be a serious, and gentile, girlfriend of Leo's.

128

Alison had a great capacity for charm – she knew how to listen and could, if she wanted, make herself interested in practically anything. Miriam and Nathan were indeed charmed by her and though initially Alison had disapproved of the dishonesty of the subterfuge, she accepted afterwards that it had been necessary. It was certainly kinder, she felt, to let Leo's parents get to know her as herself, rather than as an undesirable appendage of Leo's.

After that, dropping in to see Sarah, she often saw Nathan and Miriam. And they always asked her to stay for the next meal.

Once, when Leo visited his parents on his own, his mother broached the subject. 'I'm surprised you don't take more interest in Sarah's friend Alison.'

'But she's a goy,' Leo said surprised.

'Well, I've been thinking. Religion isn't everything – and she's so beautiful and clever – a really good coper I should think – and it's time you started looking for a wife.'

'Mum,' said Leo, laughing to himself, 'I'm far too busy to worry about all that now. I'm only twenty-four. But I'll think about it – maybe I'll ask her out some time.'


Alison went with Leo to Bath. A particularly good, though small, shop in Cumberland Place was on the market. They stayed in the old-fashioned splendour of the Royal Spa Hotel. Leo had spent the day with estate agents and his architect, while Alison contentedly wandered between book-shops and antique shops. In the early evening they walked around the elegant Georgian town, watched the Avon flowing beneath the Pulteney Bridge, then lingered over dinner in the traditional and reassuring surroundings of the Hole-in-the-Wall. It was then that Leo said:

'Angel, are you doing anything on September the fifteenth?'

'How the hell should I know, Leo. That's months away. What's happening then?' Alison asked.

'We're getting married.' Leo watched a smile spread

wide across Alison's face and she leant over the table to kiss him.

'So we are,' she murmured.

'I'm going to marry Leo, whether you approve or not, and I know exactly what I'm doing,' Alison said to her parents. They had not yet met Leo, but he was invited to lunch the following day, a Sunday. They had not yet said that they did not approve, but Alison thought that a pre-emptive statement might make things more straightforward.

'Of course,' she went on, 'I'd much rather you did like him, but I know perfectly well that he's probably not your idea of an ideal son-in-law.'

Alison's father, Charles Riley, was in many ways an archetypal successful solicitor. A senior partner in one of the leading City firms, he was three generations away from a Dublin lawyer who had come to practise in London in the 1860s. Since then the family had all been lawyers, although, until Charles, they had practised at the Bar. But Charles had opted for the other branch of the law. He felt that it would ultimately give him more scope and freedom to pursue his other interests. He was obsessed with music and sat on the board of governors of Covent Garden and, such had been his conscientiousness on the dozen or so Catholic committees on which he sat, that he had been made recently a Papal Knight of the Order of Malta. He was a deeply intelligent and perceptive man, and had recognised early in his beautiful daughter's life that she would not be led in any direction by him or by anyone else. He didn't resent her independence, in fact he admired it. He was as confident as any man could be that he had imbued her with sound values and that she had developed a sound sense of moral judgement.

His wife, less profound, simply wanted her daughter to be happy. Disappointed that she had only been able to have two children, she lavished an abundance of affection on them. Faith, not logic, had allowed her to continue to believe that her daughter would not make major mistakes or transgress too far the strong moral code by which she had been brought up. She dreaded, and therefore avoided, asking Alison too many details about her way of life. Alison now lived in a chaotic flat in Chelsea with three other girls. Her mother deliberately never rang her in the early morning for fear of being told she wasn't there, hadn't been there.

To hear that she was getting married at all was a relief. At least if she was married, she could not live in sin.

But there was no escaping the fact that Leo was a disappointment to both Alison's parents; to her father, because he had no subtlety, no finesse and was Jewish; to her mother because he was from the wrong background and was not Catholic.

Only Simon's presence at lunch made it bearable. With his natural diplomacy, he asked Leo the questions whose answers he thought would least upset his parents. He kept the discussions on the abstract topic of design, rather than the crude actualities of commerce. Leo recognised this, and was reluctantly grateful. He already knew that Alison's parents were unlikely ever to like or even accept him, and he resented them for it. Alison herself had been expecting her parents' reaction and for once was moodily quiet.

Later, when they were alone, she apologised for them to Leo, who shrugged his shoulders and said, 'Listen, they've got no idea what it's like to struggle up through the rag-trade, or any other trade. They were handed everything on a plate and are smugly happy in a world they understand and want to keep free of outsiders. Still – they did produce you.' And he kissed her lightly on the forehead. 'It's amazing, given the background you come from, you know as much as you do.'

Chelsea Register Office was in a red-brick building on the north side of the King's Road, next to a drab little open space of grassless lawn and paving stones. The small wedding party gathered there in the bright September sun. Alison arrived with her father and mother, he dignified and resigned, she confused and tearful. Nathan Freeman stood at the bottom of the steps shaking his head gloomily, while Miriam fussed happily around Leo, adjusting the white carnations that adorned his pale cream silk suit.

Alison emerged from the car looking stunning. From her shoes, to the short chiffon dress, to her little hat she was a work of art in pale blue – a shimmering, hazy Monet in the autumn sun. The inevitable horde of passers-by stopped to show their admiration, and less subtlety, the *paparazzi* moved in for what, they hoped, might make a front-page shot.

The Registrar, a homely woman who looked like a prep school matron, did a little to leaven the ordinariness of the civil marriage ceremony, and was surprised at the end to receive a kiss from a relieved and happy Alison.

Leo had rather pointlessly ordered a Rolls-Royce to drive them the two or three hundred yards to the Club Del'Aretusa where the reception was to be held. This was a much more positive affair than the marriage ceremony. There was nothing the world of fashion and show business loved more than a marriage between a very beautiful woman and a very successful man. And nearly everybody on the vast invitation list had turned up. Leo and Alison drifted around, sometimes together, sometimes solo, to accept enthusiastic good wishes amidst the euphoric cacophony. An abundance of pink and white champagne, and most of London's beautiful women, made it a party that was bound to succeed. And there was an uncharacteristic lack of cynicism about the object of this celebration. A beaming groom and radiant bride suggested that this marriage might stand a better chance than most that took place amongst these people.

Their honeymoon in Ceylon was an oasis of calm reflective beauty in their frenetic lives, and they savoured it. Leo especially found the new experience of not hurrying, of looking and listening, an elixir. He found no frustration in the charming inefficiency of the witty, friendly people. As they were driven from town to town, and sight to sight in a rattling old Morris Oxford, he developed a great affection for this beautiful island. In the rest-houses, still functioning

132

relics of Imperial Britain, they relaxed over exquisite tea or exotic cocktails after days of riding elephants and clambering around ancient royal ruins. They visited the Buddha's tooth at Kandy, where Alison had to take her shoes off and wrap a sarong around her exposed legs. They hunted for a star sapphire worthy of Alison's eyes. They played billiards in the fusty old tea planters' hill club in Newara-Elyah. They watched elephants come to water in the unpeopled game park at Yala. And there, in the heat of the day, and washed by gently lapping waves, they made love on the sand between the warm protecting rocks.

A few degrees north of the equator on their last evening they watched the sunset from the balcony of their bedroom in the Galle Face Hotel in Colombo. Great hooded crows wheeled around in front of this fiery backdrop, in the hope that some of the fruit in the bowl between the couple might inadvertently be left out. Cries from children rummaging around on the beach wafted up in the still evening air; and the smells of the sea and the abundant vegetation mingled into an exotic, unreproducible scent.

'Well, Angel, are you glad you've got the common little Jewish tailor's son?' asked Leo stroking Alison's hair.

'I'm glad I've got the only man who ever interested me and turned me on. How about you, are you pleased with your innocent convent schoolgirl with artistic pretensions?'

'Not so innocent,' said Leo.

'And you're not so common.'


The breath from the horse's nostrils and the sweat vaporising from his hot flanks mingled and enveloped Alison in a warm, pleasingly odorous cloud.

A tight, balanced canter around the circumference of Hyde Park had left horse and rider hot and exhilarated in the crisp, bright November morning. Now she had pulled him up to a walk, stretching comfortably on a long rein. The nostalgia produced by creaking saddle, winter birdsong and clean smelling air relaxed her, wrapped her in the warm clothing of contentedness.

Life with Leo was more demanding than she had guessed that it would be. He knew that she had to make a stand – but kindly – against the instinct which led him to treat her as another, very valuable, personal possession, rather than as an equal partner in their marriage. It was for this reason that she had decided to pursue actively her own interests – not so that he could not join her, but so that if he wanted to join her he must follow her. It was important that she should have aspirations and motivations of her own. Simply to be part of Leo's business equipment would be intolerable. She looked at the big black head in front of her and felt the response of the horse as she shortened her reins and squeezed lightly with her heels. She was grateful that Simon had suggested the horses.

Alison had always loved horses, as she loved almost everything rural. Though her family had lived in London all her life, she had spent many holidays with friends and cousins in Ireland, Gloucestershire and the Dordogne. And, since she was tiny, she had enjoyed riding. Unusually, this enjoyment had not waned with puberty and despite the lapse of a year or so since she'd last ridden, she had responded keenly to Simon's idea that one of his old school friends, Basil Barrington, now Adjutant at Knightsbridge Barracks, might arrange for her to exercise some of the better regimental 'blacks'.

The officers' chargers and ceremonial horses of the mounted squadron of the Blues and Royals and the Lifeguards varied a great deal, their only common characteristic being size, at least sixteen and a half hands, and blackness. They were principally Irish draft horses, though a number possessed a good proportion of thoroughbred blood. While they were intended to be pure black, the odd white sock or blaze was not uncommon. All were required for ceremonial duties but a few of the better ones were used for horse trials and hunting, usually by officers, though a number of NCOs and troopers also competed in the one-day events. It was one of the eventers that blasé young Captain Barrington had arranged for Alison to ride.

As she hacked back to the barracks she wondered what

Leo would make of Basil Barrington. She found him uncomplicatedly, if arrogantly, charming and talked to him easily about horses and mutual friends. But she knew that he would be lost on theatre or pictures, or the ebb and flow of the fashion world. He certainly would not understand Leo, or vice versa. They lived by entirely different priorities; which – she wondered – were hers?

Still musing about class and her own particular niche, if she had one, in British society, she drove her new small BMW to an address in Chelsea Square where Leo had arranged to meet her.

Having guessed that this was a house which Leo was intending to buy for them, she pulled up, full of curiosity, outside the large gates and small courtyard. These low, dark red-brick houses were built between the wars and were neither particularly beautiful, nor ugly. Endowed with a token classicism which now seemed slightly pretentious, they were large, comfortable and of an address prime enough for prime ministers, prima ballerinas or premier earls. And they were very expensive. Alison was amused, because she knew that Leo thought that this sort of house was her ideal. She was annoyed because she knew what her parents would say – and Leo's for that matter. Still, she guessed that Leo could afford it, and she decided that if he looked as though he would be happy here, she would go along with it.

Even knowing Leo as well as she now did, she was surprised by his enthusiasm and the energetic interest that he took in the decorating and furnishing of the house. He was, of course, inclined to treat the whole place as an interior design project, where notable tasteful effects were achieved and the tastes, comfort and lifestyle of the occupiers were not really considered.

Alison was not, by nature, particularly concerned about her surroundings and, though a little exasperated by Leo's indefatigable house pride, concurred quite happily with most of his ideas. Delivery vans descended on the house from diverse purveyors of furnishings and furniture – Oscar Wollens, Charles Hammond, Conran, Colefax and Fowler and Zarach – until a miniature, very expensive ideal home exhibition had been created.

The last delivery van had scarcely driven out of Chelsea Square before photographers from the fat glossy fashion magazines filled the house, and butch, bossy women journalists, purporting to interview Alison about her life-style, bellowed their own views at her and wrote what they thought she ought to have said. She laughed afterwards to read about this person who bore her name and likeness, who had such unfamiliar attitudes and aspirations. She did not mind and Leo was very pleased with the coverage. She was glad to please Leo.

# 1967 – Uganda

The Air Uganda 747 banked steeply as it U-turned over Lake Victoria to approach Entebbe Airport. Seeing this familiar expanse of water and shoreline from such an unfamiliar angle magnified the sense of unreality which Raj was experiencing in coming home.

The hot smells of Africa that greeted him as he descended from the plane to the tarmac confirmed his apprehensive nostalgia. He was very happy to be back, but he knew that his experiences in Europe had altered his perspective. His native country would never look the same to him again.

And although he had not changed in any obvious way, his family, watching from the roof of the terminal building, took a moment to recognise the tall, thin figure wearing a well-cut off-white cotton suit and a wide-brimmed panama hat. When he reached them, his parents knew from his eyes that he had learned a lot in his year away. Vishnu, though he wanted to, did not embrace his precious son, but his wife had no such qualms and hugged Raj unashamedly.

On the drive back to their grand ex-colonial house in the flower-rich suburbs of Kampala, Raj struggled to renew contact with his parents, but they seemed to be talking a different language.

'My goodness, Raju,' his father was saying. 'You certainly look the smooth man-about-town now. You'll make old Mahdvani's son look very shabby, and he's just got back from Oxford. Did you get Paintal's friend to make that suit?'

'No father. I bought it in the summer sale at Simpson's.'

'Oh, yes – in Piccadilly Street – I've seen it.'

Vishnu had made a few brief trips to England on his tractor business, but after only a few exchanges it became clear to Raj that he had not seen much of London and knew nothing of its geography or institutions. Raj felt as if he were talking to a child as he became aware just how much more he knew about these and other things than his father.

There was a big celebration that evening to welcome the returning son, and, tired and disorientated, he felt like a stranger. But next morning, waking to the bright sun and raucous bird calls, he enjoyed memories of his other, younger self. The spicy smells, the sounds of servants unhurriedly starting their day and the perpetual, distant barking of dogs were all sensations he relished because he had never noticed them before he had left for London.

He got out of bed feeling fit and energetic, and stood under an erratic luke-warm shower. Later, in the dining-room, strong-smelling coffee was waiting. He was greeted by the matronly, old, black housekeeper.

'Good morning, Effendi. You looking very well.'

'Thank you, Mary,' Raj replied absently, and then, more aware now of their difference in status and colour added, 'It's good of you to say so. How are you?'

She looked surprised. 'Oh very good, Mr Kalianji,' she said and bustled out of the room.

No one else appeared. Raj drained his coffee, and stepped through French windows on to the terrace that surrounded the house and walked by way of the lush gardens to the garage block. Several vehicles were parked, in and out, and Raj wondered which he could use.

His thoughts were suddenly jerked back to England by the sight of a dusty old Morris Traveller, parked in an inaccessible corner in the garage. He supposed that it had always been there, but he had not noticed it before – and now he remembered Diana, with the irrevocable sadness of remembering a close friend who has died. His whole affair with Diana, the visit to Dorset, the startling intensity of her passion, seemed part of an implausible dream.

Raj looked around for the man who was responsible for all the vehicles and found him round at the back of the garage, washing a big Peugeot station-wagon. He asked who was going to be using it that day, and was told that no one had asked for it. He climbed in and drove between the great white gateposts into the dusty suburban road.

He headed east towards Jinja, then south to the plantation. There was no one at the house, and only a young boy at the stableyard. Together, they located his horse and saddled it up.

It took him two hours to ride down to the lake-shore. He then followed it for several miles. The sun was very hot and uncomfortable now, but he carried on till he reached a small grove of eucalyptus trees where he dismounted and tethered the horse.

Before he saw his family and friends again, he wanted to try to come to terms with the constraints on his attitudes and actions that would be inevitable now he was back in Uganda. He lay on his back and watched the tops of the trees moving in the gentle wind. And he came to the conclusion that he would have to lock away, for his own private use, many of the ideas and memories that his time in England had generated. His father had tried to question him the previous evening about some of the stories that Paul Paintal had relayed. But Raj had avoided direct answers and now felt that the only practical policy was to lie.

He was going to have to rely on his father for several years yet, and wanted to establish himself as a political entity, which would take time and money and his family's support. He decided therefore to suppress any views that might disturb them. This would also mean hiding these ideas from his old Makerere College and tennis club friends – for, in such a small circle of prominent Asians, unconventional attitudes would very quickly stand out and be presented as dangerous crankiness. So, with some sadness, he closed the door on some powerful memories and resigned himself to conformity.

When he arrived back home for lunch, his parents

greeted him, anxiously. Where had he been? Why had he gone off on his own when he had just got back from such a long trip?

'It's all right, Father.' Raj managed a warm, open smile. 'I just needed a few hours out on the plantation to help me re-adjust – but I'm fine now.'

But he nearly let slip his mask of acquiescence when, over lunch, his father made an announcement. 'We've arranged a bride for you, Raju. I hope you will raise no objection.'

'Good Lord,' said Raj, trying to understate his discomfort, 'I don't think I'm really ready yet.'

'Oh that's all right. She's only thirteen now, so you can't be married for another five years at least, but it's good to have these things settled well in advance.'

Raj had not expected his new resolve to conform to be tested quite so soon and so severely. He summoned up all his self-control. He realised that, once he was committed, it would be very hard to back out. 'Well, my gosh. Who is she?'

'Oh, she's very suitable. Reena Patel. You've probably seen her with her parents at the polo club.'

Raj knew Mr and Mrs Patel quite well. They were younger than his parents, but Mr Patel had been very successful in the construction business, particularly in the large-scale public building programmes that had been instigated since independence, so Vishnu Kalianji had inevitably had a number of dealings with him. Raj rather liked him for he had a less restricted view of things than most of the Hindus they knew. But he was only vaguely aware of any offspring, and couldn't call to mind a particular daughter. And he couldn't stop himself from thinking of Diana. Would Reena Patel make him think, make him laugh, and make love with such enthusiasm? It didn't seem right to consider a thirteen-year-old in such terms, but he knew now that these things were important. Diana Quinn was more deeply implanted in him than he had been prepared to admit.

He looked away from his parents, biting his lips. Then

composing himself, he turned back to them. 'I'm sure she's very suitable – but I don't remember her. I look forward to meeting her.'

'There's no hurry. It's all arranged. We just thought that after being in Europe, it would be good for you to have no doubts about that aspect of your future.'

Raj's first few weeks back in Uganda passed in a kind of haze. On his own, in the country, he was quite content, but with his family and erstwhile friends he felt like a man who tries to speak but makes no sound. His terms of reference had changed so that every word he used meant to him something other than it did to his hearers. Even the one or two Indians who had been in English universities appeared to have failed to absorb new ideas and attitudes. They had studied hard and played cricket, but they had not immersed themselves in England and English people.

When friends asked him about his experiences, he found that he did not want to tell them – it would involve too much impossible explanation – and he found himself even more aloof than he had been previously. He did find one or two European lecturers at Makerere College, now the University of East Africa, who would talk to him in terms he understood, but he was suspicious of their broadly left-wing views, and they of his position in the unpopular Asian community.

So Raj threw himself into his work. His father made him responsible for financial aspects of their import/export business, and he quickly made an impression by speeding up procedures, extracting maximum benefit from exchange rates and even finding wider, less traditional markets for their robusta coffee. When British coffee traders visited, he enjoyed dealing with them, and they responded to his articulate knowledge and politeness. He could not help the wistfulness that sometimes pervaded him when he sent off letters and telegrams to London, and thought of them arriving in the great grey Portland stone City offices, set among the winter-wet, taxi-choked streets.

He could not stop himself, either, from wishing that he

might hear something of Diana, though he knew that he would never contact her again.

In time, however, he settled down and began to make something of a name for himself as an economics expert. His political aspirations, so unusual for an Indian, were noted and frowned upon – although he justified them as commercial expediency. He was aware that his outstanding abilities already meant that he was held in some awe by his father's generation as well as his own, and this increased his sense of isolation.

When his father suggested he should meet Reena, he was surprised to find that the original dread with which he had thought of the arrangement had dissipated, and had been replaced by an emotional numbness.

As it was, Reena was a remarkably pretty girl with large, innocent eyes and a charming, shy smile. Like most Indian girls, she was only basically educated and spoke bad, uncertain English. But there was, Raj thought, a spirited personality behind this traditionally suppressed exterior – and it was with some pleasure that he thought of fathering their children.

These thoughts, and his increasing confidence in his position, meant that Diana's letter, when it came, took him completely by surprise. At first he did not want to open it, but when he did, just the sight of the handwriting produced an overwhelming longing.

'My beautiful son of Krishna,' he read.

I didn't really want to believe you'd walked out of my life through Gate 13 last autumn, but I suppose I knew it. Then it was as if half of my body had been amputated, and it bled and hurt and ached so much. But nature's a great nurse. If she can't heal you, she simply makes you numb to ease the pain. How I've longed for your warm, soft hands to bring my body back to life, and your deep brown eyes to fill me with reviving heat.

Please, one day, find me. I'm going west, to New York, this September. I've persuaded them to take me on the NYT and then I hope the frenetic pace will cure me of romantic fantasy.

I still love you though,

Diana.

Sitting alone in his office, Raj hunched his shoulders and hot tears erupted in his eyes. As they dried, he sat for an hour, staring at the walls.

Then, standing up, he shook himself and made his way surreptitiously to the wash-room where he dabbed his eyes, blew his nose, combed his hair and straightened his tie before going out to a lunch-time reception being held for a visiting trade mission.

In a trance, he talked to earnest black politicians, polite English diplomats and Japanese businessmen. Without thinking, he gossiped with the other Indians, and joked with two of the young princes of Toro. But all the time, he was back in the cosy house in Cleaver Square, lying in bed with Diana.

# 1970

Leo tried to remember who had suggested that he should come to the Spring Fashion Fair in Copenhagen. Someone had said that there was a better perspective of young European fashion here than in Paris. The show, at the new exhibition halls at the Bella Centre, seemed to be dominated by London manufacturers and designers. The knock-on effect of the British Swinging Sixties and the Beatles and their successors was still very strong and it looked as if Paris might have been usurped as the centre of *prêt-à-porter* fashion, at least at the younger end of the market.

Leo had wandered around the fair on his own, warding off eager approaches from most of the British contingent all of whom either knew or recognised him. He had scowled amiably at what he thought of as blatantly exploitive tat which his countrymen were showing and was more impressed with the clean, stylish lines of the upcoming Danish designers like Margit Brandt. That was the way this market would go, once the vestiges of flower-power and the strongly represented ethnic looks had run their course.

He had been to see what he was told was Copenhagen's busiest young fashion store and had found the two Streker brothers surrounded by a bewildering selection of North African, Indian and South American costumes as well as an aura of their own glamorous self-importance within the tiny confines of Copenhagen's hip society.

Strolling curiously up the long sunlit Strøget, impressed by the standard of shops and display and the good-looking, well-dressed shoppers, Leo knew that he had also been attracted to Copenhagen by its other reputation. Since he had married Alison he had found it hard to come to terms with the restrictions this had imposed. He was still besotted with and intrigued by his wife, but a year and a half into their marriage, he occasionally yearned for the special excitement of hunting new quarry. All over this peaceful, laid-back capital, he had seen girls by the dozen that would pass muster in any top London modelling agency. And as he contemplated the legendary weakness of their knicker-elastic, he did not even try to suppress the desires which surged around his system.

Since meeting Alison, he had slept with no other woman. In London he simply did not want to go through the accepted preamble – and he certainly was not going to pay for it. But here, six hundred miles away, he quickened his pace back to the Grand Hotel in Kongens Nytorv, eager to prepare himself for the evening's chase.

The chase was not long. In the hotel bar, while he was sitting with a large whisky, deciding which clubs to go to, he found himself beside two classically Scandinavian, blond girls, perfect featured, blue-eyed and subtly, sexily turned out. Like most other Danes, they spoke more or less colloquial American English and they showed no reticence in joining him. Solvejt and Hetti, they were called. They told Leo that the place to go to was a blues jazz club called Montmartre and yes, they would both come with him.

When Leo hailed a taxi outside Solvejt's flat next morning, he felt simple, healthy elation and very little guilt. The two girls had given him no challenge, and no rest. Somehow the fact that he had not had to persuade or seduce them detracted from any sense of disloyalty that he might have felt. And there was a sense of having fulfilled one's duty in keeping two such libidinous women busy all night.

Feeling positive, aggressive and in control of his own destiny, he flew to Amsterdam where he hoped to open the first European branch of Rags.

During the short flight he reflected on his operation in

England. Now, in the spring of 1970, he had recently opened the twentieth Rags, in Exeter. Two years before, he had sold out his share of Showbiz Clothing to Nick. This had yielded a substantial profit and had avoided a head-on confrontation between him and his ambitious Greek friend. But it did mean that Leo was now solely in the business of retailing. All the garments that they sold were made by the Nottingham factory and several others that they were forced to take on as business expanded. Leo was inclined to resent the profits that they made out of him, but, with characteristic logic, he resisted the temptation to diversify into manufacturing at this stage. No, his priority was to expand his retailing empire. He was faced with a number of options: to increase his representation in British high streets; to increase dramatically the floor area and product scope of his principal stores, or to expand in Europe. The first option was the least attractive. He felt that he had as strong a geographical representation as Rags's rather specialist style would take, and the smaller provincial units yielded less interesting margins. The second option required a particular type of site, and this type was not often available, although he was constantly searching, so he had decided, for the moment, to look to the Continent.

The nature and style of Amsterdam seemed appropriate for Rags. He was aware that the Dutch press had given the look consistent and enthusiastic coverage and that the public response had shown that he had a market there. Anyway, he had visited the city once before and his instinct told him it was right.

He was, rather surprisingly, met at Schipol Airport by the property agent who had found sites for him to view.

The first shop they visited, in one of Amsterdam's more formal shopping streets, was exactly what Leo wanted. He asked the agent about the financial details and they sat together in a café, eating cake and drinking coffee for two hours. Every so often the agent was obliged to jump up and have telephone conversations from the public call-box at the back of the café. But they finished the discussion by shaking hands.

'Fine, then,' Leo declared. 'We've dealt. You look after the legalities with my solicitor in London, and I'll have a holding deposit telexed out tomorrow.'

Amazed, the neat little agent drove Leo back to Schipol to catch the next flight to London.

By the middle of that year Leo was confident that his plan to expand into Europe would work. In the face of opposition from Sarah, Liz Macintosh and everyone else prepared to express a view, he had decided to open in Paris.

In England, life could not have been better. Sales were stronger than ever and Leo's only frustration was the absence of a suitably large site in which to open his projected Rags department store. He had even reconciled himself to the restrictions of marriage, but had not been able to confine his sexual adventures to the memorable threesome with the girls in Copenhagen.

It wasn't that he was bored with Alison. Far from it. Their love-making was as fulfilling as it had been from the start – but the Danish girls had reminded him just how exciting it was to encounter fresh tastes. He was, however, fairly discreet and didn't make himself available as freely as in his bachelor days. Out of respect for Alison he restricted his field to undemanding models and ambitious sales girls; but this still provided great scope, and, in a way he didn't stop to rationalise, it counteracted the feeling of slight inferiority he felt in his wife's presence.

Alison's ability to amuse herself and pursue her own interests still made him feel inadequate, but he had learned not to argue if she went off riding, went out with her brother or disappeared for an hour on Sunday mornings to mass. He still could not relax with her family and arty friends.

So he had planned a long and luxurious trip with her to France; first to Paris to eat, club, shop and look for possible sites for Rags and then to Antibes and Cannes, followed by a cruise down to Sardinia in a chartered yacht.

147

He left the office early and drove to Chelsea Square in his new, golden, Aston Martin DBS. They were to leave for the ferry very early next morning. He wanted to be sure that he had everything correctly packed and in order.

He found Alison up in the bedroom, surrounded by a sea of multi-coloured, sequinned, braided, embroidered and appliquéd clothing.

'Christ, Angel!' he exclaimed, 'I want you to look stunning and beautiful every day for the next six weeks, but you've got enough stuff there to clothe a six-month tour of Billy Smart's Circus.' He picked up a particularly exotic diaphanous kaftan. 'And this rich hippy gear – that's really going to frighten the natives down in Cannes. Where d'you get all this ethnic stuff anyway? It's a bit played out.'

'Leo, I know you don't believe it, but a garment doesn't have to come from Rags to be beautiful, or fashionable for all it matters. I love it – and don't you worry, the natives in the South of France love to be frightened.'

'Okay, Angel. On you, a tie-dyed pillow-case would look good. But this Indian stuff, who's selling it?'

'Oh – Harrods, Feathers, Kensington Market.'

'Well, I'm bloody glad we don't. The thought of trying to do business with a bunch of turbaned curry-wallahs does not appeal.'

Leo happily jumped his way to the front of the ferry queue, and he and Alison joked their way across the Channel over SNCF steak and frites. At Calais they headed off down the RN1, touching 130 on the straight tree-lined stretches, leaving behind a string of furious and frustrated French drivers. At Abbeville, they stopped for coffee and cognac and enjoyed absorbing the Frenchness: men in berets hurtling along on mopeds; little children carrying home enormous armfuls of long bread; battered Deux Chevaux parked anyhow in narrow, cobbled streets, and a desperate gendarme trying to persuade the citizens that traffic laws should, at least, be acknowledged, if not obeyed.

Two hours further down the Paris road, Leo pulled off towards Chantilly. They had an invitation from a young English racehorse trainer, a friend of Alison's, to stay for a couple of nights and to see the Prix du Jockey Club, France's equivalent of the English Derby.

Jim Kettlewell and his pretty but predictable English wife lived in a large turreted house in a quiet street near the main Place in Chantilly. They had rented it for the duration of Jim's contract as assistant to one of the largest of the local French trainers.

Most of the English racing fraternity, thirty or forty people, and some French, had been asked to drinks that evening and Alison was struck by the British capacity for remaining British regardless of foreign surroundings. Gin and tonics, sherry, little sausages and English cheeses were served. In tweed jackets and Jermyn Street ties, most of the guests would have been more at home in a Cotswold manor-house than an elegant Paris dormitory town. But then, this town was also the centre of French racing, and wherever good thoroughbred racing is to be found, so are the English.

At the top level, racing is a very international sport. The party conversation drifted back and forth across the Channel, even across the Atlantic. Leo joined in to the limited extent to which he was able, until he began to be asked, as a businessman, how he viewed the general financial outlook in Britain with the newly elected Tory government. Leo's instincts were, of course, deeply capitalist, but, privately, he thought that Edward Heath was probably more fitted to steering a sailing dinghy than a national economy. However, the generally uncritical approval with which the new Prime Minister was regarded by these expatriates led Leo to reserve his own criticism and to agree that it was a jolly good thing.

Alison was quite at home with these people and enjoyed discussing mutual friends, life in France and horses. She arranged to ride out with one of the trainer's strings, first lot the following morning. Leo got up early too and drove to the yard with Alison, and then on with the trainer to

Aiglemont, the vast communal grass gallops used by all the Chantilly trainers. Despite the fact that one of the biggest races of the year was being held later on that day, horses still had to be exercised and in the crisp early morning air, Leo was impressed by the sight of a hundred or so racehorses, some of the best in Europe, being put through their paces by hard little stable lads and fit, arrogant jockeys. He watched with amusement, and some pride, as his wife galloped the five-furlong straight on an eager chestnut filly and a tiny saddle with just a few inches of stirrup leather. She had some difficulty in pulling up at the end of the gallop, until one of the lads called at her to drop her reins, not hook them back. Nobody had told her that young racehorses are trained to fight the bit. She did as she was told and the lightly panting two-year-old slackened and came back to her.

She hacked back to the yard with the rest of the string, trotting through the thick forest of Chantilly on wide sand gallops. When they reached the yard, she jumped off, gleaming with exhilaration.

'Sometime soon,' she told Leo, 'I'm going to have to get a horse of my own.'

'Yeah,' Leo laughed, 'we could put up a stable behind the house and you could ride round the garden in Chelsea Square. Okay, Angel, maybe we'll find somewhere for you to keep it. You sure look good on a horse and if it keeps your body in shape, that's all right by me. But the minute you grow a fat arse – you stop, all right?'

Alison's friends had reserved a table for the whole party in the restaurant behind the grandstand at the racecourse. It was one of a dozen or so set on the lawns under huge parasols. All the women were dressed in their most special summer clothes; bright flower baskets hung from every available projection; swift, efficient waiters glided across the finely mown grass carrying champagne buckets and trays of langoustines. Leo could not deny that the French did this sort of thing better than anyone. He found to his surprise that he was enjoying himself enormously, studying and discussing form, eating and drinking the best that was on offer.

They watched the races from the pretty stand reserved for members of the *Société pour l'Encouragement*. The course itself was breathtaking, looking towards the huge ornate stable block built in 1719 by Henri de Bourbon, Prince de Condé, who thought that he was going to be reincarnated as a horse, and then, beyond the sweeping right-handed arc of the race track, the Château de Chantilly was set behind its lake, gleaming in the bright sun. Wandering among the restaurant tables was a selection of beautiful girls, hand-picked by the *Pari-Mutuel* to sell betting tickets for the state-run totalisator. Leo, following informed opinion, called one over and placed a five-thousand-franc bet on Sassafras, which was to be ridden by Yves St Martin in the Prix du Jockey Club. He was as excited as all the other backers of this outstanding horse as it streaked first past the post. Praised by the other men in the party for his shrewd judgement and bold gambling, he laughed it off as Jewish luck and went to collect his winnings.

In high spirits and approving of everything French, Leo and Alison drove down to Paris that evening and checked into the Plaza Athenée. Before unpacking, they sought out Michel Biguault in the Bar Anglais and ordered a pair of his famous bloody marys to commence the evening's celebrations.

The city was still buzzing, before the annual August shutdown. Leo and Alison extracted all the traditional pleasures of Paris: they sat in cafés round Trocadero, shopped in the rue St Honoré, ate in the Taillevent, ordered the duck menu at the Tour d'Argent, and climbed up Montmartre to experience the view from the steps of the Sacré Coeur. Then, while Leo looked at possible shop sites in the sixth and seventh arrondissements, Alison visited the Louvre, the Grand Palais and L'Orangerie and wandered in and out of the art galleries along the Left Bank.

In the evenings they danced in Regines and Castels and, for those few days, they were both unreservedly happy and in love with one another.

151

But arriving in Cap d'Antibes, to stay with old Jewish rag-trade friends of his parents, Leo tightened up again. Somehow he had to be proving himself all the time to these people. The Steenbergs, like his parents, had started in a very small business, but by the time they had retired five years before, they had built up a chain of one hundred and twenty high-street dress-shops at the lower end of the market.

They knew all about Leo's success with Rags, but weren't going to let him get away with any boastful arrogance, and old Louis Steenberg constantly picked up on any remarks which, in his view, demonstrated Leo's youth and inexperience. Alison, of course, met with their approval. She was well-bred and beautiful and anyway, something of an outsider. Her natural diplomacy, too, led her away from any provocative conversations. Privately, she found the house and its furnishings ostentatious and vulgar – masses of gold ormolu and gilt Louis XV furniture – and she was unimpressed by her hosts' inability to speak French or communicate effectively with the indigenous population. She could see that their staff, and those of the restaurants they visited, considered the Steenbergs no more than a source of income and wasted no affection on them.

Conversations tended to centre on business, money and old friends. They spoke wistfully of the knighthood recently bestowed on Jo Kagan, a Lithuanian Jewish raincoat manufacturer from Yorkshire. Louis Steenberg commented that if he had stayed in England and spent all his spare time with politicians, he would have expected at least a knighthood. 'Look at the Seiffs,' he added.

'Your business was hardly Marks and Spencer,' Leo replied drily.

'Only because Louis didn't want it to be,' Mrs Steenberg defended.

The day after this exchange, Leo and Alison went to the marina in Antibes to see the yacht which they had chartered. A big bulky gin-palace, it didn't look very romantic, but Leo was well pleased with all the comforts and gadgetry, the Riva swinging on the davits and the white-uniformed crew.

They had arranged to lunch that day at the Eden Roc with a French couple whom they had met in Chantilly. They in turn were introduced to a serenely beautiful Italian, the Contessa di Martelli. Sole heiress to an Italian motor manufacturer, her young aristocratic husband had recently been killed in a light aircraft in Kenya. Leo was captivated by her and much to everyone's astonishment, before the end of lunch he had asked her to join them on the yacht. Still more surprisingly, she agreed.

Alison later asked Leo why he had asked her. 'I know you don't want to screw her, she's not your type.'

'Well, she's the sort of person we ought to be mixing with – not these rag-trade bores. You're right, she's not my type, but she's fantastic looking, and, you know, aristocratic.'

'Her husband was, she's not,' replied Alison, 'and God knows how she'll get on with the assorted mob you've invited on the yacht. You really do some odd things sometimes, Leo. Still, it's rather sweet and naïve.'

Yet the cruise was a success. Leo loved having this flamboyant status symbol under his command and revelled in his duties as a yachting host. They made their way via Monte Carlo to the Italian Riviera, then turned south, down the east coast of Corsica. Their destination was Porto Cervo, a newly built town on a natural harbour on north-eastern Sardinia's Costa Smeralda.

The Aga Khan, whose money and enthusiasm were responsible for the unique resort, had exercised rigid control over the development of this stretch of coast, and the architects of Porto Cervo had blended it into the landscape very effectively; the white, rough-rendered walls and pan-tiled roofs looked as if they were centuries old.

There were yachts in the port that dwarfed theirs, and Leo suddenly felt less important. In a town that was a playground for some of Europe's richest people he was no big deal, but he was very impressed by the style and beauty

153

of the Costa Smeralda and promised himself to come back and stay another time. Maria di Martelli, who appeared to have enjoyed the trip, though without any great show of appreciation, annoyed Leo by announcing that she had been invited to stay on at Porto Rotondo with friends whom she had met when they had all had dinner at the Pitrizza.

Alison had been amused by Leo's performance with Maria. He was so conscientiously not making concessions to what he considered her well-bred sophistication, in marked contrast to the futile fawning of the motley crowd of garment merchants, tax accountants, lawyers and their wives who were his other guests. Alison knew that Maria was leaving the boat because she wasn't getting anywhere with Leo. Leo misinterpreted her aloofness and thought it was because she was bored with him and his friends.

He decided that they would stay on in Porto Cervo for a few days. Nobody minded. The food was good, the women were beautiful, and the scope for sexual adventure seemed limitless. Once Leo had found his way around, established the pecking order and dismissed it, he relaxed. The yacht was full of people constantly coming and going.

Late one night, when his guests were all in their cabins, and the noises from the town had diminished to short isolated bursts of music or human drama, he sat alone on the deck. The air was warm and still. The bottle of Sardinian wine by his side tasted well in its native surroundings. Leo had drunk most of its contents when a noise made him look up – the sound of slow, soft footfalls approaching his boat down the quayside. A shadowy, white figure stopped at the gangway, then almost noiselessly ascended. The ethereal shape moved around the fore-deck, then, apparently searching, found its way close to where Leo sat in a wicker chair at the stern.

Leo waited until it was almost beside him, still not having seen him.

'What are you looking for?' he whispered angrily.

'I was looking for you, Leo.' The husky Italian voice of Maria di Martelli made Leo catch his breath. Now he could focus on her white-clad, over-poweringly sexual presence.

She lay down comfortably on a wide, thickly cushioned sun-deck a few feet away.

'I went rather suddenly – I want to explain.'

'Maria, it was great having you. You don't have to explain.'

'No, but I want to. Why don't you come over here? We don't want to wake everyone.'

Leo sat down by her cross-legged, facing her. Immediately he felt a hand caress his thigh.

'I had to go because I did not think I could stand being so near to you, and not having you.'

Leo was astonished. He did not know what to say. The hand continued gently to massage his thigh, up towards his groin.

'Don't you feel it too?' Maria murmured.

Up until that point, Leo hadn't. Now the warmth and urgency of her invitation were tremendously arousing. He felt his cock grow with alarming rapidity. Maria propped herself up on one elbow, withdrew her hand from Leo's thigh and flung it around the back of his neck. Irresistibly she pulled his head down towards hers.

Leo found his mouth on a bed of warm sucking softness. Her tongue tasted sweetly of sambucca. The smell of her scent mingled powerfully with her sweat, proclaiming her readiness for love-making.

Leo's motives were in conflict. His body, his physical instincts, were in no doubt where they wanted to be, but behind these was the thought that he should not be making love to this sophisticated, grand Italian lady – not with Alison lying asleep in the cabin beneath.

Maria sensed some reluctance, and her hand resumed its relentless pursuit of his genitals. She gasped with excited triumph when she found his exaggerated response.

Leo lay back and passively stretched out.

Maria's mouth left his and a short trail of saliva down his chin. Her lips caressed their way hungrily down his chest, and busy hands fumbled with his belt-buckle and zip.

A warm fist grasped him, tantalisingly, jiggled his balls. Suddenly he was enveloped in her warm, rhythmically constricting mouth as her fingers lightly stroked his granite shaft.

Leo, in a haze of deliciously distant climax, felt vaguely that he should be giving, doing something in return, but Maria seemed totally preoccupied, too busy to need anything more.

For an instant, Leo took the sudden flood of light to be some preorgasmic experience.

Alison's voice jerked his mind and eyes into sudden focus.

'Didn't anyone get you dinner tonight, Maria? You must be starving.'

Leo deflated like a party balloon with a fast leak.

Maria looked up. A trail of spittle still joined her mouth to Leo's coy, wrinkling member.

Alison glared back at her. 'I'd stick to spaghetti if I were you – I'm sure you'd find it more manageable.'

Leo was shivering in apprehension of the inevitable scene. He reached down and zipped up his trousers. Ignoring Maria's presence, he clambered to his feet and leant against the nearest deck rail.

The Contessa slowly wiped her mouth with the back of her hand. 'Maybe your husband is hungry too, or he wouldn't have been here.'

'You insolent tart,' Alison sneered. 'I know bloody well this was all your initiative. I saw how you were looking at him on the way down here. And he thought you couldn't fancy him because you were such a smart, rich countess.' She let out a snort of disparaging laughter.

'Maybe Leo finds no satisfaction in making love to someone who can't carry his children.' Maria shrugged her shoulders.

'You bitch! Who the hell told you about that?' She held up a hand and shook her head. 'It doesn't matter – I don't want to hear. Just get off this boat and out of my sight.'

The Italian woman lifted herself languidly from the deck, and without a word or a glance, walked with complete composure to the gangway and down to the quay. Alison and Leo stood looking at one another. She, angry but forgiving; he, crestfallen and confused.

'God, Angel, I'm sorry – I just don't know how it happened.'

'You're such a fool sometimes, Leo. Still at least you weren't doing anything to her. That would have been a bit hard to take.'

Leo took a couple of steps to stand in front of Alison.

'Ali – about you not having children. I don't know why you wanted to keep it from me. I've known for a long time. It hasn't changed what I think of you, what I feel for you, one bit. Believe me, Angel – making love to you is the best thing that's ever happened.'

He wrapped his arms around her, and her head rested on his shoulder. She cried a little.

'Oh, Leo – please don't ever let me catch you like that again.'

'I promise, Angel, I promise.'

# 1970

In 1969, President Milton Obote had warned that, sooner or later, the Indians in Uganda would have to go. This was an African country and should be run by Africans.

Prem Patel was a pragmatist. He and his family, like the majority of Indians in East Africa, held British passports.

The British immigration authority were allowing three and a half thousand heads of families into Britain each year on a quota system divided among previous British possessions. Uganda's share was less than one hundred. Mr Patel had applied, pulling hard on every available string, for an entry permit for him and his family and had had his application accepted. Over the preceding two years, he had systematically smuggled out everything he could, and left the remainder of his possessions in the hands of the Kalianji family for safe-keeping and future remittance.

Raj was asked to give his advice about life in England, and to discuss what was to happen about his marriage. His feelings about this were still ambivalent. In the two years that had elapsed since his parents had told him about his marriage arrangements, he had ceased to think of Diana – he had heard no more from her – and had accustomed himself to the idea of Reena as his wife. He was even worried that this might not now be the case.

But Mr Patel reassured him. Either Reena would come back to Uganda or he would fix an immigration permit to England for Raj.

'I think it unlikely that she will return here, though,' he added. 'Your father is being very stubborn, don't you think? He refuses to agree that things are only going to get worse for us here – especially now that our presence is becoming a political football. If I were you, Raj, I'd apply for a permit right away.'

Raj shook his head. 'You may be right, but I must stand by my father. To be honest, he feels that you're running away.'

Mr Patel laughed. 'Well, I'm sure you know the saying: discretion is the better part of valour.'

Driving home, Raj considered his family's position. Mr Patel was right. They, the Indians, had become a political factor in East Africa generally. Governments in neighbouring Kenya and Tanzania had been making anti-Asian noises for many years, and though Milton Obote was, on the whole, a realist he was beset by the problems of tribalism. One way of unifying the diverse peoples of Uganda was to concentrate their attention on the most obvious ethnic and cultural outsiders. It was considered that this might evoke a sense of nationalism which would make the country a lot easier to run.

Raj's own position was more complicated. He had been born and brought up in Africa, completed the most important part of his education in Europe and felt vaguely, but strongly, that his real cultural roots lay in India. He was annoyed by his fellow Indians' refusal to integrate and enter fully into political life in Africa, but was finding it hard to achieve much on his own – and, anyway, he had become very fascinated by and involved in his family's business.

'Don't you think it would be prudent to make contingency arrangements in case we are expelled from Uganda?' he asked his father that evening.

His father laughed. 'You've been taking too much notice of Patel. The Africans will never get rid of us. We run the businesses, the hospitals, the legal system and the civil service. These political leaders just talk about it to sound tough. Anyway, what has happened to your great political theories?'

'Well, I think I'm more interested in survival first – and

it would be a real disaster if we had to leave in a hurry, unprepared. We might lose everything that you've worked so hard to build up.'

'Raju, you worry too much. Mark my words, Patel will be back here in a year or two. I think in England he'll miss being the top dog.' He paused and looked across his neat lawn with its fringe of flowering shrubs, peaceful in the short twilight. 'Raju, you're a realist. You know we're too important here. They can't afford to make us go.'

# August 1972

There was a loud hammering on the elegant front door of the Kalianji house. Uncompromising, urgent and authoritative, the family knew what it meant. Their servants, Baganda, Acholi and West Nilotes had left within hours of Idi Amin's announcement. Raj's parents sat in a state of silent shock, willing the truth to go away.

Reluctantly, Raj walked to the front door to open it before it splintered beneath a rain of blows from machine-gun butts.

A tall Nubian, not unlike Amin himself, wearing the uniform of a colonel in the Uganda Rifles smiled cynically at him.

'You want some help to pack?' he asked. 'It won't take long – you only allowed a couple of cases.'

As he spoke he strode into the hall, looking around with glee. He was followed by half a dozen soldiers, jauntily toting their automatic weapons. Outside, Raj could see another group dismounting from a pair of Land Rovers and heading towards the garage block.

The colonel continued, 'I like to live in this house very much. Thank you for preparing it so well for me.' He looked around covetously at the fine colonial furniture and rich wall-hangings.

In the saloon, the soldiers pestered Vishnu and his wife. 'What you still doing in the colonel's house?'

The colonel beamed benevolently. 'Don't abuse our departing friends. They got twelve weeks to get out.'

Raj momentarily lost control. 'What do you mean by

161

bursting in here?' he shouted. 'This is private property. You've no right to harass us like this.'

The colonel grinned cruelly. 'You blood-sucking, cheating people have got no rights at all now. You leaving Uganda to be run by Ugandans.' He nodded at one of the soldiers who swung the stock of his gun crushingly into Raj's midriff. Raj gasped harshly as the air was driven from his lungs by the lightning blow. His knees buckled. His mother let out a cry as her son crumpled to the polished wood floor.

The colonel turned back to Vishnu. 'My brother is very polite. He asked me to thank you for your businesses – but you can't go to your office, or your warehouse or your farm. You are forbidden to own these things any more. You may only take some personal possessions. The government will allocate all your other things to people it thinks have more right to them.'

In the silence that followed, they could hear the sound of cars being started up and driven off amidst appreciative whooping from the soldiers.

'Tell them to leave one car so that we can get to Entebbe,' Raj rasped as he dragged himself to his feet.

The colonel agreed and gave the order. 'It has also become the property of the state and it will be searched when you leave here and arrive at the airport. Now, two of my men stay here until you leave. The telephone is cut. So – no tricks to cheat the government anymore.' He glanced round once more. 'And look after my house carefully.'

He, with all but two soldiers, swaggered out of the house and slammed the front door behind them.

The day before, 5 August 1972, President Idi Amin had told a gathering of his troops at Tororo in Eastern Uganda that all Asians were to be expelled from their country and must leave within three months. Amin had come to power eighteen months before when Milton Obote, attending a Commonwealth Heads of Government conference in Singapore, had telephoned through an order to have him arrested. As it happened, the call was taken by one of

Amin's own Kakwa tribe and a coup had been instigated and effected immediately.

At the end of 1971, he had denounced the Indian community for black-marketing, hoarding goods to raise prices, smuggling money and sugar, and for refusing to allow their daughters to marry Africans.

It seemed to Raj then that Amin was mad enough to do what none of the other East African leaders had done, and follow this threat with actions. Once again, however, Vishnu had refused to listen, and now they found themselves ignominiously huddled as prisoners in their own house, subjected to the aggressive taunts of the soldiers and facing expulsion and destitution.

Raj, talking to his father in Hindi, tried to work out a way of saving something from the wreckage, but because no plan had been made, he had to accept that there was nothing he could do. His mother managed to secrete two pieces of jewellery in her clothing, but the carrying of bulkier possessions was out of the question.

When the day came for them to join the twenty-seven thousand other Asians who had chosen to go to Britain, they drove out of the gates of their house for the last time to the delighted cheers of the soldiers.

Raj drove. His parents huddled silently in the back seat. He looked straight ahead of him when they were stopped at the road blocks and their car was searched. Their four suitcases were opened and checked for gold and currency. Raj's mother, scared speechless, was left alone but abuse and taunts were hurled at Raj and Vishnu. As they entered the airport they were jeered and spat at.

Sitting mournfully among the huge crowd waiting to be allocated seats on British Airways planes, they learned that they had suffered less than some who had been beaten openly, violently robbed and raped. Listening to weeping women and their confused complaining children, Raj thought of the last time he had left from this airport to fly to London, with all the glorious expectations of that trip.

Now, he could see, his adherence to Hindu conventions that demanded obedience to his father had led directly to their being in this plight. He had had many opportunities for transferring assets and money out of Uganda, but had not availed himself of them as his father had expressly and consistently forbidden it. Because of his father's myopic stubbornness, therefore, and in spite of his own long-held certainty of the inevitability of their expulsion, the family faced a bleak future.

The plane broke through the low cloud cover on an early evening in November, and rain slashed against the cabin windows. Raj thought of the cold English autumn. He glanced over at his mother. She sat as if in a trance, wearing a fine, very light, pink and silver sari; then at his father, who had scarcely spoken since leaving Entebbe. They really had no idea what was in store for them.

Vishnu Kalianji was completely broken. When he had finally accepted that all their property and all the possessions which they could not take with them would be seized by the government or, unofficially, by the army, and that no compensation was ever likely to be paid, his will had deserted him. In a state of sustained shock, he had had no option but to leave all the arrangements for their journey and arrival to his calm, confident and pragmatic son.

Before the plane had even touched down, the frantic bustle to gather up belongings had begun. Everyone in the plane was in the same position: they were arriving in an alien country with nothing other than that which they had been able to cram into a few suitcases, and the one or two valuables that they had been able to hide in their clothing. These few items now represented their only link with the life they had left behind in what, for most of them, had been their native country.

The Kalianjis had lost more than most. Finding himself on terms of equal destitution with all the other occupants of the tightly crowded Jumbo jet had been almost as unbearable to Vishnu as the loss of his wealth.

Raj stopped his parents from joining the undignified scramble for bags and suitcases. He insisted that they stay in their seats until the plane had drawn up next to one of the long concrete fingers that projected from the hub of Heathrow's Terminal 3. When all the other passengers had grabbed their possessions and shuffled slowly down the bottle-necked aisles, he allowed them to rise and make their way calmly out of the plane and into the long, bare corridor.

'We will achieve nothing by rushing,' he told them. 'Life is going to be hard enough without panicking, so we might as well get used to absorbing the situation in our own time, and as far as possible on our own terms.'

Wheeling the scant remnants of their wealth through the Customs on two trolleys, Raju noticed that the Customs officers were regarding them with a benevolence that had not been there last time he had entered England. Everyone was waved through. Even those attempting to declare dutiable items were discouraged from doing so. They didn't have any currency with which to pay duty, and had prepared themselves to barter with less cherished objects. In the arrival hall there were groups of helpful young English people, volunteers to the specially created Ugandan Resettlement Board. They would provide transport to the refugees' homes; some in centres set up by a government trying to put a bright face on an unavoidable inconvenience, others in the homes of Asian friends and relations.

Raj had written to Paul Paintal, warning him of their imminent arrival, and expressing the hope that there would be room for the Kalianjis in his house in South Harrow, but he had been unable to give specific time or date.

He left his parents with their pile of luggage and went to make a reversed charge call to Paul, who was out. His wife, though happy to hear they had arrived safely, was unable to come and collect them. She could not drive. She suggested that they take a taxi.

Raj squeezed his way back through the crowd of bewildered Indians, wondering how he might get a taxi when they had no money at all. An Englishman, about his own age, wearing jeans and an old tweed jacket, was trying to talk to Vishnu. Raj introduced himself to the young man, who looked relieved at Raj's concise English and evident ability to cope.

He wondered, he said, if they had made arrangements for anywhere to stay, or did they want accommodation at one of the resettlement camps?

Raj explained that they were expected at their cousin's house in Harrow.

'Oh, fine. Is it just the three of you?' asked the Englishman.

Raj nodded.

'Great. Well I can get you into my car. It's right outside – they've bent the parking rules a bit for this emergency. Here, I'll take this trolley, and you follow me.'

They wove their way out to a confusion of honking and double-parked cars. Raj's mother gazed about her at the fur-coated women, the gleaming Rolls-Royces and the spotless pavements. Eventually, they reached a small estate car and loaded the cases into the back.

Raj's parents, still silent, were ushered into the rear and Raj got in the passenger side.

As they set off for the tunnel that led out of the airport, their driver turned and spoke to Raj. 'My name's Simon Riley. Welcome to England. I'm sorry it's under such ghastly circumstances. Was the flight all right?'

Raj smiled wanly. 'The flight has been the easiest part of our ejection.'

'Fairly rough was it then? I read that the military were being pretty aggressive and pinching everything they could lay their hands on. Have you left a lot behind?'

Raj nodded. 'We had one of the biggest trading companies in Uganda – coffee, engineering and so on. Unfortunately, my father didn't think that we would ever be expelled, and so we made no arrangements. We have lost a very great deal.'

The Englishman shook his head slowly. 'God, I'm sorry. Still, at least you're safe now. I gather the Indian community has left behind about four hundred million dollars-worth of assets, and there's no hope of compensation. It's

166

extraordinary that Amin has got away with it – so far. Mind you, we tried to talk him out of it. Geoffrey Rippon, our Foreign Secretary, went over, and so did Amin's old commanding officer, Major Grahame. But I think Amin had committed himself by then. He would not back down.'

They drove on in silence for a while towards London, then Raj said, 'It's very kind of you to do this. I'm afraid we have no currency and no way of repaying you.'

The young man laughed. 'Good Lord, that doesn't matter. I'm glad to be of help. By the way, if you've got no money, what do you plan to do?'

'Well, we have a couple of pieces of jewellery. And our cousins will help us until we're on our feet. I've been in London before, and I'll look around and see what I can do. I'm determined not to be beaten by the situation. My father, though, is very confused – he still doesn't believe it's happened. So it's up to me.'

'Anything I can do,' said Simon, 'let me know. I'll give you my telephone number when we reach your cousin's. You can ring me if you want any advice or help.'

'That is most kind of you. Why are you offering such assistance?'

'Look, you people are in a bloody awful situation and I've not put myself out all that much. I really admire your determination, and it would be a pleasure to see you get settled.'

When they reached Harrow, Paul Paintal was waiting solemnly to greet them. Simon was offered a cup of tea, which he accepted, and before leaving, he assured Raj once again that he would be glad to do anything he could to help; meanwhile, he left them his phone number, wished them the best of luck and shook hands warmly.

# 1971

Rags's progress was relentless – in spite of the gloom being spread by fashion and social pundits who were busily nailing the coffin of the preceding decade. Mick Jagger's appearance in *Performance* was treated as a kind of swan song – and, to reassure their customers that youth culture still flourished, the rag-trade offered them hot-pants. Sarah and Leo refused to acknowledge this short-lived fashion, and held by their principle of ignoring mainstream, high-street trends. This served only to increase customers and strengthen loyalty.

Over the previous year, Sarah had introduced cushions, lamps, furnishing materials and other household goods into their range as well as expanding an already wide variety of cosmetics and accessories. Leo was very anxious to maximise the public's eager response. He dreamed of taking over a major department store and prowled predatorily up and down outside those which he thought might be dying of old age.

One, in Kensington High Street, was a grandly handsome art deco building, with a meticulously designed and well-preserved interior – a very pleasing example of its period. Leo would pat its pillared portico with acquisitive affection, and gaze wistfully at the uninspiring merchandise and customers within.

That spring, he started to make inquiries into the possibility of buying the store with a view to converting it into a huge Rags. He was astonished to find that United Hosiers, the group that owned it, were more interested in simply selling the property, rather than the store as a going concern. But the sum that they were asking seemed well above the current market value.

Leo tentatively sounded out his bankers on the matter of raising the four million pounds being asked. To his fury he found that Tony Scott was now their principal commercial property consultant. Guessing that it was Leo who was looking for funds, Tony promptly, and convincingly, undervalued it.

There was no real chance of using another bank. It would have involved transferring all his accounts and, such had been his rate of growth, Leo was already operating with substantial borrowings.

As the summer approached, he became more obsessed with buying this huge store. In an off-guard moment he admitted to Sarah what he was considering. He had not intended to tell her until it was a *fait accompli*, and her signature would be a formality.

Sarah looked at him aghast, as if he were mad. This meant, effectively, risking the whole business, all thirty-eight shops, on an enormous gamble. It was not simply a question of buying the property, it would involve a total refit, a huge quantity and variety of stock and a massive investment in preparatory, start-up and promotional costs.

But one by one, Leo allayed her fears. The thought of eighty thousand square feet filled with a range of goods that were unique to Rags was tremendously exciting to a designer of such commitment as Sarah. And with Leo's inspiring confidence, she was persuaded that it would work.

Their first French shop too, in the rue du Four in Paris's less traditional sixth arrondissement, had just opened to a euphoric reception from the normally hard-to-impress Parisians. *Le Jeune Chic Anglais* had found a ready acceptance among the price-conscious middle class. This strengthened Leo's case and his resolve. He determinedly set about seeking the funds required for his mind-boggling flagship, but he encountered more difficulties than he had anticipated. Although his balance sheet showed high borrowings at a time of increasing interest rates, his profit and loss account continued to show very healthy trading. But the merchant banks and institutions that he approached took the view that interest rates would rise further, that Rags was merely a survivor from the sixties and that the bubble was due to burst. They felt that the rapid growth of denim merchants like Jean Machine and Jean Junction were clear indicators of the way the fashion market was going. In vain, Leo pleaded that Rags's success had always lain in his ability to buck trends. But the City people looked at their market research and analyses, and shook their heads.

Leo had been unable to hide his frustration and disappointment from Alison. She had asked him to tell her in detail what was involved, and found herself discussing it with her brother, Simon, over lunch.

Simon had been with one of the City's bigger stockbrokers for three years. His first-class degree in economics had secured him a place as a junior analyst with particular responsibility for the property sector. Already he had an intimate knowledge of the major property companies, their state of health and the personalities behind them. After lunch he phoned Leo's secretary and arranged to meet his brother-in-law later that evening.

Leo waited impatiently in the bar at Meridiana. He had told Alison that Simon wanted to discuss something over dinner, and she had simply said, 'Why not? You go alone.'

'What does he want?' Leo had demanded irritably. 'I've got a lot on my mind at the moment.'

'Well,' Alison had replied, 'I did tell him that you were looking for a way of buying your new store – and he said he thought he might be able to help.'

'For Christ's sake, I don't want you discussing my affairs with your snotty family. What the hell can your brother do for me?'

'I don't know. But he said he might be able to do something – and right now, you haven't got any other likely deal, so you might as well be polite and listen.'

Simon, a few years Leo's junior in age, and many years

his junior in experience, had the inexplicable effect of making his brother-in-law feel inferior. It didn't appear to be deliberate; Simon was always polite and, Leo grudgingly admitted, amusing company. It was Simon's unassuming air of insuperable confidence that Leo resented. For though Simon had had a very successful time at Oxford – President of OUDS, a cricket blue and a first-class degree – he had still to prove himself in the real world. Yet he talked as if he were already a senior partner and was on familiar terms with a number of prominent politicians of all views.

Simon, apologising warmly, arrived ten minutes late, ordered an Americano from the welcoming barman, nodded acknowledgement to the slightly drunk pianist in the corner and sat down on an uncomfortably low leather sofa next to Leo.

'Sorry I didn't give you more details of what I wanted to discuss, but I don't know how much your staff know about your Kensington store project.'

'Not as much as you apparently,' Leo growled charmlessly.

Simon laughed. 'Look. Let's get one thing clear – I'm not here to do you a favour. If my introduction results in a deal for you, I'll earn handsomely, in cash and brownie points.' He paused. 'Now, in broad terms, one of the property companies we advise is very anxious to substantially strengthen its portfolio of retail properties. Word is that United Hosiers won't budge on their asking price, which most analysts think is far too high. Well, right now, a lot of retail property is too cheap, and our view is that there will soon be a big acceleration in rental and freehold values. This property you're after, eighty thousand square feet at four million pounds, represents a rent of five pounds a foot on a ten-year purchase, and that sounds about right.'

Leo nodded eagerly. 'Yes,' he said, 'that's what I reckon, and on top of that the whole place could have been custom-built for Rags – the architecture and interior are spot on as they are. That's got to save us a million in fitting costs.'

'Okay. The company that's interested is Ubiland, and they're prepared to buy it and let it to you. They'll grant a long renewable lease, with five-year rent reviews. They haven't said so, but I'm fairly sure that they'll give you fitting time and a year rent-free, if you're going to refurbish to a specified extent. They've already done their homework with your company accounts and banks. Michael Richter, who's the boss there, is quite an admirer of yours. He believes you've got a long life ahead of you.'

Leo drank too much over dinner, so relieved was he that a real deal now looked possible. He even managed to relax with Simon, and suggested that they go up to Tramps in Jermyn Street and, perhaps, see what women were around.

'Won't Alison be expecting you?' Simon asked.

'Oh, shit, I'd forgotten that you're my lovely wife's brother.' Leo laughed. 'I was thinking of finding some wild chick for you – to ruffle up your hair a bit – you know, loosen your tie.'

Simon smiled slightly and raised one eyebrow. 'No thanks. And I think it's time you went home, before you get into trouble.'

'Yeah, well, don't worry, Simon,' Leo slurred a little. 'But, thanks for Ubiland. I hope you're on a good earner with them -- you deserve it.'

They walked out through the entrance of the restaurant and Simon watched Leo speed off in his gold Aston.

On 5 August 1972, the day on which Idi Amin announced his expulsion of forty thousand British Asians from Uganda, Alison and Leo flew to Sardinia.

It had been, so far, a tricky but satisfying year. The effects of the winter power strikes seemed to have been dissipated. Leo, though furious at having either to close his shops or to light them with thousands of paraffin lanterns, had been amused afterwards to observe that industrial production had dropped only a few per cent in spite of a forty per cent reduction in the working week. And although Mr Fish in Clifford Street had gone bust,

Jim Slater was buying land for himself with impressive voracity.

The deal had been done on the Kensington store, and it was planned to open the following autumn, just in time for Christmas. The press had a field day with the announcement. It seemed as if the whole country was waiting excitedly for the opening day.

Leo had left Sarah with an army of designers and shop fitters, who breathed a sigh of relief at the absence of his manic, relentless pressure. Amidst general speculation as to whether he was engaged in an inspired gamble or an ego trip of spectacular proportions, he had decided to take a holiday. At the last moment he had been able to rent a villa on Punta Sardegna, just outside Porto Rafael on the island's north-eastern tip.

A little Alisarda Fokker Friendly took them the last leg from Genoa to Olbia, where a rented Ferrari was waiting for them.

The sun was beginning to drop behind the low mountains on their left as they drove along the winding road to Porto Rafael, thirty miles to the north. There was a pleasing freshness in the evening air provided by the persistent north-easterly wind. Passing through Arzachena, then branching off the main road where it turns towards Palau, they dropped down a narrow, sinuous road which ran between the sea and the eastern slope of the rocky spine stretched along Punta Sardegna. The barren landscape supported only gorse bushes and sharp, sparse grasses, and the twilight turned the granite rock formation into massive, eerie sculptures. There was a romantic other-worldliness to the scene, and the odd twinkles of light from villas scattered sparsely along the coast seemed hundreds of miles away. Their villa was almost at the end of the point, and they decided to stop and refresh themselves in Porto Rafael before driving the last kilometre.

The village was a cluster of houses centred round a three-sided piazza, whose fourth side was open to a small bay. Built only six or seven years before on virgin soil, there was already an established charm to the little white, vine-clad houses and shops that lined the alley down to the square.

In the bar of a pension called La Fonda, they learned from the elegant Mulatto barman that the village had been the idea of Rafael Neville, a flamboyant and successful property developer from Marbella. With backing from banker Dino Daponte and encouragement from society pioneers Joe Setton, Peter Ward, Bay Larische and his old Marbella friends, Rafael had arrived and bought up agriculturally worthless land at silly prices, and installed himself in a concrete gun emplacement, since turned into a nightclub called 'La Mittraglietta', the Machine-gun. Rafael had remained the focus of this social whirlpool and had attracted a varied and outrageous crowd of fun-lovers to his little domain.

Leo, with his customary interest in such matters, asked who owned the establishment in which they were drinking their champagne.

'I do,' a soft English voice said behind them. They turned to see a tanned, blond, fit Englishman in his early thirties. Good-looking, supremely confident, he said, casually, 'I'm Harry. Are you staying here?' eyeing Alison with undisguised approval. Alison was impressed and not unflattered by the unequivocal message in his eyes.

'Yeah,' replied Leo, irritated by this flagrant covetousness. 'We've got a villa up the track towards the lighthouse – if there's a villa there at all. We haven't been to find it yet.'

'Oh, yes, I know it. Great beach and an amazing view.' Harry paused then said to Alison, 'But if you want some excitement, there's always a lot going on here. See you around.' He walked through the serving door into the kitchen with a quick last glance over his shoulder at her.

The barman was grinning. 'What's the joke?' asked Leo.

'If that guy was a rabbit, you wouldn't be able to see the ground on this island for little bunnies. The locals here call him "*Il Stallone*". He's not too subtle, huh?'

Alison laughed. Leo scowled.

'Hey, man,' the barman chided, 'don't get peevish. He usually draws the line at pinching other dogs' dinners.'

Harry was right, though, about the view. Leo woke early, before the maid, and walked on to the terrace to watch the sun appearing from behind the hill on the island of Caprera. There were a few fishing craft on the still sea, and the early ferry plied between the little town of Palau and La Maddalena Island. Back towards Porto Rafael, just off shore, two large sailing yachts and a big silver motor cruiser lay sleeping.

Padding around in bare feet on the springy grass, Leo was amazed at the profusion of flora which had been produced by regular sprinkling of water on this otherwise fruitless land. The lawn and the house itself were surrounded by a border of riotous green, vermillion, and orange flowers and shrubs.

Alison appeared beneath the white arched veranda with a tray of orange juice and coffee, which she placed on a wrought-iron table. Still a little asleep, she looked soft and vulnerable, smiling below half-closed eyes. Leo felt that he couldn't be luckier. He drew her to him and held her tight. Then, with his arm still around her, they sat on the low wall that surrounded the terrace and looked out at the peaceful dawn.

'This reminds me of how it was in Ceylon – on our honeymoon,' Leo remarked.

'I suppose being on an island somehow removes you from all your normal hassles,' Alison murmured. 'It's good to feel you relaxed.'

'Yeah. We'll go into the village for lunch and see what's going on.'

'Leo, let's stay here, there's everything we need. We don't have to sit around in restaurants with crowds of over-rich, ostentatious trendies – you do that all the time in London.' She looked at him affectionately. 'Come on, relax. At least I'm out of the way of randy inn-keepers here.'

'He should be so lucky,' Leo laughed, squeezing her

waist. 'He'd need more than a hyperactive cock to pull you.'

But they did drive down the rutted track to Porto Rafael, and had lunch at a bar on a small headland just to the south of the village. It was staffed almost entirely by good-looking young English girls, fresh from Chelsea, and Leo felt very much at home as they sat for hours being introduced and talking to everyone who came in. Most people knew, or quickly found out, who he was, and Alison noticed, not for the first time, that he never tired of playing the part.

The hot sunshine, occasionally tempered by the fierce north-easterly, continued over the next two weeks, while Leo and Alison amused themselves. Leo managed to hire a Riva, and moor it by their villa. They would water-ski, swim, sunbathe and eat. Sometimes they took the boat round to the uninhabited island of Spargi, where they and people they had taken with them would roam the beaches unconcernedly naked and pretend the rest of the world didn't exist.

A couple of times they drove down the coast to Porto Cervo, where they found a number of friends staying in yachts and villas. They visited the yacht club in Porto Rotondo, where Johnny 'Jingles' Johnson held sway amongst the elegant Italians who favoured this resort.

One evening, meeting a crowd of English people at a small restaurant in Liscia di Vacca, just outside Porto Cervo, they joined them, then stayed for hours in a night-club hewn from solid rock and entered through a cleft in the mountainside. The club, the Ritual, was owned by a huge, bearded Milanese who had made a fortune dealing in emeralds in Brazil and had the funds to engage in this extravagant speculation. There was a large central cavern where the dance floor was, with several small caves leading off it to provide bars and little semi-private drinking areas. Heavy rock, Led Zeppelin and Status Quo, pounded up into the uneven granite cavern roof, bounded back and forth across the rough-hewn sides and enveloped the dancers in a morass of sound.

Alison, asked to dance by every man in the party,

worked herself into a voodoo-like frenzy as the drink, the sound and the primeval atmosphere of the place worked their way into her. Leo watched, danced a little, drank more, and in the early morning they drove back exhausted through the approaching dawn.

On 21 August, Rafael, founder of the village, held his customary birthday party in the piazza. People arrived from miles around, by land and sea. International fun-lover, Michael Pearson, arrived in his big black yacht, *The Hedonist*, and anchored a short way off. A tender was lowered and set off for the short jetty crowded with his prize-winning team of ravers. Famous for causing havoc in many a Mediterranean resort, here on Rafael's birthday, they had met their equals.

Leo was amazed by the familiar faces gathering in the square, most people dressed in kangas and, the women, bikini tops.

At one o'clock, Rafael appeared and fired a starting gun to announce the beginning of his fiesta. From tables around the edge of the square, his lethal *combinacion* was served, one part gin two parts Martini Rosso, cucumber peel and lemon. For the less intrepid, there were huge bowls of white sangria and champagne.

In the middle of the back of the piazza, a rock band was set up on the roof, traditionally the loudest and the worst from the local town of Santa Teresa. As the *combinacion* began to take effect, the whole party became a surreal fantasy. Startlingly beautiful women, old, rich men, danced, laughed, shouted, flirted in the square, on the balconies, on the roofs, in a kaleidoscope of vivid, printed cotton, tanned torsos and naked breasts.

Even Leo found the hubbub daunting, and resented his insignificance in this mind-blowing extravaganza. His pulse, already high with excitement ingested from the surroundings, quickened further when he saw Harry, the bar-owner, approach Alison and lead her off to join the dancing. They were soon lost in the mélée, but later he felt his stomach tighten as he saw his wife being led by the hand through an archway at the edge of the piazza.

Refusing to chase after them like a jealous teenager, he gulped down a couple more *combinacions* and looked around for something to take his mind off his fury.

To his astonishment, Leo recognised the relaxed swaying figure of Tony Mackie. Tony was a Lloyd's underwriter and the subject of many myths and legends among London's leading young socialites. There were few grand English houses and Red Ensign-flying yachts whose doors were closed to him, and he was always to be found at the best parties from Inverness to Marbella. Leo envied Tony his easy charm and had, from time to time, asked his surprisingly valuable advice on insurance matters.

He made his way over to greet him. 'Bloody hell, Tony, what are you doing here?'

'I came on that black boat out there,' Tony waved towards *The Hedonist*.

Leo noticed a quiet but coolly beautiful girl standing beside Tony. He turned to her. 'Hallo, who are you, Angel?'

'Oh, er – d'you want to be introduced? This lovely girl is, um, Françoise. This is Leo Freeman.'

'Actually,' a soft French voice, 'I'm Danielle Milinaire.' A small hand was extended towards Leo, who took it and lifted it to his lips.

'Enchanté,' he said in clumsy French. 'Do you want to dance?'

'Why not?'

Leo turned, grinned and winked at the other man. 'Could be some big renewals coming up,' he offered by way of a quid pro quo. Then he lurched towards the middle of the square, still holding the French girl's hand.

For a while they stood gyrating gently. Leo felt the excitement mounting beneath his kanga and knew that he had to have this perfect, delicate, self-possessed woman. If his wife was going to be unfaithful, he drunkenly reasoned to himself, so was he. As he pulled the girl to him he slowly felt her melting. Her hips moved with increasingly eager acquiescence. He put a hand inside her tiny bikini and his mouth to her ear and said,

'Would you like me to pull these knickers down?'

'Where?' she asked.

'Come with me,' said Leo, who hadn't the slightest idea where. As they passed a table Leo grabbed two more glasses of the unforgiving cocktail and they made their way through a gap in the side of the piazza. Walking down the alley, frantically trying to decide what to do, he found an open door and went in, gently pulling the girl behind him.

There appeared to be no one around. Leo led her upstairs and into an open, empty bedroom that overlooked the party. He closed the door and propped a rustic chair beneath the door handle.

He turned to Danielle, smiling, and untucked his kanga, letting it drop to the ground around his ankles. He was pleased to hear a little gasp of appreciation as the girl gazed, fascinated, at his whole-hearted erection.

Leo stood in front of her, and put his hand behind her back to undo the bikini top, which fell away to reveal her large, firm-nippled breasts. He lent and kissed each of them, fondling them with his tongue. Then slowly, lowering himself, slipped his lips down her body to her navel.

He slid the bikini down her legs, and as she stepped out of it, he buried questing lips and tongue amongst the golden pubic hair. The taste he found there mingled sweetly with the *combinacion*. Soon he felt her urgent growing response to his active tongue.

He stood up and, kissing her deeply, put his hands beneath her smooth buttocks and lifted her on to him.

The sounds of the party continued outside. Danielle wrapped her legs around Leo's waist and, levering herself on his hips, slid ecstatically up and down on his rigid pole. Leo had never suffered from alcohol-induced flaccidity or 'brewer's droop', but, when drunk, he took a long time to climax – and he was very drunk. He and Danielle worked their way through a dozen varying modes of entry, interspersed with bouts of greedy cunnilingus and fellatio.

Their cries of pleasure grew in volume and frequency

until, both bathed in sweat, Leo reached a shuddering climax, and they lay wrapped around each other in total, delicious exhaustion, at first unconscious of Rafael's fiesta. Then, with a sudden shock, Leo remembered Alison.

Guilt and triumph fought to dominate his state of mind and then there was anger at the thought that someone else might just have given Alison as much pleasure as he'd given Danielle. Suddenly, decisively, he released himself from her moist arms, jumped off the bed, picked up his kanga and wiped his sweaty torso with it. As he wrapped it round his waist, Danielle watched with hurt and disappointment in her eyes.

'Don't go,' she whispered. And he nearly relented – the little naked body was too perfect to leave.

He leaned and kissed first her lips, and then her overflowing vulva. 'Angel, I've got to go. I've got to see someone. I just remembered.'

'But Leo, it's a party. You don't have to see people now,' the girl said plaintively.

'I do. But I'll see you later,' he winked at her, moved the chair from under the door handle and stumbled out of the room.

Down the narrow stairs and through the house, which was still deserted, he went out into the alley and turned towards the piazza. His head was reeling with drink, sexual triumph, remorse and anger. He saw how wild he looked in the reflective window of a small boutique, and decided to go round the outside of the piazza to the bay. The few people who were frolicking drunkenly in the sea scarcely noticed him as he slipped off his kanga and dived in. The water had a calming, cleansing effect on both mind and body. After a few minutes he emerged, retrieved his simple garment and climbed up over the seaward edge of the piazza. Almost immediately, he saw Alison. She sat demurely, talking to an increasingly incomprehensible Tony Mackie. She spotted Leo and called out light-heartedly, 'Where the hell have you been, Leo? You look as though you've just swum to Maddalena and back.'

Leo tried to smile and look athletic.

'Not quite,' he replied. 'When I saw randy Harry dragging you away from the party, I thought I'd better amuse myself while you were gone.'

'Well that was an hour ago and it only took Harry five minutes to realise he wasn't going to get my knickers down.'

'That was smart of him – considering you're not wearing any.'

'I was talking metaphorically,' replied Alison. 'Anyway, Tony here is almost beyond speech, so let's have a dance.' She stood up and started to walk towards the diminishing group still dancing to the appalling rock band. As Leo followed, his sense of guilt was intensified by the sight of Danielle, looking dishevelled and desperate, emerging from a nearby archway. He pretended not to notice her, but was aware that she saw him. She walked pointedly over to Tony Mackie. Next time he looked, he saw them clambering into *The Hedonist*'s tender and setting off across the bay.

Every so often over the next few weeks, when Leo was back in London immersed in the final run-up to the opening of his new store, his encounter with Danielle would suddenly and vividly present itself and his whole body would respond to the memory. He was neither able nor willing to eject this tantalising recollection and, during the course of a meeting to finalise insurance details with Tony Mackie, he found out more about her.

Tony couldn't remember how she had appeared on *The Hedonist* in Monte Carlo. He supposed that somebody must have known her, or picked her up, but anyway, when the yacht set off for Sardinia, she was still on board. She didn't seem to be with anyone in particular. When they had stopped at Jean Castel's private island, Cavallo, on the way down, she had a blazing row with a French photographer whom she knew and who was staying there. She had gone back to the yacht and locked herself in her cabin for the rest of the voyage – to the disgust and frustration of the rest of the boat's passengers.

She had, until very recently, been the most popular photographic model in Paris, but had announced her intention of ceasing this demeaning activity and of becoming a designer. With backing from a besotted Franco-Swiss banker, she had just opened lavish showrooms off the Boulevard St Germain, and was already receiving good notices from the most chic of Paris. She was the fashion press's idol and she knew how to handle them. She had a reputation for being tough, even ruthless, in the pursuit of her career – and though she wasn't much liked, she was very admired by the French, who understand and approve of this attitude in a beautiful woman.

Leo had had no communication with her at all. He hadn't seen her since the tender had pulled away from the party in Porto Rafael. But Tony gave him the approximate address of her salon, and he decided that he ought to go to Paris to look at Rags's progress there. Alison didn't seem surprised or put out that he didn't ask her to join him.

The night before Leo left for Paris they went out to a lavish dinner at Tiberio's and met friends at Annabel's. Back at home, they made love with even more than their customary passion and Leo wondered why the hell he was going to complicate his life by following up a notoriously bitchy, over-sexed French woman.

Wearing a long pig-skin coat and a wide brimmed fedora, Leo walked slowly from the Brasserie Lip, where he had lunched with his French manager, up the Boulevard St Germain towards Danielle Milinaire's salon. When he arrived, he entered a small, expensively fitted showroom, whose air of elegant calm contrasted with the bustle in the narrow little streets outside.

Making no attempt to speak French, Leo asked an aloof, immaculate receptionist if Danielle was in.

'What is your name, please?'

He gave the information. When the girl had left the showroom through a small archway at the back, he looked at the few garments and the many photographs that were displayed. Without any conscious effort, he applied his professional judgement to what he saw. He was impressed. As far as he could see, Danielle's style was a romantic version of Feraud, less extreme than St Laurent, more Italian than French.

His musing was interrupted by a simple soft ''ello.'

He turned. She was more stunning than he had remembered, and now with the added attraction of being another, perhaps rival, garment merchant.

Leo smiled. 'Remember me?' he asked.

'Of course. What do you want?'

'I . . . I thought we might have something to discuss that could be to our mutual benefit.'

She looked slightly puzzled, and then, understanding, said, 'You are Mr Rags, no? Why not come to my bureau?'

She walked back through the archway, expecting Leo to follow. She led him down a wide, picture-clad passage to a panelled room where full-length windows gave on to an extravagantly planted courtyard, in the middle of which a classically erotic fountain played.

Danielle pointed to a large, leather chair. 'Sit down. Champagne?'

Leo nodded, but didn't sit. As she leaned down to extract a bottle from a fridge concealed in the wall panelling, he came up behind her and put his arms around her bending waist. She straightened, turned round to face him and flung her arms possessively around the back of his neck, pulling his mouth eagerly on to hers. Almost immediately, locked in an overwhelming embrace, Leo felt the startling surge of her arousal, as if she had long been starved of any outlet for her considerable passion. Gently he withdrew himself from her arms.

'Christ, Angel, I think I'd better have some champagne first.'

She turned a little petulantly and took a bottle of Krug '64 from the fridge. Collecting two glasses from a side table, she carried them to her desk, then handed the bottle to Leo to open.

Leo slowly poured the frothing liquid into each glass.

He handed one to Danielle, and clinked hers with his. 'Good to see you again. I had a lot of trouble tracking you down.'

'I don't think so.' She grinned doubtfully. 'I am easy to find in Paris.' She looked at him challengingly for a moment. 'I thought you would find me sooner.'

'Yeah, well – better late than never.' He paused. 'Can you have dinner tonight?'

'Sure.'

The evening, and the ensuing night, were well up to Leo's most fantastic expectations. Afterwards, he found it puzzling. He did not particularly like Danielle, but she epitomised his idea of the French woman of a million men's dreams, and there was a selfish voraciousness about her sexuality that made love-making with her removed from any emotional considerations.

For the next three nights, they immersed themselves in an uncontrolled, animal frenzy, though during the day Leo tried to concentrate on his work – meetings, endless phone calls to London, visits to competitors, design houses and possible suppliers.

He only had lunch once with Danielle, on the last day of his trip. By the end of the meal, he found that he had agreed that she should design a *prêt-à-porter* range for Rags, initially only for Paris, then for all his other stores.

As he flew back, he tried to work out how this had happened. Somehow Danielle had led him into it – and though he rated her as a designer, it was going to cause a lot of problems with Sarah. Anyway, Rags simply didn't need any external design input.

He wondered if he should just telephone Danielle and say that he had changed his mind, but it seemed too churlish after such frenetic mutual experiences. And then he thought about facing Alison. He decided that he would drive to his office first to try and expose himself to some normality before seeing her.

But, when he did arrive home, he sensed that she was aware of his infidelity. He knew that he was being too affectionate, so he tried to behave with his more normal light-hearted brashness. She neither asked him directly nor hinted at any suspicions that she might have about his activities in Paris. Leo ventured a pre-emptive statement. 'I'm going to have some trouble with Sarah. I've arranged for a new young French designer to do a range for us – just for the Paris shop.'

'Why have you done that? You're always telling me that Sarah and her team produce all the designs you're ever going to need. It's one of your great theories, isn't it, that an internal design team will preserve your individuality and keep you free from dependence on outside people?'

'Yeah, yeah. That's true. It's really just an experiment to prove my point.'

'Well, who is this designer anyway? Have I heard of him?'

'It's not a him – it's a chick called Danielle Milinaire.'

'Oh – I thought she was a model. Actually, I think I saw her in Porto Rafael in August.'

'I suppose she might have been there. Anyway, she's a designer now, just starting her second season and she's gone down very well, but wants to get involved in ready-to-wear – and she's keen to do it with a non-French company.'

'Hmm – is she? I didn't know you knew her. I should be careful if I were you, Leo – it sounds like a troublesome venture.'

Simon asked Alison to lunch on a Saturday shortly after this, when Leo was busy. He was, Alison thought, more light-hearted and frivolous than usual. At first, as always, he asked about her and Leo.

'I'm okay,' she replied, then, knowing that her relationship with Simon was strong enough to take it, she added, 'but I'm not sure about Leo. He seems unusually cagey – somehow guilty. I think he may have misbehaved when he was last in Paris. I didn't go with him, and when he came back he was behaving oddly.'

'In what way?' asked Simon.

'Well, he started being nice and considerate. He's given

me a load of money to go and buy horses and sort out stabling somewhere for them. I'd been suggesting it for ages but he always said that he didn't belong in the green wellie set, and that Jews who try to become country squires never get it right. Still,' she shrugged, 'he's no less affectionate and I suppose as long as I don't find out, I don't mind.'

'Oh, Ali, of course you mind. I know how strong your principles are. You should confront him with it, the bastard.'

Alison laughed. 'Of course he's a bastard, he always has been. But believe me, under the quagmire of complexes he's a good soft man, and there's no point in my confronting him – it's only a suspicion, and what good would it do? Don't worry, Si, I'm not feeling bad about it.'

'Well, if you ever do, let me know,' he paused. His expression signalled a change to a more positive subject. 'Well, I hope I'll never give my wife those sort of problems. She'd definitely take it badly.'

Alison glanced up sharply. 'What? You have a specific victim in mind for your marital plans? Fantastic! Who?'

'You haven't met her. She's an American, from Virginia. I met her when I was over there last year – and she's been to London a couple of times since. She's just gone back to spring the bad news on her family.'

'Good God! You are discreet. I'd no idea you were concentrating your attention on anyone in particular. What's she called?'

'Claire Calloway. She's from one of the old families, but very unconservative, studied psychology at university. She writes incomprehensible articles about social behaviour for funny little scientific journals. Anyway, she's a lovely girl, very pretty, and we're both very happy. I know you'll like her, and she'll like you, though I don't know about your bombastic husband.'

'Never mind him. When's she coming back? When's the wedding?'

'She's staying in the States till after Christmas, and then coming over with all her family in January. I think they're treating it as an excuse for a rampage around Europe. Then we'll be married at Farm Street in early March.'

'She's a lucky girl. I hope you've done as well.'

Simon smiled, shaking his head with embarrassment. 'No, she's got the worse deal.' He glanced at his watch. 'Look, Ali – you're the first person I've told. I'll tell the parents tonight, so don't mention it to them yet. I've got to shoot off now to help some homeless Asians.'

Alison smiled. 'You're still a boy-scout at heart, aren't you? Anyway don't worry; I'll let you break the happy news to the folks yourself. And I'm really happy for you.'

# February 1973

Raju Kalianji came up the steps of the Chancery Lane underground station and into the open. As he walked east down High Holborn, anyone looking at him would have seen a tall pin-stripe-suited, young Indian businessman, perhaps on his way to the head office of one of the Asian banks or trading companies.

In a small packet in his inner breast pocket lay his family's total tradeable wealth. He glanced over at the red-brick Gothic castle that is the headquarters of the Prudential, one of Britain's largest life insurance companies. The morning sun was reflected on the light grey slated roofs of the circular turrets. He admired the way it suggested absolute solidity, reliability. He admired the architect who had responded to his brief so effectively. It was a shame, he thought, that the British no longer had the same confidence in themselves. At Holborn Circus he crossed over to Hatton Garden. He had not visited this unremarkable street before, but had been told that here was the greatest concentration of two-way trading jewellers in London.

He walked up and down, trying to gauge the calibre of the various dealers. From the outside they all looked very unimpressive little operations. He went into the one that looked the most prosperous. There was very little glamour in the place, and nothing of value or interest on display. As he approached the counter at the back of the shop, a small old man, wearing a yamuka came from an office behind.

'What can I do for you, sir?' he asked.

'I want to buy for my wife something particularly outstanding,' Raj replied smoothly. 'What I have in mind is a large solitaire ruby pendant, nothing around it, just hanging on its own at the end of a fine gold chain. About five carats.'

The jeweller smiled unconvincingly. 'I think I might have something very suitable, sir,' he added. He disappeared into the back of the shop and whispered instructions to somebody whom Raj could not see. After a few moments another man came through the back door carrying a small black jewellery box. The old Jew took it from him and opened it.

'Here we are, sir.' He took the ruby from the box and placed it on a velvet pad on the counter.

Raj picked up the stone and its cunningly attached chain. It was very similar to the one in his pocket; perhaps it was a little smaller, but cut in the same slightly peardrop shape.

'How much is it?' he asked.

The old man looked up at him and then down at the ruby. 'That'll cost you twenty-five thousand pounds,' he said, looking up again at Raj, straight into his eyes.

'That seems a remarkably high price for a stone of that caratage,' Raj replied. 'I am a serious cash-paying customer.'

'Sir,' said the old man peevishly, 'this sort of stone is very much in demand and, quite frankly, after paying for the mounting, I'm making very little from it. I really can't bargain.'

'Well, I'm not prepared to pay twenty-five thousand for it, but thank you for showing it to me,' said Raj and turned towards the door.

He made his way up the street to what he assessed was the second most prosperous establishment in the street. He entered another uninspiring premises, which, like the first, had few of its wares on display. There were two men in the shop, standing on either side of a square table. One had a jeweller's glass in his eye and was crouched over a large, clear, glittering stone. They both looked up as Raj entered. The man who had been inspecting the stone said

189

'Okay' to the other and dropped it into a small cotton purse, which he put into his pocket. The other man moved away from the table to allow Raj to talk to what, he presumed, was the proprietor. He was stocky, five feet seven, about forty, with curly hair and long sideboards; evidently, from his accent, a native Londoner.

'What can I do for you this fine morning, sir?' he said with exaggerated *bonhomie*.

Raj took a manilla envelope from his breast pocket, opened it and took out a small bundle of screwed up velvet. He put this on the table and unwrapped it to reveal a magnificently cut Burma ruby. A small gold clasp was set into the narrower end, and attached to this was a loop through which ran a filigree gold chain.

'I would like to sell this,' he said. 'What will you offer me for it?'

'Where did this come from?' the jeweller asked sceptically.

'My father gave it to my mother when they were married in 1945; they were living in Kampala then.'

The jeweller's face betrayed his understanding of the circumstances. Raj saw this and realised that he had irreversibly weakened his bargaining position. Meanwhile, with a glass to his eye, the man was examining the stone. After a moment he took the glass from his eye, and put the ruby back on the table. He shook his head at Raj.

'If only there was a demand for this kind of stone. Of course, it's a good example, but you know people don't want these big peardrop pendants now. I'm afraid I can't offer you what you think it's worth.'

'Since I haven't told you what I think it's worth, I don't know how you know that,' said Raj. 'However, could you please tell me what you will offer.'

'Well, sir, I want to be helpful, and I'm sure a young man like you could become a customer in the future, so shall we say, eight thousand pounds?'

For a moment Raj said nothing; then he wrapped the pendant in the velvet square and put the bundle back into the envelope which he returned to his inside pocket.

'No, I don't think we will,' he said quietly.

'I'm sorry, sir, but . . .'

'I'm sure you are, and thank you for looking at it,' Raj said, and walked out of the shop.

Outside in Hatton Garden again, Raj decided to try one of the shops that displayed some of its goods in the window. The display was garish and lacked the subtlety of a Bond Street jewellers, but some fine pieces were among the cheaper, mundane diamond rings. He went into a showroom more brightly lit than the other two, and waited for a moment as a customer completed a purchase and left. An alert, intelligent looking man in his late twenties asked if he could help. Once again Raj produced the ruby and put it on the counter.

'Would you like to buy this piece?' he asked.

The young man looked down at it and nodded. 'May I take it into the back and have it looked at?'

'I'd rather you did that here,' replied Raj.

'Okay,' nodded the man, and turned towards the back of the showroom. 'Dad, can you come out?'

An older man appeared. 'What is it?' he asked in a thick German accent.

'This gentleman wants to sell a ruby pendant. Will you come and look at it?'

The old man picked up the ruby, took a glass from his pocket and inspected the stone from every angle. He took the glass from his eye and said to Raj: 'For this I will give you twelve thousand pounds and that's my best offer.'

Raj dropped another velvet bundle from the envelope. He unwrapped a delicately worked gold bracelet, set with dozens of small diamonds and four larger ones. 'And for this?' he asked.

The jeweller picked it up and looked at the stones. 'This is only nine-carat gold, and the stones aren't worth much. I can only offer you two thousand pounds.' He put the bracelet back on the desk and waited for Raj to respond.

'I would consider seventeen thousand pounds for both pieces,' Raj said.

'Sir, I don't bargain, but I will go to fifteen thousand for the two. That is the maximum of their value to me.'

'I will accept that.' Raj put out his hand to the jeweller, who shook it, and nodded to his son.

'Fetch the money, Danny.'

Danny returned with a bundle of notes.

'I really would rather have a cheque,' Raj said tentatively.

The jeweller shook his head. 'I don't want a receipt. Danny will go to the bank with you if you want to pay the cash straight in.' He scooped up the two pieces of jewellery and indicated that his son should go with Raj.

'Which bank?' asked Danny as they left the office together.

Raj pointed through the window to the National Westminster Bank opposite.

They walked through the shop and over to the bank where they watched the teller count out the money in ten pound notes, and stamp Raj's paying-in slip.

As he walked down Hatton Garden to High Holborn, Raj was satisfied he had got as much as he could expect. Simon Riley had told him that he would be lucky to get half the retail value. Bearing in mind that the retail prices he had been quoted included purchase tax, he had done slightly better than that.

He was, at Simon's suggestion, on his way now to meet him at his office. Simon had kept his word and been ready to give advice or any helpful information that he had been asked for. Since the Kalianjis had arrived three months before, the young Englishman had visited them at the Paintals' several times. It was he who had suggested that Raj wait a while before selling the jewellery, since the price of both gold and stones was likely to rise. Raj, meanwhile, though frustrated that he and his family should be recipients of the Paintals' temporary charity, had devoted his time to researching any possible business openings, and he was confident now that he knew how to invest the proceeds of the jewellery.

He turned east over Holborn Viaduct and walked up to a large office-block on the north side. He asked the uniformed commissionaire for the offices of stockbrokers Maple Muir. These occupied the top four floors and Raj went up to their reception area on the fifth floor where he asked for Simon. As he waited in the discreetly furnished visitors' room, he felt a sense of solidity and financial sureness about the place. The periodicals on the side tables and the pictures on the wall demonstrated a dedication to the profitable manipulation of capital. He couldn't reconcile Simon's humanitarian and, in Raj's view, unrealistic view of life to his job as senior equities analyst at one of London's largest stockbrokers. In the same way, he hadn't understood the LSE students' obsession with student rights, when it seemed so counterproductive to their studies.

After ten minutes, Simon strolled in. His normal jeans and old tweed jacket had been replaced by a navy double-breasted suit, white stiff-collared shirt and classic black brogues.

'Hello, Raj. How did you get on in Hatton Garden?' He greeted Raj with a firm handshake.

Raj could not accuse him of condescension, but he could not identify the reason for Simon's enthusiastic interest in him. 'All right, thank you. I got fifteen thousand pounds for them. The cash is already banked.'

'That's fantastic! I don't know how you did it. I must say, I thought you were going to get taken for a ride by those guys. Now I suggest we go and have some lunch. There's a new little French restaurant below the Viaduct. You must tell me what your plans are.'

'Are you sure you are able to? You're not too busy?' asked Raj.

'Far too busy, but I want to be in at the bottom when you've got your business going and decide to go public.'

When they were sitting and had ordered, he asked Raj if he had decided what to do. Raj was sure that there was no danger in confiding in this knowledgeable and self-assured young man opposite him. 'I've been to see the two big Ugandan Asian trading companies with offices in

England. They say they are inundated with refugees like myself wanting to work for them – and anyway, they're private companies owned by people with large families, so there's not much scope there. The money I got from the jewellery is all we've got. There's no chance of getting anything back from Kampala, at least as long as that madman is alive. So I have to find a business that can generate profitable turnover from as low a capital base as possible. Also, I can't deny that it'll be easier to get involved in an area where other Indians are already active.'

'But surely,' said Simon, 'if you haven't got the money to fund some kind of large-scale importing, that leaves you with all-night grocers and newsagents.'

'No, that's only the most visible Asian trading activity. I should have thought in your job you must have seen the headway being made by a number of Indians and Pakistanis in a much broader range of businesses: electrical goods, hotels, catering and the garment industry. Take garments; it's always been one of the more attractive activities for immigrants to England. To set up a small factory making clothes is very cheap. Location is not important, second-hand plant is cheap, and if you can identify the right customers, production is easy to sell. The main input is labour, and with each wave of immigration there's always plenty of that about at bargain rates.'

'But, Raj, this sounds very exploitative for a man of your commercial ideology,' Simon remarked with mock dryness.

'Well, it is, but that's not how I'll go about it. I'm only telling you why the Jews, the Cypriots and now the Asians have become involved in the garment industry in this country. It's just as true in New York as it is here. Anyway, the reasons for it aren't accidental. The only way the whole business can work is as a vast cottage industry. With a little foresight and a lot of hard work, it isn't hard to gain a foothold in it. I intend to get involved in it, but with some slight differences of approach.'

Simon looked at Raj thoughtfully. He nodded. 'Okay, so you're going into the rag-trade. I have to tell you it's very competitive at all levels – more than ever. You only have to walk down the King's Road or Carnaby Street or even Oxford Street to see that it's over-subscribed. I suppose Mary Quant, Biba and Rags got going in the sixties; then there was enough business for them, but now every other shop's a boutique. Of course a few individuals have done well out of the British fashion boom, but that's tailing off, and for every one that's made it, there are another nine struggling – nine and a half probably. The big high-street operators like Burton's and Dorothy Perkins have had huge chunks of their business taken from them. They're closing down factories all over the place. And until they've learned to understand the new shape of the market, they'll go on declining.'

'Simon, you're talking about retailing. Of course I've seen what's going on there, but I'm talking about the production and wholesale business,' Raj interrupted.

'What happens at the retail end,' Simon continued, 'inevitably affects the source of the product – because though more garments may be being sold, the failure rate of the retail business means that bad debts, or, at best, impossibly long payment times, are going to wipe out production margins, and these margins can't be too high simply because the retail end is so competitive.'

'I'm grateful for your concern,' Raj said, 'but these are all economic factors that are obvious and that I'm aware of. I did say that it was important to identify the right customer, and that will be the priority.'

'Well, if you definitely decide to get into the rag-trade, I'd better put you in contact with Rags. Believe it or not my sister's married to Leo Freeman who owns and runs it. He's an aggressive little shit, but he's certainly successful. They must have forty shops around the country now; they've got them in Paris and Amsterdam, and they're planning to open three in the States next year. Have you seen any of the Rags shops yet?'

Raj looked at Simon with interest. 'Yes,' he said, 'I spent several hours in the big store in Kensington High Street. It's really remarkable. It's the busiest shop I've been into in London – and the people were buying, not just looking. But I won't be ready to do business with them for a year. Perhaps then an introduction will be helpful.'

'Raj, do you know, I don't think you'll need my help, but of course it's there if you do. And the best of luck to you.' Simon raised his glass of Chablis, 'And you can drink to me – I'm getting married next month.'

When Raj arrived back at the Paintals' house in Harrow, there was no one there.

He sat down and leafed through a pile of prospectuses and brochures for English language schools. After studying them for a while, he extracted one and heavily underlined the details of a course run by the Inner London Education Authority at the college of further education in Ealing. This course, the prospectus stated, was designed to teach English to native Hindi speakers, and cost five pounds a term, one evening a week.

If Raj was going to marry Reena Patel, he wanted her to be an asset, not a liability. He knew that to achieve what he had planned, he needed all his energy and concentration. He couldn't afford to dissipate these on a totally dependent wife. She was too old to go to school here now – and her lack of English and education precluded her from enrolling on any proper course. Raj was going to insist to her father that she should be thoroughly fluent in English and conversant with western ways before they were married. He also hoped, though without much confidence, that his mother might attend the English language course.

So far his parents had been problematic. The Paintals, with no children, had apparently been very happy to accommodate three extra adults, and had sustained their welcome. But Vishnu spoke little, and spent all day gloomily reading the papers. His mother was terrified by the strangeness of England and seldom left the house, except, as today, to go to an Indian film with her husband.

Raj had no intention of telling his parents or his prospective parents-in-law about his business plans. A long drawn out, and ill-formed family debate would only cause an absurdly long gestation period for his scheme, or its still birth.

They had said that they trusted him – so let them. He would present them with a *fait accompli*.

That evening Raj had arranged to meet Jay Singh, the friend that he had made when he had been studying in London. Jay had decided to help his father in his restaurant, rather than pursuing a career in accountancy. He felt that there was a much more sophisticated way of offering Indian food to the English. So he had persuaded his father to open, near Portobello Road, a second restaurant that relied on colonial India rather than ethnic India for its inspiration. The idea had caught on. It was not used just by the fashionable English, but also by the more anglicised of the Indian community. Jay had made a number of very good contacts, and had promised to introduce Raj to some of them. The effectiveness of the cultural compromise in the restaurant impressed Raj. Large ceiling fans turned slowly over mahogany tables surrounded by bent-wood chairs and rattan screens. On the walls were sepia photographs of maharajahs and viceroys out tiger-shooting in Rolls-Royces.

When he remarked on it, Jay explained. 'The British rather like being reminded of their imperial past. It's amazing the number who seem to have had grandparents who planted tea or played polo in Calcutta.'

He took Raj over to a large round table in a corner and introduced him to the five men sitting at it. Raj took the empty chair and sat down.

'It's good of you to offer to help,' said Raj. 'I'll try not to take up too much of your time. What I really want to do is look into the textiles business. I need to know who, amongst the Asians, has made the greatest success in garment manufacture.'

An older, grey-haired Bengali on his right leaned forward. 'I can tell you that. There are several, though none of them large businesses. What do you want to talk to them about?'

Raj replied, 'Well, I have no capital, and there are no commercial openings where I can use my degree. I really don't want to get buried in the British civil service. So I thought I could get involved in the garment business – identifying markets and matching them to production, on a kind of freelance basis. It occurs to me the Asians rely too heavily on one another for their sales.'

The Bengali shook his head. 'This is from choice. We know where we are with each other. I've been importing cottons from India for seven years and I sell plenty to the English factories – but they're difficult; they think they're doing you a favour by buying from you. It makes for a very unsatisfactory business relationship.'

Raj nodded slowly. 'I don't think it helps to bring personal sensitivity into business relations. If they're buying from you, it's because you've got what they want. I feel that in the manufacturing of clothing there's a much wider market for production by Indian-owned factories – if only it's approached with real confidence and backed up by real efficiency. I could be wrong, but I'd like to research it.'

Others round the table nodded and all started giving names of people they knew in the business. Raj decided to make a list of these at the end of the meal and suggested they order their food.

Over dinner, he was bombarded with advice on how to do business in England: what banks he should use, where he could find premises, where he should live, what car he should drive. He was surprised by how much these men really wanted to help. He himself would have been very reluctant to offer so much information. But he made full use of it, and by the time he left, he had covered two sheets of paper with names of factories, banks, estate agents, cloth merchants and industrial sewing-machine dealers.

While Raj Kalianji was deciding which Hatton Garden jewellers he should enter, Leo strode into the Rainbow Room on the fifth floor of his new store. For two months decorators had been restoring it to its original art deco colours. Around the recessed, central part of the ceiling, hidden strip lights were arranged in rows of varying colours that gave the room its name.

The bars and fittings were all in cream, black and chrome, the seating upholstered in geometric patterned moquette. The dance floor in the centre of the room was polished pinkish-white carrera marble. Above it, on a high trestle between two step-ladders, electricians worked on the vast chandelier.

'Why the hell isn't everything finished?' Leo asked the nervous interior decorator who had followed him in. 'The opening party's in three days and these bloody bars aren't ready. Where are the engraved mirrors we ordered from that loony woman in Portobello Road? I gave you more time than you asked for and still it's not done. I wanted everything finished a week before the opening so we could sort out any operating problems.'

Whatever Dave Davis said would be wrong, so he said nothing, and let Leo rant on. In fact, with constant interruptions and changes of plan from Leo, he was amazed that they had got as far as they had. He admired Leo though, for the thoroughness of his brief and his enthusiasm for detail. There wasn't another room in London with as much chic and glamour. And it was going to give Dave Davis's reputation a major boost.

So he quietly walked round the room behind Leo, who stopped every few yards and complained bitterly about shabby joinery, bad paintwork, unsatisfactory seams in the carpet – anything that he could see that wasn't perfect. Dave noted it all down and knew that he would have to get it all right within the next two days, but he didn't mind. Decoratively at least, the club was going to be a triumph.

For Leo, decoration was only one aspect of making his club a glittering success. People, the right people, were what made a club. Without them it didn't matter how beautiful the surroundings were. He needed the film stars, the fashion kings, the young aristocracy, the City whizz-kids. He had been getting his PR to feed tiny morsels to the gossip columnists. He had called a press conference six months before to announce his intention of restoring the Rainbow Room and opening it as a club. This had been enthusiastically received, and since then, every few weeks there had been some mention of who was going to do what at the new Rainbow Room.

Nigel Dempster, a rising star at the *Daily Mail*, had really enjoyed the build-up. He had got his readers intrigued by the new club long before its opening; Princess Margaret's friend, Roddy Llewellyn, was re-landscaping the famous roof garden; Willie Feilding was painting a series of erotic fantasies that would hang in the cloakrooms.

After spending half an hour on his inspection of the fifth floor, Leo beckoned Dave Davis up to the bar on the top floor. This was surrounded by a half-acre roof garden. The bar looked as though it had been plucked straight from the interior of the Queen Elizabeth. It was a perfect example of 1930s taste at its best. The terrace outside, apart from the lack of seaview, could have been Cannes at its peak. The small trees around the edge of the roof meant that no buildings were visible from here and it was unexpectedly quiet.

Leo turned to Dave, smiling. 'It's fantastic, isn't it? Why those dozy old creeps never exploited it before, God knows. Do you know, I used to come up here before I got it, and there'd be a few old biddies up from Surrey wandering about and dowdy old waitresses serving second-rate teas. You've done a great job here, Dave.'

Dave knew this, but was pleased with Leo's approval. 'Yeah, well, it's the best job I've ever done. I hope your punters realise it. Finding this stuff wasn't easy, even with the money we had.'

'It was worth it,' said Leo. 'Even if the club doesn't go, these top floors are worth what we gave for the whole building. It's a shame I had to do it with Ubiland, though. Look, I'm going to the States tomorrow; I won't be back till just before the opening. Let's celebrate your efforts now.' He walked over to the top of the stairs and yelled down at Salvatore, who was to be maître d' in the restaurant. 'Bring up a bottle of Dom Perignon and we'll have a drink – you too!'

When Leo arrived back at Adam and Eve Mews, his secretary met him with a string of messages. First, Sarah was waiting in his office.

'Leo, what the hell have you done with the range?' she stormed as he walked in. 'What have you done with all the tweed? That was the main story.'

The evening before, Sarah had left the first sample of the following autumn's collection on a rail in Leo's office. Leo had said that he would go through it. He had put what he considered to be the losers on one side. He always did this on his own, sticking to his contention that selection by committee didn't work.

'The tweed's great, but it's too soon. That classic country look won't work in the high streets for another couple of years – we'll do them then.'

'But, Leo, the girls from *Vogue* were knocked out by it. You know I showed it to them unofficially.'

'Yeah, well, we know how right their predictions are. Look, don't get excited. I'm not criticising your talents, but you're locked away with your designers. You spend all your time with fashion people. It always takes a couple of years for the ripples to get from the middle to the high street. Maybe we'll run a bit of it just in the London stores next year, just as a teaser, and I suppose it'll give some of your fashion press something to write about.'

'Leo,' Sarah's voice was shaking. 'I'm sick to death of you axeing my ranges. I've worked bloody hard on this one, and it's right. It's going to be right up there with the others in Paris. Why do you always want to push me down?'

'I bloody don't!' yelled Leo. 'I didn't say you were wrong; I said you were early. You seem to forget that most of our customers are ordinary little chicks. They take time to get used to new ideas. That's why we make money and sell millions of frocks. And when has my judgement been wrong?' He checked himself. Sarah looked forlorn and

201

beaten. 'Look, I'm sorry, Angel. I know you've been working like shit.' He put his arm around her. 'You're as brilliant as ever, but you've got to trust my nose for the common taste – it hasn't let us down yet. But I promise we'll do a small run on the tweed next year. Come on, cheer up and have a drink.'

She accepted the glass of champagne he poured for her and sat looking resigned. 'Well, what's this other range of Danielle Milinaire's?' she asked. 'I don't think there's anything special about it. We've got a fantastic design team here. I still don't see what we need her for?'

Leo looked embarrassed, but fought down his immediate defensive response. 'She's a big name in Europe, and that range is very commercial. Now the interest in British fashion is wearing off it'll do us good to have a French influence.'

'That's crap. I know bloody well you've been having a scene with her. God knows why. You've got a much better wife than you deserve. Does Alison know?'

'What are you on about?' demanded Leo. 'I've only ever seen her to talk about her work. Maybe she fancies me, but that's not my fault.'

'Oh well, forget it. When are you leaving for the States?'

'Tomorrow morning.'

Sarah got up to leave. 'Will you be back before the opening?'

'Yeah, yeah. An hour before. I hope it all doesn't get fucked-up in my absence.'

'Well, have a good trip,' Sarah called sullenly over her shoulder.

Immediately, the phone on Leo's desk rang. He put down his glass of champagne and picked up the receiver. His secretary's voice said, 'It's Danielle Milinaire in Paris. She's been hanging on for five minutes.'

'Oh God, put her through.'

'Leo,' he heard her soft French voice echoing down the line, 'why didn't you call me back? I telephoned already two times yesterday and three times this morning.'

'Angel, I've only just got back to my office. I've been

running about. I'm going to the States tomorrow. If you've rung to find out how the range looks – it's great. We'll do very well with it.'

'Leo,' she interrupted, sounding peevish, 'why didn't you ask me to your party for the Rainbow Room? I've had no invitation.'

'Danny, Danny, hang on. Listen, Angel, you don't want to come over for that. It'll be a crowd of press and freeloaders. Nobody interesting will be there.'

'That's not what the papers say. It's because you must have your wife there, isn't it? I don't care about that; I'm not going to make a row.'

'Now look here, Danielle, it's nothing to do with Rags or the fashion business. You just can't come. You're coming over in three weeks anyway to work with your collection. Leave it till then, all right?'

Even over the line from Paris he heard her sigh. 'Okay, Leo,' she said, resigned, and then: 'but you are sending the samples over today, no? Your secretary has said so.'

'Yeah, sure. I think they've already gone. I'll check it out for certain. And, Angel, look after yourself. I'll ring when I get back from the States, all right?'

'Okay, Leo, goodbye.' She put the phone down.

Leo sat on his desk staring at the Aubrey Beardsley prints that hung opposite him. The door opened and his secretary came in, followed by his PR, Liz Macintosh. She ran a very successful agency of her own which specialised in fashion accounts, but Leo had talked her into covering the club as well. She didn't really have the right contacts, but felt she had done a good job so far. Leo slid off the desk and walked over to greet her with a kiss on the cheek.

'Hello, luscious Liz. What's in the papers today, then?'

The secretary left, closing the door behind her. Liz was a tough, good-looking Scot in her early thirties. She liked Leo, but found his rapid changes of mood hard to deal with.

'Nothing today, boss, I'm afraid, but did you see the *Sunday Express* yesterday?'

'That did more good for Dave Davis and his dealer friends than it did for the club.' There had been a nice little piece about tracking down art deco furniture. 'We're opening in three days – it shouldn't be hard to get something in every day. Is anyone going to mention Georgie Fame's cabaret? And what about those bloody mirrors that Lady What's-her-name's doing for us?'

'Don't worry, Leo, we'll get them all in. I shouldn't think there's anyone in London who doesn't know about the Rainbow Room by now – and those people who've bothered to reply all say they're coming. You'd better make sure you've got enough champagne.'

'All right, Liz, you haven't earned a drink but you can have one anyway.' Leo poured her a glass. 'Now, look. I'm on the nine o'clock to New York tomorrow morning, and then I've got a day looking at sites in Dallas and I'm back just before the party, so you're in charge of it all. You'd better check everything out with Salvatore this afternoon – I don't want anything to go wrong. Dave knows the place has got to be looking perfect by tomorrow night, but have a last check round with him, too.'

Liz nodded. Leo glanced at his watch. 'I'm meeting Terry Donovan at Meridiana to talk about shooting the autumn collection – do you want to come?'

They went down together and drove to the restaurant in Leo's Corniche.

At seven that evening, Leo arrived back in Chelsea Square and let himself into the house. He heard noises in the dining-room and went in to find Maria, the Filipino maid, scurrying about the table, which was laid for dinner. He groaned. He had forgotten that Simon Riley was coming that evening with Claire, his fiancée. He went upstairs to the bedroom and looked into the bathroom. Alison was lying up to her neck in suds in the big circular bath. She grinned at him and tossed her wet hair.

'Hello,' she said, 'you look miserable. Who's been baiting you?'

'Alison, Angel, I'm going to New York tomorrow morn-

204

ing and Simon's coming to dinner. He'll sit around drinking armagnac half the night. I wish you'd asked me.'

Alison leaned forward and turned on the hand shower to rinse her hair. Leo watched, always stimulated by the sight of her perfect breasts, dipping in and out of the thick foam. From under the heavy spray she said, 'If I asked you, you'd always find some reason why he shouldn't come. Anyway, if you want to go to bed early, I don't suppose you'll let your highly developed sense of etiquette stop you.'

She stood up in the bath and sluiced the suds off her fine, firm body, pointing the jet at the soapy black curls between her narrow hips. Leo watched as the water trickled down the inside of her thighs. 'Don't get out,' he said, undressing, 'I'm getting in.'

He left his clothes in a heap on the floor, and stepped into the bath, his excitement palpable. Alison playfully sprayed him all over. He put his hands beneath each of her buttocks, and lifted her up onto him. Then slowly he lowered them both into the foam-filled bath and, laughing, they rolled around the huge tub, water sloshing over the sides. Later, out of the bath, they rubbed each other down with huge towels. Leo went into the bedroom and came back with a well-rolled joint. He lit it and passed it to Alison who sat naked, cross-legged on the floor, drying her hair. She took a long drag, handed back the joint, and looked up.

'God, you're a randy sod, Leo. What are you going to do when you go to America and you can't have it for a few weeks?'

Leo grunted. 'I'll think of something,' he said, and went back to the bedroom, wondering why he looked at any other women when Alison excited him so much, even after four years. She was still the best. He looked at his naked body in the mirror as he finished drying himself. He shook his head. 'Angel!' he shouted through the door. 'For that I'll try and be nice to your brother. I'll even be polite to his snotty fiancée, okay?'

'Tell me, why is Simon the only person who seems to

205

make you feel inferior?' she asked. 'He's got a lot of respect for what you've done, and he's been really helpful to you. I mean, he introduced you to Ubiland.'

'Look, if I hadn't done this deal with them I'd have done it with someone else. He's so bloody confident and self-satisfied – and what has he achieved? He's never made any real money, but he gives me advice as if I was just starting out in business – and he still behaves as if he owned you.'

'Oh, Leo, don't be jealous. We were never incestuous,' Alison laughed. 'If you think his advice is wrong, tell him, or just don't take it. Anyway, relax now, and just try to behave yourself when they come.'

Simon and Claire arrived punctually at half past eight. The maid showed them into the drawing-room. Claire wore a knee-length dress of Indian silk chiffon, printed in great swirls of dark green and purple. Her blond hair was brushed to the back of her head, where it was fixed with an enamel slide. Some long curls had escaped and curled fetchingly down the side of her face. At five feet nine, and in high-heeled sandals, she was only a little shorter than Simon. As they stood, waiting for Leo or Alison to appear, her intelligent blue eyes swept the room, appraising, assessing. She and Simon talked quietly about the stables in Hampshire and two horses she had been to look at. After a few moments, Leo came in wearing a figured velvet jacket and a wide William Morris print tie. He shook Simon's hand. 'Hello. Sorry we weren't down when you arrived – you should have helped yourself to drinks.' He waved towards an extravagantly stocked tray. He turned to Claire. 'Would you like champagne?'

'I certainly would, thank you.'

'Simon?'

'No thanks. I'll have a whisky.'

'Look, help yourself. I'll get a bottle of Dom Perignon.' Leo went out as Alison came in. Simon walked over and kissed her on both cheeks.

'Hello, Ali. You look worryingly beautiful,' he said.

'Why worryingly?' she asked, laughing.

'You've obviously got too much time on your hands. You should be using that busy mind of yours on something more useful than buying clothes and making up.'

Leo had come back into the room, clutching a bottle in each hand, like two baseball bats. 'Listen,' he said, 'it's hard work spending the money at the rate she does.'

'Anyway,' said Alison, 'Claire obviously hasn't got enough to do either. Where did you get that amazing dress?'

'Oh, there's a far-out little guy down in Petticoat Lane who sells saris. I got some made into dresses and kurtas. The problem is a sari's about twelve feet long, so you run out of things to do with it.'

'Who makes them up for you?' asked Leo, half interested.

'A girl who makes samples for Ossie Clarke – I met her at the Escalade party.'

'You seem to have found your way about London pretty fast,' remarked Alison. 'Has Simon bothered to show you around?'

'Yeah, sure, a little. But he's strong on galleries and restaurants and weak on anything practical,' Claire said. 'Except some things, of course.' She squeezed his arm.

Leo poured drinks. Alison sat beside Claire on a sofa and asked her how all the wedding plans were going. The church in Farm Street and an elderly, mellowed Jesuit had been booked for the event. The wedding dress, nearing completion in Virginia, was to arrive a few days before the event with half a plane-load of family and friends. A room at the Connaught had been reserved for the reception. Alison wondered if they still made their peach and champagne cocktails. Then she asked Claire what she had been doing that day.

Claire believed, like all horse-lovers, that everyone else must be as interested in them as she. She described in great detail and with great enthusiasm the two hunters that she had been to look at – how they moved, their personalities, ages, colour, breeding and scope. She compared them with horses she had owned in Virginia and talked of her longing to ride and hunt in England. Simon, she said, was a natural horseman. With a few lessons in basics he could become really competent. They were going to enjoy it together. She didn't like shooting and was sure that Simon would prefer hunting.

Alison was pleased by her future sister-in-law's enthusiasm. She suggested that next time Claire was going to look at horses they should go together.

'I thought you were a metropolitan person,' said Claire, surprised, 'but I'd love it if you came.'

'Well, I've got a horse I keep out at Richmond, but there's not much you can do there so I'd be really interested to see the set-up you're using.'

They fixed a date before going into dinner, Alison organising the maid on the way. The food was adventurous, unusual and delicious. Alison never tried to play safe with her cooking, and she was a perfectionist. It still amazed Leo that she had such a talent for everything she tried. The wines that he had chosen were famous, expensive, generally inappropriate, but very good.

They talked about Leo's trip to America and the new club. Leo asked Claire her opinion as to the right cities in the States to launch Rags. She said New York, Boston and San Francisco. He said New York, Los Angeles and Dallas; that was where the money was. Claire thought that he would have to adapt the range to the weather conditions. Leo disagreed.

Simon asked about the cost of setting up and running the club. Leo told him in great detail, and what business they had to do to break even. Membership charges alone, he said, would cover this. Simon was sceptical. Two thousand members at seventy-five pounds a year seemed very optimistic.

'Look at Annabel's,' said Leo. 'They won't even take any new members. Look at Tramps, packed every night – and there's nowhere to go in Chelsea except Aretusa, and they haven't got that right. Mario's too dogmatic about how he does things.'

'But, Leo, it's already cost you three hundred thousand; you've got to see a net profit of a hundred thousand a year to make the borrowing worthwhile. Ubiland won't hang around to back you up if you don't.'

'Don't worry, Simon. It's not your money and I won't blow your valuable connections.'

'Well, let's drink to its success,' said Simon. 'The party should be great if all these people come.' He raised his glass and so did the others. 'To the Rainbow Room and all who flail in her.'

After dinner, still at the dining-table, they drank coffee and brandy.

'I had lunch today with a man you should watch,' Simon told Leo. 'He's a Ugandan immigrant who's going into the rag-trade. He's sold all the jewellery they could get out with and is going to set up a small factory.'

'The best of luck to him,' said Leo. 'I haven't yet come across an Indian factory that could make a decent garment – and there are hundreds of them at it. They haven't got a clue. They don't look at the market. All they can offer is cheap crappy production at the bottom of the market. I hope you advised your friend to try something else.'

'He's not the sort of man that takes advice,' answered Simon, 'and he's definitely in a class of his own. If he says he's going into the rag-trade, he will, and he'll make it work.'

Leo laughed complacently. 'I very much doubt it,' he said.

Over a period of three weeks, Raj Kalianji visited fifteen clothing factories, six cloth wholesalers and several suppliers of industrial sewing-machinery. He inspected a dozen vacant light-industrial premises in the Wembley area and half a dozen firms of chartered accountants.

He had approached most of the factories with introductions from the men whom he had met with Jay Singh, and others were suggested to him by those that he had first visited. All had responded positively to his proposal that he should look for business on their behalf. They had been impressed with his confident and businesslike appearance and they recognised that he was a man who would deal on equal terms with any potential customer. In each case, Raj asked to be shown all aspects of their operations. He wanted to know where they currently sold their production; how many staff they had; what machinery they used; what productivity they expected from each machinist; what sort of garments were most profitable; who was the key man in each factory; what was the state of their current balance sheet. Most of them offered the information willingly.

He came to a number of conclusions as a result of these researches. The simple garments, though attracting a low making-up price, would provide the most profitable volume of business. He had noticed that where girls had been working on the same style for some time, they were a great deal faster than those constantly being given new styles to make. In a simple blouse or shirt, there were far fewer production stages than, say, in jeans, which involved nine separate stages. He decided, therefore, that he would specialise in simple blouses.

Raj asked one of the larger factories if he could have a sample of their production. They had been subcontracted by one of the major East End manufacturers to make a basic cotton summer blouse for Dorothy Perkins. He took some on the understanding that he would use them to sell direct to the multiple retailers.

When he wasn't visiting factories or looking at premises, he spent his time in clothes shops. He went to Etam, Top Shop, Rags, Biba, Chelsea Girl, and any of the more interesting-looking boutiques he had seen. He avoided those like Monsoon, which displayed a strong ethnic theme. He had built up a good relationship with a young Englishman who owned a small but busy shop in the Fulham Road. He took his samples there to get his reaction.

'That's fine,' he was told, 'if you can get the volume. If I were you, though, I'd show them something from Rags – their styles aren't complicated, it's their cloths and colours that are special. If I could stand the hassle of setting up production, I'd just concentrate on ripping off Rags's styles and selling them to the boutiques in the sticks; maybe even some of the multiples would risk stocking it. Look at this blouse. The shape's fine, but give it a yoke, put a couple of tucks here above the tits, and make it up in maroon satin and you've got a fashion garment.'

Raj's next job was to recruit his key employee, a top-grade pattern cutter, who could also make up samples and organise the bulk cutting. In one of the factories that he had visited, he had been impressed by a calm and competent English woman in her mid-forties. She seemed to be in charge of everything. She had shown Raj a new pattern on which she was working and had explained how she went about it.

He returned to the Willesden factory where she worked. He waited on the other side of the road for her to leave at the end of the day. When she came out, she crossed over without seeing Raj and headed towards the bus-stop at the end of the road. He caught up with her.

'Good afternoon, Joan,' he said.

She turned to see who it was and smiled.

'Oh, hello, Mr Raju. I didn't see you in the factory. Were you seeing Vijay?'

'No, I haven't been there. Actually, it's you I wanted to see. Could I buy you a cup of tea in the café there? Strictly business, you understand,' he added, seeing her slight confusion.

'I don't see why not,' she said. 'The bus won't come for half an hour.'

Raj took her arm and they crossed back over the road to the brightly lit, bustling café. It smelled heavily of frying, and there was constant banter between the man and the two women behind the counter.

Raj got two teas and led Joan to the only empty table. 'Now, Joan, I'm going to make you an offer, but before I do, I want you to promise that you won't tell Vijay – whether or not you accept it. Is that a promise?'

'Yes,' she said. 'I won't tell him.' She looked worried and ill at ease.

'This is what I want to offer you. I am starting a small factory myself. It will specialise in making ladies' blouses only. I would like you to run it for me: oversee the machinists, cut the patterns, make up the samples – all the things you do at the moment, but with more responsibility.' She said nothing. Raj went on. 'Of course, you would have appropriate terms of employment. I will pay you fifty per cent more than you are paid now, and, as it's a new venture, I will give you a ten per cent share in the company.'

Joan looked interested. 'Where is it?' she asked.

'Just behind Wembley Stadium.'

'That's very near where I live,' she said thoughtfully. 'But you know, Vijay's been very good to me. He's ever such a nice man, and it would let him down . . .' She paused a moment. 'Mind you, I've taught his wife a lot – she could probably manage now.' She paused again, stirring her tea slowly. 'But if I did leave, I'd have to give them a couple of weeks' notice.'

'Of course,' said Raj. 'And I don't expect you to give me an answer today. Perhaps you would like to know more details.'

Joan looked at him and said, 'Mr Raju, I'm a good judge of character, and I'm sure you're a good businessman, and fair . . . and I know all there is to know about making up. Vijay works hard, but he only gets business from the other factories, so he doesn't make much profit. To be honest, I have had to ask him for a rise, but he says he can't.'

'What do you get at the moment?' asked Raj.

'Fifty pounds a week, and that's a long week.'

'As I said, I'm offering you seventy-five and the shares.'

'Well, it's nice of you to offer and I'll think about it and let you know,' said Joan.

'That will be fine, but when can you let me know by?'

'Tomorrow night,' she replied.

He wrote his number on a piece of paper and gave it to her. 'I'll be at home tomorrow night to wait for your reply.'

Two days later, Raj and Joan met outside Wembley tube station and walked to the factory. This was simply a large empty brick shed, seventy by thirty feet with a twenty-foot ceiling. Surrounding it were similar buildings, some forlornly empty, some occupied by a variety of small businesses.

Inside, the bare brick walls were windowless, but large perspex panels in the roof allowed in plenty of natural light. In a corner, below a cluster of power meters, was a sink with a draining-board and a single tap. The floor was dusty concrete screed. A series of neon tube lights was suspended from the ceiling. The electricity was disconnected, so these could not be switched on. Joan looked around gloomily, shivering slightly.

'Well, if you want this place ready in a week, we'd better get a move on,' she said. 'First, the girls won't work on this floor and, anyway you'll never get rid of that dust, so you need to cover it in lino. You've got your power points all round the wall so that should do to start with. You'll have to partition off one corner for a tea-room – where the sink is I'd say – and you'll need hot water. If all the lights work, they'll do.'

She continued with a list of requirements, down to the smallest detail. She had also prepared a breakdown of the machinery and equipment that she needed. She and Raj spent an hour discussing what would go where. Then she left, saying she must get back to Vijay's factory. She would give in her notice and start working for Raj on Monday week. They arranged to meet at the weekend to review progress.

Within three days, Raj had signed a lease on the premises. After a long discussion with the landlords, they granted him a rent-free period of six months. They agreed that in the current climate, and with six empty units, it would suit them to let on these terms rather than not at all.

The next day, two healthy-looking young men whom Raj had found outside the Wembley Labour Exchange were in the factory with ladders, trestles and fifty quarts of white paint. The flooring contractors agreed to supply and lay the lino, and for a small surcharge, accepted payments over three months. Raj himself checked out all the electrical wiring and put all the lights and sockets in order.

He took the list of machinery that he needed to three East End dealers. The last that he visited had recently been to a sparsely attended receiver's auction of the property of a large, insolvent dress manufacturers. By surreptitious negotiations with the auctioneer, this dealer had bought all the sewing-machines, overlockers, cutters and presses for a little under ten per cent of their new list price. Raj bought what he needed for a little under thirty per cent of list price, with an agreement that it would all be serviced, and that he would pay in four monthly instalments.

Simon Riley had phoned to see how Raj's plans were progressing, and enthusiastically volunteered to come to Wembley on the following Sunday to help Raj to install his equipment. When he arrived just after ten in the morning, Joan Wilson was already there, trying all the machines and looking around with astonishment at the transformation that had taken place in five days.

Simon, too, was impressed, as much by Raj's wisdom in recruiting Joan as by the amount that he had achieved since their discussion over lunch. They spent the morning putting heavy industrial sewing-machines in place and wiring them up, placing the huge cutting-table under the best light, and finishing off the stud-work partition that created the tea-room.

In the afternoon, they sat down around a clean Formica-topped table. Raj was asking Joan to recruit the six best machinists she knew and to offer them thirty per cent more wages than they were currently getting. She had already produced a list of fifteen, which she read through, pointing out their advantages and disadvantages. Raj favoured married women over thirty, who were unlikely to have more children and who were secure in their homes and marriages. Simon asked Raj how he intended to offer

214

competitive prices if he was preparing to pay thirty per cent higher labour rates than his competition.

'It's very odd,' said Raj. 'The British seem to have a blind spot about the obvious correlation between higher wages and high productivity. I suppose it goes back to the early days of your industrial revolution, when one labourer was pretty much the same as another. Conditions were so bad and aspirations so low, that a day's work was a day's work whoever did it. There was a rock-bottom price for a day's labour, and that's what an industrialist thought he should pay. Even though he was ready to accept that different qualities of coal, for example, had to be bought at different prices. The difference between the British today and the Americans or the Germans is that, where the British say that they will pay as *little* as they can get away with, the Germans say that they will pay as *much* for their labour as they can get away with. And what's the result? You produce a Jaguar, which is expensive and frequently unreliable, and they produce a Mercedes, which sells much better for twenty per cent more and never breaks down. So, by offering to pay more than my competitors, I can pick and choose my staff. I am convinced – do you agree, Joan? – that two well-paid, first-class women will produce at least as much good finished work as three mediocre and dissatisfied girls. On that basis, by offering thirty per cent more, I am actually saving thirteen per cent on my labour costs.'

Simon smiled and nodded, and sat back as Raj and Joan discussed production samples. Raj had bought six blouses from Rags which he wanted Joan to copy, using the machinery they had just installed. She said that she would come in and do them over the next few evenings, so that he would have samples to show that would genuinely reflect the quality that they would be able to achieve.

When Joan had left, Simon and Raj discussed accounting aspects of the new business. They established capital costs, operating costs and sales projections. From these, they derived profit and cash-flow forecasts. They then worked out the profit that could be achieved with each additional machine and machinists. Raj planned to double his capacity every three months, without borrowing, and to increase it eight-fold by the start of his second year. On paper it looked possible if the factory always worked to capacity and if all customers paid on time.

Simon was inclined to be sceptical. He had seen dozens of proposals for new businesses. They always looked thoroughly plausible, provided that everything went in their favour. In his experience, this never happened.

Raj agreed, but maintained that, provided that all the areas where the plans could go astray were anticipated, the odds against failure could be lengthened. By recruiting reliable women at premium wages, he was more certain of continuous production being available. Because they would also be experienced machinists, he could guarantee customers good work delivered on time, at the same, if not lower, prices than his competitors.

He knew that marketing his services was vital and planned to spend most of his time selling. He was confident that Joan could handle the normal running of the factory.

At six, they left the factory. Simon dropped Raj at the tube station and drove home, more than ever convinced that he was witnessing the birth of a major commercial success.

Leo swore as the oversize pink velvet bow tie unravelled itself for the third time. He had arrived back from Heathrow fifteen minutes before, and the most important social event in his life was due to start within the hour. The opening of the Rainbow Room was the high point of all Leo's efforts at the Kensington store. He didn't stop to consider the figures – the fact that however well the club went, it would only represent a small fraction of the group's total profits.

To Leo, this club would put the seal on his membership of the upper echelons of Europe's rich and beautiful.

Alison tried to laugh him out of it. As she dexterously tied his tie, she leant back and looked mischievously at him. 'And if the club dies, you die with it, I suppose. If it's a flop, you'll commit suicide. Come on – get things in perspective. Whether or not it succeeds, I am sure you'll have a lot of fun trying. I don't know why you're so hyped up about it. It's a gamble, but your future doesn't rest on it so, if I were you, I'd relax and enjoy it. There.' She stood back and laughed at her husband's angry features twitching above the absurd pink confection. 'You look like a New York ballet master.'

'Okay,' he growled, appreciatively eyeing her body, wrapped only in a small towel, 'and what are you going to wear?'

'Look, Leo, don't worry about that. The car's outside and waiting, so why don't you go on and send it back for me?'

Leo tweeked her towel off, and for a moment desire almost overcame him. Then he grinned regretfully. 'No, I can't go through all that undressing. I'll see you there, Angel.'

When he arrived in the cavernous room, there was an eerie silence as waiters flitted about in the dim light, putting the final touches to the elaborate arrangements. He walked slowly round the room, feeling like Henry V on the morning of Agincourt, quite unable to rid himself of an entirely unaccustomed nervousness.

He could not resist the temptation to walk over and push up the master dimmer-switch which produced an oval halo of multi-coloured light around the high ceiling. The effect, carefully redesigned by Dave Davis, was magical. The white dance floor took on an unearthly glow, and the recesses around it became darker and more intimate. He turned the lights off, well pleased, and walked over to one of the bars, which gleamed from within, the barmen bouncing up and down like Punch and Judy in a booth. From one of them he demanded a bottle of champagne and a glass, which he carried with him to the centre of the room.

Slowly he turned a full circle, and a large grin spread across his face. It would be a triumph. It was a festival of good taste, new and old. The seats were soft, inviting and sophisticated. The lighting was warm, flattering, mysterious. On each table a small candlelamp flickered on a single yellow rose and a cluster of glasses which would shortly be filled and refilled with pink Roederer.

On a low dais at the end of the dance floor an eight-foot, white Steinway had been placed, its lid open towards the room. Leo strolled over to it thoughtfully and put his bottle and glass on the floor. He sat on the stool and tinkled unmelodiously, listening to the discordant sounds echo round the room.

'For Christ's sake, Leo,' a rich, American voice chided him amiably from the darkness, and a tall, thin black man appeared at his shoulder. 'I think I'd better sit there, don't you?'

Leo nodded, and made way for the pianist, who sat, flexed his immensely long fingers, closed his eyes and proceeded to play a convincing imitation of Oscar Peterson. Leo smiled and put a hand across the black man's shoulder. 'That's perfect, Bobby, very classy, brings out the colours in the room.'

Salvatore, the maître d', had approached looking calm and in control. 'The first guests have arrived, Mr Freeman. We'll start opening the champagne.'

Leo's heart was pounding. He didn't want to greet the first-comers. He slid quietly on to a seat in a dark corner to watch and hear their reactions. Gratifyingly, though predictably from the early arrivals, these were full of awe and admiration. There really was nothing to criticise and these first guests gave the impression that they were very privileged to be there.

A steady stream of people began to flow into the club, and the noise of their increasingly loud conversation began to muffle the piano player's complex arpeggios. The atmosphere was one of fulsome appreciation. Leo saw that everyone had made an effort. They knew they were going to be seen, and even those notable for not caring had made sure that they looked unconcerned in a photogenic way. To Leo's eyes, all the women looked stunning, helped by their clear enjoyment of the event, the champagne and the warm light.

When he felt that half the expected guests had arrived, he emerged and started to greet them. He was thrilled by their deference, even from the most hardened socialites, and his burgeoning sense of having pulled off a major achievement was crowned by the arrival of Alison.

Her long dark tanned legs projected from an uneven hem of half a dozen sharp points of printed silk scarves, above which was a small plain dark red bodice.

It was a dress that on almost anyone else would have looked dated and home-made, but on Alison was riveting. It displayed a contempt for any prevailing fashion ideas and enhanced all her outstanding features: her almost black hair and blue eyes, her golden unblemished arms and shoulders, and her very air of knowing something that no one else did.

When the room was full and all the tables occupied by groups of laughing people, Leo signalled Bobby to stop playing the piano and, to the sound of Bowie's 'Space Oddity', the rainbow was gradually lit. There was a discernible diminution in the noise being made by the guests, even an audible murmur of appreciation. The vibrations heightened, and the party was really on.

Without exception, everyone was having a good time. It was the only place to be in London that night, and, for many, simply being seen there was a pleasure. Even the rock stars, the young earls and the professional famous faces happily succumbed to the demands of the frantic *paparazzi*. Notorious newsworthy men quite readily grasped the waists of the wives of other newsworthy men, and enjoyed the confusion this would cause that night at the gossip editors' desks. Leo himself, glowing with the sensation of complete social stardom, was snapped hugging or kissing a dozen different beautiful women. And Alison looked on indulgently, prepared to overlook her misgivings – at least for that evening.

She was untroubled by the sight of Leo's erstwhile girlfriend, Sammy, with whom she had done the shampoo commercials five years before. The American girl was clearly pleased with the spin-off of having once been involved with the star of this event. But Leo scarcely seemed to notice her constantly touching hands, such was his preoccupation with the crowd in general.

Sarah, too, seemed agreeably resigned to the reflected glory. Though she had been luke-warm about the very idea of the club, she was prepared to admit that, this night at least, it had worked. She danced with uncharacteristic enthusiasm with the many frustrated men who pursued her.

Leo saw, and wondered idly if, for once, she would go to bed with one of them.

Then he devoted himself to making sure that anyone of the slightest importance was being looked after. He chivvied the waiters till the sweat poured off them. He joked with the men, flirted with the women, smiled benevolently on everyone.

Meanwhile, the club throbbed with excitement. There was no doubt, that night was a huge success.

By the time the last guests left, at nearly six, he was too drunk, too happy to care. He couldn't take himself away; didn't want to leave the scene of such a major triumph, and finally fell asleep on a sofa, in a glow of ambition achieved and a haze of pink champagne.

From his office window, Leo saw Danielle Milinaire arrive in a black taxi. The cabby willingly unloaded the Gucci luggage, and carried it into the reception area on the ground floor. Danielle, calm but energetic, elegant but sexy, preceded him. Leo went down to meet her in the conference room that doubled as a showroom.

She was already looking through the samples of her range when he entered. She glanced over her shoulder, said, 'Hello,' and turned back to the clothes on the rail. Leo walked round and sat at the large oval rosewood table. Danielle picked out one of the short satin dresses from the rail. She held it up on its hanger and inspected the detail and the cut.

'That's worked well, hasn't it?' said Leo. 'That'll be the winner. Are you happy with the colours?'

Danielle nodded, put the dress down, picked out a couple more garments and applied the same scrutiny to them. Leo watched and said nothing until she had examined the whole range. Eventually she turned to him accusingly. 'Who made the alterations?'

'What alterations?'

'Look. Here, for example, the tie at the back is lower,' she said, holding up a classically simple wool jersey dress, which used the age-old technique of tying at the small of the back to achieve the most pleasing fit at the front of the waist and hips.

'Oh, well, Sarah may have made a few allowances for local consumption – but they're your styles. What do you think?'

'I want to see them on a model.' She sat opposite Leo at the table. 'But first, you must tell me where I am staying. All my baggage is here and the girl outside didn't know where it should go.'

'I told my secretary to book you into Blake's, a suite. You'll like it there; it's very laid back.'

'Leo, why didn't you ring me? You said you would when you got back from the States. That was more than two weeks ago. I only did this collection because you asked me, and now you won't talk to me.'

'What are you talking about, Danny? I'm here now, talking to you – and we'll have dinner tonight, okay? I've been really busy. We're opening the New York store in the autumn and I've been on the phone the whole time.' He leaned across the table and took her hand. He squeezed it tightly and smiled into her eyes. 'Don't worry. We'll have a good time while you're here. But look, don't let Sarah know there's anything between us. I asked you to do this range because we need a Paris connection, but if she thinks there's any other reason, she'll be difficult. You're spending the rest of the day with her and the other designers, so for God's sake, use your head and be discreet.'

221

Danielle picked up Leo's hand, pressed it to her cheek and kissed it. 'You are a bastard, Leo. I don't know why I like you.' She let go of his hand and sat back in her chair. 'Okay, let's look at the dresses on a model.'

After an hour's critical inspection, Leo called Sarah over from the studio. He left the two girls together, exhorting them to do a hard day's work.

Back in his office, he pulled out the plans for the New York shop on Madison and 62nd. It was smaller than he had originally planned, but he had had to agree with the wisdom of his American advisors. They felt it would be dangerous to open on a large scale before the New York public had a chance to get to know the Rags style. He had stood firm, however, on opening in Los Angeles and Dallas, and he had already bid for sites in both cities.

He had opted for a large store on Rodeo Drive, Beverly Hills' most expensive street, and Old Town Drive in Dallas. The staggering spending power in that corner of LA had been his justification for committing four or five times what would have been needed for similar premises in London. Meanwhile, he had dispatched Dave Davis to New York to start work there.

He buzzed his secretary and asked her to send in Michael Morris, his accountant. They had organised a credit line of a million dollars in the US to cope with all the costs of opening three stores. He wanted to be sure that this wasn't going to tighten things too much in the UK.

Although the business was turning over just under thirteen million pounds a year, the rate of expansion meant that there was no liquid cash. Leo already resented the deal that he had been forced to make with Ubiland on the Kensington store. He certainly didn't want to find himself needing further favours from them.

Mike Morris was a first-class accountant in his mid-thirties. He had left Arthur Andersen's to join Rags the year before, on Leo's promise of a great future and a degree of autonomy which had not, as yet, been granted him. A quiet, conventional man, he nevertheless enjoyed the pressures of Rags and the informality that let him work in jeans and a sweater.

He had all the figures in his head. 'In the profit and loss account for the year ended March '73, we should show a trading profit of 1.2 million, and the balance sheet will show a greater improvement with the revaluation of the old leases. But we're showing all the money spent on the club as a net capital asset to earn itself back over five years from the rent payable by the Rainbow Room operating company – and if you want my opinion, that's pretty unlikely.'

'Well, I didn't want an opinion, I wanted facts,' Leo said curtly. 'I've already told you. If the club doesn't work, there'll be plenty of buyers around for the premises. What I asked was whether or not the million-quid line that's been diverted to the American operation will leave us with an adequate facility over here.'

'Well, Leo, that depends on how many other new ventures you start, or shops you open. If you level off the expansion programme over the next eighteen months or so, I don't see a problem – that's assuming a ten to fifteen per cent rise in sales over the next year.'

'Okay, and what about the plan to buy out Ubiland at Kensington?' asked Leo.

'If you're opening the American shops, you won't have enough to finance that kind of borrowing. I told you, it had to be one or the other, not both, and the draft accounts bear me out.'

'Okay, Mike, thanks,' said Leo. 'Just put all that and the figures on paper for me, because I'm not sure that a million quid is going to be enough.' He held up his hand to stop Mike protesting. 'Don't worry, my neck's always stuck out a long way, and it's still in one piece. See you tomorrow.' He walked over to the door to show the accountant out.

Then he picked up the phone to talk to his secretary. 'Ring Tratoo and book me a table for two at nine tonight. Not in the gallery. And give me an outside line.'

When he heard the dialling tone, he rang his home

number. Alison answered. 'Hello, Angel. What are you doing?' he asked.

'Claire's coming here any minute. I'm going down to Hampshire with her to look at horses.'

'What time will you be back?'

'I don't know – seven I should think. Why?'

'It doesn't matter. Look, I'm going to be tied up in the design meeting all evening – I won't be back till late. Why don't you go out with Claire and Simon and I'll see you when I get home.'

'Okay, don't work too hard.'

'You enjoy yourself with the gee-gees. Bye, Angel.'

He put the receiver back and stared thoughtfully at the closed door of his office.

Johnny, Leo's young, long-haired driver, took the Rolls to Blake's to collect Danielle at 8.30. She sat in the front where she could be seen as they drove slowly and silently up Gloucester Road and along Kensington High Street to Abingdon Road. In the narrow street outside the restaurant, Johnny leaped out and ran round to open the door for her. As she got down from the car, the few people who were in the street couldn't help noticing her, though famous and glamorous faces were not unusual in this part of London.

Leo sat at the bar inside. He jumped from the bar stool when she came in and helped her to take off her coat. He gave her bottom a pat that ended in a squeeze as he passed the heavy mound of fox fur to the sultry cloakroom girl. 'You lovely, clever girl. I hear the session with Sarah went okay – but you don't look a bit exhausted . . . yet.'

Leo pulled over a stool for her to sit on and poured her a glass from the bottle of champagne on the bar. Danielle leaned towards him, put her hand on his knee and kissed him. 'You look very naughty tonight,' she whispered.

Leo glanced round to see if anyone had noticed them. But he saw only the waiters and, if they took any notice of their customers' infidelities, they never showed it.

Once they had finished the bottle of champagne, Leo

had relaxed and didn't really care what anyone saw or said. No man could be blamed for wanting to spend an evening with this soft, sweet-smelling siren. They ate tagliatelle and bollito misto and drank two bottles of Carema. The strong, heavy wine from the foothills of the Italian Alps lulled them into a mood of tingling sensuality. Danielle looked at Leo with obvious excitement. He knew that he wouldn't be back at Chelsea Square till very late.

She ran her fingers through the thin blue flame that burned the coffee beans floating on her sambucca.

'I want to see your Rainbow Room now,' she said. 'Sarah told me everyone is going there. You must be pleased to be king of a new success.'

'Yeah, we'll go there on the way back to Blake's.' He looked at his Piaget. 'It should be steaming by now.' He beckoned a waiter. 'Mario, can you ring Salvatore at the Rainbow Room and tell him to keep a table for me? I'll be there in about twenty minutes.'

When they arrived at the club, it *was* steaming. All the people that Leo had hoped would use it had been in the first few weeks. Most had been back for more. An advantage of the bright light in the centre of the room was that everyone could see and be seen. The gossip writers found it a useful source of space-fillers, and most evenings there were one or two photographers hanging around the entrance.

Liz Macintosh saw Leo come in and pushed her way through to him. A professional and interested glance at Danielle evoked an introduction from Leo. 'This is Danielle Milinaire, the designer I was telling you about. Danny, this is Liz Macintosh. She does PR for Rags – oh, and this place. You can see she's done a good job.'

'My God, Leo. Don't tell me you're satisfied,' Liz laughed.

'Of course I'm not, but it's not your job to get these arseholes to pay their memberships so I can't blame you that they don't. Anyway, what's happening tonight?'

'Michael Caine and Shakira are somewhere around, and Robert Plant, and Georgie Best, oh – loads of people. I

225

haven't checked the book, yet. Are you staying long? I wanted to ask you about a shoot that *Harpers* want to do here next week – it's for the opposition, though.'

'Who's that?'

'Janet Lyle, Annacat.'

'Good God, that's not opposition. 'Course they can do it. No money, I suppose?'

'No, but full credits.'

'Okay, fine. Anything else?'

'Yes, there's a hairdresser called Heinz Schumi who wanted to know what we'd charge for him to hold a show here. I gave him the usual rates but he backed off.'

'Well, get back on to him and offer him half-rates.'

'But, Leo . . .'

'Never mind "But, Leo",' he cut in, 'Schumi's only just started and he's going to be very big. Let's be associated with him now. And anyway, we'll still make money.'

Liz shrugged, 'Okay, Leo.'

Irritated, Leo looked around. 'Now, where's Salvatore? He's supposed to have a table for us.'

Leo led Danielle through the laughing, drinking crowd. He found Salvatore by the bar, calmly surveying the noisy swirl of people and directing his flock of waiters to thirsty customers. A table had been kept free for Leo by the edge of the dance floor. People looked up as he and Danny sat down and ordered champagne. Some nodded and smiled or greeted him as they walked past. An aggressive little fashion photographer who had been pestering Leo for work came and sat down at their table, but got up again fast when Leo shook his head and snapped, 'For Christ's sake, not now, Charley.'

Danielle was used to being looked at and paid no attention to the interested eyes surrounding her. She drank her champagne and caressed the back of Leo's neck. 'These people aren't very beautiful – it would be better at Castel's,' she said.

'Well, Angel, it's the best of the local crop, and I'm not complaining. Do you want to dance?'

'Okay.' She slid off the sofa to her feet and walked

lithely to the dance floor. When Leo joined her, she stood with feet still and slightly apart, slowly gyrating her hips and swinging her hair across his face. Leo, oblivious to anyone watching him, moved close to her, put his arms around her and pressed his hard, excited body to hers, soft and yielding.

When they got to Danielle's suite at Blake's they undressed each other hungrily. In the warm rooms they made love everywhere – on the floor, on the bed, on the window seat, under the breakfast table, on the sofa, in front of the fire. Danielle had no inhibitions and loudly showed her eagerness and excitement, a series of rhythmic groans announcing each climax. Nothing existed for Leo outside the highly charged parcel of physical energy that their two bodies composed.

Afterwards, he lay on the floor while Danielle stroked every part of his naked, exhausted body.

'You're a dangerous woman,' he said as he slowly raised himself on his elbows. He leaned over and kissed her damp breasts and softened nipples, then got to his feet. 'I'm going to have a shower.'

She reached out and grasped his ankle. 'Oh, Leo, don't go now.'

He shook his head, eased his ankle free and wandered slowly to the bathroom. He stood for five minutes in a wide, high-powered jet of steaming water and felt the sweat running off his skin. Wrapped in a towel, he went back into the bedroom where Danny lay gazing reproachfully at him.

'I've got to go, Angel,' he said.

She lay without moving and watched him dress. As he pulled on his jacket, she turned to lie on her back. She held out her arms, moving her hips slowly from side to side. It was too much. He got down on his hands and knees, straddling her. He kissed her. She tried to pull him to her, but he resisted.

'I'm really going, Danny.' He stood up and looked down at her briefly. At the door he turned back and blew a kiss at her naked body. 'I'll see you tomorrow.'

He had told his driver to take a cab home and leave the car keys with the porter. He collected these and found the car parked right outside the hotel. Slowly, he drove himself home. When he reached Chelsea Square, he turned the engine off and for a while sat listening to the silence. He tried to shut the door quietly, but winced as the faint clunk echoed round the square. He let himself in, went to the kitchen and poured himself a large glass of milk. He drank it slowly, then crept upstairs. In the bedroom, Alison seemed to be asleep. Thankfully, he undressed and slipped in beside her.

The next morning, he leaned over and kissed her cheek. Her eyelids lifted and she looked at him through her bright blue eyes.

'You must have got back late. I didn't hear you,' she said.

'Yeah, I did. I tried not to wake you.'

She smiled and stretched. 'Well done,' she said. She jumped out of bed to go to the bathroom. Leo lay listening to the flush of the lavatory and the sounds of her washing. Then he thought of Danielle. He turned and lay on his stomach, and buried his face in his pillow. The taste of the night's encounter still lingered in his mouth.

At Etam's head office in Oxford Street, the receptionist was no match for Raj's persuasive charm. Not to connect this beautifully dressed, good-looking man to the office of the buyers with whom he wished to speak was unthinkable. He had brought nothing with him. His aim was specifically to identify and establish a rapport with the right people and to persuade them to commit themselves to an hour's appointment at the earliest opportunity.

Two days later he returned with Joan's samples to the buying office.

The tough, uncompromising women there saw dozens of manufacturers every week. In Raj they recognised the single-mindedness and sense of commercial reality that are the hallmarks of the successful factory operator. They were impressed by the styling of the samples and their crisp, neat finish. The delivery time Raj quoted seemed very optimistic, but prices were low enough to be interesting.

They gave him a trial order of fifty dozen blouses. This order was strongly conditional on the production matching up to the quality of the samples – which they asked him to sign. And he had to keep within the two-week delivery time. They would supply the cloth, which would arrive at his factory the following Monday.

Joan and the girls they had selected arrived on Monday morning. Keen and intelligent, the new employees were enthusiastic about the factory and everything in it. Raj asked them to sit around a table in the tea-room while he delivered a short speech of welcome and outlined his plans for the coming year. He explained that he intended to start his second year with forty-eight machinists, and he hoped that each of these original six would head up a team of seven others. Each of these teams would be monitored and bonuses would be paid on comparative results. These bonuses might add ten per cent to their wages, enough to create friendly, not bitter, rivalry. And the staff as a whole would be in a profit-sharing scheme that could reasonably be expected to add a further thirty per cent to their income.

He then announced that the first docket was due to arrive that morning and asked them all to start checking their machines, and make sure their chairs were the right height. Then they started to practise on the calico toiles of the garments that Joan had cut. The blouse that they were to make was fairly simple, but Joan went through each stage with them in detail. When the cloth arrived they all laid it out on the table and helped with the cutting.

When they were ready to start machining, Raj told them that the delivery time he had promised was two weeks. He wanted to halve that. There were six hundred garments to make. The last one was finished, checked and pressed in four days.

Raj asked the driver of the van that he had hired to telephone when he had a signature for the receipt of the blouses at Etam's warehouse. When he had got the call, he phoned the buyers to ask them to have the production quality checked. They agreed and called him back an hour later. The quality was excellent and if he came up next week there would be a second, larger order for him.

Over the next six months, Raj's company, West Textiles Limited, produced garments for several of the major high-street fashion retailers. There were no complaints about the service that he gave, and the volume of business grew as he had projected. He resisted the temptation to take on more work than he had capacity for. On the few occasions when there had been gaps between orders, he made up a fast-moving style that he supplied on sale or return to one of the Margaret Street cash and carry wholesalers. He had copied what he had guessed to be one of Rags's winners. His garments only differed from the original in that it was better made and retailed at half the price. Although this was speculative, none of the stock was ever returned, and because he had bought the cloth himself, he earned higher margins for it.

By September, the factory employed twenty-five machinists, Joan and a van-driver. Now Raj felt that he was ready to approach Rags. Although he saw Simon Riley at least every few weeks, he had decided not to use his offer of introduction to Leo Freeman. Instead he used the technique that he had now used several times to obtain an appointment with Min Cooper, the production buyer.

When he arrived for his second appointment, he was met in the conference room by Min and two others. They were sitting around an oval table on which lay two blouses. Raj knew that they were his copies. At the head of the table, a very pretty dark-haired woman in her mid-twenties stood and walked round to him. She wasn't tall, but her well-proportioned body moved firmly under the tight, faded jeans. She held out her hand. 'Hello, Mr Kalianji, I'm Sarah Freeman.'

Raj bowed slightly, took her hand and shook it firmly. 'It's a pleasure to meet you. I'm a great admirer of your designs.'

Sarah leant over and picked up one of the blouses from the table. 'So I see.'

Raj didn't look at the blouse. He stared into her dark brown eyes, and said nothing.

'It's difficult and expensive to sue people for plagiarising clothing designs, especially one as simple as this. But it's not impossible. You look as though you know that.' Raj saw the beginnings of a smile in her eyes. 'Why don't you sit down?' she said. 'Would you like coffee?'

'Thank you, yes.' Raj sat in the offered seat.

The third girl poured from a percolator on the sideboard. Sarah sat down again, still holding the blouse. 'You know, we had a lot of trouble finding out from Nick the Greek who made this – and by the way, he won't be taking any more from you.' She turned it inside out, looking at the seams. 'It's better than ours, isn't it?' she said, handing it to Min, who nodded.

Raj refrained from acknowledging this, or that the blouse came from his factory. 'I've brought along some samples of my production for Chelsea Girl and Etam,' he said, producing two styles from his briefcase. 'These will give you an idea of the quality.'

Sarah waved them away. 'We know all about your quality. We're told you're very quick.'

'Well, we're never late,' replied Raj evenly.

Sarah turned to the younger girl who hadn't yet spoken. 'Jan, get the three styles we want Mr Kalianji to quote on.' When the girl had left the room, she turned to Raj. 'Now, Mr Kalianji, what's your first name? I hope we'll be doing business with you, so we might as well get to know each other.'

'Raju; call me Raj.'

'And you call me Sarah. And this is Min Cooper – well, of course, you met her before. Jan, who's just gone out, is Min's assistant.' She paused and leaned back in her chair. 'Right, Raj, we think you should do some work for us. But there are two conditions. First, you stop ripping off our styles; and second, you stop working for the wholesalers – their margin takes away the price advantage. Would you agree to those conditions?'

231

'No, not without a quid pro quo,' replied Raj. 'What had you in mind to offer?'

'A minimum of five hundred dozen pieces a week.'

'And?' asked Raj.

'A premium of ten pence a garment – that's six hundred pounds a week for doing nothing,' said Sarah. 'And of course, we'd want your undertakings in writing.'

'Of course. As I would want yours. For what period of time are you prepared to commit yourselves?' Raj asked.

'A year at a time.'

'All right, but I'd need six months' notice of your intention not to renew.'

Sarah nodded. 'Okay. Now, I'm supposed to be a designer, not a hustler, so I'll leave you with Min to go through the details. Would you like to come up to the studio afterwards, when you've signed?'

Raj smiled at her. 'Yes,' he said, 'I would.'

An hour later, Raj waved down a cab in Kensington High Street. As it rattled its way through the West London traffic, he was trying to come to terms with an unfamiliar sensation. It was now a few years since he had been troubled by his emotions over Diana Quinn. It had been a struggle, back in Uganda, to evict her from his thoughts. But since then no one had replaced her.

His attitude to Reena was fondly dutiful – he knew that they were to be married, and he had completely accepted this. And he admired her for the efforts she had made in learning English and in trying to understand his activities; he admired her, too, for her undeniable good looks – but he didn't love her.

But what he felt now reminded him sharply, like an unusual scent, of Diana, and for a moment his thoughts strayed back to the last day he had spent with her – and the row in the shop with the dark, curly-haired man. Rags, in the King's Road. And here he was five years later driving through London with a contract from them – from Sarah.

He felt a turmoil in his chest, his guts and his loins. It was alarming, exciting, scaring – like driving a car that for twenty years had behaved perfectly, then suddenly, it won't decelerate, and the brakes have gone.

Sarah Freeman had looked into his eyes, understood him and wanted him. None of his defences had worked, or even been deployed. In the half-hour that they had sat and talked in her studio, a rapport had evolved that both of them knew would develop beyond their control.

Raj felt no guilt about his emotions. He wasn't betraying Reena, because he had never shared that experience with her. While he knew that whatever was going to happen between him and Sarah was completely inevitable, it wouldn't in any way change his attitude to his future wife. He was alarmed because this was something that he hadn't planned or remotely foreseen. But he was certain that whatever did happen, he wouldn't let it interfere with his new commercial relationship with Rags.

He decided not to go straight back to the factory. Instead, he asked the cabbie to drop him at a large detached house in Winchester Avenue, just off the Harrow Road. Set in a small, well-kept garden, it had been built in the 1930s when the suburb of Sudbury had first appeared. Raj had just exchanged contracts on it and he had the keys in his pocket.

The house had been occupied by the same family since it had been built and Raj had got a bargain. When the previous owner had died, his executors were a small firm of Norwich solicitors. Raj's accountants had, from time to time, advised the family on financial matters, and, as they were the only local professional firm mentioned in the executors' files, they had been asked to organise the disposal of the house.

It had never been on the market. The Norwich solicitors were pleasantly surprised that a four-bedroomed house could fetch £20,000. In Norfolk they would have been pleased to get £15,000.

Raj let himself in and walked around the house. The sound of his footsteps on the bare boards echoed loudly. With a deliberate effort, he pushed Sarah Freeman from his mind and started to make a list of all the jobs that needed doing in the house. But, out in the garden, listening to the birds singing their late-summer songs, he leaned against a mossy apple tree and let his mind return to her. He felt his pulse rate increase and a gentle throbbing in his groin. He wasn't going to see her again for two days.

'My God,' he muttered to himself, 'I must, *must* control myself!'

After a few moments' contemplation, he drew in a deep breath, straightened himself and went back into the house to finish his inspection. He left soon afterwards, taking a quick satisfied glance back at the house, and found a cab to take him to his factory.

Later that afternoon, at Adam and Eve Mews, Leo came into his sister's studio to see if she had any interesting developments to tell him about.

'Hi kid. What's new?'

'We had a visit from the phantom copier today.'

'Fantastic! How did you track the bastard down?'

'We didn't really. He tracked us down. He came to see Min last week, just to get an appointment, and when she started asking around to see what anyone knew about him, Nick the Greek admitted that he'd been buying rip-offs of our styles from him.'

'Great,' said Leo, grinning, 'I hope you scared the shit out of him and sent him packing. Did you tell him we were going to sue him?'

'I told him we were considering it, but he didn't seem very impressed. But I did get him to sign an undertaking that he won't make any more copies.'

'Christ, the pathetic little creep. How did you make him do that?'

'By giving him a production contract for five hundred dozen pieces a week,' replied Sarah.

Leo stared at her, his eyes burning. He grabbed a wooden ruler and smashed it down on Sarah's drawing-board. 'You did *what*?' he yelled. 'Are you telling me that some little rip-off merchant comes crawling in here and instead of kicking his arse up to his Adam's apple, you give him six grand a week of business? You women are bloody mad! What the hell did he do to you? Who is he, anyway?'

'If you stop yelling and smashing up my studio I'll tell you,' said Sarah, just controlling herself. 'And you know bloody well the production has improved by miles since me and Min took it over. So calm down and listen for a change.'

Leo took a deep breath, sighed and walked over to the window, looking down into the mews. He turned back to Sarah. 'Don't you know the reason we're where we are is because I don't let people walk over me? No one. Ever. The minute you let that happen you know you're losing control. And if some guy turns up here admitting he's stolen our designs, we don't kiss his arse and give him a contract, we shit all over him to make sure the others know what'll happen to them if they try it. Now, tell me who this bastard is and I'll veto the contract.'

'No, you won't. His production is better and quicker than any we're getting. We've given him a very tight contract and it'll be easy to control. He's the most business-like manufacturer I've ever met.'

'Who the hell is he?'

'He's an Indian called Raju Kalianji.'

'Oh God! Not a fucking Indian. They haven't got a clue. He must have conned you. Where's the contract? You ring him right now and tell him you're cancelling it – think of a reason – there's nothing he can do about it.'

Sarah got up and walked over to the rail where Raj's copies were hanging. She picked one up and thrust it under Leo's nose. 'See this,' she snapped. 'Raju Kalianji is selling these to Nick, who's selling them to every crummy little boutique, and they're selling them at half the price we are – and they're better made. I don't know how he does it for the price, but he does *and* I'll take any bet you like that he's not losing money. He knows bloody well that we can't sue him. What's your solution? And anyway, we need production like his. This way we win twice – a new source of good production and no more copies. I wish you'd stop and think before you come in here and start yelling at me.'

She hung the blouse on a chair next to Leo and went back to sit at her drawing-board, waiting for Leo to respond. She knew that once he'd looked at the garment and found a way of climbing down without losing face, he would agree with her.

But he didn't look at the blouse. He stared stubbornly at Sarah. 'I tell you, I've never yet met an Indian who ran a good factory. Why haven't I met this one before if he's so bloody good?'

'Because he only started the factory six months ago, and he wanted to have enough capacity to do big runs before he came to see us. As far as I can tell, he planned everything right and it's working. And if you can see through the racist fog round your head, you'll find he's a very clever, sophisticated man, and tough. He's also very beautiful.'

'Oh my God!' Leo groaned. 'So that's it. Some randy Indian comes in here full of eastern promise, and you women are so busy wetting your knickers, you don't even suss him out properly. So he goes trotting back to the family sweat-shop clutching our contract and laughing his turban off. They'll probably bung a bit of caviar in the curry tonight to celebrate.'

Sarah strode to the door. Turning back, she said, 'I'm not going to sit and listen to this crap. When you've looked at that garment and started thinking logically, maybe we'll discuss it. And your prejudice amazes me, Leo. For years you've been grumbling about the idle English goys in the cloth-trade, and now at the first sight of an Indian who's got it right, you're screaming Alf Garnett abuse at him. I tell you, this guy's going to be very useful to you – and that usually makes you like people.'

She left the studio. The door banged shut behind her. In the ladies' lavatory on the ground floor, she leaned on a hand basin and looked at herself in the mirror, shaking, aching with rage at Leo and, beneath that, like an earth-quake in her guts, rumbled the excitement she had felt from the first moment she had set eyes on Raju Kalianji.

236

# October 1973

Leo took Alison and Sarah to New York for the opening of the first Rags in America.

They arrived at JFK on a clear, bright day. When they came out of the terminal building into the open air, they were met by a fierce, cold north-westerly and a tacky, rather faded Cadillac limousine. Seven hot, cramped hours had combined with Leo's nervousness about the opening to make him very edgy. As they drove through the flat, ugly sprawl towards Manhattan, he grumbled incessantly about the people he could see, the buildings and the cars. Alison sat in the middle of the back seat with Leo and Sarah on either side. She didn't speak as they argued across her.

'For God's sake, Leo,' Sarah was saying. 'If you hate America and Americans so much, why did you want to open here?'

But as they drove down the Long Island Expressway towards the Queens Tunnel, and the Manhattan skyline came into view, Leo's mood changed. Suddenly he was excited and enthusiastic again. When they reached 42nd Street, he told the driver to take them slowly up Park Avenue, and he looked around with relish at all the obvious wealth bustling up and down the sidewalks and in and out of the stores.

By the time they drew up outside the Pierre Hotel by the Park on Fifth Avenue, all his normal energy and optimism had returned. He yelled happily at the porters and Liz Macintosh, who was already there to meet them. He told Alison and Sarah to go on up to their rooms; he was going straight round to the new shop with Liz.

'You tell your boss if he can't produce a cleaner car than this, then don't bother sending another, all right?' he told the chauffeur, and turning to Liz, 'Come on Liz, we'll walk – it's only round the corner.'

As they walked, Leo checked details with his PR. She had used a New York firm to help her, and they had promised the earth. 'I don't know if they'll deliver, though. They spend so much time talking in this place, they don't have any time left actually to do anything. But I've seen or spoken to all the fashion editors of the big papers and they seem really keen – I think we'll get all the coverage we want from that point of view. And Jake Hascher says . . .'

'Who the hell's Jake Hascher?' interrupted Leo.

'He's the head of the PR firm we're using. He reckons we should get some good general coverage. He's been using all the stuff I gave him on your career and lifestyle and whatnot.'

'Only the clean bits, I hope.'

'He thinks it's worth hinting it was a bit cut-throat early on. They like all that over here. And a couple of magazines are doing features on the Rainbow Room. And Dolores Nicholson from *Womens Wear Daily* says she'll do a page feature if you interview well. She doesn't mind a hint of naughtiness either, and if you can think of something funny to say she'll use it. But for God's sake, don't start slagging off the locals.'

The windows of the Madison Avenue shop were blanked out with sheets of gold and maroon paper. The Rags logo over the corner entrance had been ostentatiously covered up. Leo hoped that there was nobody who didn't already know what was underneath. He hammered on the door, and Michael Rappacioli, the New Yorker who was to run the store, opened it himself. He took Leo's hand and pumped it ingratiatingly. 'Leo, welcome to Rags, New York. Come on in and tell us what you think of it.'

Leo walked into the dimly lit, much-mirrored and spacious shop. The Rags image – art nouveau, bent-wood hat-stands, maroon, black and gold – had been sharpened up, a little more pronounced for American consumption. But it was still subtle. Reflector spot-bulbs made little pools of light around each fitting, leaving the spaces in between in a soft, warm glow. The changing-rooms at the back of the shop were framed by a vast proscenium arch, and the pelmet from an Edwardian theatre curtain.

Leo sat down on one of the deep-buttoned velvet chesterfields and looked around, nodding his head and smiling. 'It's great. For once it's better than the designer's drawings. Dave is incredible. Where is he now?'

'Man, Dave has aged six years in the last six weeks. I guess he's back at the Pierre right now in a bath of champagne, but he said he was coming by again at eight-thirty.' Michael Rappacioli laughed. 'You know, Leo, if you'd seen this place a week ago, you would not have believed it possible.'

'Yeah, I would. That's why I use him, poor bastard. Still, he loves it – he's an adrenaline addict, which is the only profitable kind of addict to be. Right now, before I satisfy my addiction to the champagne I want to go through this whole place with you in detail, from petty cash to stock control. Let's take a look at your office.'

'Okay, Leo,' said Michael. 'I've got everything ready. All the first stock's here and it's all checked.' He led Leo up a flight of wide stairs to the first floor. At the back, hidden by a wall panel that swung open, was a large well-equipped suite of offices. Leo looked with approval at the array of closed-circuit television surveillance monitors, the telex and accounting machines. An hour later, he was satisfied that everything that could be done to make the operation work had been done, and it only remained to get the customers through the door.

He found Liz, who had been sitting on the phone, chasing up guests to the opening show, which was to be held in two days' time.

'All we need now,' he told her, 'is a shop full of punters with hungry plastic, so I hope you and your Mr Hascher get it right. Make me a list of everyone who's said they're coming to the show. And I want to have a look at the venue tomorrow morning. I hope the Plaza's the right place.'

In her room at the Pierre, Sarah was sitting with Alison. Both in silk kimonos, they lounged on the mock French-renaissance furniture, drinking strong, spicy bloody marys. Leo had told them they were going down to Greenwich Village for dinner. A car would collect them at nine.

They had both bathed, washed their hair, and sluiced off the feeling of cramped tackiness caused by the long flight. They were similar women, and recognised the strengths in each other; the different perspectives of their relationships with Leo had made them close to one another. Sarah, though a year older, looked on Alison as a big sister and tended to canvas her support both in her rows with Leo and in other crises in her life.

Alison got up, stretched, found some jazz on the radio, and looked down at the lights and traffic swirling around Grand Army Plaza, then across the blackness of the park to the great apartment blocks and the synagogue on Eighth Avenue. 'Well, how do you think they'll take to Rags over here?' she asked.

'I don't know, but Leo's obsessed with the idea of making it in the States. I mean, the reaction's been amazing when Americans have been to see us in London, but that may be just because we're in London, I don't know. This autumn's been bloody good in Europe: we've had great coverage, and we're selling more than ever – relative to floor space, that is. But I'm still not sure about the States. I wanted to wait a bit before we opened here. And the trouble is, Leo expects me to charge around giving interviews and being a showman like him – and I hate it. You know, I love the designing, and putting together a range that really works, but all this hype!' While she was talking, she leaned forward in her chair. Now she flopped back again. 'Oh, don't worry,' she went on. 'Once we get into the show I'll be as optimistic as he is. I hope to God Liz has booked the right models. Trouble is, over here the models haven't just got to be the best-looking, they've got to be the ones all the big names are using. That's the problem with New York. In this part of the city it's practically a crime to be unfashionable – you've got to go to the right restaurant, the right hairdresser, the right shows, the right shops . . . shops are like shows over here. If they're not a big hit first time, they never will be.'

She stopped and swirled the remains of the bloody mary round the bottom of her glass. Alison held out a hand. 'Here, I'll make a couple more. Let's forget all about the opening and enjoy ourselves. There should be a guy arriving any minute with some really good dope. I found a phone number we used last time we were here, and he produced some great stuff then.'

As she was putting together the ingredients for the drinks, there was a knock on the door.

'Who is it?' called Sarah.

'James,' said a soft New England voice.

Alison nodded. 'That's him. Let him in.'

A tweed-jacketed ivy-league type in his early twenties came into the room. He saw Alison and smiled. 'Hey, how are you? I'm glad you called, we've got some great shit at the moment. You'll love it.' He pulled a hard little packet from his pocket and handed it to her. 'There you are,' he said. 'One troy ounce. That'll be a hundred dollars please, ma'am.'

Alison looked at Sarah. 'I've left my bag in our room. Can you lend me a hundred?'

Sarah pulled a note from her purse and passed it to the improbable-looking dealer, who placed it neatly in his wallet.

'If you two ladies would like something to wake you up and keep you going, I have some other goodies,' he said tentatively.

'No thanks. We'll let you know. And thanks for the prompt service,' said Alison.

When he had left, she abandoned her bloody mary, and started to prepare a fat, three-paper joint.

'Is that guy really a dealer?' asked Sarah. 'He looks like a schoolmaster.'

Alison laughed. 'He came highly recommended. I suppose as long as he looks like that he's got a greater chance of staying in business. Anyway, this stuff smells very promising.' She was holding a burning match to a corner of the small black cube, crumbling it into the tobacco below. She finished rolling the joint and lit it. They sat side by side on the bed, their backs against the huge, velvet-padded headboard and dragged deeply. After a few moments of appreciative silence, Sarah spoke. 'Did Leo tell you about Raju Kalianji?'

Alison thought and slowly shook her head.

'Well, he will. He's an Indian who's just taken on production for us. He's really beautiful – a good-looking version of Omar Sharif. You know, he's like those liquid-eyed film stars you see on posters for Indian films down in Southall. God knows what he's doing in the rag-trade. When he came to see Min and me, I couldn't believe it when he walked in. When he looks at you he doesn't stare, he sort of scours the inside of your head. He came up to the studio afterwards and sat and talked about patterns and stuff, but all the time I felt myself going hot and cold. I nearly fell off my stool when he touched my hand. Isn't that amazing? A hardened old bitch like me!' She paused, took another long drag on the joint, and grinned vaguely at the middle of the room.

'Well . . . did you do the same to him?' asked Alison.

'I don't know – I really don't know. I don't know if he looks at everyone like that, or just women he fancies. He didn't say anything about it; he just seemed to want to know about bloody frocks. I tell you what, though, he's a very strong character. He wouldn't take any shit from anyone.'

Alison giggled, took Sarah's hand and squeezed it. 'Sarah, it's great, you've got a real old-fashioned crush – and all he's done is talk about dresses and touch your hand. Do you know what'll happen next?'

'No – no idea. But if he makes a move, I shan't stop

him.' Sarah gurgled. 'Leo'll go mad. You know what he's like, especially about people who are better at anything than him. And he's got such a hang-up about being Jewish, he's more racist than Hitler. Oh well, sod him.' She looked at Alison. 'If you know what I mean.'

'Don't worry about him. If he makes a fuss, tell me and I'll sort him out,' said Alison. She stretched, swung her legs over the side of the bed and stood up. 'Well, I suppose we had better get dolled up for any vagrant members of the New York press corps. Apparently we're celebrities this week.'

Sarah passed her the joint. 'There's room for a last toke on this,' she said.

Alison took it. 'Wow, this is great dope,' she said, shaking her head slowly from side to side. She wandered to the door and let herself out, then popped her head back. 'It's great about you and the Indian. You must push it along when you get back to London.'

When she got back to the suite where she and Leo were staying, Leo was already there, wearing a soft beige silk shirt and a pink silk scarf. He was on the telephone, holding a glass of champagne and shouting at the hall porter. 'Listen, we're not going to come down and hang around the lobby like a hookers' convention. Just tell your doorman to ask which is my limo and buzz me – okay?' He slammed down the phone. 'It's all bullshit about American efficiency. The service you get in these places is in direct proportion to the column inches you're getting. I hope they'll be running around like blue-arsed flies by the end of the week.' He filled a glass for Alison and handed it to her.

'How does the shop look?' she asked.

'Fantastic. Dave has been amazing. It's the best-looking store in New York – no argument. You and Sarah must come and see it tomorrow after we've been over to the Plaza. Right, now this car's supposed to be here in twenty minutes, and Liz has booked a table at a restaurant in the Village. We've got to meet some guy called Jake Hascher there – he's the New York PR we're using. It's supposed to be this month's restaurant. I hope to God the food's worth eating – not like that hake cooked with cider and bilberries we had last time.'

'Don't worry, Leo, you can always send out for steak and chips. Anyway, I'm ravenous. It's three o'clock in the morning for us. I hope you're not going to want to hang around in clubs all night.'

'Angel, we've got a busy schedule tomorrow. So it's dinner and then into the sack with my beautiful sexy wife.' He slipped his hands under her kimono, fondled her buttocks, then ran his fingers through her pubic hair. He kissed her on the lips. 'But, right now,' he said, 'you'd better get some clothes on – if you want to eat.'

The next morning Leo, with Alison and Sarah, walked across to the Plaza. In the lounge on the ground floor, they met Liz with Jake Hascher. Jake introduced them to Tony Lenz, who was choreographing the show. Leo's initial scepticism of the small, gay Jew dissipated fast, and was replaced by enthusiastic admiration. Tony Lenz came from a theatre background, and he used this to the full when putting on major fashion shows. He had cancelled six of the eight girls that Jack Hascher had booked. 'All the Europeans have used them this season,' he said dismissively. 'We don't just want a copy of the St Laurent show.'

He had selected four tall, blonde Texans, two ultra-thin, high-cheekboned black girls and two full-mouthed, dark-eyed Puerto Ricans.

'The Rags look is too romantic to hang on these gaunt Park Avenue models. We want warm-blooded women to show it at its obvious best – and, you know, the fashion writers really would like a change,' Tony told them. 'And the music has got to be British. We're using Purcell and Greensleeves and Vera Lynn and Pink Floyd and David Bowie. Relax Leo,' he said, as Leo, looking annoyed, made to interrupt. 'I've played the whole tape through half a dozen times. It hangs together really well.' He looked around him. 'Quite honestly, I wouldn't have chosen this venue, but then, everybody knows you're new to this side, and maybe somewhere less obvious would have been thought just too clever. Anyway, they're starting to put it all together on Thursday morning, and the set is already finished. Do you want to see the drawings?' He leaned over and picked up a portfolio lying beside him, and pulled out some sketches of what appeared to be the palm court of a pre-war ocean liner.

'If it looks like that,' said Leo, 'they'll either be knocked out, or piss themselves laughing.'

'Don't worry, this is New York. People only laugh if they think they are supposed to, so it doesn't matter either way. Now, the commentary's being done by an old British actor who's in New York at the moment, Charles Gregson, who used to be the butch young lead in British films in the early fifties. Anyway, he's aged wonderfully, and he's wearing white tie and tails. By the way, Leo, you should wear something neutral, formal and British. Everyone in the fashion trade round here seems to wear falling-apart jeans, or oriental robes with all sorts of symbols hanging round their necks. What would be perfect would be an old-fashioned double-breasted dinner-jacket, with an absolutely plain black bow-tie. Actually,' he said, putting his head to one side, appraising Leo, 'it's probably what suits you best anyway, and the fashion ladies will think it's wonderfully eccentric.'

He turned towards Sarah and Alison, who shook her head. 'Oh, no, we're not part of the show. We'll look ravishing, but normal.'

'Yes, well,' said Tony, 'I'm sure you will.'

'Have you checked the running order?' Leo asked. 'It's got to show the development of the philosophy behind Rags.'

'My God, Leo,' laughed Liz. 'What's that supposed to mean? Look, we've tried to work towards a climax without downgrading any of the styles by comparisons with each other. We're using the models and the music and the lighting to put across the appropriate mood for the different outfits. I think it's going to be the best show we've ever given.' Her Scottish lilt was becoming more pronounced with her enthusiasm.

'The amount of bread it's costing,' Leo broke in, 'we should sell tickets and do a six-month run, so it'd better be.' He turned to Tony. 'Okay, when's the rehearsal?'

'Don't come till the final run-through,' Lenz ordered. 'That'll be at three o'clock.'

'On Thursday? But the show's at five. Won't you need more time?'

'No, I won't, Leo. And it's bad enough having to book the girls for a whole day when the show only lasts twenty-five minutes. We're cost-conscious too, you know.'

Over the next two days, Leo and, to a lesser extent, Sarah, were exposed to a round of press conferences, interviews, television appearances, and radio shows. Liz and Jake Hascher had done their work well. They had sold the American media the notion that here at last was a major British fashion talent, combined with a commendable, and demonstrable, degree of commercial skill. Shots of the Rags store in Kensington and examples of the Rags look were presented side by side with charts and graphs depicting the phenomenal growth rate of the operation. Pictures of Leo with famous faces from show-business and the English aristocracy had been brought over by Liz and eagerly grabbed by the gossip pages. Photographs of these and other famous faces quenching their thirst at the Rainbow Room headed articles about Leo's influence on the way the Swinging Sixties had swung on into the seventies in London. The pundits all forecast a spectacular and prosperous future for Rags in America.

As the guests arrived for the show, they were handed a glass of champagne and a programme bound in maroon silk satin, ragged around the edges. They were ready to be impressed. From the moment Charles Gregson walked on to the apron stage that projected into the room, and the lights on the set came up, they were going to be. It was in many ways the oddest, most incongruous and naïve show they had ever seen, and they loved it. Tony Lenz

246

had broken all the rules and, by doing that, had made a statement that they would all remember. He hadn't just offered a page from *Vogue* with music and movement. He had shown that Rags was high, romantic fashion for any woman.

The press response was overwhelming. A short piece was even networked by CBS; the New York dailies covered it in detail. The headline 'A little black dress in Madison Avenue – $20!' and others like it headed up articles about the Rags philosophy of chic on the cheap.

By ten o'clock on Friday morning, the shop was packed and the changing-rooms quite unable to cope: the New Yorkers loved it, and the tills rang without a break. Leo walked back and forth through the store, his pulse racing, numb with the thrill of success. If he saw a customer dithering, he strode up to her and closed the sale, laughing, cajoling, reassuring. Every hour or so, he went up to the offices to check the takings, and stared at the pandemonium on the closed-circuit TV monitors.

Sarah and Alison went down for the first hour or so. Sarah watched girls trying on and buying clothes she had designed and muttered constantly about their wrong choices.

'I think these chicks are mad. They just seem to want to buy anything, whether it suits them or not. I hope they don't blame us when they get home.'

Leo turned on her. 'Christ, Sarah, what do you want? They're buying this stuff by the truckload. They love it. Stop moaning and be positive for a change. Your frocks have just passed the ultimate test. Relax, then get back to your studio and design some more.'

They left the seething crowd of customers and decided to walk across to the Plaza for a coffee. Sarah took Alison's arm.

'Ali, I'm worried. Those punters are all in there for the hype, not the clothes – and hype wears off. Sure, we're going to take a load of money for a while, but you can tell by the way they're buying they just want to be first with a Rags dress because everybody's talking about us. I mean,

Leo just can't see that's a danger.' She stopped and looked over at the Pierre. 'Look, I don't think I want to hang around and watch. I'm going back to London today.'

'Sarah! You can't! You must come to Dallas and LA Maybe you'll get a calmer view of it there.' She paused. 'Probably not though. But Leo'll be really upset if you don't come.'

'Like hell he will. He won't even notice five minutes after I'm gone. He'll probably be relieved. He doesn't want me chucking cold water on what he thinks is his greatest success to date. He's certainly not going to stop and think about what I'm saying. I'll book the first flight I can – and you tell him, okay? He won't leave that shop until it's shut and they've cashed up.'

'Okay,' said Alison reluctantly. 'Though I don't know for certain that I can take two weeks of Leo like this myself. I'm glad Liz Macintosh is coming along. At least she's sane. But look, let's have a drink at the Plaza first.'

Sarah nodded and they carried on walking across the square in the bright sharp morning sunlight. When they sat down in the Palm Bar, several heads turned, recognising, and a tall, effete man in a pinkish dove-grey suit came over and held out his hand.

'May I congratulate you, Miss Freeman. I think underneath all the ballyhoo and razzamatazz you're a very clever designer. Your brother's a lucky man. But, if you ever feel like spreading your wings and leaving the nest, give me a call.' He handed her a card. He was president of one of the major national store chains.

Sarah managed a weary, blasé smile. 'I'm not really such a fledgling – but thanks,' she said, and put the card in her bag.

They had lunch in a little French restaurant on 54th Street. The Cadillac took Sarah to Kennedy Airport in time to catch the six o'clock flight to London.

When Leo arrived back at the Pierre, it was already nine o'clock, and, although he had been on his feet since nine that morning without lunch or any kind of break, he was looking as fit and energetic as ever. The adrenaline was still pumping round his system. His eyes were bright and reckless-looking.

'Angel, we've cracked it here! We sold two thousand pieces and took thirty-seven grand! At that rate we'll take twelve million bucks a year. That's about half what we do in the whole of Europe! Tonight we celebrate. We're going to some new club that Jake says is the one place in New York everybody wants to go. We're meeting some mates of Andy Warhol's, and a few other English faces, Hockney and that faggot earl.'

As he talked, he undressed and ran a bath. 'Open a bottle and come and talk to me,' he shouted to Alison from the bathroom.

Alison thoughtfully took a bottle of champagne from the fridge and opened it. She wanted to tell Leo about Sarah and her misgivings, but she knew that he was on a plane of his own now, where logic and objective judgements couldn't reach him. She had always found Leo's tremendous self-confidence exciting and challenging to deal with, but this time, she was worried. Since they had left London he had hardly seemed to notice her or indeed anyone who wasn't specifically talking about Rags. She had never seen him so obsessive. Slowly she filled a couple of glasses and took one through to him.

Later, they squeezed past the colourful and outrageous queue waiting noisily to catch the doorman's eye and be let in to this latest shrine to late twentieth-century liberalism. Leo and Alison, with Jake Hascher, were deferentially waved in and found their table.

The music mingled cacophonously with the yelling and laughing. The lights throbbed. Waiters weaved amiably among the tables, stopping every few yards to talk to their friends among the customers. In here, the waiters were the celebrities. Leo was loving it. He danced with two silver-sheathed girls whom he found already sitting at their table. Alison was pounced on by Jake, whose hot, clammy hands wandered up and down her back and bottom as they walked to the dance floor. She managed to keep her distance as he leered at her, and after a couple of minutes, she said, 'Okay, Jake, that's your ration,' and strode off the dance floor to where a group of long-haired, tight-panted rock-and-rollers beckoned.

'Whose fantasy have you just escaped from?' asked one in cockney English. He took her hand and led her back to the dance floor. She noticed Leo glance over, but carried on dancing, letting her body absorb the heat and the pulse of the music and the strobe lights. As the man danced with her, his hips moved slowly from side to side, and his eyes smiled into hers. She had not said a word to him.

He moved towards her, put his arms behind her and pulled her up against him. She felt his hard cock inside the tight cotton trousers, and a sudden surge of excitement ran up from her groin. He put his mouth on hers, and for a moment their tongues twined around each other. Then, instinctively, she backed off. 'Don't get too excited, you may not get the chance to follow through,' she murmured in his ear.

His eyes opened wide. 'What's this? The reluctant debutante?' noticing her English accent. 'Don't worry, doll, I'll keep him at bay,' he laughed, glancing down at his crotch. 'Come and have a drink.' Not waiting for an answer, he led her back to a corner where his friends were sitting, and ordered her a tequila sunrise. 'Meet the rest of the band. What's your name?'

'Ali. What's yours?'

'I thought you'd know that, being another Brit. We are', he said, sweeping his arm round to include the other four, 'the talent behind Rod Stewart. We've been backin' his tour.'

'Well, sorry. I don't look at *Top of the Pops* these days. Anyway, what are you all doing sitting around like a bunch of rugger-buggers on a piss-up? I thought you guys spent all your spare time screwing fans.'

'Well, we're having a night off – unless you fancy a gang-bang? We're all knackered so we won't tire you out.'

'In that case,' she said, getting up, 'I think I'll go and

find someone who will.' She ruffled his blond hair, 'And try and keep that thing in its cage,' she said, pointing to the bulge in his trousers.

Before they could get her back, she was making her way round the edge of the club to where Leo was sitting with the other girls and an odd assortment of men. Leo looked up. 'Hello, Angel, you look flushed. Who's been poaching? Here, have some of this, it'll cool you down.' He poured her a drink, shook off the girls on either side of him and stood up. He seemed annoyed. 'I'll see you later,' he said and pushed his way towards the cloakrooms.

A short, slightly made-up, very blond man, who had been sitting quietly at the end of their table, also got up and followed him into the lavatory. As Leo was peeing, the blond man took a small mirror from the bag he was carrying. He laid it next to the wash-basins and spooned a little pile of fine white powder from a silver snuff box on to the mirror. Then, with a silver blade, he divided the powder into two long thick lines.

'Do you want a line, man?' he asked Leo, who was just zipping up his fly.

'Yeah, sure,' said Leo, who had never tried cocaine, and watched as the American put a thin ivory tube to one nostril and sucked the powder up through it into his sinuses. Leo leaned down and did the same, and felt a perceptible surge of energy and well-being flood through his body. He smiled and shook his head appreciatively. 'That was great, thanks man,' he said.

'Hey, that's all right, any time. You want another line later, just ask.'

Leo walked back into the club feeling on top of everything. When he reached their table, he waved to Alison to join him dancing.

Three hours and two lines later, they climbed into the back of the Cadillac. The driver sleepily asked them where they wanted to go. 'Just cruise up the East River Drive,' said Leo. 'And put "Dark Side of the Moon" into the cassette deck.'

The next day, Leo asked about Sarah. It was already midday. He and Alison had just woken. Alison told him.

'What the hell do you mean she's gone back to London?' he yelled. Then he stopped, held his head, shook it vigorously. More quietly he said: 'Why didn't you tell me last night. I wondered where she was.'

'Leo, you didn't ask. You didn't notice a damn thing going on around you. You were up on cloud nine, and that was before you started snorting all that coke. She said you wouldn't notice. I didn't believe her, but she was right. Do you know something, Leo, you're a self-centred shit sometimes, especially since we've been on this trip.'

'My God!' Leo cried. 'We've had one of the best openings they've seen in this bloody city. The whole place is crawling with people who want to see Sarah and interview her. All she had to do was hang around and be nice – it's not much to ask after all I've done. What's wrong with her? . . . No!' He held up a hand. 'Don't talk about it now. If she's gone, she's gone. She was being totally negative yesterday morning. The shop was busier than any of our shops have ever been, and there she was moaning that the punters were buying the wrong things. I don't know what's got into her. The sooner she finds a geezer to give her a good seeing to, the better.'

'The way you crowd her and put her down the whole time, it's not surprising she's got a problem. But you watch out, Leo. She's got a stronger character than you seem to realise, and one day she'll stop taking all the shit you dish out. In fact, when she does get it together with a man, that'll probably give her the strength to turn round and walk out on you – and I think you sometimes forget she's your biggest asset.'

Leo looked stunned and hurt. 'Look, if it wasn't for me, she'd be getting five grand a year from Chelsea Girl or somewhere. As it is, she owns twenty per cent of the fastest-growing retailers in Europe. Even if she felt like it, which I don't believe, she wouldn't walk away from that.'

Alison sighed. 'There's no point in arguing with you. If you don't want to take any notice of what I say, then don't.' She looked at him. The combination of vitality and well-disguised vulnerability that had attracted her to him so strongly were still there, but before his confidence had been built on realities, and, if forced to, he could rationalise his arguments. Now he was making judgements based not on what had happened in the past, but on what he thought was going to happen in the future. The media were surrounding him with myths about himself and his career, and he actually believed it all. There was a hollowness to his vitality, and his vulnerability was less well disguised. She thought that he probably needed her more than ever, but she knew for certain that he didn't think so.

Sarah arrived back in her house in Portland Road, Holland Park, at eight in the morning.

She had not slept on the plane. She never could. She hated the idea of being seen asleep by strangers, with her eyes shut, her mouth open, maybe dribbling the way some other people did on planes. She had quickly and effectively fended off overtures from a fifty-year-old American banker who was sitting next to her in the first-class cabin. She wasn't exactly rude; she simply had a way of looking at people that made it perfectly clear she didn't want to communicate with them.

Her huge brown eyes, neat little body and mass of dark gently curling hair conspired with a full, slightly pouting mouth and her obvious independence, to make her attractive to almost any man. She was used to – and bored by – attempts to pick her up. She had long ago stopped being surprised by the paucity of the range of clichés used by men who sought to interest her. Occasionally, if a man was original and made her laugh, he would be rewarded with a smile, seldom more. Because she was talented, and had become fairly famous for it, she noticed that men's attitudes to her fell into various categories: those who found success in a woman unattractive; those who admired it but didn't know how to cope with it; and those who, while admiring it, were anxious to demonstrate how they were, in fact, rather more successful.

So she had reached the age of twenty-six without ever having had a long-term lover. And when she was alone in her elegant house, she could not think of a man whose presence would enhance it. It was the sameness, the predictability that irritated her, and prevented her from really looking closely at any man.

Sitting in the 747 for seven hours, though, she really wanted a man to cling to. Her brother was so insensitive in his domination of her. Everything in Rags revolved round him, and she was just one, quite important satellite. She had always done what Leo said, and, when they were teenagers and the family were despairing of him, she had always stood behind him, backed him up, encouraged him. He used to notice it then. Now, however, he behaved as if her own very talent had been kindly loaned by him to her. Leo boasted and swore by his instincts, which had often been born of her ideas. Right now, her instincts told her that Rags in the US was going to go wrong. She felt emotionally exhausted by the few days in New York and she had no regrets at having curtailed her trip.

As she brooded with the whistling drone of the jets in her ears, and the sharp, cloying over-oxygenated air in her nostrils, her thoughts kept returning to Raju Kalianji. Around this strong, calm and startlingly handsome man, she began to weave a passionate fantasy. By the time the plane had landed on the wet, grey runway at Heathrow, she was having his children in a world that transcended all the mundanities and frustrations of her previous life.

When the plane stopped moving and the engines were silent, the business of collecting up her bags and wandering through the hard, noisy corridors of the terminal building seemed like a rude intrusion on the serenity of this fantasy. But slowly, as she clanked up the M4 in a black cab, past the familiar Lucozade bottle and through the rush-hour hustle of Hammersmith Broadway, reality imposed itself, immoveably, and a deep depression descended on her.

At home she made herself a huge cup of French chocolate and sat cross-legged on her bed, staring out of the window at the bedraggled sparrows hopping around the leafless plane tree in her garden.

After a while, she lay down and slept. She did not wake until five o'clock. She showered, then telephoned the office. Min was surprised to hear her voice, but said that she would be glad to stay on so that Sarah could come round for a chat, to catch up with any developments.

An hour later, they were sitting at a table in the upstairs bar of the Rainbow Room with a bottle of Mosel between them. Min told as much as she knew of sales figures and style movements. She also gave a detailed up-date on the sampling for the spring ranges; and, at last, just when Sarah thought she would have to ask, Min announced, 'Raju Kalianji is coming in tomorrow with some production samples of those dresses we gave him.'

She was not surprised that Sarah gulped a little before replying quickly, 'Oh, good. What time's he coming? Perhaps I'd better be there.'

Min smiled. 'Yes, perhaps you'd better be. It'll give him a nice surprise. He asked on the phone today whether you would be there. He sounded put out when I said you were not back for at least another week.' She paused, looking over at Sarah. 'You really fancy him, don't you?'

Sarah looked back, tightened her lips and nodded.

A day's sleep and the drab winter London had brought her fantasies down to earth, but Raj was well established at the back of all her thoughts, and, she knew, he wasn't going to leave easily.

She changed her mind about being there when Raj arrived, and asked Min to mention, as casually as she could, that she was back in her studio.

She heard a gentle knock on her studio door. Her heart leaped, her pulse quickened. She gripped her drawing-board to keep her hands from shaking. It was him. She knew it. All day she had been preparing herself, but she wasn't prepared. Her voice was huskier than usual as she called, 'Yeah? Come in.'

Raj opened the door. He came round it slowly. Sarah

stared at his dark, long-lashed eyes, the fine, black hair falling a little across his face from his neat parting. He stood there for a moment, slim, elegant, beautiful and, so it seemed to her, a hundred miles away. When he spoke, his voice was soft and even more mellifluous than she had remembered. 'Hello . . . Sarah. I gather you flew back sooner than expected. It's a pleasure to see you again. Min told me you asked to see me about something.' He walked a little way into the room, a very slight smile about his mouth as he asked, 'What can I do for you?'

Sarah bit her lower lip, and swung round ninety degrees on her stool to face her drawing-board. Without looking at him, she said, 'Well, I really wanted to go through a number of the late spring styles. Some of them are quite tricky, and I thought it would be constructive for us to go through them together, in detail.' She swung back to face him again, and forced herself to look him full in the eyes. She managed to control the quaver in her voice. 'The thing is, it'll take a bit of time and I'm hoping to be tied up all day here. I wondered if you'd mind seeing me at my house this evening? It's not far from here,' she added quickly. 'Just off Holland Park Avenue.'

Raj relaxed and nodded his head slowly. 'Fine, fine,' he said, 'but I'm afraid I won't be able to come till about eight-thirty. I hope that won't be too late.'

'No, that suits me. Will you have eaten? I could organise some dinner; we might be a few hours.'

Raj would have eaten. He was committed to a family gathering to discuss his cousin Vijay Paintal's wedding arrangements, and these discussions were always accompanied by vast and various feasts.

'No,' he said, 'I won't have eaten. A light dinner would be very welcome. Thank you.' He looked down at the sheet of meaningless doodles on Sarah's drawing-pad, 'If you give me your address, I'll see you later and leave you to get on with your work now.'

Sarah tore a corner off her drawing-pad and scribbled her address. She handed the piece of paper to him and, trying to smile casually, she said, 'See you then . . . then.'

'Okay. Goodbye till this evening.' He turned back at the door and looked at her for a moment before leaving. Then he closed it gently behind him and as Sarah heard his footsteps fade away down the corridor, she thought, he knows. God, he *knows*.

Alison tried to make her voice heard over the deep gurgling roar of the seven-litre AC Cobra and forty watts of Led Zeppelin. She and Leo were driving into Dallas from Love Field Airport. He had insisted on putting the hood down and Alison, in spite of the bright sun and a thick coating of fox fur, was feeling the bite of the Blue Norther blowing over the prairies from the Arctic. But Leo's blood was up. New York had been a complete triumph, and the Texas media were all ready to take the torch and keep running with it.

He zig-zagged in and out of the heavy, slow-moving traffic, laughing at the wheel-spins every time he changed down and hit the throttle. He finally screeched to a halt outside the Fairmont Hotel in downtown Dallas and was ready to sleep with every woman in Texas if anyone thought that that would help Rags take off.

He leaped over the side of the car, and doubled up the stairs to where Liz waited with a crowd of press-men and local PRs.

'Christ, Leo, we nearly heard you all the way from the airport,' said Liz. 'You're not going to get a very good press by killing off the local population – you didn't hit anyone I hope? Good, because these fellows are all on your side. They had a big splash with those Texan girls we used in New York. As it happens, they were all from Dallas, so it made a great local story.'

Leo smiled his big warm smile and shook hands with everyone within reach. The press cameras were happily clicking away at this energetic Britisher, who seemed to epitomise American ideals of dynamism and success. And their attention was caught by the tall beauty with the dark, wind-blown hair who stepped out of the Cobra and made her way calmly up the hotel steps.

'Leo, Leo!' the photographers yelled. 'Let's have you with your wife.'

Leo willingly reached out, took Alison's hand and drew her to him. A rich, flamboyant man and his beautiful wife, arriving in Dallas to open a new place for spending money and bolstering feminine egos – this was a good, clean uncomplicated story. Their editors would love it.

When eventually they shook off the press and found some privacy inside the hotel, Liz told Leo that KRLD, the local CBS affiliate, had confirmed an appearance for him on that evening's seven o'clock chat show. They were sending a car at six.

'Maybe,' said Liz, 'Alison should go with you – people seem very interested in her too.'

Leo glanced at Alison. 'Do you want to go?' he asked doubtfully.

She shook her head. 'This is your party, Leo. If you hadn't driven Sarah away in New York she could have gone with you. But it's nothing to do with me. I'm not going to be paraded around as your mascot.'

Leo looked relieved. 'Okay, Angel. Don't worry, I'll manage.'

Alison knew he liked to present himself to the public, macho and independent, unfettered by marital ties.

When Leo and his entourage had left for the television studios, Alison decided to go down and have a few martinis in the cocktail bar. She was impressed by the surprising lack of brashness in this fairly new Dallas hotel, and she was pleased by the friendly politeness of the staff, especially after the frenetic hustle of New York. She sat at the bar and ordered her drink. As it arrived, she was joined on the next stool by a tall good-looking man of about fifty. He held out his hand.

'Evenin' ma'am. Can I have the pleasure of buying that drink for you?' he asked in broad Texan.

Alison studied him for a moment. He had thick, grey hair, bright blue eyes and a perfectly tanned complexion. He wore a western shirt under a light beige Texan-cut

258

suit, with a yoked jacket and narrow trousers from which protruded a pair of sand-coloured, ribbed, sharp-toed high-heel boots.

Alison smiled, nodded slowly and gave him her hand. The Texan shook it. 'My name's Ross Blackwell.'

'And I'm Ali Freeman,' she said.

Ross Blackwell stepped back in overstated surprise. 'And what's a beautiful British lady doing in the Lone Star State?'

'Well, I'm here with some people who've got business to do, but I don't have to help. So I'm looking for something to occupy myself,' replied Alison.

'What'd you like to see; where'd you like to go? I'd be honoured to arrange anything for you,' said Blackwell expansively.

'We're only in Texas a few days, I'm afraid; but in England I've just started buying horses. I thought I'd like to see some western horses while I'm here.'

'Hey, well, you're asking the right man. I've got more'n twenty quarter-horses out on my ranch in Denton County. Matter of fact, we've just had two foals by Jet Deck. He's one of the world's leading quarter-horse stallions; five-thousand-dollar stud fee. They are beautiful little movers. You'all come on out and stay a couple of days. It's one of the prettiest ranches in Texas.'

'I must say, you Texans really are very hospitable, to ask a total stranger out to your home. That's very kind of you. I think I'd love it, but can I let you know later?'

'Course you can, and I got a feelin' you and me ain't gorna be strangers too long.' His eyes sparkled. 'Now, let me get you another little martini.'

They talked on for another half-hour. Alison wanted to know all about his horses, and quarter-horses in general. He told her the history of the breed; how they had been selectively bred for nimbleness and manoeuvrability; how the cowboys still used them, and of the excitement and money generated in racing them over a blistering two furlongs – the quarter mile, which gave them their name. He told it well, and although she didn't trust him, she

259

warmed to him and to his enthusiasm for the horses. She thought that eventually she had better tell him about Leo. 'Well, Ross, thanks for all the information. I really will try and get out to your ranch. Can you give me a telephone number where I can reach you?'

'Why? You're not going now, are you?' said Blackwell.

'I'm meeting my husband and his hangers-on for dinner here, and I just want to go up to my room first. So I'll call you tomorrow, if that's all right?'

She could see the disappointment and the anger at the back of the bright blue eyes. But he took a slim wallet from his jacket, pulled out a card printed 'Ross Blackwell – Realtor', with a Dallas phone number and handed it to her. She thanked him warmly for the drinks and the invitation and walked casually from the bar, turning to give him a smile when she reached the door.

Leo was ecstatic over dinner. He had given a great interview, which had been preceded by some footage of the Plaza show featuring the four local girls who had been in it. A press conference had been called for the next morning at the just-completed Rags store, which was part of a brand-new development in Old Town Drive, just east of the rich, exclusive suburbs of Highland Park and University Park. With the success of that evening's television appearance, the conference was likely to be very well attended.

Alison had to wait a long time before she had a chance to say, 'I've been asked to look at some quarter-horses. How long are we staying here?'

'I told you, Angel, only three days. You won't have time,' Leo said carelessly, and Alison didn't refer to it again during dinner.

Later, though, when they were in the Venetian Room Club, she spotted Ross Blackwell lounging moodily with two blond and very dumb-looking girls. Leo was amusing himself, comparing this sedate, old-fashioned club with his own Rainbow Room. Here, all the men wore jackets and ties and the average age was about forty-five. But he grudgingly gave them points for the quality of the neo-Italian baroque decorations. And the local PR eagerly pointed out, and put a price-tag on, those of Dallas's leading socialites who were there.

Ross Blackwell was making his way across the room when he noticed Alison. He changed direction and headed towards Leo's table, beaming and exuding *bonhomie*. 'Hello again, ma'am. You must introduce me to the lucky guy who married you.' He looked expectantly at Leo, who cast him a quick dismissive glance.

'Leo, this is Ross Blackwell; Ross, this is my husband, Leo Freeman. Ross very kindly asked me if I wanted to see his quarter-horses.'

'Hey now, if Leo would like to come too, that'd be a real pleasure,' Ross addressed Leo warmly. 'I'd rather have her come out with her husband than not at all,' he said laughing. 'What d'you say? Y'all are welcome.'

'Thanks, man,' Leo said vaguely. 'Would you join us for a drink?' He waved at an ice-bucket.

The Texan squeezed himself down between Alison and Liz, and accepted a glass of champagne. Alison glanced over to where he had been sitting and saw the two girls looking at him, and talking nervously. They obviously didn't know what to do, but they didn't approach Ross or leave the night-club. Alison smiled to see confirmation of her first impression that Ross Blackwell was an untrustworthy womaniser.

Blackwell asked Leo what he was doing in Dallas. Leo by now expected everyone in America to know who he was and what he was doing. 'We've just been opening another store here,' he answered airily.

'Oh? And what store is that?' asked Blackwell.

'Well – Rags,' replied Leo, as if surprised by such a stupid question.

'And what will that sell?'

'The same as it sells in New York and all over Europe,' said Leo impatiently.

Blackwell smiled thoughtfully. 'You must think I'm real dumb, but I don't know what you sell in New York or

Europe. They're both a long ways from here. If I came to London, do you reckon you'd know what I was selling?' he asked.

'Yeah, sure. Cattle or oil,' said Leo.

Blackwell shook his head and grinned. 'Neither of them. But you haven't told me what Rags sells.'

'Fashion, a sense of romance, the enhancement of the normal feminine characteristics. You know, frocks.'

Leo turned to Liz. 'Maybe you'd better give him a press kit. I've answered too many questions tonight.'

Alison noticed Blackwell's angry sideways glance at Leo, and sensed an increase in tension; but she knew that he wanted to keep it under control, and admired the way he said charmingly, without losing face, 'Well, I wish you every success here in Dallas, and if I can do anything to help – you tell me and I'd be glad to.' He stood up to leave the table. 'And don't forget, you're very welcome out in Denton. Your wife's got my number, so you just call when you want to come.' He turned to Alison. 'It was a real pleasure seeing you again. Be good now.' And with a big smile he turned and made his way towards the lobby.

'Where'd you find him?' Leo mocked. 'He definitely thinks he's on to a good thing. These bloody cowboys are as subtle as a herd of bison.'

Liz, who had been quietly studying Blackwell, said, 'Well, I thought he was really dishy, and what a charmer! Those eyes! You can't have him, Ali, so you'd better pass him on to me.'

Leo laughed. 'Christ, Liz, no wonder you're still a spinster if that's your idea of a dream man. I should think he treats a woman pretty much the same as he treats a two-pound steak.' He turned to Alison. 'Anyway, where did he pick you up?'

'He bought me a couple of drinks in the bar while you were on the telly. I asked him about quarter-horses and he gave me a half-hour lecture. I think it'd be great to go and see his ranch. Apparently it's a replica of a Mexican hacienda, full of Spanish furniture and doors from San Simeon. It should be worth seeing. And if you're going to fuss about him chasing me, why doesn't Liz come too, as a willing decoy?'

'Oh, yes. I'll be a decoy,' Liz giggled. 'I love being treated like a steak.'

'Okay,' said Leo, 'call him tomorrow and tell him we'll come out the next day. We were going to have a couple of days to kill in LA anyway. I called Dave this evening. He says the shopfitters won't be out till Sunday.'

The following morning, after a full and positive press conference, Leo, Alison and Liz had lunch at Mariano's, a Mexican restaurant nearby in Old Town Drive. The margaritas there were famously potent, and Leo insisted that they all have several before lunch. He followed this up by drinking neat tequila to counteract the mouth-burning Mexican sauces.

A guest list of local social luminaries had been drawn up for a small exclusive opening party for about two hundred. Leo had been against the idea, but the PR man in Dallas had said that any success in fashion had to filter downwards from the top.

As he got progressively drunker, and closer to the five o'clock start of the party, Leo began grumbling loudly about the provincialism of Texas and the lack of imagination which, he claimed, made it impossible for people there to make up their minds as to what they did or didn't like. 'Why the hell should these lovely long-legged Texan chicks only want to come to Rags if a handful of blue-rinse biddies from the Dallas Country Club tell them it's okay?' he demanded of anyone who might be listening.

'Leo, for God's sake,' said Liz, 'we haven't asked the blue-rinse biddies, just the young wives and daughters of the oil aristocracy – some of whom are in this restaurant right now, beginning to wonder who the hell you are. If you can't sober up, don't come to the party and insult them all. They're on your side – so far.'

Alison looked on, amused. She liked to see Leo told the truth by someone other than herself. And knowing the risk Liz was running, she admired her for doing it. 'Don't worry about him, Liz,' she said. 'He'll be fine as soon as he gets back to a shop full of eager punters.'

A limousine bore them back the short distance to the elegant and simple new shopping mall, where Rags had taken two adjoining nine-hundred-square-foot units. The two-storey buildings were half timber-clad, and laid out around four paved piazzas, full of shrubs, flowers and fountains. A lot of money had been spent in establishing and maintaining a permanent show of colourful blooms throughout the year, and the whole area had an atmosphere of quiet, suburban elegance, unexpected in this big, bare-knuckle city.

The Dallas Rags was small by comparison with most of the European branches. Nevertheless, Dave Davis had employed the same techniques that he had used in New York. Behind the rows of hanging baskets in front of the shop-windows, the strong romantic look was unmistakable. Entering the dark intimate shop from the sunlit plaza was like stepping into another time.

The free-standing fittings, the bent-wood hat-stands had all been removed to make room for the party. A small dais had been placed and spotlit at the back of the shop, and a continuous, informal show was going to be presented throughout the party.

The guests soon started arriving. The PR people had done their job well and it became clear that everyone who had been asked had come. The unbridled Texan enthusiasm quickly made itself heard, and the response to the show was genuine and spontaneous. Leo's moodiness, as Alison had predicted, turned into an elated *bonhomie*. He received the congratulations and good wishes of the rich and surprisingly glamorous women with his special brand of sparkling wit. The Dallas society ladies loved him and his beautiful wife. Invitations were issued from every side. Leo dealt with them skilfully, and it was arranged that he and Alison would join a group later that evening up at the Dallas Country Club.

As soon as the last guests had left, cleaners came in and

the staff of the shop began setting everything up for the first day's trading. The adrenaline had dissipated the effects of the tequila, and once again Leo examined the shop in minute detail and lectured Lucille, the manageress, on how to deal with Dallas customers. Lucille had been dealing with Dallas ladies for twenty years and knew better than anyone how to treat them, but she seemed happy to be told. She nodded attentively, as if she were hearing it all for the first time.

At last, Leo followed Alison and Liz back to the Fairmont, where they bathed and changed before going to the Country Club. Alison called Blackwell's number and left a message with a brisk-sounding secretary. The three of them would be coming out to Denton next day, and would Mr Blackwell call if that wasn't convenient.

Dallas Country Club isn't in the country, although, in the quieter parts of the vast park around it, you could imagine that you were. It is surrounded by the ultra-rich suburb of Highland Park, and is considered a vital pass-key to Dallas society. As in many clubs in provincial America, there were few Jewish members and the names on the membership roster were principally Anglo-Saxon or Irish. When Alison and Leo arrived in the bar, there were a number of members of the big local families – Hunts, Dealeys, Caruths, Crows.

Leo fell happily into conversation about real estate, oil and money, while Alison found plenty of people ready to talk to her about horses, the history of Texas, or fashion in Dallas.

Their attention was caught by a row in a corner of the bar, where two men were angrily shouting at one another across a table. One of them was Ross Blackwell. He hadn't seen them, and casually Alison asked about him. Only a little information was forthcoming. 'Ross Blackwell isn't a member here. I don't know who brought him in. Nobody knows enough about him. He just appeared a few years ago with a pile of money from God knows where. But he's got a ten-thousand-acre ranch out in Denton Country, a couple of Lears down at Love Field, and some very fine quarter-horse brood-mares. He's been in here before, but doesn't usually misbehave like that.'

As they were talking, Blackwell wound up his heated discussion and stormed from the bar. Alison was relieved that he hadn't seen her, but her interest in the colourful, roguish man was increased. She was looking forward to going to stay with him next day.


Raj left the Rags offices after his meeting with Sarah and retrieved his new Cortina Estate from the car park on the corner of Kensington High Street and Earl's Court Road. Driving back to his factory, he was scarcely aware of the other traffic on the road.

His emotions about Sarah were mixed. He had been almost dismayed to find that his excitement at seeing her again had grown even more intense since their earlier meetings before she had gone to New York. He was in no doubt now about her feelings towards him. He was determined to keep control, at least outwardly, but could do nothing to contain the pulsing in his body that antici- pated the evening's meeting.

Another cause for excitement was his certainty that he could build a long and profitable business relationship with Rags. He was aware that Sarah would not be giving him such orders just because she fancied him; Min Cooper was just as committed to his production and she was, Raj thought, a lot tougher than Sarah.

He had the impression, from the way the women re- ferred to Sarah's brother at their meetings, that Leo posed some kind of threat. It hadn't been articulated and, never having met the man, he had no idea what form it took. But although Leo's presence pervaded the whole business, Raj was confident that the two women held enough power in the organisation to choose their own suppliers.

He mused over this unknown, potential adversary who clearly possessed a very strong and dynamic personality. Rags buzzed with a very personal energy that must, he thought, be generated by Leo Freeman. But why should this man, who didn't even know Raj, apparently resent him? Was he jealous, or was he simply racist? Whatever the reason, Raj knew he could deal with it. He had prepared himself for their first encounter.

And if he found himself Sarah's lover, that would add spice to the event.

At the Paintals' that night, Raj saw Reena for the first time since he had met Sarah Freeman, and he could not stop himself from resenting her, pretty and charming though she undoubtedly was. While it was accepted that he could not marry her yet, it was understood that as soon as his business was on a thoroughly sound footing a wedding would take place. This inevitability now seemed to surround Raj like a cage, and he was annoyed by Reena's naïvety and slavish adherence to her parents' wishes and their culture. Her sister, Gita, who had been only twelve when the Patels had arrived in England, was much more emancipated and, to her family's disgust, imbued with western attitudes. Raj could not help thinking that if he was going to be forced to marry an Indian, Gita would have been a better bet.

With Sarah at the back of his mind, he found it impossible, for once, to maintain his polite charm. The people at this gathering were puzzled by his uncharacteristic curtness that evening.

At the end of the long meal, the ceaseless talk had arrived at the conclusions that they had all expected. Raj excused himself on the truthful grounds that he had a business meeting and set off with eager curiosity to Sarah's house in Portland Road.

Sarah was wearing a silk hand-painted kimono and a nervous smile. When Raj entered her elegant drawing-room, he saw a delicate Japanese meal laid out on a low table between two sofas. A coal fire glowed in the hearth, and paper-shaded lamps lit the room.

Sarah extracted a little porcelain jug from inside another filled with hot water.

'Saké?' she asked. When Raj nodded she poured some

into a delicate china cup. 'I thought that if we had a Japanese meal we'd be on neutral territory – I hope you don't mind?'

Raj smiled. 'Not at all. It looks delightful, and not too heavy.'

He accepted the cup and sipped the warm fluid. The effect was almost instantaneous. He didn't normally drink a great deal and in his excited state the rice alcohol met little resistance.

'I thought we'd eat first, then go down and look at the drawings and samples in my workroom,' Sarah said tentatively.

The meal was delicious, and the air of sexual anticipation was as potent as the Japanese wine.

In the gentle light, with Raj's dark brown eyes looking steadily into hers, Sarah found that she could speak her thoughts with uninhibited clarity – she knew they were being heard and understood. She poured out her ideas about everything: design, philosophy, the Bomb, religion, race and Leo.

Raj didn't interrupt much. He knew that he wasn't expected to. He did understand her, though he couldn't see why she felt so strongly about some issues that had little bearing on her own life. He was interested to see how she trusted his judgement and how pleased she was by his confirmation of her views. She seemed, he thought, a little in awe, and deeply respectful of his Indian culture. The only time she talked about him was when she asked if he didn't have an overwhelming urge to go to India and seek his roots. But Raj had no such urge – only a mild curiosity. The history of his race was irrelevant to his need to make a living in western Europe, but he didn't say so.

Raj was still surprised and a little flattered to be so obviously admired by such an intelligent and good-looking English girl – especially one who could do more for the growth of his business than anyone else. And, physically, he wanted her with an aching hunger. All his instincts were aroused and ready, all the pent-up energies of the years since he had made love to Diana Quinn were bubbling at boiling point.

Calmly, during a brief pause in Sarah's monologue, he took a deep breath and said, 'Shall we make love before we look at your drawings?'

Without saying anything, Sarah pushed the low table to one side revealing a big, square, Chinese silk rug between the two sofas and in front of the fire. She slowly undid the wide cummerbund around her kimono, which she then shrugged off to reveal her pale naked body, and, with a simple gesture of the eyes, shoulders and hands, she offered herself to him.

With all the inventiveness, and more confidence than he'd had with Diana, he made love to Sarah. Time and time again he gently, strongly, entered her in hazy, endless variations.

The fire had died down to a few red embers when they finally moved apart. Sarah tenderly stroked his glistening brown body with her kimono as he gently kissed away her perspiration and then draped her garment round her. As he reached for his own clothes, she said, 'Wait', and left the room to return a moment later with another, larger silk robe which she offered to him. 'I couldn't bear you to put on your shirt and trousers; they'd be like a barrier.'

They sat side by side, Sarah wrapped in his arms. She asked him about himself. He did his best to tell her what he knew she would like to hear – and such was his feeling of tenderness towards her that he almost believed himself.

A little later, they went to bed where the love-making continued – more languorous, less urgent, more gentle.

And, having hardly slept, they rose early, energetic and ready for work.

There was no need to refer to the night before, no need for mutual reassurance.

So they looked at Sarah's designs, her skilful drawings. They discussed the reasoning behind her new collection. Raj's commercial instinct could only be impressed by her grasp of the market, her understanding of its moods and her very practical approach to designing.

Having established the effect that she wanted to achieve, she would only consider her job half done. She would then painstakingly seek the simplest way of constructing the garment and the most economical way of using the cloth without detracting from her original concept.

Raj was full of admiration for this inventive logic – and marvelled that it should be possessed by such a passionate and beautiful woman.

By the time he left, he had a real insight into her creative attitudes, and knew that in hitching his enterprise to the Rags bandwagon, he had not erred.

Sarah watched from her drawing-room window as he drove away. She pirouetted girlishly round the room, giggling, hugging herself with glee.

Raj drove straight to Wembley in an aura of elation, triumph and fulfilled ambition, constructing bold lies to tell his parents about his absence from home that previous night.

Leo wanted to drive the Cobra the sixty miles out to Denton. This was strictly a two-seater, so Liz had to hire another car and drive herself. But first, Leo wanted them all to call in and see how the shop was doing.

They left downtown Dallas behind them, and burbled deeply up Highway 75 to the University Park exit point and round to the shop. It was busy, not frantic, but it didn't appear to worry Leo. He had now convinced himself that a low-key opening was more suitable for this location.

He drove up the Northwest Highway feeling very much in the mood for the wide open spaces of Texas. Liz managed to keep up until they hit Interstate 35 and headed north. It seemed absurd to hold the Cobra back and, oblivious to any speed restrictions, Leo put his foot down and felt the seven-litre engine rocket the shining, curvaceous metal beast up to a hundred and thirty m.p.h.

After about twenty miles, he decided that they shouldn't

270

arrive too early and pulled off the highway at the Lewisville turn-off.

'But what about Liz?' Alison protested.

Leo laughed. 'Well, she can have old Blackballs all to herself for a bit.' He carried on down to the quiet rural road below. They found a little restaurant-bar and had a quick lunch of fresh catfish and hushpuppies with a bottle of Coors beer. Then they headed back to Interstate 35 and drove on up over the empty, forest-fringed Dallas Lake and through the reddish, rolling, cypress-dotted country. At the Krum turn-off, they left the highway and drove until they saw a sign saying 'Blackwell Ranch'.

Turning into the dusty track, they caught their first glimpse of the ranch a quarter of a mile away on a slight rise in the ground. They drove past acres of white-railed paddock, past a guest bungalow and through a rock entrance into a dirt paddock. Leo parked the car in a long, low building open on two sides. To their left ran a stable block with twenty boxes, to the right, the house itself. The massive double front doors were of solid carved oak, sheltered from the sun by the overhanging shake-shingle roof.

The door was opened from the inside and Blackwell appeared, hands outstretched in welcome. 'I sure am glad y'all could make it,' he beamed and shook hands with both of them. 'Your little Scotch friend's been here a while, and she's been telling me all about you, Leo. I didn't know you were such a big wheel back in Europe; it seems you've got some pretty good people around you. Anyway, welcome to my little abode. Let me show you around.'

He put his arm around Alison's waist and led them into the hall. A Spanish influence pervaded the whole building. The internal doors were eight feet high, also of carved oak. The lights were all great wrought iron candelabra, invisibly adapted for electricity. The ceilings were lined with grape arbour stakes and the floors were of traditional Spanish terracotta tiling. Substantial oak furniture, large armorial crests and thick woven rugs reinforced the illusion that this was the house of a Mexican grandee. The building ran four sides round a wide, thickly planted patio, onto which most of the rooms had access.

Blackwell directed his cowboy henchman to carry the bags into a large, light bedroom that gave onto the patio. Beyond lay a beautifully sited lake surrounded by carefully planted saplings.

Alison kicked off her shoes and exclaimed as her feet touched the tiled floor. 'This floor's heated! And there must be some kind of underground heating in that patio. Those flowers couldn't be blooming at this time of year otherwise. God, what a hysterical place!' She looked at the huge oak bedhead, carved with a plausible version of an aristocratic coat of arms. 'I wonder where he found all this stuff. He seems to have accumulated an awful lot for a man who appeared from nowhere four years ago.'

'Yeah, this sort of place costs a lot of bread, even out here. I wonder what he's really into. You say he's got a couple of Lears down in Dallas. Well, there's four Piper Aztecs parked up beside the garage, and all these cowboys wandering about don't look as though they do much cattle herding – and I didn't think legit cowboys still carried guns.' He took Alison in his arms. 'I just hope he doesn't want a shoot-out over you!'

Alison smiled. 'I think the willing decoy will do her stuff. She's very determined.' She stroked Leo's face. 'Anyway, a couple of days out here will do you good. You've been so uptight recently, I thought you were going to flip.' She wriggled free and walked through to the bathroom to shower, and Leo collapsed on the bed.

In the saloon, Liz was trying to talk politely to a surly blond Texan woman in her early thirties. She had introduced herself as Betty. She was Ross's personal, confidential secretary, she announced in a proprietorial way that suggested she took more from him than dictation. She was certainly not keen to encourage any poaching on her territory, and seemed to sense that Liz had set her sights on Blackwell.

'I don't know why Ross has got all you people visiting right now. He's got plenty of business on and he don't need any distractions,' she said. 'He should have stayed on in Dallas to wind up a couple of deals, but he said if Mrs Freeman wanted to see the horses, he was going to show them to her himself.'

'Well, I think that was very gallant of him,' said Liz. 'He seems a very charming and thoughtful man.' Her clipped Scottish lilt contrasted with Betty's Texas drawl.

'Gallant, bullshit!' growled Betty. 'The man's a no-feeling bastard.'

Behind them, Blackwell's deep laugh boomed. 'Are you building up my public image again, Betty? I've told you before, you ain't in charge of the public relations. But I've got a job for you that you can do: you've gotta get on back to Dallas and meet those gentlemen from LA, seeing as how I gotta look after our important British guests.'

Betty looked at him furiously, but Liz saw the angry iron glare in his eyes. A little, excited smile touched her lips. Betty would have to go.

During the simple steak dinner, cooked, it seemed, and served by one of the cowboys, Blackwell was charming and informative about everything except himself. He talked about the early days of independent Texas, the founding of the great oil dynasties and the hi-tech manufacturing businesses that were beginning to establish themselves in the state. Blackwell had an encyclopaedic knowledge of who had made how much from what. He mentioned only in passing that he had interests in real estate in Houston and Dallas.

After dinner he and Leo played a game of backgammon, which Leo won, gaining a modest sixty-four dollars. When Blackwell suggested a replay, Leo put forward Liz as a substitute. He and Alison were going to bed.

Alison sat in front of the dressing-table in their bedroom, taking off make-up and combing her hair. Leo filled the deep, wide bath and settled down in it to read all the news magazines. An hour later, he came back into the bedroom to find it in darkness, with a gentle breeze rustling the curtains on the patio windows. Alison seemed fast asleep.

273

He silently climbed into bed and lay beside her. He could hear quiet, half-whispered talk from across the patio. After a while he identified the talkers as Blackwell and Liz and, grinning to himself, he wondered what sort of progress was being made. He didn't have to wait long. Shortly after, the talking stopped and a perceptibly rhythmic series of breathless gasps, slowly building in length and strength reached him through the quiet night.

As the tide of moans and whispers ebbed and rose, he thought of Liz's firm little body yielding to the powerful incursions of the big Texan.

Now big and pulsing hard against Alison's thigh, Leo turned towards her. His fingers explored the warm crispness of her pubic hair. She wasn't asleep, and the dampness between her warm, vaginal lips told him that she had been listening too.

Soon they forgot about the sounds from across the patio and were immersed in a rhythm of their own. Later, hot and spent, they lay back and listened to the still night time, and the breeze rustling the curtains.

The next morning, they had breakfast round a large table in the kitchen. Coffee and eggs were being cooked by a grey-haired old woman of about sixty, who swore happily at the half-dozen or so men who wandered in to eat. Leo came down before Alison, and had been there a while when Liz walked in, beaming and bouncy. She sat next to Leo, who asked innocently, 'How did you get on?'

'Och, he'll be back for more,' she said quietly.

Leo laughed. 'Well, Angel, you were due that, but don't let it take your mind off your work.'

Then Blackwell came in. He strode over and shook hands with Leo, then kissed the back of Liz's neck.

'Your public relations advisor is a very skilful lady.' He winked at Leo from behind Liz's back. 'Now,' he went on, 'I've laid on some of my finest horses for you and your wife. My head man's going to take you up over the hill to the woodland, and back down our training gallops. But they ain't at peak fitness, so that shouldn't stretch you none.'

Leo had never been on a horse. 'Not me, thanks, Ross,' he said. 'I sometimes look at 'em, but I never get on 'em. But Ali will. She loves it – must be her Irish blood.'

'Hey now, Leo, that's no problem, that's no problem. We'll give you one of the stock horses. They never do anything you don't want 'em to, and my man'll make sure y'all have a good time. Uh-huh,' he said, aware that Leo was going to protest. 'You can't come out to the Blackwell Ranch and refuse to ride.'

Leo submitted. To have protested further would have been an admission of cowardice. And, anyway, it might be interesting to find out why Alison got such a kick from it. If those ya-hoo friends of Simon's could do it, he was bloody sure he could. 'Yeah, you're right. It'd be stupid to come out to cowboy country and not be a cowboy for a day; but I'll need the right gear,' he said, looking dubiously down at his jeans and Gucci shoes.

'Great. We'll find you some boots and chaps; a lariat and a pair of forty-fives too, if you want them,' said Blackwell, who had by now sat down to devour a plateful of fried eggs and corn hash. He looked at Liz and asked, 'Are you worried you're gonna lose your boss? He'll be fine.'

Liz laughed. 'You can give him your fieriest steed for all I care. He'll survive.'

At eleven o'clock, they all gathered by the stable block. Four gleaming quarter-horses and a mule were hitched to the rail that ran along the front of the block. Three of the horses had narrow bridles and European saddles and stirrups. The fourth had an elaborately tooled, deep-seated western saddle, with wide leather-covered wooden stirrups. The mule was loaded with two large panniers which contained a picnic lunch.

Blackwell beckoned to Alison, and led her to the first of the horses. A dark chestnut gelding, his head was not dissimilar to the thoroughbreds that she was used to. But his deep chest and greatly developed quarters showed he had been bred for a different job. He stood at just below sixteen hands, and Alison accepted the cupped hands that Blackwell offered for a leg-up.

Leo walked his horse round the paddock, trying not to show his apprehension. He certainly looked the part in a stetson and silver buckled chaps, though he wore English jodhpur boots; western boots, Ross said, tended to get stuck in European stirrups.

Alison already felt quite at home on her horse. The lightness of mouth and the well-controlled energy in its quarters belied her previously received knowledge of quarter-horses.

The four of them, the man using the western saddle leading the mule, set off at a walk through the stockade gates, then turned down a dusty track towards the lake. Skirting this, they headed on up towards the brow of the ridge behind the ranch. On all sides of them lay large white-railed paddocks, mostly empty at this time of year. As they topped the rise, the paddocks gave way to enormous wire-fenced areas, dotted with a five-hundred-head herd of Herefords. For four miles they trotted on through flat and featureless country, with more large cattle enclosures on either side.

Leo reluctantly took advice from Alison and found that his horse's pace allowed him to rise and fall comfortably with alternate strides. By watching Blackwell's head man, he found a suitable way of holding his reins. After a while, he began to relax and feel confident that he would get through the day and enjoy it.

Alison chatted to the two Texans, who were happy to tell her all she wanted to know about the horses and how they used them. They told her that most of the animals kept at the house were specifically racehorses, although, it was claimed, any of them could be put to work any time. Over at the stock farm another twenty working horses were kept – no mechanical substitute had yet been found for handling large herds over this terrain. But again, some of the working horses found themselves performing in local rodeos and barrel races, and most of the men took a pride in the versatility of their particular mounts.

When they reached the edge of the small plateau, they looked down into a shallow river valley. The river meandered slowly down its flood plain from the west, sometimes hidden from view by small clumps of trees.

Wayne, the head man, pointed up the valley. 'We'll take the riverside track about six miles up into the wood. We can pull up and eat there.'

They picked their way down the valley side and joined the track. Wayne, in front, broke into a gentle canter. Alison followed. To his alarm, Leo found that his horse decided to keep up without his asking it. Alison turned round. 'Just sit hard into the saddle and move with the horse,' she shouted.

They weren't going fast, and Leo's confidence returned a little when they dropped back into a trot, then a walk. He was able to look around at the fast-flowing, rocky river as it hit rapids. Colourful, unfamiliar birds darted from tree to tree. Down in the valley, the wind was hardly noticeable and the sun shone strongly. He began to enjoy the smell of the horses' sweat, the creaking of the saddle, the quiet, rhythmic footfalls.

The valley rose and the wood thickened with tightly clustered pines. The path narrowed and they were brushed on either side by protruding lower branches. Leo looked back. The man leading the mule was quietly walking along about half a mile behind. Looking ahead once again, he was startled to see the hindquarters of Alison's chestnut disappearing up the track and to find his own horse breaking into a canter. He tried to slow it by pulling back sharply on the reins, but this only seemed to make it quicken. In order to avoid branches that grew across the path, he had to lean right forward along the horse's neck, which gave him even less control.

The horse was travelling faster and faster, almost at full gallop now, and every time Leo opened his eyes after another stinging swipe from a needle-covered whip, he could see no sign of Alison. By now he was terrified, and had abandoned all hope of regaining control of the horse. He knew that the only thing that would stop it was the horse in front. Where the hell was Alison? She must have known that this would happen.

Two minutes later, they had covered another mile and the horse was bolting in earnest. Leo was growing weak from the exertion of trying to stay on and avoiding the trees. Suddenly, looking ahead, he saw a fallen pine tree lying across the track. It was about two and half feet off the ground and, almost directly above it, stretched a branch too thick to push aside.

'Oh, shit,' he muttered into the horse's mane. He turned his head sideways, trying to duck as the horse leapt. His head struck the solid, unmoving timber full on the side of his skull. Leo's unconscious body, plucked from his saddle, hit the ground at the side of the path just beyond the fallen tree.

Just half a mile ahead, Wayne and Alison had pulled up and dismounted in a clearing where the path ran up alongside the river. Their horses were blowing heavily.

'You couldn't do that on no English thoroughbred,' Wayne grinned.

But Alison looked back down the track anxiously. Her heart sank as the riderless horse galloped into the clearing and, panting wildly, trotted round in circles until Wayne caught it.

Alison started to run back down the track.

'Hey honey!' Wayne called. 'No need to go back down there. Jerry's followin' up behind with the mule, and if your husband don't want to walk, he can hitch a ride with him. You jest come on back here, sit down and have a smoke.'

Alison seized the offered cigarette with trembling fingers. She felt terrible remorse at having thought that it would teach Leo a lesson if he didn't find the riding as easy as he imagined. He may be a selfish bastard, but I don't want to be without him, she told herself. Tears formed at the corners of her eyes.

Wayne broke into her thoughts. 'Hey, honey. I can hear Jerry now.'

The sound of approaching horses became louder and she looked up as the other cowboy rode into the clearing, leading the mule behind him. Leo lay slumped belly-down across the mule's back. Alison jumped up and rushed over.

'He's as unconscious as a county judge,' said Jerry. 'But he's alive. He jest banged his head a little; ain't even no cuts or nothin'. Let's jest lay him down against that old tree and give him a little whiskey.'

The two men lifted Leo off the mule and propped him against an old willow. Wayne took a whiskey bottle from one of the panniers and opened Leo's mouth to force some in. Jerry strolled over to the river, filled his hat, and threw half a gallon of water straight into Leo's face.

With intense relief and inexplicable irritation, Alison saw Leo's eyelids flicker a little then slowly open. She knelt in front of him, put her hands either side of his head, and gently shook it.

'Leo, darling, are you all right? Can you hear me?'

Leo nodded slightly, and blinked his eyes full open. He put his hand up to where a discernible lump had formed above his right temple, prodded it and winced.

'Jesus Christ,' he hissed under his breath, 'I'm never doing that again.'

After ten minutes, he had recovered enough to stand up, stretch and test his limbs. As Jerry had said, there was no more damage. He had been unconscious and completely relaxed when he had hit the ground and, mercifully, his horse's galloping hooves had missed him. But he hadn't forgotten the terror of those few minutes, the lashing branches and the unavoidable obstacle in his path.

The two Texans opened the panniers and produced thick rolls of cold beef. From an insulated container they took iced cans of Coors beer. Alison and the two cowboys ate hungrily, but Leo left his food untouched. Alison turned to Wayne.

'Don't you think Leo had better go back to the ranch with Jerry?'

Wayne nodded. 'If Jerry leads him back the horse ain't gonna bolt again. Okay, Jerry? You be sure and don't get out of a walk now.'

'I don't know if I want to get on the bloody animal at all,' said Leo. 'Still, he seems to have calmed down. Ali, were you all right on yours?'

'Fantastic. He's a beautiful horse. His mouth's as light as a feather and nothing seems to faze him. Do you mind if I carry on with Wayne?'

'No, of course not,' said Leo, a bit too quickly to be convincing.

Alison watched Jerry lead Leo and the mule back down the track. She knew from the way that he slumped in the saddle that his pride was probably more hurt than his head.

Wayne started off again up the valley. They walked slowly along the narrow path, still surrounded by trees. After a mile, the trees stopped and the track led twenty feet up the side of a steep gully, then turned south across a red, dusty, undulating plain. Alison trotted to catch up with Wayne and rode alongside him. He told her that they would trot on another three miles, then head east back towards the ranch. Then, he said, about two miles before they got back they would find a three-quarter-mile strip of cleared earth that was used for galloping.

'Have you ever had one of these babies take off from a standstill? There ain't no faster horse in the world from a standing start than a quarter-horse. I want to see how this youngster will do against the boy you're on. He's one of the best; his daddy won thirty times at four hundred and forty yards, and he's doing almost as good.'

When they reached the long, straight strip, they pulled up. The thirty-foot-wide track of level ground stretched in front of them, with a few white markers and nothing else on either side. A four-horse starting-stall had been wheeled to one side; only this and the innumerable rough-terrain tyre marks showed that anyone ever came up here. They weren't going to use the stalls, not with just the two of them there. Alison followed Wayne's instructions closely.

She shortened her stirrup leathers so that her knees could nearly touch above the horse's withers. Then she backed up her mount until she had him bunched up, back arched like a spring, dancing on his front hooves, his hindquarters well down. Then Wayne yelled, 'Let him go!' and the horses jumped off.

Alison felt as if she had been shot from a catapult. Within four strides they were at full gallop, travelling at nearly forty miles an hour. As the horse settled into its stride, Alison managed to crouch, bent double like a Z, head, shoulders and torso lying almost along her horse's outstretched neck.

The wind and the dust bit into her eyes, but she noticed no pain in the thrill of this completely new experience. It reminded her of the excitement of her first gallop across the Galway Sands as a twelve-year-old on a Connemara pony. This, though, was the ultimate!

Wayne, hunched and driving, was half a length ahead. He half turned and yelled, 'Ask him now!'

Alison had not thought that a horse could go faster, but she squeezed her heels into the horse's side. She felt it surge forward, up beside, then ahead of the other, and, a length apart, they streaked past the quarter-mile marker, where Wayne had told her to pull up. She relaxed into the saddle and gently brought her horse back to her, slowing to a canter, then to a trot.

Continuing up the gallop at a long-striding, leisurely walk, Wayne came up beside her, grinning appreciatively. 'This boy'll have forty-five pounds less on him when he's running. He'll be all right, but he only wants a quarter of a mile, or maybe just three-thirty yards. Well, did you enjoy yourself?'

Alison smiled and nodded. She appreciated now why the racing bug could take such a hold, and why the breeding of these animals was so fascinating. Walking back slowly to dry the horses and bring them home relaxed, she was warm with the glow that comes after a great new sensation.

As they rode into the stableyard, Ross came out of the house.

'How was it, honey? Did my little beauty give you a good time?'

Alison nodded, still tingling with exhilaration. Ross extended a large, leathery hand to help her down from the quarter-horse, and led her through the great front door, across the hall, and into a small den. He kicked the door to behind him, and firmly pushed her down on to a deep, old-fashioned armchair.

Alison was tired. She was happy to relax and accepted Ross's concerned hospitality and four fingers of bourbon.

'Have you seen Leo?' she asked.

Ross shook his head. 'Seems his ride took a little too much out of him. He's out cold on the bed.'

Alison started to lift herself from the chair, but Ross restrained her. 'Don't worry, honey – he's fine. He's just taken a handful of drugs to kill the pain. There ain't nothing you can do . . . for him.' There was a lascivious gleam in his eye. 'But there's plenty you can do for me.'

He put his knees either side of her slender legs and leaned his bulk over her, into the armchair. 'Because I've wanted to have you ever since I set eyes on those beautiful quarters of yours, and them cheeky tits, and big lips waiting to be kissed.'

Alison was taken completely by surprise. She beat his chest pathetically with her fists.

'For God's sake, Ross, what are you doing? You know you can't do this – anyway, it's Liz you want, not me. We heard you last night.'

He grinned, running his tongue along his upper lip.

'Just because I'm a greedy man don't mean I don't have no favourite dishes.'

'Come on. Stop fooling around,' Alison said laughing shakily. 'You can't be serious.'

'Oh, but I am. I intend to have you, and no one's gonna stop me.'

He started to kiss her neck with thick, sucking lips. When he lifted his head, his eyes were lightly glazed, trance-like.

Alison panicked. She was going to be raped.

Her scream, long and piercing, penetrated the closed door, echoed through the rough-cast hall and passages.

Ross laughed. 'I love a screamer. And by the way, my men never interrupt me; your husband's dead to the world, and your little Scotch girl is way down by the lake. She won't hear.'

He put his brawny arms behind her back, and pulled her up off the chair towards him.

The door of the den clicked open. 'Get off my wife, you bastard.' Leo's voice was soft and calm. He stood white-faced, just inside the door. Ross glanced round, and Alison took her chance. With all the strength and speed her anger could muster, she brought her knee up into the Texan's groin.

He yelled at the sharp and sudden pain, released Alison and fell sideways, clutching at his balls.

Alison flopped back in the chair exhausted and Leo took a few paces into the room. Ross slowly clambered to his feet, and Leo was almost blasted back through the door by a short glare of unbridled, naked hatred. It was as if a lion had been robbed of his haunch of gazelle before he had taken the first bite.

Leo gazed, mesmerised at the struggle going on behind the furious eyes; and then a blind was drawn over them, and the hatred was replaced by bland affability.

'Hey, man – don't look so sore. Me and your wife were only fooling, weren't we honey?'

Alison said nothing, and Leo slowly started to walk towards Ross, clenching and unclenching his fists. Leo always avoided physical fights, but this time, Alison knew, he was past considering the two or three stone weight difference and the undoubted experience of the Texan.

'Leo,' she said urgently. 'It's okay. Ross was only teasing. Don't be an idiot.'

Leo stopped, confused.

'That's right, fella,' said Ross, watching warily. 'You don't want to hit old Ross, now, do you?'

He released his crotch and put out a firm hand towards Leo. 'Come on – take it. Forget it.' In a daze from the pain-killers, and his first real experience of insane, but controlled, hatred in another man, Leo took the hand and found it warmly reassuring. He thought he must have imagined what he had seen in Ross's eyes.

Later, that evening, though the nights were cold, Blackwell had organised a barbecue dinner. A long, glass-sided building connected two wings of the ranch house. It was full of plants and coarse-cut timber furniture; one side had been opened onto the patio, where a large, rock-built barbecue had been installed. A wide bed of red-hot charcoal grilled slabs of steak and chickens on a spit.

They sat round a table munching meat and sweetcorn, with bowls of spicy rice and black-eye beans. Three dark-skinned, dark-eyed Mexicans appeared to have been added to the household. Leo assumed they had arrived earlier while he and Alison were out riding. He attached no significance to them. It was obvious from the house that Blackwell had strong Hispanic connections. There was nothing surprising in the presence of a few Mexican hands.

Blackwell had skilfully and irresistibly dispelled the tension from the earlier incident and, during dinner, Leo asked him more pointedly than before what business he was involved in.

Blackwell looked over at him blandly. 'Like I told you, real estate, mostly in Houston, now more in Dallas,' he said.

Leo nodded appreciatively. 'Well, you must know what you're doing to have put this place together. Have you got connections in Mexico as well?'

Blackwell paused before answering. 'Well, I have had a few dealings down there. Crops, chemicals, personnel, stuff like that. But mostly I'm here now. I like it here and it's not too far from the race tracks in Arkansas.' And having changed the subject, he stayed with it and asked Alison her opinion of the horses. She had no trouble in being genuine in her admiration, and managed to disguise her lingering revulsion. The rest of the dinner was spent in discussing racing and the prospects for Blackwell's horses the following year.

Around midnight, in an aura of almost believable *bon-homie*, Leo and Alison left Liz with Blackwell and went to bed. They planned to start off early next morning for a final meeting in Dallas before flying to LA.

They had lunch the following day at Les Saisons down by Turtle Creek. As they watched couples strolling among the cherry trees and willows to the riverside, they tried to appraise the reception of Rags in Dallas. Holroyd, the local PR man, felt that they had aimed a little too far up-market and that ultimately they would find their business coming from the young, middle-income wives and daughters. But, he said, there was no harm done in the long run. Leo, still subdued, was happy to agree. Anyway, he accepted that after the ecstatic, high-profile reception in New York, anything would seem an anti-climax.

Over brandy, Leo asked Holroyd if he knew anything about Blackwell. Holroyd confirmed what they had already heard, but when he was told of Blackwell's claims to dabble in crops, chemicals and personnel in Mexico, he roared with laughter. 'That was surprisingly indiscreet for him. I think you'd find he deals in marijuana, cocaine and wet-backs – though he's never been indicted for anything.'

Leo laughed with him. 'I knew he was talking bollocks! And he can be a vicious bastard under all that charm.' He glanced at Alison, then at Liz to see her reaction.

She shrugged and simply said, 'Well, I couldn't care less. He may be crooked, but he's a real man.'

They finished their liqueurs and returned to the Fairmont before flying out of Love Field for LA.

Whilst Alison was sitting down to lunch with Leo at Les Saisons, her brother Simon was sitting down to dinner with Claire, his wife of eight months, at Chez Victor in London's Wardour Street.

Simon had thought his American wife would enjoy the brusque Frenchness of the little, old-fashioned restaurant with its '*le patron mange ici*' on the door, red and white checked table-cloths and unselfconsciously tatty interior.

Simon's job and his political activities took up a lot of

his time, and in order to expurgate the guilt that he sometimes felt about not being with Claire, he would frequently ring her from his office or a meeting and tell her to take a cab up from their little house in The Billings, by Chelsea football ground, to join him in a West End restaurant. He reckoned that way they could have at least two or three hours in which to really talk to each other.

He was probably right. They talked to one another with as much animation and mutual interest as when they had first met two years before.

In the absence of any suitable offers for her services, Claire had given up psychology and had thrown herself into a fine arts course at the Victoria and Albert Museum. She found that she had a real affinity with the subject and was happy with her studies and her marriage to an intelligent and considerate man. Her eagerness for knowledge about England, its history and its people, had been effectively deployed, but with typically American energy, she was always ready to see more.

When they had finished dinner that evening she suddenly said, 'Do you realise, I've never been to Leo's famous Rainbow Room. Why don't we go along there tonight? I feel like dancing.'

Simon did not. 'Oh, Claire, it'll be packed with mindless horrors – all seeing and being seen. Do you really want to?'

'Come on, Simon. Don't be so boring. It'd just be harmless fun. And I'm in the mood for seeing and being seen.'

Her husband smiled indulgently. 'You're worth seeing. Okay, we'll go. I suppose I'd be interested to see how it's doing. It still seems to be very popular; sometimes London clubs only last a couple of months. But I'm still convinced it will cost Leo money in the long run.'

'Well that's his problem, and anyway, he's got plenty of money. Let's just enjoy ourselves and – do you realise – it's our eighth wedding monthiversary so you can buy me some champagne.'

They walked to Simon's car through the noisy streets of

London's tiny Chinatown and drove to Kensington. Up above Rags's huge store, the evening was in full swing in the big, colourful club. A first-class chef had been employed at great cost and people had decided it was a good place to eat, as well as to dance and drink.

Simon and Claire found a table, and were soon joined by people that they knew. Simon woke up a little and enjoyed the champagne and a large Davidoff. Now and again they went to the dance floor and moved around to the music.

While Claire was engrossed in conversation, Simon looked round the crowd. He noticed Raj Kalianji dancing easily and gracefully with a girl whose face was obscured by her long, curling hair and by Raj's shoulder. The schmaltzy track which had been playing ended and was followed by more energetic funk. Raj moved apart from his partner. It was Sarah Freeman. Simon was amazed. He also felt vaguely alarmed. He had not heard from Raj for a few months, and had assumed that he was satisfactorily making his own way. He felt that the Indian's pride would prevent him from asking too many favours and anyway, it was now evident that he wasn't going to need Simon to introduce him to Rags. But it seemed to Simon somehow dishonourable that Raj should be using his obvious attractiveness to ingratiate himself; Sarah was plainly very absorbed and had eyes for no one else.

When Raj and Sarah left the dance floor, Simon excused himself and strolled over to their table.

Raj smiled politely. 'Hello Simon – you know Sarah?'

'Yes, of course. Hello, Sarah. How are you?'

'Glad to be back from the States – and nose down to the drawing-board. Ali's still out there.'

'I presumed she was, but she's not a good postcard sender.' He looked quickly back and forth between them. 'How do you two know each other?'

'I might well ask the same,' Sarah laughed. 'Raj is doing some production for us in his new factory. And you know how these business discussions run on.'

Simon glanced at her exquisitely made-up features, her

bouncing fresh hair and party clothes. 'You don't look dressed for business, but I believe you; I can also tell you that you won't get Raj to drop his production prices by turning on the charm – will she?' He turned, smiling, to Raj.

'But I don't mind her trying,' Raj said drily.

'It's a long time since we had one of our lunches,' Simon went on. 'Are you free some time in the next few days? I'd like to hear how it's all going.'

Raj nodded. 'Thank you, Simon. Would Thursday be suitable?'

'Great. See you then – do you want to come to my office? Fine.'

Raj frowned slightly as he watched Simon wend his way back towards Claire.

They lunched, as they had several times, in the small restaurant below Holborn Viaduct. From the start, Simon was aware of Raj's constraint. He was used to his aloofness, but now there was something positively covert about him.

After Simon had asked about progress in the factory, how the girls there were getting on, and how Raj's parents were, Raj suddenly announced, 'Simon, it was good of you to take an interest when we first arrived, but we've been here a year now and, as I told you I would from the start, I'm standing on my own feet now. I don't need any outside assistance.'

Simon was taken aback and embarrassed. 'Good heavens, Raj, you never needed any help from me anyway. I always said you wouldn't – remember? But I thought you found it useful to sound out your ideas on someone.'

'I did. But it's all right now.'

There was an awkward pause.

'I see you didn't need an introduction to my brother-in-law, Leo,' said Simon at last. 'That's good. How are you getting on with Rags?'

'I think I'll do a lot of business with them. It's very pleasing to work with such a successful company and the styles are well-designed, not too complicated. Sarah

288

Freeman and Min Cooper are very good at their jobs.'

'How do you get on with Leo? I should think he's fairly tricky to deal with – though I'm sure he wouldn't get away with trying to bully you.' Simon grinned. 'I must say I'd love to see you together.'

'I haven't met him yet,' said Raj carefully, 'but I think he already has some bee in his bonnet about me, from what Sarah says.'

'Good God – I'm amazed you got a new contract out of Rags without Leo's approval. Maybe he's learning to delegate properly. When is he due back from the States?'

'I think soon. I believe he's opening a new shop in Los Angeles at the moment, then he comes back – and we shall see.'

A few of the taller buildings in downtown Los Angeles could be seen dimly through the dirty orange smog as the 707 lost height over Pasadena, aiming at LAX airport. Leo could just make out the huge white sign on the Hollywood hills, obliquely lit by the evening sun. He was looking forward to the next week. Here they took celebrity very seriously. The last time he'd visited, he had been just a rich rag-trade nobody. This time he was founder of Rags, owner of the newest store on Rodeo Drive. His face and voice had filled many minutes of air time; photographs and descriptions of his products had filled thousands of column inches. There wasn't a fashion writer or gossip writer in the whole of California who wouldn't want to talk to him.

They were staying at the Hotel Bel Air. Lush quiet gardens surrounded the low building. Like everywhere in Beverly Hills, money and glamour were on view, but here at least it was private and Alison thankfully lay out by the pool and declared that she didn't want to move that evening. Liz and Leo had work to do, so together they drove off down to Rodeo.

Leo felt itchy. He wasn't in the mood for a quiet dinner *à deux* at the Bel Air, so he phoned Alison to tell her that he wouldn't be back till late. After a few cocktails at Joe Allen's, he ate with a group of English expatriates he had met at the bar. They all worked, or claimed to work, on the fringes of the movie business, and Leo enjoyed all the talk of wheeling and dealing. He didn't believe a quarter of it but it was a language he understood and, being on the outside, he had nothing to prove. He happily got talked into going on to the Troubador on Sunset. It was full of musicians and somehow he found himself talking earnestly to a black bass guitarist and studio engineer called Robinson.

Robinson was bright, likeable and from Detroit. He had come out here to work with one of the big sound studios and had quickly found himself in demand for both his technical and his musical skills. Twenty-eight years old and ambitious, he was certain that if he opened his own studios he could keep them fully booked. But he also knew that if he was to attract the big bands, he would have to endow his studio with some special and unique features. And these would cost money.

All sources of speculative finance had long queues at their doors and there were half a dozen proposals a week for studios, so Robinson was looking hard for money from outside. It only needed Leo to say how much he liked the life in LA and how he wished that he had more reasons for coming here for Robinson to come right back with an excellent reason.

He told Leo his plan for a two-centre studio: a long-term residential set-up in Papeete, Tahiti, with a short-booking sister-studio right here in Beverly Hills. In this way he could handle bands doing albums and any afterthoughts, re-mixes or over-dubs that they might want to do as well as commercials and movie soundtracks.

Leo was impressed by the financial logic, the energy and the sought-after skills of the charismatic young musician. In an odd way, he was flattered that Robinson had asked him for backing. And the notion of regular trips to Los Angeles with a musical involvement appealed to him very much. He asked Robinson to bring his written proposal to the Bel Air in two days' time, after the Rags opening was over.

The LA opening, though a little later than planned, went off without any problems. The response was less emphatic than in New York, but was as good as could be hoped for. The buying public in Beverly Hills was always ready for something new, and Rags was quite unique in Rodeo Drive. There was something novel about being able to walk into a fashion store and walk out with a frock and change from a hundred dollars. A lot of women who had longed to be able to shop in that famous street found that for the first time in their lives they could, without having to lie to their husbands. This time, Leo was relaxed about it all, and it showed in the interviews he gave. He wasn't trying so hard, and his spontaneous wit and elusive charisma were more evident.

Alison noticed this and was pleased to see it. But she determinedly kept away from the various functions and PR trappings that now seemed unavoidable in an American launch. She lay by the pool at the Bel Air or drove out to spend the day with friends by the beach at Malibu. She had had enough of the States and was looking forward to getting back to the familiar greyness of an English winter.

When Leo told her that they were staying on for an extra couple of days to talk to a man about a studio, she didn't argue. She just booked a seat on the next plane out. Leo, she felt, had changed their plans without consulting her just once too often. She wanted to go back now. Leo wanted to stay. So she would, and he could.

Leo watched her pack. He knew that there was no point in arguing. Alison, finally, always did what she wanted to do. And although she hadn't helped in LA, there was no doubt that she had been useful in New York and Dallas.

He shrugged, kissed the back of her neck as she bent over the suitcase and said quietly, 'Okay Angel, see you in London.'

Robinson arrived, as arranged, the next morning and, as Leo had guessed, his proposal and figures bore out everything that he had said in the Troubador. The projections were realistic without being unattractive, the cash-flow forecasts understated the pluses and overstated the minuses but the deal still looked good. Leo told Robinson that if he would forward a heads of agreement to London and an appropriate contract were drafted, he would provide the two hundred and fifty thousand dollars needed to get the project going and he anticipated no trouble in raising a further half-million for the next phase.

From his crocodile briefcase, Robinson produced a clear, concise eight-point letter of commitment for Leo to sign. It stated no more than Leo had just agreed to. He signed.

The manager of the Rainbow Room was able, honest and conscientious. A hard-working Englishman in his late thirties, he had not enjoyed any of the discussions or meetings that he had had with the club's proprietor. Now he sat behind his desk, impotent and frustrated, staring blindly at the photographs of celebrities on the wall without even trying to fend off the torrent of irrational anger directed at him by his furious boss.

'Look, you bloody little bureaucrat,' Leo was shouting, 'what the hell do you mean by telling me you're going to bill Rags for their Christmas party? I own both companies and it doesn't matter a *toss* which one pays.'

'Well, Leo, it does matter to me and the company I run for you. I don't want to preside over a business that makes bloody great losses because its owner wants to entertain the whole world without paying. Do you realise that if you or any other of your companies had paid all the bills run up by Rags's staff or models or journalists that you've okayed, we might be showing a profit? It's totally demoralising working my arse off while the club's haemorrhaging on your orders . . .'

'Listen,' Leo broke in, 'I'm knackered. I've been running round all over the States expanding the business that pays your wages, and I'm not interested in your book-keeping problems. Christ give me patience! First you tell me I can't take over my own club for a night because

292

it will annoy members who aren't invited and then you say I've got to pick up the tab!' Angry that the other would not look him in the eye, he advanced on the desk and slammed both fists down on it. 'It's my bloody club!' he yelled. 'Do you understand? Mine – and I can do what I want with it. I couldn't give a rabbi's foreskin what the members think. They're not interested in me and I'm not interested in them.'

'Leo,' said his manager, now looking straight at him. 'If that's your attitude to the club's customers and its finances, then it's never going to work. You made all sorts of promises about my profit-sharing – well, let me tell you, there aren't going to be any profits for me to share in, and I'm off '

He rose and walked round the desk. 'If you think you can use this place as a tax loss to offset against your rag-trade profits, forget it – it never works. A place like this is either a healthy viable entity in its own right or it folds, and I'm not hanging around to watch.'

'What the hell do you mean? You can't walk out! You've got a contract of employment.' He took a step towards the departing manager, his fists clenched.

'You thump me and I'll sue you.'

'What! You sue me?' Leo spluttered. 'I'll sue you for non-performance under the terms of your contract.'

'Listen you demented megalomaniac, you've got two choices – sue me, or stick my contract up your arse. I suggest you take the second option. It'll hurt you less because it'll cost you less.'

He slammed the door as hard as he could behind him. Outside, he bumped into Liz Macintosh.

'I wouldn't bother going in there, lassie. I think your boss – my ex-boss – is suffering from serious jet-lag. He's left half his brain somewhere between LA and New York.'

'Oh Christ,' said Liz. 'Has he sacked you?'

'No, he bloody hasn't – and the best of luck to you.'

Liz watched him walk away and waited a few moments before knocking on the recently slammed door.

'Yeah?' A dejected yell.

293

She went in to see Leo sitting behind the desk, his head on his hands. He looked up. 'Oh, it's you. Did you gather I'm minus a manager here?'

'Mm,' she nodded.

'Do you think I'm a demented megalomaniac?'

'Mm,' she nodded again and grinned. 'Don't you?'

'No – not demented, anyway,' he replied.

He asked Liz to take over as best she could, then walked back to his office, too preoccupied to acknowledge other people's greetings. He had arranged a meeting with Sarah and Min to review sales and production progress, and the two women were waiting for him in the boardroom with all the appropriate figures prepared and a display of the final production samples of the spring '74 range.

Leo was impressed – first with the figures. European sales to the end of November were up nearly thirty per cent on the previous year, pro rata floor space, and the lines they had pushed hardest had gone very well; the run-up to Christmas was looking very healthy.

'Perhaps I should go away more often,' he joked predictably. Sarah and Min didn't disagree.

Then he looked at the finished collection, which seemed to him as strong as any they had produced. He couldn't really fault it, though he grumbled about the colours. 'They're the same as last year's! I told you before I want to move out of these purples and petrols.'

'Leo,' said Sarah, not very patiently, 'they're paler than last year's and anyway, we were just a bit too early for the mass market then, and you're the one who's always shouting about not getting too far ahead.'

'Well, the sales figures say you're getting it right, so maybe you're learning.' He had picked a number of garments off the rail and was fingering through them. He inspected a forties-style cocktail dress with neat little pin tucks on the sleeve.

'Your dad's production is getting very snappy,' he remarked to Min.

'Oh, that's not dad's – he's only doing skirts now. It's easier for him and cheaper for us,' she replied. 'That's

294

West Textiles. We've given them most of the tops and some dresses.'

Leo looked blank. 'Who's West Textiles?'

'You know – Raju Kalianji,' said Min. 'He started making for us in October. We've had four deliveries now and they've all been perfect.'

Leo carried on fingering the dress in silence, then he put it down and walked round the room to the other end of the long table and stared down it at his sister.

'I thought I told you to cancel his contract,' he said quietly.

Sarah defiantly looked back at her brother, noticing without surprise his clenched teeth and heavily gathered brow. 'You did tell me and, if you recall, I refused. And what's more,' she went on, her voice rising, 'I was bloody well right.' She took a deep breath. 'Our decision was based on straightforward commercial reasons, not idiotic prejudices. So unless you've got very sound reasons, don't try and override us again – or you'll find yourself without a designer or a production director. Just remember, there are over five hundred people working in this company now, not just you, and a lot of them besides Min and me have got loads of enthusiasm and a lot of bright ideas – and, God knows why, a lot of loyalty. But if you carry on pushing people around and trampling all over their individuality, they're just going to walk away and, as I say, that includes me. All right?'

She glared at him, quite ready to carry through her threat. And he knew it.

'Okay,' he said, after a momentary struggle. 'It's a great range. The production's fine.' He paused. 'I think I'm going to go home and flake out.' He turned towards the door, then looked back. 'By the way, Liz Macintosh is looking after the Christmas thrash. That prat of a manager's walked out of the club and she's in charge of that too, for the moment, so if you need her, you'll find her there.'

Sarah sighed as the door clicked shut behind him. 'Poor Leo! He does hate to be beaten.'

Nobody missed the Rags Christmas party if they could help it, whether or not they had received an invitation. These parties had become legendary, and Leo had found that he had to employ special security guards to detect and eject gate-crashers. Furthermore, this was the first to be held in his own Rainbow Room, so expectations were high.

The room was decorated with dozens of stylised gold and maroon Christmas trees and art nouveau reindeers. Leo had arranged for a truck-load of mistletoe, plundered from the Herefordshire orchard of a friend in the cider trade, to be hung in a huge bundle over the centre of the dance floor, and the ceiling was criss-crossed with gold and maroon streamers.

Before the guests arrived, a thousand small dishes were laid out and filled with caviar. Case upon case of champagne was opened and the bottles placed in half-barrels of chipped ice. The barmen and their auxiliaries were busily pouring hundreds of 'Rags' cocktails, the varying viscosity of the multi-coloured ingredients producing a drink that was deep golden at the top, changing through a rich red to maroon, almost black, at the bottom of the glass. It was a fearsome drink, unlikely ever to be copied, and now traditional at these parties.

With only two weeks to go before Christmas, people were already in that mood of inexplicable euphoria which prevails, even among the godless, at the time of the feast of Christian rejoicing and this, and the party's reputation, predisposed them to believe that they were in for a good time – and there was no sense of anti-climax.

The spark of the gathering was the mix of guests. Besides the usual crowd of the rich, glamorous and fashionable, everyone who worked directly or indirectly for Rags, and who could get there, was there – shop assistants from Bath or Edinburgh even; trainee machinists from Nottingham; switchboard operators, secretaries and window dressers. It was their party, the outsiders were lucky to be there. The influx of eager, quite often pretty women, not normally seen in the London circuit, gave the party an extra and unusual dimension as they mixed among the models, journalists, photographers, television personalities, rock stars and young millionaires.

In keeping with the style of the place, Leo had booked the Pasadena Roof Orchestra. A curious cabaret act consisting of two geriatric drag queens occupied the supper interval and afterwards the strobe lights throbbed to the music of Led Zeppelin, Rod Stewart and David Bowie.

Leo, high on champagne, a little cocaine and the party's success, was enjoying himself. When he had stood up to welcome his guests and introduce the cabaret, he had been greeted with tumultuous applause, into which he read affection and approval. People were constantly approaching him to congratulate him and thank him, and any rows or disagreements he may have had with them were temporarily forgotten. He even managed to have a polite conversation with Tony Lonsberg, the up-and-coming denim merchant, fast emerging as his main rival for prime high-street sites.

His mood of *bonhomie* was rudely jerked out of gear later in the evening when he saw his sister sitting at a side table in earnest, animated conversation with an elegant, black-tied and undeniably handsome Indian. He approached their table and without waiting for an introduction from Sarah, thrust his hand across it. 'I'm Leo Freeman,' he said and sat down in a vacant chair before he'd finished his aggressive handshake.

'I'm Raj Kalianji. Thank you for this splendid party.' He waved his now free hand disdainfully around the room.

Sarah sat between them apprehensive and angry. 'Raj owns West Textiles, who are making for us now,' she said unnecessarily.

'Yes,' said Leo, his eyes fixed on Raj, 'I'd worked that out.' The Indian's voice had been badgering his memory cells. Then he remembered. 'We've met before,' he said. 'Years ago in King's Road.'

'Yes,' agreed Raj calmly.

'You tried to tell me how to run my business.'

Sarah looked at Raj, amazed. 'You never told me that.'

'It was an unimportant incident, and we weren't introduced. Anyway, I wasn't certain until now that it was your brother.'

'Not many secrets between you two then?' Leo asked Sarah with sarcasm. 'I hope you won't let your friendship affect your judgement.'

'For Christ's sake, Leo,' she hissed. 'We've been through all this. Raj's factory is turning out a bloody good product and you know it – so don't push your luck.'

'Well, as long as he doesn't start telling me how to run my business again,' said Leo.

'So far as it affects me, I assure you I will,' replied Raj in a matter-of-fact tone.

'You're bloody sure of yourself for a Paki who's only been in the business five minutes.'

'Oh God, Leo. Don't make a scene now. Just piss off and let all those phoney friends of yours fawn all over you.'

When Leo didn't move, Raj turned to Sarah.

'Would you like to dance?'

She nodded, and they left the table.

Leo glared after them and Alison, who had noticed the last part of the scene, came over and sat down.

'What's the matter with you? Did he get the better of you?' She put her hand on his, but he withdrew it. 'Come on – enjoy yourself. Don't antagonise Sarah. I presume that was the famous Raju Kalianji with her?'

'Yes, it bloody was. It's bad enough having greasy wogs manufacturing for us, without Sarah letting them inside her knickers.'

'Leo, why are you always so jealous of Sarah's boyfriends? She's your sister, for God's sake.'

'I'm not jealous of him – I just don't want to see her fucked about. She thinks she's so tough but she's bloody vulnerable. And she's deliberately gone after that Paki because she knows it'll annoy me.'

Alison laughed. 'You flatter yourself. God knows you deserve to have your nose put out of joint, but she fancies Raj for much more positive reasons than that. He's certainly very beautiful, and a change from all the other shmucks that chase after her.'

'Well if he's out of order once, with her or with his production, he'll bloody well hear about it from me – and that's a promise.'

Min Cooper tentatively knocked on the door of Leo's office. She had wanted to talk to Sarah before seeing him, but Sarah was having a couple of weeks' holiday with Alison in Marbella over Easter, and the problem that had cropped up incensed her so much that she wanted to deal with it immediately herself.

A large consignment had arrived from West Textiles, on time and of faultless quality as usual. But checking through the delivery, as she occasionally did, she came across a factory cutting docket muddled in with the delivery notes. Idly she had wondered why, and was about to throw it away when she noticed the cloth costings.

The arrangement that Rags now had with Raj – and this was unusual for them – was that he would supply complete garments at a price that included cloth and trimmings. Raj had suggested, quite logically, that it was much easier for him to plan production if he were in direct contact with the cloth merchants and manufacturers, so orders were placed with West Textiles specifying the garment and the cloth to be used, as well as the precise yardage required for each garment. This was referred to in the trade as the 'costing', and on the basis of this costing, an inclusive price for the garment was reached.

What was clear from the production docket was that the factory had used about seven per cent less cloth than had been stipulated for the garments. By making a comparison with the production sample and their own design sample, she could not see that the garments in the delivery had been skimped to save cloth. The hems were a fraction narrower, but not enough to make a difference to the finish or, as far as she could see, a significant difference to the amount of cloth used.

It was Min's view that a factory was honour-bound to

inform a customer if they had achieved a tighter costing than had been the basis of the original order – certainly, in her parents' factory, clients were always told. It created greater trust and strengthened a factory's case on the occasions when they considered the costing that they had been given to be impossibly tight.

She felt, in view of Raj's close, albeit newly-forged, relationship with them, that he should have told them of the savings he was making. Because Raj dealt direct with cloth suppliers, he was presumably only ordering sufficient for his costs and saving himself the difference. She estimated that on ten thousand garments a week he could be earning an extra five or six hundred pounds – twenty-five thousand pounds a year. Min was hurt and outraged to discover it, so she hadn't waited until Sarah returned. Her loyalty to Sarah lay second to her loyalty to the company.

Leo answered her knock sharply, but looked up and smiled when he saw who it was. 'Hi, Min. What do you want?' He looked at his watch. 'Do you want a drink?'

Min nodded. 'Yes, a large vodka – I need one.'

Leo poured a long measure of Stolichnaya and added some tonic and ice from the fridge.

'What's the trouble – are you pregnant or something?'

'No, no. It's to do with West Textiles' latest delivery.'

Leo tensed up. 'Has that greasy brown bugger been short-delivering? Christ, I'll have his bollocks!'

'No, he wouldn't do that – deliveries are always spot on,' said Min, alarmed at the intensity of Leo's reaction. 'It's not as bad as that. It's just that one of his production dockets is mixed in with the delivery notes and he's used a seven per cent lower costing.'

'What, he's trimmed off the garments?' said Leo, delighted anger in his eyes. 'That's just as bad.'

'No,' said Min, 'The garments are perfect. He obviously somehow managed a tighter costing.'

'There's no way he could get in by that much, is there?'

Min shook her head. 'I don't see how.'

'Right. I'll get him round here and find out what the hell

300

he's up to.' He pressed the intercom to his secretary. 'Get me Raju Kalianji at West Textiles – right now.'

A moment later, the phone tinkled once and he picked up the handset. 'Mr Kalianji? It's Leo Freeman. We want you round here, like immediately. There's some discrepancies on your latest docket . . . You come round here and I'll tell you what discrepancies . . . What do you mean you can't? We're your best bloody client and when I say come round, you come – okay? . . . I don't give a damn if you've got a date with the six-armed dancing goddess. You come here. You'll just have to be late for your chicken ring-stinger and chapatis . . . If you think I was offensive then, you wait . . .' He looked up furiously. 'Shit! The bastard's hung up.'

The next morning, Raj was already sitting in the reception area at the Rags offices when Leo arrived. When he saw Leo, he uncrossed his legs, folded the *Financial Times* he had been reading and stood up.

'Mr Freeman, if you want my company to carry on producing for you, I think you'd better explain your outburst on the telephone last night.'

Leo was about to yell at him, but stopped himself. Staff were still arriving. Various suppliers and other commercial visitors were waiting around for appointments. He led the way to the office and waved Raj to a leather-seated chair. Then he placed Rags's original order, with all its stipulations, on the desk in front of Raj and beside it a photocopy of the West Textiles production docket.

Raj glanced at them, then at Leo. 'Is there supposed to be something significant about these two documents?'

'Bloody right there is! Look at the difference in costings – nearly seven and a half per cent, and presumably you've been pocketing it.'

'I haven't pocketed anything. I've merely ordered sufficient cloth to fulfil the orders you've placed with me.'

'Thereby making an extra seven and a half per cent on cloth costs,' said Leo exasperated.

'Rather more than that, actually. I am in the happy

position of being able to pay cash on delivery for all my cloth requirements, for which suppliers are prepared to grant me a three and three-quarters per cent discount, so, in this particular case, I was saving some twelve per cent – sometimes it's more, sometimes less.'

'How the hell are you able to reduce so much on our costings?' demanded Leo.

'As I remember you pointing out to me last time we met at your lavish Christmas party, I am a mere pipsqueak, a newcomer to this industry – though, incidentally, I am not a Pakistani – therefore, it should come as no surprise to you who are an old hand in the trade that it is possible to alter a costing quite substantially in a very long lay. We use a forty-foot cutting-table, and with a lot of concentration and ingenuity we can usually improve on the costings stipulated.'

'Okay – so you find you're producing cabbage, that's normal; one or two per cent maybe – but that cabbage is ours.'

'Cabbage' was the term used in the trade for garments cut from a client's cloth surplus to the specific quantities ordered.

'Mr Freeman, what you are saying is both wrong and irrelevant. First, there is a medieval common law precedent for a garment manufacturer to retain title to any over-cuts – "a tailor is entitled to his cabbage". Secondly, since you are not supplying the cloth, that particular question does not arise. If you order a hundred dozen pieces of a particular style in a particular cloth, that's exactly what you get – at a pre-negotiated price. If you aren't happy with the service we are giving you, I suggest you look elsewhere.' Raj got to his feet. 'Please let me know if you'll be sending any further orders. You are not the only retailer who wants what we can offer – and I do not have to swallow your offensive, ignorant abuse in order to stay in business.'

Before Leo could answer, Raj had left the room and closed the door behind him.

The first half of 1974 presented a wildly fluctuating graph of high points and low points for Leo.

On the up side, to his surprised relief, Danielle Milinaire's collection launched as 'Danielle at Rags' in Paris, was well received there and seemed to broaden the store's appeal. Even Sarah grudgingly admitted that it had worked, and discussions about its introduction into the UK and America were initiated. Leo considered it the possible basis for a wholesale range now that, in his view, Rags had saturated its UK retail market. Of course, they would go on introducing the broader non-clothing lines into those shops big enough to accommodate them, but he could see no further scope for rapid growth in his British retailing operation.

Sarah was sceptical about entering the wholesale market. It was subject to a very different set of rules. She was accustomed to designing direct for the consumer without the intermediary input or veto of the store-buyers, and Leo was accustomed to running a business with high margins and constant cash flow.

But the need for increased production would continue to force Leo to accept that Raj Kalianji's contribution was vital, and in a perverse confusion of loyalties, Sarah overlooked her scepticism and tacitly concurred with Leo's views.

The American operation meanwhile seemed to have got bogged down. It was covering its costs, though not servicing its investment, and these costs seemed to be rising uncontrollably. Salaries were enormous and all the ancillary costs – lawyers, accountants – were far higher than Leo had budgeted. They were selling a lot of product by European standards, but making no money.

Leo had flown over a couple of times to try and plug the leaks. On his second visit, in LA, he had been confronted by a sour-faced Robinson, the studio entrepreneur, demanding the first tranche of a quarter of a million dollars that Leo had agreed to invest.

Leo could no doubt have found some get-out from the commitment that he had made in signing the heads of agreement, but the very fact of his US operation's lack of profit made him irrationally anxious not to lose face, so he arranged funds, at unsatisfactory rates, through his New York bank and Robinson was suddenly all smiles and enthusiastic bear-hugs.

At home, Alison found Leo's moods becoming even more volatile and he was less forthcoming than usual about his business preoccupations. She was also fairly certain now that he was having an affair with Danielle – at least on his trips to Paris. Sarah, when they had been in Spain together, had more or less confirmed it, even suggested that she might perpetrate a jealousy ploy, but Alison had shaken her head. 'When I married Leo, I accepted him for everything he was – good and bad. His standards aren't mine – and I don't see what right I have to insist that he changes them. On the other hand, I'm not going to lower mine. Anyway, I'm simply not interested in any other men sexually, and I feel guilty that I haven't been able to give him any children.'

She had, instead, thrown herself among her art and theatre friends and her horses. She kept two fine, very expensive thoroughbreds in stables in Hampshire. Claire, her sister-in-law, had a horse there too, and Alison had grown to enjoy her company.

She had also recently developed an interest in Andalusian horses. On trips to Seville and Jerez she had been impressed by their elegance and intelligence.

She had been introduced to one of the better-known Spanish breeders who had invited her to his stud for a closer inspection. There she had enjoyed the experience of riding a fully-schooled Andalusian.

On a subsequent trip, she had arranged to buy two mares and a stallion, which were now ready to be shipped to England. These, too, would be stabled in Hampshire. She intended to breed from them and then school the offspring herself. Both activities were, to her, absorbing challenges and provided an escape at times when her husband's moods became too oppressive.

In spite of Leo's reluctance to divulge details of his

business circumstances, she did gather the gist of his problems and she exulted in the good news and sympathised over the bad. But she couldn't understand his obsessive animosity towards Raj Kalianji. She knew from Sarah, who was probably biased, and Min, who wasn't, that Raj's company had, inside a year, become a vital, almost irreplaceable source of production. Usually Leo was inclined to like and generally promote the people who contributed to the continuing success and profitability of his company, but in the case of Kalianji, he evidently found this impossible.

When Alison asked him why, he was evasive and unclear. 'I resent the way that he insinuated himself into Rags through Sarah. The trouble is, he gives a bloody good service and Min is right behind him. He's talked her out of her resentment over that costing business. I told her and Sarah dozens of times that it's dangerous to be so reliant on one particular factory, but they argue that his prices and production are worth the risk and they won't back down.'

Alison had also heard Simon's revised – and disappointed – opinion of Raj. But Simon, less acrimonious, had a more rational opinion. 'We can't judge him too harshly. After all, against heavy odds, he's achieved what he set out to, and more. He's received no real help or encouragement from us, and he's had to put up with a lot of envy and prejudice. If he seems less idealistic and more aloof, I think the English people he's had to deal with are as much to blame as anyone else. Especially people like Leo.'

Alison agreed, but wondered aloud if Raj wasn't deliberately taking advantage of Sarah's adulation.

'He'd have to be a saint not to,' replied Simon.

That autumn, Nathan Freeman died of pneumonia after suffering a heart attack.

Sarah was too upset to be of comfort to her mother and Alison stayed for three nights with Miriam in the house in Highgate. She knew that Leo was more distraught than he had expected to be, but he was unable to demonstrate this to Miriam. Alison felt a vague alarm, as well as sadness, at the passing of old Nathan for, although Leo ostensibly took no notice of his father, she knew that many of Nathan's more commonsense attitudes lurked at the back of Leo's consciousness, and that somehow he had always harboured a need for his father's approval. His death had severed an umbilical cord and Alison was concerned for her husband's stability. No one besides Miriam understood her concern, and it was as much for her own sake as her mother-in-law's that she stayed in Highgate.

The funeral was a dismal affair. It was cold, windy and drizzling. Several of Nathan's old staff, whom Leo hadn't seen for years, stared at him across the open grave, resentfully – even accusingly – as if he had caused his father's heart attack!

There was a mournful little wake at Miriam's house. Leo left early, pleading inescapable business commitments, which he thought everyone would understand. They didn't, of course. Alison tried to persuade him to stay and Sarah scowled as he left.

When he reached his office after a slow, thoughtful drive back, he was greeted with a piece of news that was both good and bad. Raju Kalianji had just informed them that he had contracted to buy the total production of a factory in Hong Kong with a quota of half a million garments per annum into the European market.

This quota was set under the auspices of the Multi-fibre Arrangements, and was supposed to protect the indigenous textile industries of the developed world from 'unfair' competition from countries with lower labour costs. There were loopholes and there was scope for abuse but, on the whole, it worked, and the quota system had a, no doubt predicted, by-product: it made the imported garments more expensive. Because there was so much competition for quota in exporting countries, quota itself had become a marketable commodity. Indeed, a producer who had managed to have himself allocated a substantial quantity of exportable garments under this system, could often make more money by shutting down his factory and selling his quota. The going rate might be HK$1 per unit, adding some twenty-five per cent onto the exported price of a garment.

So Raj, in buying a business with a fairly substantial allocation, had been prepared to pay well. His intention, however, was to make and export garments to the ready-made markets which he had in the UK, and to Rags in the US.

All the same, he had no plans to drop his prices, but had been forced to inform Rags and his other clients that he was going to use Hong Kong product, since he would need their orders earlier in the season, and the law required that garments were labelled with their country of origin.

Since there was still, in Britain, an unwarranted association between Hong Kong and cheap, shoddy garments, Leo was insistent that he would accept Hong Kong production only for the simple garments from the bottom end of the range and would pay substantially less for them. He congratulated himself on recognising that Raj would have to accept this since he was committed to selling his production, and all his customers would be saying the same thing.

So pleased was Leo at the end of the meeting which had resulted in Raj climbing down over prices, that he was almost affable in his offer of champagne. It was only a very minor victory for Leo, so Raj inclined his head and accepted with no display of disgruntlement.

Leo laughed, 'I'll grant you this, Raj, it takes a good businessman to recognise the inevitable.' And for once there seemed to exist a mood of cooperation between them.

Since Prem Patel had arrived in England with his family in 1969, he had successfully established himself as an importer and wholesaler of electrical and electronic goods.

He had recently moved into a large Edwardian house in a pleasant suburb of Ealing, in West London. Patel prided himself on his independence and freedom from what he called the 'ghetto mentality'. He had encouraged his daughters' efforts at school and had many friends and contacts who weren't Indian. He nevertheless preserved a traditional attitude to his family and their morals.

Raj had been invited over ostensibly for an informal dinner, but, as he well knew, he was going to be grilled over the state of his business, and his attitude to the proposed marriage with Reena.

Mr Patel greeted him with a hearty handshake. 'Have a beer, old man,' he said, 'or a Scotch?'

The two men settled in armchairs in the Patels' large, very English drawing-room. The women had not appeared.

'I hear things are going very well with West Textiles.'

Raj nodded and Mr Patel went on. 'Gita tells me that the clothes you are making are all the rage – I'm afraid she won't be seen dead in a sari now.' He laughed. 'Her mother is very worried, but after all, she's been at school here for five years. Reena, on the other hand, is very much the traditionalist. She's left college, you know. She's a secretary with one of those big companies in the Uxbridge Road. But when she gets back from work, there's nothing she likes better than a gossip with her mother and aunts while she's cooking a fine meal. She's making dinner for us this evening, by the way.'

Raj knew that he was supposed to approve of this evidence of wifely qualities. In general he did, and a good secretarial training could do no harm.

Mr Patel carried on. 'But about your position, now. You must be ready for marriage. After all, you're twenty-eight and business is good, isn't it?'

'Well, Mr Patel,' said Raj cautiously, 'I am being very careful not to draw profits out of my business. It is developing according to my plans, but I don't anticipate being in a position to support a family for a year or so.'

'But, my dear chap, we will of course be helping to provide. Naturally, you will be wanting a house of your own – and I've already been looking at some with you and Reena in mind.' His eyes twinkled. 'No mortgage millstone round the neck of my son-in-law!'

'Even so,' Raj said hastily, 'I still won't be prepared.'

'But it can't surely be that your business isn't on a sound footing? I've heard about this trip to Hong Kong you've made, and the factory there.'

'Well, that's the point really. I had to pay a high price to the Sindi who sold it to me, and I'm very highly geared at the moment. Hong Kong money is not particularly cheap.'

Mr Patel nodded appreciatively. 'You've not bitten off more than you can chew, then?'

'No, but it will take a year to see a return on the investment.'

'All right, though with Reena coming up for twenty I was hoping to get a date settled. But I can see you are a sensible, cautious fellow, so I won't push the issue for the moment; though you know your parents are just as keen.'

Raj nodded. He knew.

Mr Patel rose and walked over to the door to call the girls and their mother. When Reena came into the room, Raj was impressed again by her striking but serene looks. She shook hands with him coyly, returning his greeting with an embarrassed murmur. He wondered how on earth she coped with brusque English bosses.

Gita, only fourteen, was bouncing with enthusiasm, demanding if Raj had brought any free samples of clothing. She spoke English with a thoroughly English accent and idiom and had none of the reticence of the normal Indian girl. She was, with her vivaciousness, at least as attractive as her sister.

Over dinner, as Raj chatted with them and they listened to his stories of the fashion business and his travels to the Far East, he constantly compared his relationship with Sarah to the kind of relationship that he could expect with Reena. At least, he thought, Reena would make few emotional demands on him and would undoubtedly be dutiful – and by marrying her, he knew he would be doing his duty to his parents.

It had been at the launch party for the Rags wholesale range in the autumn that someone suggested to Raj that

309

he should have a look at the increasing demand for sophisticated western clothing made from traditional Indian cloths. There was no doubt that what had started in the sixties as a specifically ethnic look of questionable finish had developed into an established look that co-existed with mainstream fashion. European designers had gone to India and made contact with manufacturers who were prepared to up-grade to the standard of production demanded, and an identifiable and not unsizeable market had revealed itself.

The look, strongly represented by firms like Monsoon and Anohki, relied on the practical application of the vast variety of traditional Rajastahni prints to relevant western garments. There was, in northern Europe particularly, a continuing fascination with the shapes and colours of these hand-block prints upon fine, cool cottons.

Raj's commercial reaction to the suggestion was that it involved a complicated series of stages to supply a minority market of doubtful future. But there again, it could prove very profitable, and he harboured a nagging desire to see if his increasingly dismissive attitude towards his Indian culture was justified. It would, at least, be interesting to look at the possibilities, perhaps on the way back from his next visit to Hong Kong.

Sarah was enthusiastic when he mentioned it to her. 'Of course, that look's not for us,' she added regretfully, 'but there could be one or two things that would fit in – accessories, maybe scarves or bags. You're right, though, there is still a strong feel for that kind of thing. If I were you I'd at least research it a bit. Don't you think it would be great to have the excuse to go to India? You could explore your roots. I'm sure you'd find it very inspiring to be surrounded by the living evidence.'

Raj shook his head. 'To be frank, I doubt it. The people I know here who have come from India don't appear to be all that inspired. Their main preoccupations are with Japanese cars and stereo systems. Still, I'm interested enough to stop off. I'll go there after the New Year.'

Raj's indifference to what Sarah considered such a rich

cultural and religious heritage puzzled her. She was convinced that his self-possession and supreme confidence were products of an inherent spirituality, and it was this, above all, that allowed her to give herself to him so completely in mind and body. She would have loved to accompany him on his first trip to India, but felt that it was something he should do on his own – and anyway, she had learned by now that, in their relationship, initiatives came only from him.

She discussed Raj's proposed trip with Min and Leo. Leo was sceptical about the commercial viability, but remarked, 'At least it shows that there's a human heart buried in his super-cool exterior.' For he had slowly and grudgingly conceded the Indian's abilities, and could not deny that Raj had made a significant contribution to Rags's sales and profitability over the past year.

The existence of a finished and marketable wholesale range had been largely due to the Indian's rigorous efficiency and attention to details. He had been instrumental in turning Danielle Milinaire's range from a high-price, minority product into a commercial mass-market range, by inspired compromise on styling and cloths.

While the press were ready to be enthusiastic, given Rags's spectacular track record, the other retailers were inclined to be as critical as they could – but, once again, Leo's instincts had not let him down. Danielle's range was sufficiently removed from Sarah's look to silence any objections that other stores which stocked it would simply be competing with Rags's own shops. There was a pronouncedly Italian feel to it which set it apart from the Englishness of Rags.

And so the stores had bought, for Spring '75, and Leo was hailed as having launched another winner. But he knew, Sarah and Min knew, and Raj knew, that it was due to West Textiles and its Hong Kong production that the collection had been such a success.

# February 1975

The airport in Delhi had a very decrepit air about it at two in the morning. Long queues shuffled slowly past khaki-uniformed immigration officials. Raj tendered his British passport, was scrutinised with a cold stare, and asked in English the purpose and duration of his stay.

He picked his way fastidiously through the crowds and out past disinterested Customs. He was quite unprepared for the sights and smells when he emerged from the arrivals building. Hundreds of ragged men squatted and leaned on the ancient, battered, vaguely English saloon cars that served as Delhi's taxis. Small braziers glowed here and there, and the smell of cheap petrol was overwhelming. His turbaned porter, carrying one suitcase on his head and another in his hand, led him arbitrarily to one of the waiting cars. The driver demanded the name of Raj's hotel and set off wildly through the car park, heedless of pedestrians and other vehicles. As they drove through the wide boulevards of New Delhi, Raj was amazed by the number of people walking at the side of the road at this time of night. What he saw appalled him. Everything seemed so shabby and unkempt, and the people so poor. The only sign of his much-vaunted cultural heritage were three gaudy plastic statuettes of the gods Krishna and Ganesh stuck on the top of the car's dashboard.

The Taj Mahal Hotel seemed like an oasis of civilised calm, and with relief Raj sank into bed.

The next morning he asked the hotel to book him a seat on the next flight to Jaipur and was told there was none to be had. He decided to try and change that by personal haranguing and took a taxi to the Indian Airlines office.

As they crossed the great wide avenue that leads through India Gate up to the old Viceroy's palace, he told the driver to turn into it and drive him up through the magnificent complex of Lutyens' government buildings. This is grand indeed, he thought, and the bloody British built it. The uncompromising magnificence of the neo-classical, slightly oriental iron-stone buildings were enhanced by their imposing position atop a gentle rise. The lush gardens of the old Viceroy's – now the President's – palace could be glimpsed through fine wrought-iron gates. Raj was impressed by the richly flowered roundabouts and well-groomed margins of the avenues around the diplomatic and governmental residences – but, he thought, it owes nothing to Indians.

With very little pressure, he secured himself a ticket for the afternoon flight to Jaipur, then told his taxi-driver to take him to the famous Red Fort of Old Delhi.

This Delhi was a startling contrast to the new city. Narrow streets lined with dilapidated buildings were crammed with trucks, buses, bicycles and pedestrians. The little motor-rickshaws, driven with grim determination, seemed to put their passengers' lives in jeopardy every few minutes, but no one was alarmed.

When at last Raj reached the great Mogul fortress, he was impressed by this very different style of magnificence. Three, four hundred years after they were built, the great marble pavilions within still demonstrated a power and opulence that must have been utterly overwhelming to the people of the time. The Moguls, of course, had not been Indians either. They were Muslim raiders from the Hindu Kush who knew how to kill, mused Raj, but they had also had a remarkable appreciation of the arts and had used their might to sponsor great architects, poets, artists and craftsmen.

On his way back to New Delhi, he found himself unable to reconcile this past cultural greatness with the squalor of the crowded streets around it, and it was in a state of frustration and apprehension that he boarded the little passenger plane to Jaipur that afternoon.

The Rambagh Palace had been remodelled by the reigning Maharajah in the 1920s in order to provide accommodation for part of his vast household and many European guests. The demise of the Indian princes and the reduction of their power and privy purses had forced economies on Jai Singh, the previous maharajah, and in the late fifties the Rambagh Palace had become one of India's finest hotels.

The great rooms and the terraces were impeccable. The building had been converted to the highest level of luxury, with all the modern features which that entailed but with little loss to the inherent character of the palace.

On the evening he arrived, Raj strolled around the grounds, and then sat contemplatively on the wide, cloistered terrace beside the Polo Bar and looked out across the lawns to a fortress perched on the top of a nearby rocky hillock. The calm air was pierced by the occasional shriek of a peacock, but even these and the harsh voices of excited American tourists couldn't detract from the sounds of sitar and tabla drifting from the open dining-room windows.

This, thought Raj, is India.

The next day, he took a taxi through the old Pink City of Jaipur to visit a small workshop that had been recommended to him by contacts in London.

Here, in the old town, the original beauty and the evidence of thoughtful planning by its founder were not entirely obscured by the crowds on the streets. What astonished him most was the number of animals: hump-backed cows, protected by their holy status, wandered everywhere; monkeys scampered along the roof-tops, engaged in never-ending territorial skirmishes; placid, bored-looking camels trudged slowly in front of heavily laden two-wheeled carts and small boys, perched at the front of flat-top trailers, urged their short-striding, fast-trotting ponies with competitive wielding of long sticks.

Weaving among these and the bullock carts, the bicycle-rickshaws plied for trade, their riders hungry enough to be undaunted by the prospect of three or four large women clambering onto the back seats of their tricycles.

The shops and stalls were seething with people. Everyone seemed to be tremendously busy. The city's economy was thriving, but at such a low level as to make this incomprehensible to someone now accustomed to a welfare state and the safety net that it provided for the poorest in most western societies. Here, the only unemployed seemed to be limbless or leprous beggars. Raj wondered if any of London's jobless would be prepared to pedal shoppers up and down Oxford Street. He doubted it.

Raj's contact was an English girl, a designer, married to a Jaipuri. This couple had set up a line of supply from weavers, through dyers, hand-printers, block-makers and tailors' workshops that allowed them to control the designs and colours of the prints as well as the style of the finished garments.

They arranged to have Raj driven fifteen or so miles out of the town to a village where a family had occupied themselves for generations in the preparation of vegetable dyes and their application to locally woven cotton.

These dyes were painstakingly printed with amazing accuracy on to the cloth with small hand blocks, perhaps six inches square. The blocks had been carved with great intricacy and detail into the grain of shallow slices of *shisham* or rosewood. Charity Singh, the English girl, was constantly thinking up new variants of the traditional Rajastahni prints, and would draw the two or three different coloured components of the design on to tracing paper. The block-makers, with fine chisels, would then chip them into three-dimensional existence.

The garments they produced at that time still leaned heavily on the past decade's western understanding of Indian prints and their uses, but there was no reason why more currently marketable garments should not be produced. Raj gave them two dress patterns. By the next

315

day samples had been made and costed. He was very impressed with the finish – and the price.

They discussed at great length his access to large European retailers, and the Singhs, with a strange reluctance, agreed that it would probably suit them to deal with him. Raj realised that Charity was the only European woman he had ever met who didn't either talk down to him or patronisingly over-compensate. It was his first experience of dealing with a white woman for whom difference of race was completely irrelevant. Oddly, this slightly disturbed him: he felt somehow more transparent and slightly less in control than he normally would have been.

These were not serious misgivings, however, and having assured them that he would involve them in styling as much as possible, he offered them two return tickets to London to organise the beginning of a range for production in Jaipur.

Raj rang Sarah the day after he arrived back in London and asked her to meet him for dinner at Jay's restaurant in Westbourne Grove. He told her what he had seen and what he planned to do, for he was certain he could make Jaipur an effective, though limited, source. He acknowledged, and thanked her for, her enthusiasm in persuading him to go.

'But, Raj, you must tell me how you found it – whether you felt an affinity with what you saw,' Sarah said.

'I'm relieved to say I didn't,' he replied.

Sarah looked shocked, affronted even.

'Look,' he soothed, 'India is a very large, very poor country. The main preoccupation is with getting enough to eat, and this doesn't leave much time for the spiritual introspection you're so keen on. I'm sure there are many admirable *sadhus*, you know, holy men, but I didn't see any, and to be quite honest, they don't seem all that relevant to India's problems today.'

'But didn't you feel some kind of sympathy with what you saw? Didn't you feel you belonged?'

Raj's eyes focused for a moment on an unseen horizon,

then he turned back to Sarah. 'To be honest, I don't feel that I belong anywhere,' and, watching Sarah's reaction, 'but please don't feel sympathy on my behalf – it is a great source of strength to me.'

Leo was in a telephone booth in the California Yacht Club in Marina del Rey. He heard the London number he had dialled click and crackle its way through the transatlantic cables.

Why the hell was Alison so stubborn? Why did she make herself so difficult? She had refused to come to LA for the opening of the first part of Robinson's studio, and Leo, waiting impatiently in the bar to meet some English friends, had impulsively decided to call and insist that she join him. A slight diminution of the clicking down the line told Leo that he was through to the London telephone system, then he heard the unmistakable sound of a crossed line joining his. When this interruption ceased, he heard a breathless, female voice ask, 'Hello, hello. Is that King's Cross?'

Leo groaned. 'No it isn't. This is the California Yacht Club – in Los Angeles.'

The caller was indignant. 'But I dialled King's Cross – and you're English.'

'Look, lady, I'm in LA trying to call my wife in London, and you've got a crossed line – so put your phone down and try again,' Leo bellowed. The line went dead and Leo, swearing, was preparing to re-dial when he felt a hand fall heavily across his shoulder and heard a laugh and an English voice say, 'Good old Leo, giving some innocent old biddy a hard time?'

Leo turned and saw Tony Lonsberg and a friend grinning at him. Both were in the jeans business in London. Leo had heard they were in Marina del Rey and had telephoned Tony to suggest they meet up.

Tony had recently bought a seventy-five-foot, aluminium-hulled ketch from the widow of a San Francisco businessman who had driven his Cessna into the side of a mountain. He was, in easy stages, sailing it back to Lyming-

317

ton in England, and had invited a few friends to join him on the LA to Acapulco leg of the journey.

'Come on board and have a drink,' he said. Leo abandoned the telephone and they walked from the clubhouse down a long pontoon where the ketch, *White Fin*, was moored in the prime position on the T at the end.

She was a spectacular and businesslike vessel, with a main mast of one hundred and ten feet and an inverted sawn-off transom. A crew of five hefty, blond Californians were busy polishing, repairing and making ready for the long trip. A long-legged, six-foot American girl was sitting in the stern cockpit, rubbing oil into her tanned thighs.

'Meet the cook,' said Tony waving a hand towards her. He produced bottles of Coors beer and they sat in the warm spring evening trading gossip and trying to cap each other's stories of their more outrageous activities.

'How did you get involved in this studio?' Tony asked, 'Isn't it a bit outside your sphere of interest?'

'Not really. One trading operation is much the same as another – and there are big bucks in the music industry out here. All the big rock stars and writers from England come over here to work. And there's a lot of spin-off from the movie industry.'

'Yeah, but you know what you're doing in the rag-trade – do you know anything about the music business?'

'Not a lot, but I'm learning. And Robinson, the guy who's setting it up, knows it inside out.'

Tony looked sceptical. 'I wouldn't like to be relying so heavily on one man. What has it cost you so far?'

Leo looked uncomfortable. 'Oh, not too much – it's all come out of the profits of our US operation.'

Tony was doubtful, but didn't go into it further.

Leo asked them to come up to Sunset for the studio party and, in return, was invited to sail with them for the first day down to Newport Beach. Later that evening they went to have dinner in one of the steak restaurants that surround the marina. They found a group of three girls having dinner on their own and, without much difficulty, persuaded them to join their table.

Leo by now had drunk a lot, and his earlier annoyance at Alison was replaced by an inebriated lust for one of the girls they had picked up. While he was in the lavatory, Tony, in the next stand-up, said, 'You'll be all right there. They all suffer from weak knicker elastic in this town.'

Leo offered to drive the girl home.

'Just across town,' she said, but in Los Angeles that meant thirty miles or so. When they arrived in Leo's rented Ferrari at the extravagant portico of the girl's apartment block, to his astonished anger, she refused to invite him in. And wriggling out from under his groping arms, she heaved herself out of the low seat and slammed the car door shut. 'Listen, asshole, I just wanted a ride home, and that doesn't entitle you to ride me.'

She strode quickly up the front steps of the building, let herself in and disappeared before Leo could clamber out and catch her up.

Leo drove back to the Bel Air, bitterly frustrated. He saw this rejection as something of a bad omen. He was already nervous about his businesses in America, and he knew very well that he was getting out of his depth with Robinson's studio.

In his suite, he drank half a bottle of Scotch before he could get to sleep and, next morning, feeling terrible, was even more depressed. With an effort, he forced himself into a positive frame of mind and after several pints of fruit juice and coffee, drove down to spend the rest of the morning at the Rags store in Rodeo Drive.

The shop was busy, and Leo couldn't complain about sales. The new accessories and household lines were also doing very well there. But when he was sitting stretched out on a sofa in the manager's office, the physical discomfort he was already feeling as a result of the previous evening's excesses was suddenly worsened by a sinking of his stomach at some news the manager had for him.

'We may have a problem, though, boss,' drawled the deceptively laid-back young Italian American who ran the store. 'A lot of the boutiques on Sunset and Santa Monica are selling identical copies of our gear – same cloth, same make; some have got no brand names and some have got Rags labels. And some of the cheaper ladies who came in here at first have started to buy these copies. The Rodeo Drive ladies ain't gonna carry on buying when they know the stuff can be bought for a third of the price in the down-town stores.'

Leo stood up, his temples throbbing and his eyebrows knitted in an angry band across his forehead. 'Where the hell are they coming from? Are all the deliveries checking out here?'

His manager nodded.

'Somebody's got to be nicking them – how are your stock checks?' demanded Leo.

'They're fine – we've very little shrinkage. It can't be that. No, this gear's being shipped in in quantities. I don't know if it's only in California, but we've had such consistent coverage of our styles in the fashion magazines that they're very hot now and the other stores are moving the copies real well.'

'Well, can't we sue them for selling stuff with our labels in?' asked Leo.

'That's hard – and could take a long time, and lawyers are very rich round here. Maybe if you could prove it had been stolen from you you would get some action from the LAPD.'

'Yeah. Well, it doesn't look as though it *is* stolen, does it?' He paused, his head in both hands. 'Oh, shit!' he moaned, then, 'Okay – I'm going to find out who the hell's doing this and then I'll have their bollocks.'

His manager raised an eyebrow. 'Be careful, man. There are some heavy guys in this business, and if they're making a lot of money out of ripping off your styles, they're not going to give it up just because you ask 'em.'

Leo spent the afternoon doggedly trailing round the stores and boutiques where he had been told Rags's styles were being sold. When he first encountered the copies, he was horrified to see how good they were; they could have been straight from his production.

But in finding their source, he got nowhere. He hadn't

told people who he was, but he couldn't disguise his anxious fury. Those store buyers who he managed to talk to would tell him nothing, though he gathered from one garrulous sales clerk that they, maybe, emanated from wholesalers in San Francisco.

Exhausted and depressed, he drove back to the Bel Air to change and try to get himself in the right mood for the studio party. Before he left for it, he went into the bar and ordered a couple of dry martinis in quick succession. He was just gulping down the second when a voice next to him boomed, 'Well, Leo how you'all doin'?' Leo turned. There was Ross Blackwell's craggy, wicked face grinning down at him.

Leo had scarcely thought of Blackwell since the visit to his ranch. He still occasionally joshed Liz Macintosh about him, though his references to 'the wrinkled cowboy' produced no more than enigmatic smiles from her. If Blackwell had been in touch with her or anyone else at Rags, Leo didn't know about it.

At the moment he was in no mood to renew his acquaintance with this wheeler-dealer of obscure credentials and hard, guarded eyes, but was obliged to accept a drink from him. They talked for a while and, without really meaning to, Leo found himself asking Ross along to the party.

It was much like a hundred other parties that were probably going on at the same time in the northern half of Los Angeles. Robinson had arranged it well enough. Most of the people he had hoped would come had done so: record company executives, television producers, record producers, musicians and ad agencies. And the studio itself was impressive enough; the reception area and rest lounges a predictable jungle of foliage, metal, glass and leather.

Leo was introduced to scores of people who regarded him speculatively and were surprised to learn that he was English and didn't even live in LA. Ross Blackwell seemed quite at home and even appeared to know a number of the other guests.

Eventually, Leo found himself beside the large Texan who nudged him. 'D'you want a line of this fine snow?' he

321

asked, producing a large silver pill-box filled to the brim with white powder.

Leo did want, and noticed that cocaine was being taken quite openly by a number of the guests – as normally as they might have drunk a glass of champagne.

He snorted a long line, and instantly felt better. He hadn't used much coke in London, where it was still something of a novelty and a rarity. He hadn't realised how efficiently cocaine could dispel a mood of negative gloom. A short while later, he greedily ingested another line. A sense of euphoric optimism overtook him and he was able to laugh at his own misgivings about the studio project and his whole American operation. He sought out Robinson and congratulated him on the job he was doing. Ross Blackwell looked on with amusement.

The following morning, however, Leo was appalled by his optimism of the previous evening. He was well aware now of coke's ability to block out undesirable realities.

Depressed and feeling out of control, he tried to call Alison but was told that she was down in Hampshire with the horses. Late in the morning he made his way to the bar where he found Ross lounging in a rattan chair, drinking Coors and reading the gossip column of the *Beverly Hills Gazette*. The beaming Texan beckoned Leo to join him. Leo was in need of someone to talk to, so he did.

'That was a great party! The studio should do real good. A lot of the guys there reckoned your man Robinson's the best – and they'll use him.' He stopped and gave Leo a hefty slap on the back, 'Hey, why d'you look so sad?'

'I'm okay. Yeah, the studio's fine. I've got a problem at Rags, though.'

'What, business not so good there?'

'It's not that; sales are fine. But we've discovered that somebody's pushing out a lot of copies of our product to all the other stores and little boutiques and undercutting us very heavily. And in the rag-trade, cheap copies are very bad for business.'

Ross nodded. 'That's true of any business. Who's doing it?'

Leo looked at him, unable to disguise his desperation. 'I wish to God I knew. Of course, nobody wants to tell me.'

'Aha,' said Ross, 'of course they don't. Well, sounds as if we're a bit more in my territory than yours. Y'all better leave it to Uncle Ross.'

Leo felt a lot more positive by the time he joined his British friends on *White Fin*.

He had called into the studios where an ebullient Robinson told him the bookings were already coming in, and at Rags, where there was some relief at the news that Leo had an apparently experienced ally in his search for their prolific plagiarist. But he had also vowed to himself that he would keep his use of cocaine in moderation.

He needn't have worried about any temptations to indulge in drug-taking on *White Fin*; Tony Lonsberg would not even allow cigarette smoking below decks, and apart from a reasonable intake of beer all other abuses were frowned on.

And sailing this great, elegant white boat, there was no need for additional stimulants. They slipped their moorings and motored to the mouth of the Marina before hoisting the mainsail, and then, heading south, they ran out a two-thousand-square-foot spinnaker to catch the constant northerly that swept the whole way down the west coast of the continent.

The crew and guests on the yacht were a healthy contrast to the posing depravity of Hollywood. And, as Leo quite readily joined in heaving sail sheets and working the 'coffee-grinders', which raised the sails, he wondered why he was so attracted to the flagrant materialism and mindless bullshit of West Coast America. Alison hated it; these people on the yacht despised it, but, nevertheless, the Angelinos spoke a language which he understood.

It took three hours of gentle sailing to reach Newport Beach. Leo disembarked, sorry that he wasn't going further, and took a taxi ride back to pick up his car at Marina del Rey.

His mood was lightened by finding a completely unexpected message waiting for him at his hotel. Danielle Milinaire was in LA, God knows why, and had tracked him down. He called her straight away at the Chateau Marmont where she was staying, and arranged to pick her up later.

Danny was as interested in Leo as she had ever been. The number of their encounters had in no way diminished their mutual sexual responses, and Leo's continuing unavailability sustained her obsession with him.

For Leo it was very uncomplicated. He knew that as long as she was doing the chasing, and his performance in bed didn't flag, she would be around when he wanted her. That evening he wanted her.

He needed to crowd out the confusing, disruptive notion that the single-minded worship of mammon might ultimately turn out not to be a rewarding pursuit. He wanted to lose himself in LA's relentless lust for ostentatious pleasure. And what better than to do that with Danny? In this town, liberally stocked with sex symbols, she stood out. She possessed all the obvious physical qualities and had the added elusive ingredient of European chic, an abstract characteristic to which the American girls hopelessly aspired.

Leo buzzed all evening, on champagne, on the envy he saw in other men's eyes, and in anticipation of a night of unrestrained sexual adventure free from all inhibitions or emotions.


'How is Leo behaving at the moment?' Sarah asked Alison. 'He's been more manic depressive than ever in the office.' They were lunching that day at Scott's in Mount Street. They had found that a dozen Belon oysters and a fine '71 Chablis had a catalytic effect on their more intimate conversations. 'Since Dad died, it's got worse, like you thought it would.'

'Yes,' Alison replied. 'Sometimes I think I've lost contact with him completely. And he seems to be racked by conflicting moods of guilty self-doubt and his old super-confident arrogance. When the wholesale range did so well, it was as if he thought he didn't really deserve it. He didn't, I suppose, in a way. After all, Raj was really responsible for getting it all together and he seems to be Leo's current *bête noire*.' She paused and smiled. 'Sorry, that wasn't meant to be a pun. And it was designed by Danielle, who's his mistress.'

'Oh God, Ali. Is that still going on?'

'Sure. But it doesn't really matter. He doesn't take any liberties, and she makes it so easy for him. As a matter of fact, I don't think he likes her much, but he's incurably vain.' She thought for a moment, swilling the white wine around her glass. 'I suppose I'd find it more demeaning if I didn't know that our sex life is very healthy. It's never got boring for either of us, I'm sure of that. If only my wretched tubes worked.' She looked bleakly at her empty oyster shells. 'I'd love to be able to have a baby.'

Sarah nodded compassionately. 'I wonder if I still can,' she said, 'after years of oestrogen. Though God knows if that will ever be relevant.' She apparently changed the subject. 'You know Raj is going to get some production in India, in Jaipur?'

'I'd heard,' said Alison.

'He's found some great people to do it with. They've got the whole thing organised, designing their own prints and garments. With Raj's abilities and the reputation he's already got himself in the trade here, it could be a very interesting new line. He's got the people coming over here, and then he's going again in July. He asked me if I wanted to go. Why don't you and Leo come too? It'd be a real change for you both – you could relax, do a bit of sightseeing; I think Leo would enjoy it.'

'In July? Won't it be hot as hell then?'

'Well, I suppose it will be in parts, but it'll be monsoon time – apparently it's at its most beautiful then in Rajastahn.'

'But won't Raj mind if Leo comes?' said Alison, attracted by the idea of visiting India. 'After all, Leo's been very tricky with him.'

'Well, he might. I don't know,' Sarah mused. 'He never

refers to that side of their relationship and he's always perfectly civil to Leo now. Anyway, you two can go off on your own a bit. Raj will have some business to do that Leo won't want to get involved in – it's nothing to do with Rags.'

To Alison's surprise, when she tackled Leo on the planned India trip, he responded enthusiastically. He seemed glad to find an excuse to get away from all his businesses for a while. His visit to America had left him frustrated and exhausted and this time he was glad to tell Alison about most of the problems he'd had there – leaving out any references to cocaine and Danielle Milinaire.

The Ross Blackwell connection seemed to her a sinister sort of coincidence, but Leo was insistent that Ross genuinely wanted to help in rooting out the problems of the fake garments – no doubt expecting a fee or a favour in return.

'As long as I'm not the fee,' said Alison.

Leo laughed. 'No, no. He was talking about coming to England in the autumn and carrying on where he left off with Liz. I think that was a bit more than a one-night stand.'

Raj raised no objections to Leo and Alison joining them. He was going to Hong Kong first and, as he had about a week's work in Jaipur, suggested that the three of them meet him there when he had completed it.

Shortly before they left for India, Alison had lunch with Simon who, characteristically, produced a contact for them – one of the sons of the Maharana of Mewar, whose family owned a series of palaces in Udaipur.

'In spite of being relatively poverty-stricken, they're still very grand and very affable. And they have one of the finest palaces in Rajastahn.'

'Trust Simon to know some Indian nob,' grumbled Leo when Alison told him. 'Considering he thinks he's so socially enlightened and forward-looking, he's got a very good working knowledge of the world's high and mighty.'

They had barely three hours' sleep in the Taj Mahal Hotel in Delhi before being awoken at five to be driven to the station. Sarah had insisted they take a train from Delhi to Jaipur so that they could get some feel of the country before they arrived at the Pink City. The manager of the hotel, with deference and efficiency, had provided a man to accompany them to the station to find their train and their seats. They drove through the wide empty streets in the early dawn to arrive at the huge, rust-coloured fortress-like Northern Railway Station.

Outside and in, it was seething with people. Leo's party followed the man from the hotel and two porters through a maze of platforms, picking their way between unidentifiable stacks of hessian-covered cargo and past rows of sleeping people, wrapped in sacking, lying on the bare platform. One man sitting up in his ragged nest was carefully shaving. They located the pink Jaipur Express, and were disappointed to find that these metre-gauge lines did not have the magnificent carriages of the grander five-feet-six-gauge main lines.

The first-class carriage consisted of rows of plastic-covered airline-type seats and slightly tatty curtains pulled across the tinted windows. But when at last they pulled out of Delhi, the sun just rising on their left, the journey became worthwhile.

The land to the west revealed itself as a flat expanse of hedgeless fields of grain and pink-stemmed rice. Scattered between the fields were isolated trees, twisted stooks of straw and tiny, tumbling huts. Ghostly figures wrapped in white glided through the rippling corn. In every farmstead by the railway were cows, camels and small, hairy-spined pigs. At the stations and in the villages, the track was lined with people, ragged in tunics and *dhotis* or ancient western suits. They were just hanging around, spitting, coughing on their *bidis*, or crouching for their morning crap.

Birds were everywhere – lumbering grey-hooded crows, flashing jays, and, always in pairs, green parakeets playing airborne games or perching side by side on the telegraph wires.

Past Mewari Junction, hills, small mountains appeared to the west, the beginning of the Rajastahn Uplands, naked, red-rocked, sometimes topped by little white sentinel posts.

The other passengers in the carriage were smartly dressed Indian businessmen, their faces buried in the *Times of India*, or the *Hindustan Times*, some reading Indian novels, their covers lurid with scenes of glamorous western violence.

On the few roads they passed were hundreds of cycling peasants, big garishly painted trucks, bullock wagons and camels pulling their rubber-tyred carts. After five hours, the railway line swung west around the southern end of the range of hills that overlooked Jaipur. Next to the track as they approached the city was a ribbon-development of tented hovels, made from grubby bits of old sacking and any other available scraps, housing families of innumerable unwashed children, with goats, chickens and small hogs shambling between the tattered dwellings.

At Jaipur Station, they were besieged by gnarled old porters, wearing bright red, flat-topped turbans, who tugged at their sleeves, pointing at the luggage, then raised the cases to their heads and carried them to a rank of eager taxi-drivers.

The chaotic traffic of Delhi had not prepared them for the suicide tactics of Jaipur road-users. If the Indian Government produced a highway code, no one here had read it. Somehow, however, they arrived unscathed at the Rambagh Palace, and were shown to their rooms overlooking the north-east terrace. The temperature was a hundred degrees, but inside the palace it was comfortably cool.

Leo was impressed. He had been more than ready to find fault with everything, but here the service was as good as, and a lot better than, many European hotels, and all the public rooms were decorated in appropriate good taste.

It was too hot to venture out, and they spent the afternoon watching preparations being made for a wedding and reception that was taking place that evening. A dais with two thrones had been placed on the veranda, and archways made of thousands of flowerheads were raised over the route of the marriage procession. One of the open-sided pavilions had a bower constructed within it, surrounded by silk cushions for the witnessing families to sit on. Shortly before sunset, a young man in a white silk suit and a jewelled, pink silk turban arrived upon a heavily caparisoned wedding horse, dangling and jangling with gilt and mirrored embellishments.

They watched from the edge of the crowd of wedding guests as a brahmin harangued the couple seated in the bower, and instructed them through a series of ceremonies involving food, incense and sacred oils. It was a colourful and happy scene, accompanied by much laughter and encouragement from the families. Then followed a long, elaborate feast. Leo, Alison and Sarah were fascinated, and even found themselves joining in the reception by the time Raj arrived at the hotel.

The four of them then sat down in the magnificent dining-room to dinner. Even Leo, who never ate curry in England, agreed that, here, it tasted right.

The next day was a Sunday and Alison decided she would find a Catholic church and go to mass. 'Feeling better?' said Leo with a smile when she arrived back at the Rambagh in a little motor-rickshaw. He respected her dogged adherence to her religion, and though she had been unable to make him understand it, he would have thought less of her had she shown signs of giving it up.

Raj arranged for a car to take them up to the palace and fortresses of Amber. This was where the maharajahs of Jaipur and their entourages had lived until the time when a diplomatic understanding with the Mogul emperors of Delhi had been reached, allowing the Maharajah Jai Singh, in 1727, to found a new city down on the plain.

The state apartments of the old palace at Amber, although they had been empty for centuries, were well enough preserved to give a vivid impression of the lavish richness and artistry with which the older rulers liked to

329

surround themselves. Exquisite painted and mirror-inlaid chambers looked out through intricately carved marble screens onto the expanse of artificial lake in the valley below and the sinuous fortifications that ran the full length of the crests of the valley sides. These fortifications descended to the narrow mouth at the north end of the valley, which opened to allow a view of twenty or thirty miles in the direction of Delhi, from where, normally, any potential invaders would have come.

Here, even Raj became mildly enthusiastic, and he and Leo discussed ways in which the maharajahs had been able to generate the funds for projects of such huge scale. Certainly, the economics of it were staggering. It was with an increased respect for his ancestors that Raj drove with his party down the hill to Jaipur.

Sarah had been keen to see all the traditional crafts involved in producing the cloths and prints so it was arranged that they should be taken out to the village of Bahgru, where much of it was done. Their guide was a handsome, round-faced young Hindu. Wearing neat, faded jeans and white leather training-shoes, he had a slightly curling moustache and surprising grey eyes. He was a bright and well-informed BSc in textiles and painstakingly answered every question they asked, however irrelevant.

At the workshops they were amazed by the crudeness, but had to admit that it produced results. Some of the prints were magnificent in their inventiveness and execution. Leo grudgingly admitted that perhaps Raj had made the right contacts, although he questioned again the wisdom of getting involved in a specialist look of such limited scope.

The small twin-propellered Indian Airlines plane flew at a few thousand feet from Jaipur to Jodhpur, and then to Udaipur. The monsoon had already begun, but the afternoon was bright and clear. The effects of the rains could already be seen in the hint of greenness that seemed to have been dabbed with a wide paintbrush into the valleys below them.

They arrived at the very basic facilities of Udaipur Airport and found a taxi to take them to the town. They were greeted in Udaipur by a riot of vivid flowers in the parks and gardens and a deferential boatman, who ferried them from the lake-shore to the gleaming white palace, reflected in the placid waters of its lake. Beyond the far shore, to the west, the green hills rolled away into hazy distances. Their rugged russet crests were fringed with short spiky trees, like the bristles on an Irish horse-coper's chin. Close by, on the peak of a three-hundred-foot ridge, a white fortress perched.

The Lake Palace was fairly empty of guests and they were given the two best suites in the hotel. The tourists didn't seem to know that Rajastahn was at its most beautiful during the light, air-clearing monsoons when the rain would patter gently on the lake for a short while and then move on to reveal a fresh and lucid landscape. Leo and Alison installed themselves in the Kush Mahal, one of the original rooms of the palace where ladies of the family used to stay. Its most elaborate feature was a stained glass window, which faced east and came into its own in the morning sun. Now, in the late afternoon, Leo opened the windows and looked across at the palaces ranging down the lake-shore. The light stone was turned to honey-gold by the dropping sun, and Utrillo might have painted the image it threw on the rippling lake below them.

Alison sat down and gently swung on a small cushioned seat suspended in the window by brass chains linked by festive elephants. She smiled at Leo and at the serene and solid building across the water. He winked and, holding the chains, leaned down and kissed her lightly. 'I don't think you'd have lasted long in Purdah, like the women who used to live here,' he said with fondness.

'You'd have loved it though, wouldn't you? – to have loads of silent obedient women at your beck and call.'

Leo looked hurt. 'I'm not that bad, Ali.'

'I know you're not. Are you enjoying this trip?'

Leo nodded. 'Yes, it was a good plan, I didn't think I would enjoy it, having no work to do. But it's good for me to be away from the business. It reminds me of our honeymoon in Ceylon. That was good for me too, remember?' He grinned.

'Remember the beach at Yala?'

'I certainly do!' He smiled down at her, then lifted her from the seat and laid her on one of the low silk-covered divans that edged the salon.

Slowly, warmly, relaxed now, they undressed each other.

On the west side of the palace, Raj and Sarah were in the Sajjan Suite. Sarah sat on the terrace and gazed at the hills silhouetted against the amber-pink sunset. Flocks of pigeons winged their way hurriedly across the lake to roost on the ledges and cupolas of the palace. Above them, flecks of back-lit clouds floated high above the dusty-orange skyline. From the shore, the pulsating sound of ceremonial drums drifted across the water and mingled with the noise of angry starlings, jockeying for limited space among the bushes in the courtyard.

Sarah had steeped herself in the history and religions of India. She was captivated by the heroism of the great warriors, their grandeur and their devotion to the many and multi-faceted Hindu gods; the constant cross-references between nature and the deities, the seasons and the feast days.

When Raj joined her, she enthused, eyes bright and senses alert to every fresh nuance in the evening air around them. He smiled at her, indulging her as a father might, and she loved him all the more for his knowing strength and the ineradicable connection between him and this enchanted land.

At the end of the sixteenth century, the Maharana Udai-singh, riding out with his courtiers and soldiers from the great fort of Chittor, came across a *sadhu*, a holy man, seated on a rock a little way above a valley. This valley had been dammed and flooded a few hundred years before by the *Banjaras*, the grain carriers, to make a suitable crossing and stopping place on their mercantile journeys.

Udaisingh descended from his horse to pay traditional respects to the *sadhu*, who rewarded him with the advice that, if he was looking for a site for his new palace, this very rock would make a most auspicious spot.

And so around that rock a building of great magnificence was built with views up and down the valleys and across the wide plain to the east and the mountains beyond. Over ten or so generations, the palace had spread southwards down the sloping lake-shore, each maharana determined to leave his mark for posterity.

Only a handful of Indian sightseers were there as Raj's party walked through the ornate, echoing courtyards and galleries. They saw lavish mirror-work, borrowed from the Moguls of Delhi, fine filigree carved marble, fountains and rooms full of paintings of the lives and histories of great maharanas.

When they reached Shiv Niwas Palace, where the incumbent maharana lived, they presented themselves and the letter of introduction which Simon had written only to be told that the Maharana's son, the Maharaj Kumar, was in England for Ascot, polo and Wimbledon. This brought them down to earth a little, but they were offered a drink and the opportunity to be amazed at the continuing, albeit diminished, opulence of these now powerless princes.

Sarah lay with Raj on the wide bed in the Sajjan suite. His arm encircled her and her head lay on his shoulder. Only a fine cotton sheet covered them. She gazed out of the window where the sun had dropped below fast-dispersing clouds, carriers of a recent short, heavy shower. The silence was exaggerated after the noisy pattering of rain on the lake, and served to magnify her sense of peace and fulfilment. They had come back from the lake-shore palaces and gone to bed for a siesta. Raj had made long love to her with his customary controlled and wordless passion. And, just now, she belonged to him, to his world, this world of gentle sunsets and ancient sounds.

She lovingly trailed her finger round the bulge of his smooth brown pectoral muscles, stroked his nipples and sought his chin to turn his mouth to hers for a lingering soft-lipped kiss. There was a mingling of brown and white limbs, and a final long embrace. Then Raj untwined himself and climbed from the bed. He pulled on a pair of loose white trousers and a silk Kurta and stood in the opened doorway that led to the terrace.

Sarah felt a tiny pang of rejection, but chided herself for her unreasonableness. She leant over the side of the bed and picked up a kimono which she put on demurely, then joined Raj in the doorway.

He moved out on to the terrace and she followed. They sat on delicate white chairs at a small table. Sarah wanted to talk and took his hand. She told him how it was the time of the Teej, the festival when ladies ask blue Krishna for a good husband; a time when women should be with their lovers.

'We timed it well, didn't we, being here now, together.' She smiled and stroked his hand.

Raj was silent, thoughtful for a moment.

'When I'm married, I shall have to remember that.' He shook his head slowly. He stood up and walked to the stone balustrade above the waters of the lake which lapped against the rock foundations. 'I hope my proposed bride isn't fretting too much.'

Two homeward-bound geese flew lazily across the setting sun. Sarah watched her lover's back, in silhouette. 'What . . . what are you asking . . . saying?' The words, completely uncertain of their destination, betrayed excitement and doubt.

Raj turned towards her and looked at her with even eyes.

'My family arranged my marriage, ages ago in Uganda. And soon, in September, I must go through with it.'

He shrugged and gave no sign of what reaction he expected from her.

Sarah sat completely still. It was as if distant, unseen forces were pulling in different directions on each of her four limbs, opening up a huge empty chasm in her. She felt all her blood drain away.

Raj saw the whiteness of her face, the blankness of her eyes. 'Sarah – are you all right? What's the matter?'

She did not, could not, answer.

Raj lifted her hand. It was heavy and lifeless.

'Good God, Sarah, what's the matter? My marriage won't affect us.'

Suddenly her eyes blazed and the colour pumped back into her face. She tore her hand from his, rose furiously from the chair and walked to the other side of the terrace.

She looked, for hours it seemed, at two pigeons bickering with one another on a ledge below, a few feet above the waters of the lake. The lucky things, she thought. All they've got to care about is who's going to roost where.

She still felt as if all her insides had been removed.

How the hell had he fooled her so thoroughly? How had she been able to credit him with such honesty, when all the time he must have known that he was going to have this arranged marriage? Just how wide was the gulf of misunderstanding between them?

Good God, no misunderstanding on his part! Or did he really believe that his marriage wouldn't affect them? Were their terms of reference so utterly different?

She turned back to face him. He had not moved and his features betrayed no emotion.

'What the hell do you mean – your marriage won't affect us?' she hissed. 'Or do you think you're merely conforming to your own Hindu culture by having a wife *and* a concubine?'

Raj said nothing.

'Did you seriously think I'd hang around for you when you weren't with your wife? . . . Giving her dozens of kids no doubt to carry on your precious business – God damn it!' she yelled. 'I wanted to have your babies!' She stopped and stared at him. Her shoulders shook. 'We've been talking a different language for the last eighteen months! We're miles apart! God help me for indulging in romantic fantasy.'

She saw Raj wince, just slightly.

Tears erupted in her eyes. 'Oh Raj . . .' She moved

towards him, supplicating. 'Say you don't have to do it. You're your own boss . . . you're completely independent . . . you don't have to do what your parents want . . .'

Alison and Leo were sitting in the ornately tiled bar. She decided to go up and knock on the door of the Sajjan Suite to find out what had happened. Raj called back, 'I'll come down; I'll see you in the bar in a few minutes.'

'Where the hell has Sarah gone?' Leo asked Raj who had come down, looking uneasy. 'We saw her piling on to the Palace launch with her case and heading for the shore.'

Raj took a tentative sip of his vodka and tonic. After a moment's study of the bubbles in his glass, he looked over at Leo and said smoothly, 'We seem to have had a misunderstanding.'

'That sounds like an understatement,' said Alison softly. 'She looked very angry. Where's she gone?'

'She said she was going to get a car to drive her straight back to Delhi and that she'd take the first plane she could to London.' He paused. 'I'm sorry to have spoiled her trip.'

Leo spoke quietly and under control. 'You'll be more than sorry if you've really upset her. I don't have to remind you – do I – that she's your main contact with your biggest client? It was pretty damned dumb of you to risk losing that.'

'Oh, Leo,' said Alison, 'don't bring that into it for God's sake. For some reason or other he's made Sarah very unhappy – she must be to have packed up and gone like that – and it's got nothing to do with Rags, has it Raj?'

Raj shook his head. 'No, it hasn't. To be quite frank, I don't think it will affect our business relationship. She's capable of being very detached if she has to be. But of course,' he added, 'that's up to her.'

Leo shook his head slowly and looked over at Raj. 'Oh, God,' he groaned, 'I knew there was going to be trouble.' He got briskly to his feet and turned to Alison. 'No reason why you should have your trip spoilt. You stay on for a couple more days if you want. I'm going to Delhi to catch up with Sarah.'

'I'll come with you,' said Raj.

'No – no, don't do that. I don't think Sarah will want to see you at the moment, do you?'

Raj shrugged.

'You arrogant bastard . . .' Leo's voice rose.

Alison put her hand on his arm. 'No, don't yell now, Leo – it won't help. You catch up with Sarah. We'll settle things here and take the plane to Delhi tomorrow afternoon. Do you agree, Raj?'

He nodded.

'Right.' Leo bent and kissed Alison. 'I'm going. I'll see you in London. And you,' he turned to Raj, 'you'd better keep out of the way for the first few days. I'll ring you when I know how much disruption you've caused.' He walked out of the bar, through the hotel's reception area and on to the landing-stage where the launch was tethered.


Alison explained to Simon what had happened when he and Claire dropped in at Chelsea Square a few days after her return from India.

'But surely,' Simon said, 'Sarah must have realised that something like this would happen? Certainly, I knew it was always on the cards that Raj would make an arranged marriage.'

'But he's so utterly sophisticated and westernised,' protested Alison.

'There's nothing unsophisticated about arranged marriages. One way and another, until very recently, they've gone on in Europe for centuries. But it's also got something to do with Raj demonstrating his respect for his father – if he can't respect his father, he can't respect himself. I'm afraid it was naïve of Sarah to let herself get so involved.'

'But he didn't do anything to discourage her,' said Alison.

'Well, he's a man and Sarah's very attractive. And it has to be said that she's contributed substantially to the success

337

of Raj's business. But I wouldn't forgive him for deliberately using her.'

Sarah herself fought with conflicting emotions and logic. The irony of her being a major factor, though not the only one, in Raj's spectacular rise to fortune was what most hurt her pride. At the same time, she knew that using his factories had been a completely sound, commercial decision. Min Cooper had commiserated, had completely understood. She had offered to deal with Raj on her own in order to save Sarah more hurt. But Sarah declined. She was, as Raj had predicted, determined not to let her emotions affect her professionally.

But before she saw him again, Leo arranged to meet him at his factory in Wembley. For one thing, Leo had never been there and, also, he felt that he could use this tactical lapse of Raj's to re-establish domination in their relationship – perhaps exude a proprietorial air over Raj's business.

But, once there, Leo was deflated to see just how much production Raj was handling for other retailers. There was no reason why this shouldn't be so. Provided that competitors weren't given access to patterns or anything that would allow them foresight of what Rags were doing, Leo was in no position to object. He also realised just how capably and efficiently Raj had set up his factory and recruited his staff. Leo was surprised to see that there were very few Indian machinists and that key staff were English and clearly very committed.

One startlingly beautiful young Indian girl was checking through a rail of finished garments, frequently glancing over to where Raj was showing Leo around. When they reached the point where she was working, Leo noticed that she was dressed entirely in Rags garments. She was obviously only in her teens, but possessed none of the coyness of her age or her race. She smiled challengingly; Leo smiled back and winked. 'Hi – who are you?' he asked.

She giggled, and suddenly looked very young. 'I'm quality control,' she said.

'Are you sure you shouldn't be at school?'

'Don't go back till next week.'

Leo turned to Raj. 'What's this – child labour?'

Raj looked, for once, a little awkward.

'This is Gita Patel, the sister of my – er – fiancée.'

Leo turned back to the girl.

'Ah, family. You seem to like our clothes, Gita. Does Raj give them to you?'

'No,' she pouted. 'He said if I want them I have to buy them from one of the Rags shops; I can't afford to get many.'

'Quite right,' Leo laughed. 'Tell you what, we might have a few spare press samples you could have. Come on up to the office and see me about it.' He handed her a card.

She took it eagerly and was about to fix a date and time right then, but Raj waved her irritably away.

Leo shrugged and grinned at her, and he and Raj continued their tour.

'Leo,' said Raj, 'I would be grateful if you didn't encourage her. It worries her mother if she gets too – advanced.'

'Is that so? Well you tell her mum she'll get as advanced as she wants, with or without my encouragement. She's a bloody good-looking chick. We might be able to use her for some modelling.'

Raj's voice was quiet, and ice-cold. 'On no account will she do any modelling for you, and her parents will forbid her to visit your offices. I'll make sure of that.'

Leo looked at him, interested. 'Mm, we'll see,' he said. 'And, talking of visiting our offices, it seems that your misunderstanding with Sarah hasn't affected her commercial perspective, so you'd better arrange to come up soon to start on next spring's numbers.'

Raj inclined his head.

When the tour of the factory was over, Raj saw Leo out to his waiting Rolls. He extended a hand. 'Glad you came down to the factory. I shall be in touch with your sister soon. And, please, remember what I asked. Do not encourage Gita.'

Leo smiled broadly, and shook hands. 'Glad we've sorted out your problem,' he said, and climbed into the car.

Everyone at the wedding – there were only family and a few Indian friends – agreed that it was a most auspicious union. Raj was already held in some awe for his obvious and rapid success, but, because he was family, it was their success too. Reena was considered an exemplary bride: alert and educated enough to make the most of what was on offer in England without having succumbed to the temptations of European decadence. She was also very beautiful and fairly rich. Raj was lucky, she was lucky, they thought.

The ceremony passed without mishap, and Raj, though taciturn, gave no sign that he felt anything other than the happiness that his parents obviously felt.

At Rags, no one was quite sure whether or not the wedding had taken place. Raj ventured no information, so eventually Min Cooper asked him in the middle of a production meeting. He looked up from the garment that he was inspecting. 'Yes. I was married two weeks ago.'

'Congratulations,' said Min.

Sarah said nothing. She managed to keep her eyes fixed on Raj without blinking, without giving away any of the agony she felt at this horrific and final news.

Raj said, 'Thank you,' and displayed no emotion. He turned his attention back to the garment and the meeting continued as if nothing had been said about the wedding.

Raj drove on to the City afterwards.

In the three years since he had arrived in England, the single-mindedness with which he had pursued the re-establishment of his family's wealth had not been deflected at all. The rebuffs which he had encountered on account of his colour had fuelled his determination to prove that he was more than equal to the indigenous people of his host country. The outright abuse he had suffered from Leo had germinated a strong desire to put

340

Leo in a position where he, Raj, could control the success or failure of Rags.

Physically, he missed Sarah, but he had always regarded her attitude towards him as unconsciously patronising, and he was in no doubt that he was being used to satisfy both her bodily needs and her philosophical aspirations. At times when he had seen her since her return from India, he had still felt some sexual yearning, but this was easily relegated to insignificance beside his commercial and personal ambitions.

Reena was proving, anyway, to be a very satisfactory wife. They had moved into a house in Ealing which Mr Patel had bought, and although Raj felt slightly uneasy about leaving his parents, they had not objected. Reena had been, as he had known that she would, a virgin, but she had soon learned to make love with a submissive passion which Raj found uncomplicated and satisfying. He realised that he had nearly mishandled Sarah to the point of seriously damaging his business, but his assessment of his own importance to Rags and her strength of character had been correct. None the less, he had learned a lesson.

He was on his way now to meet a commodity broker to whom Simon had introduced him soon after his arrival in England. Because Raj's early commercial life had been dominated by trading of coffee, he had continued to watch the market and the peripheral factors which influenced it. He was certain that prices were in a trough, perhaps just turning the corner, but with scope to soar to unprecedented heights. The profits of his manufacturing, importing and property companies allowed him to speculate quite comfortably with fifty thousand pounds, which he planned to use as a deposit for one hundred five-ton lots of coffee. The broker looked doubtful of Raj's creditworthiness, but gladly agreed to deal on his behalf on presentation of a bank draft for the total amount.

Raj left the broker's office utterly confident that he would treble his money in a year and, to underline his confidence, before driving back to Wembley he stopped in Hatton Garden and made his way to the jeweller to whom he had sold his mother's Burma ruby.

The young man who had greeted him on his previous visit recognised him immediately and so did the father, who shuffled out of the back room just after Raj had entered the shop.

'Good morning,' he said. 'Have you got another fine ruby for me?'

'No,' Raj said briskly. 'This time I am a buyer.'

But when he reached home that evening with a necklace of gold and small garnets in a little padded box in his pocket, he was greeted not by Reena, but by his father-in-law. Prem Patel looked thunderous. 'What have you done to Gita?'

Raj looked blank. He had not seen Gita since the wedding. He assumed that she had gone back to school and was once again subject to the rigorous regime that her parents tried to impose.

'Nothing. Why? I haven't seen her for two weeks.'

Patel didn't believe him. 'She says you took her up to the offices of your Rags friends – and they got her drunk, and kept her out all evening. She came back at one o'clock in the morning, covered in make-up in a taxi with bags full of clothes.'

Raj, now, was also coldly furious. 'Leo!' he hissed. 'He's done it deliberately. After he'd been to the factory, I told you he'd asked her up. I told you, and I told her not to go on any account – and I told Leo Freeman not to encourage her. He'll pay for this. I'm sorry, Prem. I had no wish for her to get mixed up with those sorts of people.'

Patel appeared to believe him, and grief replaced anger.

'Her mother is so upset. She just can't understand her. It's so difficult, these kids going to English schools – they just don't know where to draw the line. I'm sorry for thinking you were responsible, Raj. But I'm afraid we can't let her do these holiday jobs at your factory. Not until she's shown that she's sorted herself out.'

Raj readily agreed. He had not wanted her there in the first place.

'Would you like a drink?'

Patel accepted a large whisky and was suitably impressed when Reena was presented with her necklace. 'My God, Raj, very handsome. You really are becoming quite the whizz-kid.' He nodded at Raj's new Mercedes parked in the drive.

Alison, too, was furious about the episode with Gita. She knew that Leo had taken her up to the Rainbow Room and introduced her to the least restrained of his friends simply to spite Raj. It was only her intervention that had sent Gita back in a taxi before something serious happened. She was used to Leo's flirting, but it had angered her to see him doing it with a fifteen-year-old girl, using her to make up for his sister's loss of face. She decided that this time he wasn't going to get away uncensured.

'Leo, that was utterly shameless,' she said when they got back home that night. 'She's only just fifteen, and a schoolgirl, from an Indian family. She's completely unprepared for dealing with people like you and your friends, and you got her hopelessly drunk. It's not just demeaning for me to sit by and see it – it's degrading for you. The whole thing was a bad, horrible joke.'

'Bollocks,' Leo slurred. 'The fact that she's Indian doesn't stop her being a randy little nymphette. Nobody was going to make her do anything she wasn't going to like.' He giggled. 'We could have brought her back here and you could have given her a few lessons.' He looked at her angry face. 'You look like a teacher now. Come on, get that gear off and try and look like a woman.'

They were in the bedroom, and Leo drunkenly lunged towards her, but she side-stepped and he landed face down on the bed. Alison walked to the door. 'I'm not sleeping with a drunk, snoring pig. I'm going next door, and tomorrow I'm taking a trip.'

She slammed the door behind her and locked herself in one of the spare bedrooms.

Leo was incapable of doing much about it. He hammered on the door for a while, then went back and fell on the bed and into a deep, noisy sleep.

When he awoke, Alison had gone.

'Where did she say she was going?' he bawled at the maid.

'Didn't say, Mr Leo. Just went with case in taxi.'

'Well, why the hell didn't you ask her?'

The little Filipino shook her head and started to cry.

'Oh for Christ's sake,' Leo groaned, then, resigned, went to find something in the kitchen to cure his hangover.

Of all the refuges Leo might have thought Alison would seek, she went to the least likely. Marie, an old girlfriend living with an American photographer in Malibu, California, had always told Alison it was open house for her there.

She felt only relief on the long polar-route flight. She arrived feeling fresh and positive enough to cope easily with the time change. Her friends welcomed her, not at all surprised or put out by her sudden appearance. The next few days she spent calmly, walking by the seashore and talking with the enthusiastic and inventive people who seemed constantly to drop in to the beach house.

Marie didn't even ask her why she had just turned up – guessed it was something marital and probed no further.

When, finally, Alison volunteered her reasons, they were ambivalent. On the one hand, life with Leo, his hang-ups, his pressures and his ego was becoming intolerable; on the other, she felt guilty about her intolerance and her barrenness.

'After all, Leo is no worse than he was when I first met him – he's even mellowed a little. And I married him knowing it would be hard work. But I hadn't reckoned on letting him down over babies. Somehow it's more difficult to be a willing martyr when some of the faults are your own.'

'Well, Ali, you just stay around here till you feel you know what you want to do. Recover your emotional strength, then decide. Maybe you should pretend you're single again – we'll invite some guys round to meet you; it might get things into perspective.'

'No – don't do that. I don't want to get involved in a

tit-for-tat scenario. And though I know Leo isn't very faithful, he certainly doesn't love anyone else.'

She didn't know what made her look in at Robinson's studio. She was up in West Hollywood and it occurred to her that it was nearby. She hadn't been there before but somehow, because it was connected with Leo, she found herself wanting to see it.

Robinson was very pleased to meet her and welcomed her to the premises, and although he was surprised when Alison asked him not to mention her visit to Leo, he assured her that he wouldn't. 'Anyway,' he went on, 'I don't talk to Leo that much. He calls every two or three weeks, and I don't often need to call him.' He led her into the lavish rest lounge, with all its greenery, and poured her a drink. 'Want anything more stimulating?' he asked, tapping a snuff box.

Alison tried not to look disapproving. 'Nope.'

'Okay,' said Robinson. 'Look, if you want to hang around, we should have a great session starting in an hour or so. Wolf Amadeus is working on an album here. We've put down all the backing tracks, and he's going over the vocals. D'ya wanna sit in?'

Wolf Amadeus was a gravelly-voiced middle-of-the-road singer, something like Neil Diamond and with a similar following. Alison wasn't particularly enthusiastic about his sort of music but she liked some of his songs and was certainly interested to watch him recording. Robinson led her through to the control room and bantered amiably as he and his engineer got the mixing desk set up for the session. After three-quarters of an hour, Wolf arrived with his musical director, his manager and his chauffeur/bodyguard.

The singer went straight into the recording booth and put on the waiting earphones. His MD also went in, shuffled music around on a stand and demanded a play through of the previous day's session. When the track ended, Wolf's voice boomed over the speakers in the control room, 'Man, that was all shit. I'll retake the whole thing.'

'I don't think that's necessary,' his MD, now in the control room, whined down the talk-back. He took his finger off the cue button, so that he couldn't be heard in the recording booth. 'That's the best take we'll ever get of that track.'

'It doesn't matter,' snapped the manager. 'Keep him happy; keep yesterday's take and let him do another if he wants to.'

The musical director shrugged, and pressed the talk button again. 'Okay, Wolf. We'll take another one.'

The sound of the prerecorded backing track filled the control room and the rock star began to sing his vocal track over it, stopping every so often to say, 'Shit! Drop me back in.'

And phrase by phrase, sometimes word by word, he worked his way through the song. Alison was amazed by the result. It sounded like one straightforward rendering, not twenty-odd sections welded together by the backing. Wolf had an obsessive desire for perfection in every note – its pitch, attack, timing and timbre.

By the time they had selected the best parts from each of the two versions he had recorded, she began to appreciate why he was considered such a pro and why his fans stayed loyal. The final result was a lot better than the previous day's recording, and Robinson and the musical director both agreed that the singer had been right to retake.

'But, hell, would the people have known any better?' grumbled Wolf's manager. Two hours in the studio was as much as he could stand. And there was the cost to consider.

'Oh, they would,' said Wolf Amadeus, pushing his way into the control room. 'They can tell the difference between something that's okay, and something that's real good.'

He saw Alison, and his eyes registered lazy interest. 'Hello, honey, who are you?'

Robinson was suddenly between them, introducing. 'This is Alison Freeman from London, my partner's wife. Ali, this is, as if you had not guessed, the yodelling cowboy – Wolf Amadeus.'

Wolf looked sour. 'Okay, thanks, Robinson.'

He sat down next to Alison, right next to her so that their bodies touched from shoulder to knee.

'Get me a beer, please somebody,' he said to the room in general. The chauffeur scuttled off. 'Well honey, what d'you think?'

'I think you're right. This member of the public could tell the difference between something that's just okay and something that's really good.'

Wolf grinned. 'My, you sure are British. That's good. The British have got fine judgement; they buy a lot of my records.'

His chauffeur came back and handed him a can of beer. He tipped it to his mouth and drained it, then threw it into a waste can on the other side of the studio, belched loudly and put his arm around Alison.

'You hang on in here for the next track, I might want some advice.'

He got to his boot-clad feet, hitched in his belt another hole in a huge silver buckle and made his way back to the booth.

They went through the same process as before with a new track. Alison perched on the edge of her seat so she could enjoy a better view, and watched, more fascinated now, as the tall, broad-chested singer set to work again.

Total concentration showed in his wide blue eyes, as, every few minutes, he looked up and flicked a hank of blond hair from across his face. While he sang and listened to the play-backs, there was a total and self-critical absorption in his work. He was no prima donna, he just knew when he had, or had not, got it right.

His face – thought Alison – was remarkably healthy, considering the stories of hell-raising and debauchery which the press wove around him. And although his eyes expressed absolute confidence in himself, they weren't without innocence.

And he loved to sing. It showed in every inch of his all-American film-star features.

It seemed only a short while before it was early evening and Wolf came out of the booth for the last time. He

347

strode into the control room. 'Okay, that's it. Six hours is enough for this boy's vocal cords.'

They listened to play-backs of the day's recordings and everyone was satisfied, including the singer who turned to Alison with a broad, easy grin.

'I think I deserve a reward, don't you – so I'm taking you to dinner.'

They were given a prime table at Ma Maison, where Wolf showed a surprising appreciation of the culinary talents of Patrick Terrail. Alison had him down for a T-bone and fries eater, but she was beginning to learn that there were many unforeseen aspects to the singer's character. Although he was as big a star as could normally be seen in the public places of Hollywood, he took surprisingly little for granted. He treated doormen and restaurant staff with a genuine friendliness. Alison remarked on the contrast here with his less than courteous behaviour at the studios.

'Well, there's a reason for that. First – I don't like the guys anyway. Those sorts of people are necessary in the music business, and if they were nice people, they'd be lousy at their jobs. Second – they actually want their artists to behave like that. And another thing, I may be no J. S. Bach, but I do have some kind of musical integrity. Some of those guys don't know a major seventh from a diminished ninth, or one octave from the next.'

Then he asked Alison about herself. She didn't refer much to Leo, but when she did, she was quite matter of fact. She told Wolf about her life in London, her trip to India, and her horses. All along, the singer listened, fascinated by Alison's perspective and the wit with which she told her stories. She was neither flirtatious, nor over-awed, and as the rich Cabernet Sauvignon grapes of the Nappa Valley took their effect, her colour heightened and her eyes grew bright. When they talked of horses, Wolf responded. Like most romantic Americans, he had always wanted a ranch of his own, to recapture some of his ancestors' pioneering lifestyle. And of course, now that he had the money, he had wholeheartedly indulged his fantasy in a huge acreage in New Mexico, with herds of short-horns and stables full of cow horses.

When Alison mentioned the visit to Blackwell's Texas hacienda, Wolf's eyes narrowed. 'That mean bastard's a dangerous man.'

'He was hospitable to us,' replied Alison guardedly, 'I'm not quite sure what he was after, but whatever it was, he hasn't had it yet. Leo said he saw him in LA last spring.'

The singer nodded. 'Yeah. He gets over here. He does a lot of business in southern California.'

'Oh. What sort of business?' asked Alison. 'Nothing too straight, I suspect.'

'You suspect right. Not the sort of business that a healthy country boy like me wants to be around.'

They were having a final calvados, and Alison was expecting the inevitable request.

'Well, honey,' it went. 'You wanna see Laurel Canyon in the moonlight?'

'Well, where is it?'

'Just a little ways north of here.'

'Sounds a long way from Malibu.'

'Don't worry – I'll have someone drop you back there in the morning.'

'Listen, singing cowboy, don't make life difficult for yourself. There must be thousands of girls round here who are a lot more willing and easier to pull than I am. I guess all you have to do is dial a couple of numbers.'

'Sure, but that's no fun.'

'Well, you're barking up the wrong tree. There's no pussy at the top of this one.'

A lazy smile spread across Wolf's face. 'We'll see – but not tonight, honey.'

With considerable charm, he helped her from her chair and into the back of his limousine. 'Tell him where to go,' he said, nodding towards the chauffeur. He leaned into the car and kissed her, very lightly on the lips. As the car pulled away, she looked back through the tinted rear window, and saw him standing in the doorway of the restaurant wearing a slight and thoughtful smile.

She was impressed. Somehow he had given the idea, in seeing her off, that he was rejecting her. Clever, sexy bastard.

And this was the first time that Alison had even considered being unfaithful to Leo. Just thinking about it, she found herself growing hot and receptive. Lounging in the back of the huge car as it cruised along the Pacific Coast Highway in the moonlight, Leo, his problems and his hang-ups seemed far, far away.

The next morning, Alison brought her urges sharply to heel.

She was crazy to let herself be so excited about a man she had only met once; a man who, in spite of his charm, must surely have a very spoilt and angry side to him. But he was overwhelmingly attractive to her and the challenge of bringing that big, powerful ego under control was almost irresistible.

But this wasn't why she had come to California, and she did resist. And the resisting brought with it a sweet joy of longing. For three days she held out, and then he rang her.

Robinson would give no clues and he had had to send his chauffeur back up to Malibu to find out who she was staying with, and the telephone number. Did she want to come up to the studios that afternoon?

She did, and was surprised by the tenderness with which he greeted her. He even stopped right in the middle of a take to come through to the control room when he saw her arrive.

When he had finished singing, and the post-mortem on the day's recordings had been completed, he asked her gently, as if prepared for a refusal, if she would mind coming up to have dinner with him in Laurel Canyon.

'I wanna show you that a simple New Mexico boy can cook as well as the fanciest, tallest-hatted chef in Paris.'

Alison accepted, aware of the inevitable sequel, without reluctance. The sheer anticipation of hitherto untasted

fruits of infidelity filled her with a tingling sense of wicked-
ness. Wolf drove them in his perfect, white XK 150 back to
his house in the Canyon. It was perched quite privately,
high up the steep valley-side, so as to provide an air of
detachment from the muggy sprawling city below.

The dinner was good, gastronomically and emotionally.
They chatted easily, wittily, through Wolf's careful preparation of a pair of simple tournedos. A fine Californian
claret accompanied the tender steaks, which they ate at a
low table in front of a superfluous but enchanting open
fire.

There was no question that Alison wouldn't agree to
Wolf's eventual suggestion that they go to bed.

She laughed when she saw the huge bed and the great
expanse of thick brown-grey fur that covered it. 'That's
just too unsubtle – a Wolf in wolf's clothing.' She turned
to him, suddenly coy. 'But you're not really such a wolf,
are you?'

He looked back at her smiling, slowly shaking his head.
'No, honey – I ain't. Here, come and sit next to me a
while.' He patted a spot beside him, where he sat on the
edge of the bed. Alison did as he asked, in a state of
meekness with which she was completely unfamiliar. He
put a large arm around her shoulders, which heaved a
couple of times, and he brought her head round gently to
face him. 'Ali – are you sure you wanna do this?' There
were slight tears in her eyes, and she didn't try to stop
herself from biting her upper lip. She didn't speak: found
that she could neither shake nor nod her head. Wolf still
looked into her eyes, understanding. 'You want to, but
you don't want to – right?'

Alison nodded, found his hand with hers and squeezed
it. He hugged her shoulders. 'Listen, if you just want to
sleep right here beside me – just sleep. That's okay, I
promise. You're too special to play with.'

Alison smiled gratefully.

They did just sleep, surprisingly well. In the morning,
as she drifted back to consciousness, Alison was glad she
hadn't succumbed before she was ready. The frustration

she felt was dissipated by the knowledge that, when it did happen, it would be *extra* good. She thought that her overwhelming inhibitions would somehow be eroded by the restraint she was now exercising.

But she did want to hug him.

She stretched out across the huge bed. He wasn't there. She sat up rubbing her eyes, feeling cheated, and then he walked back into the bedroom. He was already dressed in jeans and a buckskin jacket.

'Morning honey.' He leant over the bed to kiss her lips. When they touched hers, it took all her resolve not to fling her arms around him and pull him down on to her.

He straightened himself, and looked down at her affectionately.

'Man,' he said, 'I didn't know I possessed so much willpower. How I laid by that beautiful body all night without touching it, the Lord knows. But now, I've got to go. I'll tell the maid to bring you in breakfast, and you call me at the studio when you're ready. We'll have lunch down by the beach some place – okay?'

Alison smiled at him as he strode from the room.

An hour or so later, she had eaten, bathed and made up her mind. She dressed and wrote a note which she pinned to the bedhead.

Wolf,

Sometimes the emotion of wanting something really, really badly is completely destructive, even if the thing you want is good. I suppose that's because the want is never fulfilled, because what you want is not the thing, but the idea of the thing – and that's a product of your own mind, not necessarily at all like the real thing.

And sometimes, I think you know, the depth of longing is a product of the knowledge that you shouldn't really be wanting at all. I'm pretty sure that, in itself, loving you would not be a wicked thing to do – but, right now, for me, it seems it still is.

I'm not leaving California for a while, but I'm going

up to stay in San Francisco – maybe I'll sort out what I should or shouldn't want, and why.

I hope you'll talk to me when I get back!

You're some deceptive Wolf!

Love Ali.

Her friends in Northern California kept her busy. There was a lot going on – exhibitions, concerts, parties peopled by a seemingly limitless supply of tweed-jacketed, self-consciously thoughtful and unAmerican Americans. Alison was, on the whole, entertained and kept on her intellectual toes. The dinners and discussions were similar to those she had liked to hold in London – and, in spite of her determination not to, she found herself being constantly reminded of London, and Leo.

But she was still quite unready to go back to him, so, after three weeks in San Francisco, she rented a car and drove down the coastal highway back to Malibu. Two days of wandering up and down the beach on her own solved nothing. She decided to let events take their own course, and rang Wolf.

There was only warmth, sympathy and tenderness in their meeting – no recriminations, no hurt pride, no overbearing lust.

They were in one of the quieter West Hollywood restaurants as Wolf had ducked out of a gala premiere and didn't particularly want to be seen. He looked across the table at her with understanding, and disappointment.

'Honey, I guess I know you weren't ready to make a break – maybe you never will be. I think if you've made a promise you like to keep it. So, you're gonna keep your promise to Leo. He's a lucky man.' He raised his glass. 'But I sure as hell wish I'd got to you first.'

He saw her off from LAX airport the next day. In the VIP lounge, he kissed her for a last, lingering time. 'Thank you, honey, for adding a new colour to my rainbow.'

'Hello Sarah, it's Ali. Can we meet? Lunch?'

Alison had arrived home in the early morning to find

that Leo wasn't there. Later, when she had phoned the office, his secretary had told her that he was in Scotland looking at a factory.

He's been pining, she had thought. He always worked harder when he was miserable.

'Don't tell him I called,' she had told the secretary. 'I'll see him when he gets back.' And then she had rung Sarah. 'Of course,' Sarah said when Alison asked her not to tell Leo she was back. 'I'm not speaking to him much anyway at the moment. He's got a mad scheme to set up our own production so we'll be less dependent on West Textiles. This personal war that he and Raj are waging is going to end in heavy casualties.'

Their lunch lasted until late into the afternoon. Sarah had guessed what had happened, and what Alison was probably doing. She had even guessed that she had gone to California.

'Leo wouldn't mention it the first week. Then he said you'd gone to Spain. Then he said you were coming back via Rome and Vienna. Everyone knew it was balls. Of course, he thought I'd know the truth and went mad trying to get it out of me.'

'Yes, I suppose he found the whole thing very demeaning,' Alison sighed. 'Still, it might have taught him a lesson.'

'I don't think so. You know as well as I do how insecure Leo is. I'm afraid this has only increased his paranoia. I mean he'll forgive you all right; I should think he'll be running all over the place trying to please you, in between mad rages of jealousy and thwarted influence. The trouble is, he hates and loves your independence and you've thrust it a long way down his throat.'


Leo walked into the drawing-room at Chelsea Square. When he saw Alison sitting on the sofa, obviously waiting for him, he went over to the drinks tray without a word and poured himself a whisky. As soon as he turned to face her, Alison saw that this gesture of defiance was a failure.

354

There was, in his attitude, a meek penitence which co-existed uncomfortably with his customary arrogance.

He took a large gulp of his drink and Alison waited for him to speak.

'I heard you were back. Had a good time?' he asked.

Alison shrugged her shoulders. 'Interesting, necessary, frustrating.'

'Well, it would be frustrating, wouldn't it, without me for a month.'

'Frankly, Leo, it was a hell of a relief to get away from you for a month. But, for the time being, I've sorted myself out and I'm back. You know perfectly well why I went, so, if you give a damn about my feelings, you'll know how to behave in future.'

Leo struggled with himself, then became unexpectedly contrite. He put down his drink and sat beside his wife on the sofa. He put an arm around her and squeezed.

'Angel, I know. I'm sorry. I had a lot on my mind. I know that's no excuse. But don't worry – I've found the answer to the problem I had.' He laughed, unconvincingly. 'You know I always do in the end. And now I'll spend more time with my beautiful wife.' He looked at her hard. 'God, you really are beautiful.' He paused, and spoke with a change of tone, as if the thought had only just occurred to him. 'I guess wherever you've been, there were plenty of men around to tell you that. How did you manage to fight them off – or didn't you? I suppose it was good for your poor neglected ego to have a flock of randy bastards all sniffing round. And I suppose you gave a few of them what they were after.' His voice was rising as he convinced himself.

Alison shook off Leo's arm, got to her feet and walked to the other side of the room. 'Your jealousy is very touching, Leo – about as touching as the high regard in which you appear to hold my sense of loyalty.'

Leo had also risen. He spread his arms in submission. 'I'm sorry, Angel – I'm sorry. It's not what I wanted to say to you.' He put his hand in his jacket pocket, and pulled out a small box. 'Here, I raided Butler and Wilson for you.' He gently lobbed the box to her. She opened it and found a pair of silver-gilt and pearl art nouveau earrings and a matching pendant – absolutely her taste, perfectly chosen. She looked at Leo and smiled wanly.

'Don't think this lets you off, but it earns a temporary reprieve. Now for God's sake, let's forget that I've been away and try to live like a couple of adults.'

Leo grinned. 'That's my Ali – let's go and have a bath!'

# 1976

Ross Blackwell flew to London on a cold, wet day in January. He checked in and settled down in his large, finely furnished room at the Connaught. After a shower and half an hour with a masseur, sent to him by room service, he poured himself four fingers of Black Label and dialled Leo's number at Rags.

It was late afternoon, and a furious discussion had just ended in the boardroom. Leo had confirmed that they were taking the lease on a bankrupt factory near Greenock in Strathclyde. He justified this decision in several ways, the last of which were the substantial grants and assistance offered by the local development agency. Mike Morris, his financial director, had winced. There were too many bankruptcies in the air that year, too many properties begging for buyers. 'Leo, I must have heard you say a dozen times that if the government gift-wraps a project, it isn't worth having because it means nobody wants it. Frankly that's too much of a generalisation, but in this case it's accurate.'

'What are you talking about, Mike? We'll be rent and rates free for a year. A third of the first year's wages are paid, and we're getting most of the plant for nothing. That's not gift-wrapped, it's a bloody great Christmas present.'

Sarah groaned. 'Oh Leo! You're bullshitting again. Most of the plant's useless to us. It's all jeans production. And we'll lose far more than a third of our wages retraining the machinists. You know all this – why not face facts?'

Min was nodding her head in agreement. Leo turned to

her. 'It's all very well you nodding away like a coot with a twitch. How long have you been trying to find alternative production?'

'For years, constantly. But there's nowhere that will touch West Textiles on price and quality. And I can't see the point of changing just because Raj Kalianji's got up your nose. After all, if Sarah's prepared to go on dealing with him after what he did to her, I don't see why you can't.'

'That exactly makes my point. First, we're getting completely dependent on Raj and, secondly, if we want to get out from under, we'll just have to set up our own factories where we control price and quality.' He held up his hand as Sarah tried to interrupt. 'And let me tell you, if we don't do it pretty damn quick, that brown bastard's going to have us by the bollocks. And when he does, he's not going to stop squeezing just because we're screaming.'

After that, the meeting had descended into mayhem. Arguments and abuse had been hurled across the table with no one listening to what the others were saying until, eventually, Leo had stood up and bellowed, 'Listen – I run this bloody company. I'm chairman, managing director and majority shareholder. And I've decided that we go ahead with this Greenock factory – and that's that.'

He had stormed out of the room, leaving the others looking drained and helpless.

He reached his office and his telephone rang. The switchboard was closed and the call had come straight through.

Leo picked up the handset. 'Yeah, what?' he snarled into it.

A southern States accent drawled, 'I wanna talk with Mr Leo Freeman.'

'You've got him. Who the hell's that?'

'You're sounding real sore, Leo. This is Ross.'

Leo took a couple of long breaths. 'Oh. Sorry, man. The switchboard must have gone home – you came straight through.'

There was a deep laugh. 'That's all right. Say, I'm in

358

London, at the Connaught. Y'all come round for a drink and I'll tell you the news.'

Leo was sceptical. He hadn't heard a thing from Ross for nine months and had written him off as a source of information.

'What news have you got?'

'Tell you the truth, not much. But come on round anyway. I'm in one-o-five. See you in thirty minutes. Bye.'

Leo found himself mumbling goodbye as the line clicked dead. Tetchily, he went down to his car, couldn't find his driver, so he left a note and set off using his spare key.

Blackwell was waiting for him in the lobby and together they went into the American Bar. Barry, the ginger-haired barman who had made the peach and champagne cocktail for Alison eight years before, had moved on to preside over a less formal, noisier bar in Chelsea. Leo was annoyed to see that there didn't seem to be any staff, or guests, who knew him. Ross ordered their drinks and they sat at a table in the corner. 'Well, young fella. Is your business in LA still suffering from the copy-cats?'

'Well, they tell me that though there are fewer fakes around, the damage has been done. I don't know yet. The figures in the Rodeo Store look pretty good, and we still get the press coverage. Trouble is, you have to take a bomb there all year round just to cover costs.'

'Gettin' you down, is it?'

'The rest of the business is good.' Leo tried to look unconcerned. 'We can carry it for a while.'

'Well. I may just have slowed down the phoney merchandise for you. I was able to lean a bit on the guys in San Francisco who're bringing it in.'

Leo looked up. 'So – it was coming from there then?'

Ross nodded.

Leo was puzzled. 'But – they were making it there?'

Ross thought for a moment. 'No, no. They weren't making it there.'

'Well, where the hell is it being made?'

Again Ross paused. 'I don't know.' Smiling. 'But don't worry, the stuff'll stop coming.'

There was some truth in Ross's claim that there was less fake merchandise around so Leo felt that he owed him, but what he didn't know. Impulsively he asked him to join a shooting party the following weekend.

Leo had decided to take up shooting in an effort to find a country pursuit to complement Alison's equine activities. Simon had welcomed the idea, and at Leo's behest had already arranged a couple of days for him. Leo, however, refused to take lessons and his progress was slow. This coming weekend, Simon had booked a day's shooting at Catton Hall, in Derbyshire. They would arrive on Friday night to stay at Catton, shoot on Saturday and drive back on Sunday.

Leo was paying for it all and had invited a few friends and acquaintances but had not yet filled his complement of eight guns.

Ross was very pleased.

'Is there a lady you want to bring with you?' Leo asked. 'Well, don't blame me if you get lonely in your four-poster bed.'

They arranged that Leo would pick up Ross from the Connaught on Friday afternoon.

It was an oddly assorted party that gathered at Catton that evening: Leo and Alison; Simon and Claire; John Scott-Jones (who was a partner of Tony Lonsberg's) with his angry Italian wife; Lawrence Klonaris, who combined the talents of a top portrait painter with those of an enthusiastic shot; an impoverished but stylish earl with his demure countess; Leo's accountant; another minor rag-trader with his completely inappropriate model girlfriend; and Ross Blackwell.

Catton and its shooting weekends were run by Robert Nelson whose family had lived there since 1405, though the present hall had only been built in 1745. Robert was a surprisingly up-to-date-looking man in his early thirties, not at all the old buffer Leo had imagined. He and his beautiful wife, Catherine, greeted the guests with easy affability. Simon, of course, already knew them, and very

soon the finely painted ancestors on the walls of the subdued, elegant drawing-room were looking down on a
relaxed and garrulous champagne-drinking group.

The young Nelsons had the gift of being as comfortable
with the stuffiest shires colonels as with the trendiest of
the Metropolitans. They had had their times in London
and hadn't lost touch, though now Robert was a full-time
farmer, running the large estate and a game-rearing
business. He had realised early on that to keep the fine
house, its park and land in good order, he would have
to supplement the cost of upkeep by trading in the
fine shooting that lay across the estate, and the quiet
elegance of the warm, red-brick hall. He achieved this,
however, with goodwill and good taste. The cuisine, which
Catherine oversaw, and the wines were always excellent,
never flashy. The rooms up to which the party went to
change for dinner were all furnished with four-poster beds
as they might have been two hundred years ago, but
with the addition of twentieth-century plumbing and
heating.

Leo was almost overawed by this grand but muted style.
As he pulled on his dinner-jacket he looked around the
room.

'It's all very well living in a place like this, but have they
got any money? Things must be pretty tight if they have
to take in PGs.'

'Oh, Leo, stop worrying about other people's finances.
They look pretty comfortable to me. Anyway, I think they
really enjoy it. And don't tell me if you had an asset like
this you wouldn't want to make it earn its keep.'

'Yes, I suppose so.' He scowled at a sombre portrait of
one of Robert's ancestors. 'That guy Robert's almost too
good to be true. He was talking to me about the rag-trade;
he was talking to Simon about the City; he talked to Ross
about Texas – and he seemed to know what he was talking
about. And he's a bloody farmer, stuck out here miles
from anywhere.'

'Just because people don't live in London doesn't mean
they only know about potatoes and cattle. Anyway, now

you're here, try and behave in keeping with the surroundings.'

It was a clear, crisp and cloudless January morning when Alison drew their bedroom curtains. The windows faced south over the park, which consisted of a wide, shallow valley beside the River Trent. A small flock of sheep grazed among the venerable trees.

Low, wooded hills stretched away to the south and east and Leo, joining Alison at the window, wondered vaguely where the beaters would flush the first birds.

After a breakfast of kippers and kedgeree, the party gathered outside the front door of the house. Alison and Claire, already stocked and breeched, were going off for a day's hunting with the Meynell on horses the Nelsons had arranged.

The guns, Purdeys and Holland & Holland, were placed in the Range Rovers, and Robert brought round a tray of small pewter tumblers filled with sloe gin. As each gun drained his cup, he could see a number etched in the bottom – his first stand number – and he would move up two numbers after each drive. Leo drew number four, between Simon and the earl.

They walked down through the old coachyard where dogs were prancing around excitedly and Robert checked with his keepers, father and son, that all was ready for the drive. Local villagers, employed as stops, had been sitting around the edges of the woods since early morning to keep the birds in.

Eventually the convoy of cross-country vehicles moved off down the drive, a short way along a lane in the valley bottom, then off the road, east along a rutted track and into a shallow hollow below the northern end of the long Catton Wood, which stretched southwards down the back of the hill. The oak and ash, carefully tended over the centuries, planted, spaced, felled and re-planted, allowed enough light to the woodland floor for thick ground cover to flourish. Here the pheasants felt safe. Robert placed the guns.

Ross Blackwell, who had drawn number one, was a walking gun, allocated a field of winter wheat to the east of the wood. He looked expertly at the lie of the land, the nearest coverts and checked the prevailing south-westerly wind. 'Not too many little fellas are goin' to cross my path,' he said patting the butt of his borrowed gun. 'But if they do, they won't get far.'

Leo found himself at the bottom of a hollow between the end of the wood and a small but inviting covert by a pond. Simon, thirty feet away up a small rise to his left, called over, 'Lucky man, in the hot spot.'

When everyone was in place, Robert blew a whistle. His call was answered by the keeper, already with his fifteen beaters at the far end of the wood. The sound of timber tapping timber and shouts of 'Keep in line' echoed through the trees.

Then the first birds broke and flew: three swung west, high into the wind, over Lawrence Klonaris, the other walking gun, who dispatched two with a left and right, to the delighted shouts of the other outlying guns. Half a dozen more birds flew straight out of the wood, high over Leo and the earl. The earl calmly followed the first pheasant's progress with his gun, and shot it when it was almost overhead, then swung back to take another. Leo fired twice, and watched his targets glide unscathed into the top of the spinney behind him.

It was a good and exciting drive, the wind and the contours of the land lifted the birds and provided great sport. A little before the end of the drive, perhaps sixty pheasant had been shot by seven of the guns. Leo had fired fourteen cartridges and hit nothing. Then, from the north-eastern corner of the wood, a bird broke low to glide across the top of the winter wheat. Leo, desperately, doggedly followed its line for a second. Just before it was out of range, he fired and watched it crumple into the crops.

As it fell, there was a loud bellow from around the corner. 'Mother-fucker!' Ross appeared, picking at his jacket. 'Who the hell fired that? I almost got peppered.'

Simon called down: 'For God's sake, Leo, what are you doing? You can't shoot a bird that low. Not with other guns walking up.'

Leo felt himself redden and mumbled an apology.

And now the drive was over. A whistle was blown and the beaters appeared from among the trees. The pickers-up behind delivered the fallen birds to the game cart. One of them gave a quiet cough of disapproval as he passed Leo.

Robert came over looking slightly pained. 'No luck then, Leo?' After all, Leo was paying. 'Look, don't get desperate and try to hit anything just for the sake of it. Relax, take your time, and see how you get on in the next drive.'

They moved on.

Leo stood at his peg, keyed up and waiting. Carelessly, incompetently, his safety catch was off and his finger was on the trigger. For a few moments they heard the beaters tapping their way up the wood. Suddenly, just to Leo's right, a large cock pheasant ran out of the side of the wood and took off. Leo swung his gun round and fired. This time the yell was more muted – Leo had just missed the earl. But by now, birds were beginning to evacuate the woods, coming fast and high, and all the guns (including the nearly-hit nobleman) were concentrating their fire-power on them. But not Leo – he stood despondently, shuffling his feet like a reprimanded schoolboy as Robert told him that if he took another shot like that, he would have to ask him to stop shooting.

'Leo, you're a businessman. Well, you must understand that it's very bad for *my* business if people come here to shoot and end up getting shot themselves.' Looking up at a new burst of birds, he said encouragingly, 'Look – quick, take that nice high one now – concentrate, follow it through – oh, well done!' as the pheasant's wings folded and it plummeted earthwards.

It was Leo's only bird that drive, and after a stop for bullshots of beef consommé and vodka, he experienced two more blank drives. Yet on all sides of him his guests were dropping them by the dozen, calling congratulations

364

to one another and occasionally, noticing their host's poor performance with, 'Oh, bad luck, Leo.'

Lunch was eaten around a long deal table in one of the vaulted basement rooms of the hall. A huge log fire was blazing, winking off the brass handles of the gun cupboard that lined one wall. A strong stew and large carafes of claret were served and most of the party ate and drank well, laughing and ragging each other. Ross sat next to Leo. 'Were you trying to kill me this morning?' he growled. 'There's plenty of guys would like to do that, but I ain't given you a reason – yet.'

For a spine-chilling moment, Leo thought he was being serious, but then noticed what he took for a glimmer of humour in Ross's eye, so he tried to laugh and apologised once again. 'Listen, mate, if I'd been trying to shoot you, I'd have got nowhere near. Did you see how many birds I hit?'

'Didn't look like too many.'

Leo nodded gloomily. 'I thought this game would be a doddle. If all these Hooray Henrys can do it, I didn't think I'd have much trouble.'

His other guests offered their regrets over his morning's performance and wished him better luck in the afternoon drives – but to no avail.

At the end of the day, the party had shot over three hundred and fifty birds. Leo's personal bag consisted of the two low birds and the one high one. He slunk off as quickly as he could and soaked in the bath, with a tumbler of whisky to cheer him up. He heard Simon and Ross arranging to go out and have an hour's duck-flighting by one of the ponds. He envied them as he watched the gold and pink winter sunset through his bathroom window.

Alison came back, her beautifully cut hunting-coat and white silk stock completely bespattered with mud after a perfect day's hunting up in the south Derbyshire hills. She didn't sympathise with Leo when he told her of his disastrous day for she had told him several times to take lessons, and it was still in a mood of embarrassed despondency that Leo went down to dinner.

This was a magnificent affair of game and claret. Everyone but Leo was in a high-spirited mood. Afterwards, the party divided up. Leo went off to play billiards with Simon and two of the other men. Ross nudged Alison. He had been treating her with great charm and no trace of the manic lust he had briefly displayed at the ranch in Texas.

'Let's get out of this crowd and find somewhere quiet to talk horses.'

Alison, with considerable misgivings, allowed herself to be led to the library. They sat on a sofa by a well-made-up fire in the empty room.

At first to her relief, they did talk horses and swapped stories about their latest acquisitions. Then, abruptly, Ross turned to look meaningfully at Alison. 'I hear you ain't such an angel as you were making out back in Texas a couple of years ago.'

Alison looked blank, then realised what he was talking about.

'I may not have sprouted wings, but then I haven't been particularly devilish either,' she said blandly.

'You weren't on your knees praying, were you, those times you spent with the mighty Wolf Amadeus.'

Alison laughed. 'You can think what you like, believe all the gossip you want. I was with him in a few restaurants, where they discourage their clientele from getting on their knees to pray.'

A smile spread across Ross's face. 'Honey – I know you were in a few restaurants . . . and a few clubs, and in a big house at the top of Laurel Canyon.' He took her hand and, squeezing it, put it on his thigh.

'You ain't so tight-tailed as you pretend – are you, honey?' And, grasping her chin with his free hand, he jerked it round to face him, close to his cruel, twitching lips.

Alison managed to pull her face free. 'Whatever you may know, or think you know, you'd better believe one thing – I'm pretty damned selective.' She tried to get up from the sofa, but he pulled her back, easily, with one hand.

'I know what I know – but does Leo know?' He grinned. 'Nope, I didn't think he did, and you really don't want to hurt poor Leo's feelings, do you? So, honey, you may as well lay back and enjoy it.'

He plunged an arm down the top of her silk chiffon dress, and filled his hand with her naked breast. With his other hand at the back of her head, he pulled her against him, and started kissing her throat, her cheeks, her lips.

He let his arm relax for an instant and Alison tore away from him, felt her dress rip down the front where the Texan's hand still clasped her breast. As he got up she kicked him as hard as she could, driving a sharp pointed shoe into his ankle.

He swore loudly and fell back onto the sofa, clutching at his lower leg. Alison stood in front of the fire, her hair a shambles, and a twelve-inch rent down the front of her dress, when Leo bored with billiards, ambled in. She looked over, feeling fear, shame and relief. 'This Texan yobbo's been trying to maul me again,' she said, catching her breath. 'He's your bloody guest. Deal with him.' Then she fled the room, leaving the door open behind her.

Leo walked round to face Ross who still sat, scowling and nursing his ankle.

'What the fucking hell d'you mean by trying to rape my wife – you drunken cowboy!'

Ross's eyes were very cold. His voice was little louder than a whisper. 'Don't you call me names, boy. And that lady may be your wife, but she ain't your property – or didn't you know that?' he sneered.

Leo's head felt as if it had burst. 'You bastard – you fucking lying bastard.' He lunged at Ross, and tried to hit his face. But the big Texan had no difficulty in warding off the amateur punches. Leo fell on him and started to wrestle futilely.

A small crowd was gathering just inside the open door and Robert pushed his way through.

'Leo, what's the trouble?' He tried to sound reasonable.

Leo let go of Ross's dinner-jacket, which he had been clutching by the lapels, and staggered to his feet.

'The trouble is,' Leo was breathing heavily through clenched teeth, 'that I come in here and find my wife standing here all messed up, her frock in shreds, because this geriatric cowboy's trying to rape her.' Simon strode over and took Leo's arm. 'Listen, old chap, don't lose your cool completely. You're not going to get anywhere screaming or trying to fight him.'

Ross laughed. 'That's right. You know the score.'

Simon ignored him, 'Look, Leo, go and see Alison. Give her a drink or something. I'll deal with Blackwell.'

Robert nodded, and led Leo, white-faced, from the room. Simon turned back to the Texan. 'Whatever happened here, it was your fault. You're Leo's guest and this is Robert's house. You are no longer welcome here. We'll arrange a car to take you and your belongings to a hotel in Derby. I suggest you go up to your room and start packing.'

Ross glared at him. 'Listen you pompous, limey horse's arse, who the hell d'you think you're talking to?'

'An ill-mannered, loud-mouthed Texan drunk.'

The rest of the gathering in the room murmured with nervous approval. Ross got to his feet and limped with unmistakable menace towards Simon, who took a pace back from the large, raised fist.

'If you start trying to hit me, or anyone else, it won't be a hotel you'll be spending the night in, it'll be a cell in Burton police station – full of other Saturday drunks and stinking of piss – and you'll probably have to get there in an ambulance.'

The other men in the room moved in, preparing to overwhelm by sheer number.

Ross dropped his hands and stared around the room.

'You poor dumb bastards . . .' he growled, then pushed his way through them to the door.

In his office the following week, Leo stared at Robinson's letter.

The studio had been operating for nearly a year. It had, said Robinson, been booked to eighty-five per cent of its capacity. The accounts which accompanied Robinson's letter confirmed this. They also confirmed that Leo had loaned $250,000, and was standing as personal guarantor to the banks for a further $300,000, and the studio had made a net operating loss to date.

Robinson explained that this was always bound to be the case until the sister studio in Tahiti was built – then they would be able to establish themselves as *the* studio that all the big bands would want to use, and the LA set-up would pick up all the post-production and mixing work; and then they would be able to start charging fancy rates.

It was perfectly clear to Leo that studio time was being sold at around half the brochure price, on which all the original projections had been based.

Oh, Christ, Leo groaned to himself, of course he's eighty-five per cent booked; he's undercut every other studio in LA. Theirs must be the cheapest twenty-four track set-up in the West Coast; and now, of course, he wanted more money – this time $750,000 – so that the property could be bought and a new studio built in Papeete.

Leo wearily called in his secretary and, with his head in his hands, dictated a letter to Robinson. There would be no further injection of money until the LA studio was generating the turnover and profits that had originally been projected. And, in future, no bookings were to be taken for less than the brochure price. They would lose less money running at fifty per cent capacity at full rate.

He ended: 'You may surprise yourself. It's a good product you're selling and, in the end, people are always prepared to pay for quality.'

Half-convinced that he had solved the problem, he called in Mike Morris, his financial director, to discuss the funding of another project.

When Leo had finished outlining his proposal, Mike shook his head and looked at Leo hopelessly.

'You can't be serious. With all the money we're spending in America and on the Scottish factory and bailing out the club, the bank is going to think you've gone mad in proposing to buy a stud and all its inmates – half a million quid, with running costs of seventy grand in the first year, and no sign of a return for at least two. For God's sake, Leo, do you ever read those management accounts we prepare?'

'Look, Mike, we've done all the spending we're going to do for some time, and now we're consolidating – right?'

'Right, but you want to buy a stud.'

Leo hated himself for having to whine to his own accountant, but he wanted to buy this stud for Alison – to show her that he cared about her; and that he could still afford to make this gesture.

'Mike, for Christ's sake, you know that we'll deal with our debtor position out of cash flow. Half a million is less than a week's turnover, and it'll be great PR.'

'Leo, I don't understand you. It goes against everything you've ever preached about running a business. We will only get our current position under control if there's no let up at all in sales. If we drop as little as five per cent on projections, we're stuffed. You know the auditors are worried.'

Leo was getting annoyed. 'What do they know, those pin-stripe-suited little bureaucrats? It's my bloody company, and I'll make my own decisions.'

Mike stood up. 'If you're going to take that view, you can leave me out of it. It may be your company – mostly – but it's the bank's money and they're beginning to make noises about wanting it back. Leo, why not accept that things just aren't good at the moment? We're far too over-extended with too many loss-making projects in the group. It would be totally irresponsible to take on another now, and commercial suicide.'

For a moment there was defiance in Leo's eyes – then bleak acceptance. After a minute he sighed and looked down on his desk at the details of the fifty-acre Berkshire stud. 'Yes, you're right. We'll forget it.'

As he drove home that evening, Leo was aware of the world closing in, teeth bared. He was losing control over his business, over his wife. He was still fairly sure that Alison had engaged in some amorous adventure in the month she had been away, but he had been too frightened to confront her with it. Since that previous autumn, she had shown no signs of straying again, but she had been less affectionate towards Leo and more preoccupied with her arty friends and her horses.

He felt powerless. He couldn't reprimand her, couldn't let her know that he suspected, without chastising her somehow. He had never been able to dominate her in that way – and especially not now.

Instead, he wanted to give her things, but even as he made plans to buy her loyalty, he knew that he was wasting his time.

Over a morose supper, he told her that he wasn't buying the stud.

She looked very disappointed, but only said. 'You're right. Business should come first.'

'Ali, it's not that. I know you want it badly; I'd like it too, but it would be very hard work, you know, and it's a hell of a big investment for a hobby. It's not that we can't afford it . . .'

Alison looked at him doubtfully. 'Okay, Leo, but you know it's more than just a hobby.'

Leo knew. For her the horses were a substitute for the children she couldn't have. And as time went on, they would become even more important to her.

He walked round the table and stood behind her, then put his hands on her shoulders and leaned down to kiss her. She did not turn round to him, so he kissed the top of her head, squeezed her shoulders and carried on walking round the table. 'You're right, Angel. Business isn't the be-all and end-all; we'll buy your bloody stud.'

Alison looked up, pleased but worried. 'Are you sure you can?'

'Of course I can,' Leo said quickly.

'That's wonderful, Leo. I promise it'll be earning its keep within a year or two. Just as long as you're not jeopardising your business.'

Leo laughed. 'Don't worry Angel – I think we'll manage.'

# 1977

Ross Blackwell sank back comfortably in his chair in the bar at the Connaught. One booted foot rested across his knee. He smiled broadly at his guest.

Raju Kalianji, bland, inscrutable, looked back at him.

The barman arrived with two beers and Raj waited for the Texan to speak.

'So – you're Raju Kalianji?' He took a sip of his drink, and, when Raj didn't reply, went on. 'I learn from friends in San Francisco that you manufacture garments in Hong Kong.'

'No,' said Raj. 'To be strictly accurate, I am committed to buying the total output of a factory there. It is difficult, legally, for outsiders to own manufacturing businesses in Hong Kong.'

'I also find that you have a factory here in London supplying a lot of stores.'

Raj nodded.

'Which stores?' Ross asked.

'Mr Blackwell, where is this leading? I would be grateful if you could tell my why you wanted this meeting.'

'Okay. Do you do any business with Rags – with Leo Freeman?'

'Yes, a substantial amount. They are one of my bigger customers.'

'Yeah – so I'm told. And how d'you get on with the dynamic Mr Freeman?'

Raj said nothing for a moment, but kept his eyes fixed on Ross's.

'Why do you ask?' he said finally.

'Aha,' said Ross, his grin widening as his eyes narrowed, 'I see you don't get along with him. That's good – nor do I.'

'Mr Blackwell, we do not belong to a very exclusive club. There must be thousands of people who don't get along with Leo Freeman. To me, though, he's an important customer, and my personal views about his manners and character are irrelevant.'

'Well, my personal views about his character are very relevant to me – he owes me, and I intend for him to pay. Now it seems to me that there may come a time when we could help each other. After all, you're an ambitious man, aren't you?'

Raj did not reply.

'I know you manufacture here, and in Hong Kong and India; you distribute into Europe and the States; you supply eighty per cent of Rags's stock. You've also got three property companies, a major share in a commodity brokers, and you do a lot of commodity dealing in your own right. You're well spread, Mr Kalianji, making a lot of money, but you'll always be ready to make more, right?'

Raj was unimpressed. 'I am a businessman, Mr Blackwell. My family lost everything in Uganda, and I am determined to re-establish our position. All the information you have is either common knowledge, or on file at Companies House.'

'No, not all of it, but that's beside the point. Now, like I say, we could be allies. I could put Leo Freeman in a position where he'd be begging you for mercy.' He looked at Raj's emotionless face. 'Look, he's very exposed and you know it – you've got to protect your investment.'

'That's my problem, I'll cope with it in my own way.'

'Now, don't you be proud. You and I know he's losing a lot of money in his new factory in Scotland and that he'll go on pouring money in because he hates depending on you as his major supplier. They tell me his club is incapable of making money because he agreed with the people who owned the property that they have twenty-five per cent of the takings instead of a fixed rent. And this studio in LA –

he's too far away from it to make it work. The guy he's got running it is a good operator, but he's no businessman. Leo's got real problems in the States: he's selling the merchandise but making no money – and somebody's been flooding the market with cheap copies of his stuff . . .'

'. . . And he's just committed himself to buying a stud farm for half a million pounds,' Raj supplied. 'Yes, Mr Blackwell, he has problems. But I don't at this stage see how you can help me, though I will give you some advice. From what I know of your activities, it seems to me it would be advantageous to you to re-establish yourself on good terms with Leo. Try and overlook whatever has upset your relationship, and make friends again. Leo Freeman cannot resist people who eat humble pie in front of him.'

Ross nodded. This was a plan he understood – appease-ment, an offer of friendship, and then, the sting.

Simon welcomed Leo into his office, above Holborn Via-duct. He studied his brother-in-law's face for a moment. The heavy brows were gathered, throwing deep, vertical ridges up into his forehead. There was none of the usual sparkle in his eyes. His face was thinner; his gut hung heavy.

'Well,' said Simon. 'What brings you here? Do you want me to throw my weight behind a planning application?' he laughed. He had just been elected to the Greater London Council as a Tory member for Kensington and Chelsea.

Leo tried to raise a responding smile. 'No thanks, Coun-cillor. But congratulations all the same. I'll let you know when I want access to the corridors of power.' He paused, and looked embarrassed. 'Look . . .' He surprised Simon with the almost whining appeal in his voice. 'I think I've got a problem. It's not my bloody fault,' he went on quickly, 'but Ubiland – you know, the freeholders of the Kensington store – seem to have got into real trouble. Something's happened to their shares. They're about a fifth of the value they were six months ago and they've got to unload some of their bigger properties. Including mine.'

374

Simon shrugged. 'So what's the problem? You'll just be paying rent to someone else.'

'There is a problem. Business there has been great, but we've spent a load of bread on other projects which aren't going to show returns for a while, and I've been really strapped for cash.'

Simon raised an eyebrow. 'But you've only just bought that stud in Goring. Alison's already taken Claire there. I hear it's spectacular – and filling up with some very expensive horses.'

Leo groaned and nodded his head. 'I know, I know. I had to get it for Ali. It's hocked up to the clouds, but for God's sake don't tell her that. The point is, I got into arrears on my rent at Kensington, and then, to buy a bit of time, I negotiated a deal where they take a percentage on turnover, like they do on the club. I convinced them that in the long run they'd be better off. I mean, they'd already served a notice on me for non-payment, and the bank wouldn't give an inch, the bastards. All over me they were when the money was rolling in, and now because I've borrowed a bit to treble the turnover and profits, they're screaming "Come in, Mr Freeman, your time's up!"'

Simon looked at Leo doubtfully. 'Come on, Leo. From what I can gather you've borrowed more than a bit. I don't know what you've pumped into the States, but if I were the bank who'd lent it to you, I'd be worried. It's over three years since you opened in New York; that's a long honeymoon, and they're probably looking for offspring now.'

Leo pushed a fringe of straggling curls from his brow with a trembling hand. 'It's going to come right in the States – I know it. I've sorted out all the problems, and we should make money this year for sure.'

'Well, let's hope you do. But there's the studio, and this Scottish factory. How's that going?'

'Oh, we're getting there. The production coming out of it is great.'

'As good as Raj Kalianji's?'

'Yeah.'

'The same price?'

'Well . . . not yet. But as soon as we get the throughput up it will be.'

'Hmmm.' Simon was non-committal. 'Anyway, why have you come to see me?'

'Because I haven't signed the new arrangements with Ubiland yet. It's all agreed and everything, but we were just about to sign when they told me they were going to have to unload the place – and they can't do that without a tenant with a decent covenant and everything paid up; or vacant possession.' He looked bleakly at Simon. 'Either I pay up or get out. That place brings in about twenty per cent of our UK income. I've got to hang on to it and I just haven't got the bread to pay six months' arrears, and another quarter's rent. It's all I can do to keep up payments to my suppliers and I've got Customs and Excise frothing at the mouth over some late VAT payments.'

'Won't your suppliers extend their credit a bit? After all, it's in their interests to keep you in Kensington.'

'Raj? Extend? He's tight as arseholes. He's got us by the short and curlies, and he knows it.'

'You still haven't told me why you've come to see me – or did you just want to talk?' Simon had assumed an attitude of patient sympathy.

'Talking's not going to help. No – I thought you might know something about Ubiland shares. I don't know why they've taken such a dive. They were one of the few companies to come through the worst of the crash. I know they're sound.'

'Didn't they come unstuck on shopping mall developments in Florida?' Simon asked.

'Yeah, but not that disastrously – not enough for people to be unloading shares so fast. Once that started, it snowballed and now the banks are calling in their loans as fast as they can because the company's share value doesn't even cover them. So, they've got to sell, and most of their properties are in mid-development. The Rags store is one of the easiest to shift. But I can't see what started this run on their shares! There's not much wrong with their portfolio and they're paying out a few divis. I think there's something dodgy going on.'

'Yes,' agreed Simon. 'I also detect a strong odour of rodent. All I can tell you is that a major shareholder dumped a whole pile onto the market about four days ago. Property isn't the flavour of the month at the moment and there weren't enough takers. As well as that, about six months ago, they announced the start of a huge new commercial and residential development on the Côte d'Azur; that shot the price up, and now stories are emerging that the Mayor of Nice and his cronies are sitting on it and won't let it happen – so, along with the Florida fiasco, Jo Punter and the more nervous fund managers are all pulling out.'

'But they're crazy!' said Leo. 'There's nothing wrong with the company. Can't you persuade some of your bigger clients to start buying? – I mean the shares are a bargain, and if the price came up a bit, the pressure to sell my store would ease up.'

'You're probably right, but the kind of clients that could afford to buy enough to make a difference have got minds of their own. They're prepared to be influenced, a bit, but this Ubiland situation doesn't smell good, and I won't be able to talk them into it – even if I thought it was a good idea, which, at the moment, I don't.'

Leo looked back at him sourly. 'You're a brave man, aren't you? You're never going to get there first if you wait to see which way the wind blows before you set sail.' He stood up to go. 'Their share price will come back, no question. Meanwhile, I'm stuffed – but don't worry, I'll get myself out of it without your help.'

As he walked towards the door, Simon said, 'There is one thing I could do for you: I'll talk to Raj. I'm sure I can persuade him to give you more rope.'

Leo turned round, furious, lips trembling to shout his disdain for this offer. Then suddenly he sighed and nodded. 'Okay. You do that. But you don't stand much chance of getting anywhere. He's loving it, watching me struggle.'

'Rubbish, Leo. He's a businessman. To be honest with

you, I'm afraid he's become so obsessed with making money, I don't think he gives two damns what you think or feel, as long as you keep providing him with business.'

There was a low heavy sky over London, letting through barely enough light to reflect on the wet streets. Leo felt like a fox running before hounds, with no earth to go to, nor woods nor water to confuse the scent. As he drove back, every red traffic light seemed aimed at him; every other driver seemed to invite confrontation. He envied the people on the streets – the pressure-free existence of the meter-maid, the uncomplicated problems of the scaffold erectors, the minor financial dilemmas of the little men shuffling in and out of the bookies.

His energy, enthusiasm and uncompromising optimism had brought him face to face with disaster. He had been overtaken by his boldness, like an ambitious puppeteer who finds himself with twenty puppets to control. He needed help, but there was no one he wanted to ask. He was incapable of reversing years of braggadocio; people wouldn't believe him – and they would be right.

Alison had moved too far away. He could see her highly developed sense of loyalty struggling with the contempt that she was beginning to feel for him. But it was too late for him to change. So he carried on with his customary bravado, always dismissive of the little man, the weak man, the poor man – but he knew that now he failed to convince, even himself. Alison had been thrilled with the Goring stud, but he knew she knew he couldn't afford it. She let him go ahead because it would teach him a lesson. Leo wanted to show her that he didn't need the lesson. Sarah effectively ignored him, and as for his mother, she just shook her head when he went to see her, her eyes showing wet and helpless.

But when he walked into his office building, there was a large smiling face to greet him.

Confidence and friendliness shone from Ross Black-well's eyes as he walked over to greet Leo.

'Leo, my friend, I've come to apologise.'

He held out a large welcoming hand, and Leo took it.

It was nearly a year since the fracas at Catton, and Leo couldn't connect this large, warm laughing man with the demonic spitter of venom who had been driven off into the middle of a windy Derbyshire night. Here was a face that looked at Leo with appreciation and admiration; enveloped him in trust. A strong, long arm was round Leo's shoulder.

'Am I forgiven?' A deep soft drawl in Leo's left ear.

Leo found himself nodding. 'Yeah, yeah – of course you are – you randy old cowboy. Alison said you'd just got too pissed.' He felt the arm stiffen, then relax.

'Come on up to the office, and have a drink to it,' Leo invited and, cheered by the prospect of a temporary haven from the baying hounds, he led Ross upstairs.

Leo poured out champagne and all his troubles. Ross was sympathetic, helpful, constructive. They opened a third bottle of Krug, and Leo's problems had shrunk. He could cope; he would compromise. All these people – the banks, the landlords, the suppliers – they all needed him as much as he needed them. And Ross agreed.

Ross also agreed with the rotund, balding man who sat opposite him in the Geneva Yacht Club. Michel Disch was around fifty, and a man of limited interests. He loved only two things: money and Danielle Milinaire. In spite of the tremendous, dynastic banking wealth to which he had been born, he had never lost his enjoyment in increasing it. He had also developed a fascination for women who combined the ability to make money with the capacity for satisfying his considerable and particular libido. Furthermore, he was prepared to deploy the full resources of his power, influence and money in the pursuit of the current object of this fascination.

Ross looked outside at the *Jet d'Eau* fighting with the rain for recognition as the banker told him why he had decided to fund Raj Kalianji's property companies.

The little Swiss spoke with harsh, guttural Rs. 'Raj is

one of the most capable entrepreneurs I have met. We handle all his off-shore business. He has a real Midas touch. With his judgement and sense of timing, he will not fail. He would be the best poker player, you know.'

Ross nodded. 'And he's the best route you could find for getting at Leo Freeman.'

Michel Disch looked embarrassed. 'My involvement with Raj is only business. It is true that he may have some more success to the cost of Mr Freeman, and I would not personally be sorry for that.'

'And if Leo bites the dust, you think you'll have Danielle all to yourself?'

Disch grinned. 'What a delicious thought.' He licked his lips over the idea and his last spoonful of sorbet. 'And what's your interest in Mr Freeman?'

'Only business, long term,' Ross said slowly.

When Raj walked into the bar at Wedgie's, the club that had taken over the old Aretusa premises, he saw Leo engrossed in overt and overworked flirtation with two well-tanned ex-models, girls who had been the object of a fifteen-year game of pass-the-parcel round London, Barbados, Monaco and Ibiza. They read the gossip columns, not the financial pages, so Leo Freeman still presented an interesting and possibly fruitful test of their skills. Raj saw them responding.

He walked over and greeted Leo. The two girls appraised him, expertly, expectantly: an Arab, maybe, and very good-looking – what a bonus.

Raj suggested that they have their discussion at an isolated corner table and saw the confidence slide like a rubber mask from Leo's face.

'Why the hell did you want to meet here?' he asked sullenly.

'It's neutral. And we won't be overheard,' Raj waved towards the large thumping speakers.

'Okay, so what's this news you have for me?'

'News and a proposal,' Raj corrected. 'They're both good, and you won't like either of them. And in order to avoid any misunderstandings or face-saving gestures of defiance on your part, I should say that I am aware, as you will be, that you will have no option but to accept them.'

Leo scowled at his drink, then, without much strength, at Raj.

'All right then, get on with it,' he said to help himself to sustain the illusion that he was still in command.

Raj smiled a rare, indulgent smile. 'Yes, sahib,' he paused; then, in an even voice, went on. 'First, I am your new landlord at Kensington. I have bought the freehold. And, as your landlord, I am prepared to accept the new terms of occupation that you had worked out, but not signed, with Ubiland.'

Leo's face went white. A muscle in his cheek twitched, but otherwise he showed no emotion. Fury at finding himself in this relationship with Raj mingled explosively with relief at knowing that one of his biggest problems was solved. His confusion and frustration prevented him from reacting outwardly. Inwardly, he wasn't sure whether he wanted to kill Raj or himself. He knew that he wanted to kill someone.

Raj looked at him calmly, waiting for an outburst. When none came he continued, 'Secondly, I am aware of the cash-flow difficulties you are encountering and, given certain conditions, there is a way in which I am prepared to assist.'

'I don't need your bloody assistance.' Leo was making a visible effort not to shout. 'Just because you're the landlord of one store doesn't mean you own me. I do have seventy other shops around the world.'

Raj raised both eyebrows, like an angry classics master. Slowly, deliberately, he ran his fingers down the creases of his trousers. 'Leo, don't waste your breath posturing. I know exactly what your position is. I am prepared to help you because it is commercially expedient for me to do so, not because I like you. However, I don't intend to get into a shouting match here, so I'll tell you what I propose and leave you to think about it.'

Leo sat back and tried to hide his resignation.

'Right,' said Raj. 'My proposal is intended to allow you

to reduce your borrowings to the bank, retrench and consolidate your position. From where I'm standing, your business is haemorrhaging at four points, and these should be stopped. These points are your American retailing operation, your studio in Los Angeles, your night-club and your Scottish factory. The stud in Goring is your own affair, but I can't see how you hope to support it over the next two or three years. So, you must get rid of those four losers, and I will undertake to supply all your British and European outlets on a consignment basis, on sale or return, payment against weekly sales. Title to all stock in your current inventory which has been supplied by me will revert to me, and you will be credited in full. I will pay that credit in cash. I am supplying around eighty per cent of your product, and I am sure that your other suppliers will extend your credit by an extra thirty days, if you explain this reorganisation to them. If you take the measures I suggest, and accept my proposal, I would say that within a year you will be operating a profitable business with a healthy balance sheet. However, I am a businessman and, as I said, I am not proposing this because I like you, so there will be a ten per cent surcharge on all stock placed on your premises on consignment by my company.'

He rose before Leo could yell his instinctive response. 'And I must emphasise one thing: you must undertake to get rid of those loss-making millstones before the deal can commence. I will not supply stock on sale or return to your American stores.' He held out his hand. Leo, slumped in his chair, ignored it.

'Well, I expect to hear from you tomorrow,' said Raj, and walked quickly through the now crowded bar.

Leo sat on, silently, staring at the room's decorative details. He had never noticed them before. He wondered how the artist had been able to paint such tiny leaves on the pillars right down to the floor. He must have lain on his stomach. He looked at the backs of the two mercenaries to whom he had been talking earlier; they were engrossed in conversation with a vacuous-eyed, loud-laughed racing-driver turned property developer.

Eventually Leo got up and left the bar without speaking

to anyone. He decided to walk back to Chelsea Square, leaving his car to be picked up later. It might give him a chance to come to terms with Raj's *fait accompli*.

It was only nine o'clock when he reached the house. Alison was holding a dinner-party for an assorted crowd of artists, musos and literati. Leo only knew the painter, Lawrence Klonaris, although he recognised one of a pair of hugely successful writers of stage musicals. The guests scarcely noticed him, he was of another world to them. They did not expect him to join in their well-informed banter and competitive repartee.

He went into his study and poured himself a large Scotch, then, surreptitiously, to counteract his gloom, took a small packet of cocaine from behind his copy of *Who's Who* and snorted a long, fat line.

Feeling fortified, he went in and took his place at the dinner-table. He tried to affirm his position as master of this household, but his guests left him in no doubt that he was an intruder. Alison looked at him from time to time, sorrowful and worried, but he ignored her glances and subtle warnings and became louder in his condemnation of the arts as a serious occupation.

'It's all very well, you people having great and wonderful ideas and talents, but they're no fucking good unless someone a bit closer to the ground goes out and sells them, or finances them, or tells you where the market really is. You can sit there sneering at me because I buy and sell things, but let me tell you, there's a load of talent that would never have seen the light of day if it hadn't been for me.'

The successful ones in the group agreed, but protested that the artist and the businessman were equally and mutually dependent. The unsuccessful ones shouted that businessmen and entrepreneurs simply deflected the true course of art.

A hopeless and irresolvable shouting match developed across the table, but fairly soon Leo was identified as the common enemy. As they guzzled his Chateau Margaux '66, and Chateau d'Yquem '67, they all turned on him, reviled his philistinism, and placed his contribution to society at the level of road-sweeper or sewer-operative.

Alison was alarmed to see that he could not fight back. She almost wanted to go to his rescue, but he always provoked these arguments and, however much he hurt himself, it was his own fault.

In the end, Leo rose from the table in fury. 'While you're all sitting about getting pissed on my wine and my cognac and smoking my cigars, I've got to go and do some work to make sure they don't all run out.'

He slammed the front door and found a taxi to take him to his office. He let himself into the empty building and wandered around in the dark, letting all the familiar things reassure him of his own strengths and achievements.

He sat at the head of the boardroom table, lit only by the street lamps outside. He had to stop himself weeping over the erosion of his control of his diverse empire.

His business was his child.

It had been conceived in his mind, born of his optimism. He had struggled, relentlessly, through the labour pains which it caused and tended it night and day, until it could stand on its own feet and had grown into a robust adolescent. But now it had a mind of its own; it refused to be controlled by him. It had become wilful and self-destructive, like an unruly teenager.

And he was being told that he must share custody of it with a man he hated, that he would be only partially responsible for the continuing upbringing of his own off-spring.

He walked up to his own office and turned on the lights. He unlocked his desk and took out the current management accounts and balance sheets of his businesses and started to formulate his response to Raj's proposals. He assumed, although it had not been stated, that Raj was offering him an all-or-nothing package; that his continuing occupancy of the Kensington store was dependent on acceptance of the sale or return stock deal and disposals of the stipulated businesses.

First, he had no intention of disposing of anything, but reckoned if he removed the offending companies from under the umbrella of the main group, Raj could not object.

He could not disagree with Raj that cash flow would improve enormously under this revised arrangement, and he felt he could persuade the banks to continue to support the other businesses if he personally guaranteed them, using his shareholding in the parent company as security. He would form a new, entirely independent off-shore holding company, which would buy the American operation, the factory and the club from the existing Rags group. It could not then be argued that they hadn't been disposed of. He was sure Raj would continue to supply the US shops on the old terms. They represented, after all, a lot of business. He was confident that these shops would start making money now. And, at the studio, Robinson had followed Leo's instructions and found that bookings had scarcely dropped. They were making an operating profit, though it would be a long while before the investment could be said to be fully serviced.

If he hung on to the factory, he would eventually be in a position where he would be less dependent on Raj and, with the consignment and surcharge deal, this was more important than ever.

Looking at the figures for the Rainbow Room, there was no commercial justification whatsoever for hanging on to it – but it was, Leo persuaded himself, an invaluable PR tool for his main business; and it wasn't losing that much.

As for the stud, he could not face telling Alison that he had to sell it. He would have to transfer it to his own name and hope for the best.

With the assistance of a lot of cocaine and coffee, he spent the next eight hours preparing his presentation for the bank. The Spanish cleaners arrived at seven and were astounded to find him at his desk, elated and talkative. He offered them a drink and asked after their home lives and families. Then he took a taxi to the Connaught for breakfast.

He didn't return to the office until late in the afternoon but, by that time, he had seen his auditors and his bankers and had received their assurances that they would support his reorganisation. He summoned Mike Morris and Sarah to his office to tell them what Raj had proposed and what he had arranged. He didn't wait for the congratulations. He was opening a bottle and offering champagne before they could give their reactions.

Mike said, 'I must say, as financial director of the main group, that the price your holding company is paying for these businesses scarcely represents the group's original investment in them.'

'So what?' said Leo. 'I own both companies; it doesn't really matter if one sells cheap to the other.'

'Excuse me, Leo, but Sarah owns twenty per cent of Rags. Are you proposing that she has twenty per cent of the holding company?'

Before Leo could reply, Sarah said, 'I don't want any part of this new holding company and, as a shareholder of Rags, I'm bloody delighted to be shot of all those loss-makers, even at the prices Leo's proposing to pay. Let me tell you, it'll be in the company's interest in the long run. They'll never make any money.'

Leo said simply, and with relief, 'Well, that's your opinion and your decision. If you're happy, I am.'

Sarah looked back at him, shaking her head. 'You're mad, Leo. If you want to fund those businesses out of your own money, that's up to you. But Raj was right to identify them as major disasters. And he won't mind if you've disposed of them to yourself. That's probably exactly what he thought you'd do. He knows how you think and react and he'll be waiting to bail you out, on his own terms, when you get over your head in debt again. Raj Kalianji is a calculating, brilliant bastard – I should know – but you continually underestimate him. Frankly, I'm past caring, and, much though I resent the man, I can't help thinking that this business will be a lot better off for his closer involvement. You won't listen to me or Mike or anyone else, and if you find yourself in the shit again, don't blame us. Now – where do I sign the papers?'

# March 1978

To celebrate his adoption as Tory candidate for Fulham to fight the General Election in 1979, Simon Riley held a party in the genteel surroundings of the Hurlingham Club. Fulham had always been a Labour seat, but the interior design shops, delicatessens, and tile and cushion emporia that were springing up all round the New King's Road and the Fulham Road suggested that this would not be sustained. And so did the opinion polls, for the young professionals responsible for the relentless gentrification of the terraces of little Victorian houses were thought to be solid Tory polling-booth fodder.

Alison welcomed this milestone in her brother's career and was certain he would win and find himself at Westminster a year or so hence. She found Simon's wife, Claire, and reassured her that, although this might be the beginning of an important political career, it was not necessarily the end of her family life. Claire knew this really, and felt guilty about complaining, especially as she saw the look on Alison's face when she asked after Leo. The two of them, though, carried on chatting amiably until Alison spotted Sarah whom, since Alison was spending so much time at the stud in Goring, she had not seen for a couple of months. She made her way over to her.

'Hi, Sarah. What's brought you here? It's not exactly your kind of scene.'

'I've been feeling rather miserable and sorry for myself recently, and there is something amazingly reassuring about your brother's civilised optimism. So, as he'd asked me, I thought I'd come – it makes a change from rag-trade traumas.'

'Well, it's great to see you. I'm sorry we haven't been in touch. How are things at Rags? I haven't had the heart to ask Leo much – he's been a complete manic depressive for the last six months, and he never gives me a straight answer.'

'How much has Leo told you about the new deal with Raj?'

'Oh, bits and pieces. He says Raj isn't as smart as he seems and he's going to miss out in America. But I'm afraid I don't want to know any more. I've had ten years of it. But tell me your version.'

Sarah succinctly outlined the current position and was surprised that Alison was so uninformed.

When she had finished, Alison frowned. 'My God, poor Leo. I simply hadn't realised how exposed he is. I'll have to get him to sell Goring.' She looked very disappointed. 'Though, as a matter of fact, we've almost turned it into a paying proposition. But how do you cope, having to see so much of Raj?'

Sarah looked back at her, sad, frustrated, resigned. 'That's the hell of it. It's really weird; I never thought I could do it, but when I see him I can talk to him and behave absolutely normally. I just don't believe he knows how I still feel.' She looked down at her glass. 'I still want him desperately, every time I see him – and I hate him for encouraging my illusions, for being such an utterly mercenary bastard when I was convinced he had so much depth. I suppose as much as anything, I hate him for ever thinking I would tolerate his marriage to Reena. I mean, I don't blame Reena. She's a lovely woman, but she obviously doesn't understand the first thing about her husband. But then, she doesn't need to. Did you know they'd had a son? Well, they have, and when Min asked Raj about it, he spoke as if a prize brood-mare had given birth to a potentially valuable colt. He's completely devoid of emotion, and I mistook that for spirituality – my own fault, really.'

Alison felt warm sympathy for her friend. They seemed both to have lost out to ambitious men of entirely different types, but at least Alison felt in some way in control of her own destiny. 'Why don't you get out of it all? You're rich enough. You don't have to work. Take off; do something entirely new.'

Sarah smiled. 'Well, for one thing – without flattering myself – the business still needs me, so I wouldn't stay rich for long if I left it; and for another, I'm not going to run away. I derive a certain amount of strength simply by knowing I'm facing my past lack of judgement head-on. Anyway, let's be more positive. I came here to get away from brooding over my own affairs. How do you think Simon will get on at the election?'

'Simon is one of life's quiet, industrious winners; that's why Leo is so awkward with him. I would say he stood a very good chance of getting into Parliament and, once he does, the sky's the limit.'

'If I lived here, I'd vote for him.'

'He'll be delighted to know that.'

Sarah grinned. 'And what about the horses? You say your stud's almost a paying proposition. How have you done that?'

'Not from breeding, yet,' Alison said. 'Though I think that will come. What I've been doing is a lot of real old-fashioned horse-coping. I've found a very rare specimen – an Irishman who knows all about horses, and who's honest. We're bringing six to ten horses a month over from Ireland, putting them through their paces here, then selling some as hunters and keeping back others to bring on as eventers and show-jumpers. And so far, we haven't gone wrong at all. We've made an average of fifteen hundred quid a horse over the last six months. I'm practically making more money than Rags!' She laughed. 'Mind you, I expect we'll start getting it wrong now – the luck can't last. But at least I'm justifying my own interest. My Andalusians are looking great. I've got six top brood-mares and three more being covered this year – so, if I can convince a few more people of their potential, I should start making something back from them. Trouble is, English people aren't that interested. Still, the Americans are and they're beginning to come and look when they're in Europe . . .'

Suddenly, Simon materialised at her elbow. 'Why are the two most beautiful women in the room huddled together talking about horses? I only asked you as decoration, so it's time you wandered round and did your job. Where's your over-working, over-playing husband, Ali? Or does he still refuse to have anything to do with politicians, even if he's related to them?'

'He's over-working somewhere – at least, that's the rumour. But he mumbled something about "Good luck – he'll bloody need it," when I told him about the purpose of this celebration. Anyway, this is a good piss-up and your Party Faithful look full of admiration and enthusiasm for you. Here's hoping their trust is not misplaced!' She raised her glass and smiled.

'I'll drink to that,' Simon said, 'and I don't think they'll be disappointed on the big night.'

Leo wasn't over-working, though he was drinking as hard as he could. Sitting with a couple of loyal lieutenants in the Rainbow Room, he surveyed it hazily, trying to forget that this was an episode that was about to end. The room was fairly empty. It was some time since it had been anything else. London's fickle club-goers had found new watering holes. Membership had become too wide and unexclusive; the novelty had long since worn off and the competition for parking space in Kensington Square had become too keen. For whatever reason, people had stopped coming.

Now that Leo could no longer top up the club account from Rags, he'd had to face the inevitable and accept that he must sell it. Then, of course, he had found that he didn't really have a lease to sell, only a licence to occupy, plus some doubtful goodwill, and some rather stale fixtures and fittings.

Raj Kalianji had offered him an absurdly small sum, but as the landlord, he was the only serious potential buyer and once again Leo had had to accept a humiliating defeat.

Sometime, not now, maybe next week, he would have to make an announcement that the club would be closing. Raj intended to invite Vijay Singh to operate it as a kind of Indian brasserie. It was such a bizarre idea, and Vijay's existing following was so strong, that it would probably work. Anyway, the club was closing and Leo supposed that hundreds of angry members would start demanding refunds on unexpired subscriptions. He had no illusions about the hostility with which many people viewed him and the pleasure they would take in kicking him in his fallen state.

Leo glowered when he saw Raj walk into the club with Vijay and several other well-dressed, and self-confident, Indians.

'Here comes the curry Mafia,' he growled to his companions, 'deciding what colour flocked wallpaper to put up.'

'Oh, I don't know, Leo, I've seen the plans – it's a great idea,' one of them replied.

'Bollocks. Whose side are you on? What the hell do they know about what the English punters want?'

He was staring at Raj. He tried not to look away as the Indian spotted him and strolled over to his table.

'May I join you?' Raj asked, and sat down without waiting for a reply. He called a waiter and ordered a cup of tea.

'For Christ's sake, Raj, what are you trying to prove? Have a proper drink.' He took a bottle of Krug from an ice-bucket and waved it around. Raj shook his head. 'No thanks. I've an early start tomorrow – and so have you, Leo. I've got to talk to you first thing in the morning; I'm leaving for the States at midday.'

'What now?' asked Leo. 'I seem to have done nothing but sit in meetings with you for the last three weeks.'

'I think you know what it's about.' Raj turned to the waiter and cancelled the tea, then stood up. 'I'll see you at your office, then, at eight.'

Leo was there, before eight.

He did know why Raj wanted to see him, and felt he might cope with the meeting a little better with the aid of a short line of cocaine.

He was still snuffling when Raj arrived. He looked up as the door opened, and said with assumed briskness, 'Morning, Raj. Okay – let's get on with it.' He waved the Indian to a chair on the other side of his desk.

Raj sat, and placed a fat folder on the red leather desk top. He studied his manicured hands for a moment. His eyes flicked up and he noticed with disdain a pale trace of cocaine on Leo's lapel. Leo found himself holding his breath, waiting.

At last, Raj looked directly at him. 'On the whole, our sale-or-return arrangement appears to be functioning satisfactorily – as far as your retail outlets are concerned. However, as you must be aware, things seem to have got rather out of synchronisation on the wholesale distribution. Your people have been very diligent in supplying the weekly unit sales details – and very good figures they are, too – but you've been less diligent in enclosing your weekly payment. You've performed properly on your own retail sales, why not on the wholesale? After all, the agreement we have covers all sales.'

Leo managed a smile, and, chiding, said, 'Come on, Raj. You know the score. With the retail I get the money and a fatter margin as soon as the goods are sold; on my wholesale sales, after I've taken into account your ten per cent surcharge and our selling and distribution costs, there's not a lot of profit left, and I have to wait forty-five, maybe sixty days for payment. On that basis, if I pay you within a week of dispatching and invoicing and then have to carry debtors for a couple of months, there's sod-all left and I might as well pack up wholesaling altogether. You wouldn't like that, would you? It represents a big chunk of our business.'

Raj shook his head. 'If I'm not going to be paid, it represents a big chunk of rotten business that I can do without.'

Leo's eyes blazed. 'Who the hell says you won't be paid? Of course you'll be bloody paid – but it's only reasonable that you should wait until we are.'

'What is reasonable in these circumstances is a matter of opinion. And my opinion is that you should stick absolutely to the sale-or-return terms that we have agreed. If you don't keep your side of the bargain, I'm not obliged to keep mine. By putting in stock on consignment, I have more than halved the capital requirement of your business and I expect that contribution to be recognised by your responsible adherence to the undertakings you have given me. You are four weeks behind in payment of your wholesale turnover. This represents . . .' He paused and opened the folder in front of him, then read from the top sheet. 'Two hundred and thirty-two thousand pounds, including VAT.' He looked over at Leo. 'May I have your cheque, please?'

Leo heard himself trying to be conciliatory. 'Come on, Raj, I haven't got it. I haven't been paid for those sales yet. Be reasonable.'

'You should have anticipated that before you agreed to my terms. If your margins are too low and your credit control too inefficient, it is your concern, not mine. If you can't, or won't, pay me for these sales, then I shall have to cease supplying you altogether.'

'Don't give me that cobblers,' said Leo angrily. 'You're getting your money on time for seventy-five per cent of the stock you sell to us. You're not going to give that up. And you know you'll get your money for the other pretty damned soon.'

'Of course I want to go on supplying your shops, but I have the right, in view of your default, to change the terms of our agreement by allowing you only to sell my stock for retail, and not for wholesale.'

'I don't think you want to lose that business either.'

'Well, we've been through that. However, I do have a proposal. My company will take over the wholesale distribution of Rags's product, and, in order to deal with the outstanding current position, we will take over your trade debtor ledger.'

'Don't be mad!' yelled Leo. 'I'm not going to give up my profit on the business I've been doing.'

'But you've told me there's hardly any profit in it anyway – and I'm prepared to pay you a royalty on all sales achieved with your styles or label, all to be approved by your design department. And I propose to pay a cash advance against that royalty, in return for an exclusive, worldwide, five-year contract. I have an agreement and a cheque with me.'

He took a narrow, folded, legal-looking document from the folder and slid it across the desk to Leo.

'I'll leave you to study that, and consult on it, and will expect your reply when I return from America.' He got to his feet and gathered his papers. 'If I may summarise the position, you have three options: one, bring your payments up to date immediately and keep them up to date; two, you accept that I will not supply consignment stock for wholesaling, and you pay the outstanding amount within fourteen days; or three, you sign that royalty agreement and accept my cheque.'

Raj flew to Houston via Miami.

He felt an unmistakable physical excitement, anticipating the prospect of doing business in the world's leading capitalist nation. There was an uncomplicated boldness about the way the Americans did business – especially the Texans. They weren't subtle; they were gamblers, and they moved fast. There was a lot of money to be made by getting into their slipstream.

In one sense, Raj was already there. His finely tuned commercial antennae had picked up the significance of the Bunker Hunt's move into the silver market and he was in it too, in a big way, and very ready to get off the roller-coaster just before it reached the top of its loop.

His constant monitoring of world economics told him that there was still enough boom in Texas to engage in the kind of property development he liked best: large scale, prestigious and expensive offices. And Michel Disch's bank was right behind him.

Ross Blackwell, who had first proposed the idea to them, had had his people scour Houston for a possible site. It had now been found and paid for. A leading New York architect had been appointed and had produced drawings and models that expressed the muted and tasteful flamboyance for which he was noted and which Raj felt that the large Texan corporations would think that they should like. Raj was going to Houston to arrange funding for the building of the property and to find tenants for it.

A suite of large rooms at the Hilton had been rented and invitations sent out for an extravagant presentation of the scheme. A slick audio-visual show was accompanied by the best champagne and catering that Houston could provide. The press, hard to impress in Texas, came because they were unused to Indians doing this kind of business in the States. They were fascinated as much by the few personal details they had managed to glean about Raj as they were about his proposed building.

One of the journalists had a particular interest in him. She was a network news reporter for NBC, but she didn't have a camera crew with her. There was no story here her editor would want.

But when she saw Raj enter the room and mount the small dais to introduce his presentation, she felt a numbing horror. She wanted to get up and run away but, as in a bad dream, her limbs wouldn't respond. Then she heard his precise and mellifluous English and her thoughts flew back to London, to Paris, and to her parents' house in the West of England. She didn't absorb a word he was saying; she sat and watched his eyes, his calm, complete self-assurance, and she observed a calculating coldness in him that filled her with dread – as if she was watching a ghost, or a man whose body had been occupied by an alien from another world. And as he raised his hand to indicate the model beside him, she felt her whole body turning at once hot and cold at the memory of those long tapering fingers, touching her, exciting her.

In ten years, he had scarcely changed, yet he was an utter stranger – a totally other person. She couldn't meet

395

him. He had not seen her. She would slip away quietly during the AV show and try to forget the whole event.

But the lights dimmed, the presentation commenced and was over and she was still there. Then, when she thought that he had spotted her and was walking towards her, she sat petrified like a night-time rabbit in the glare of a hunter's lamp.

With relief and disappointment she realised that his eyes were focused a little beyond her. She turned to see a short, balding man standing at the back of the room with an aloof and stunning woman, a few inches taller, on his arm. The man gave Raj a quick smile and an approving raise of eyebrows.

'Michel, Danielle, it's good to see you,' she heard Raj say as he passed within a few inches of where she sat. 'I thought you hadn't been able to make it.'

She watched as he joined in an earnest, no longer audible, conversation with the unlikely couple. She decided that she would stay a while; see if she could find out how Raj had arrived in the position of a Houston property developer. This, and the soullessness of his demeanour seemed an awful long way from the idealistic young student whom she had loved so fiercely and for so long.

She stood up and joined the crowd of people milling around the display of the development, and acknowledged the greetings of the one or two newsmen she knew. She leafed through the press kit to find any personal details about Raj which she might have missed, but found only: 'Mr Raju Kalianji, born in Uganda, graduated from the London School of Economics and settled in Britain in 1972. Since then he has built up a private corporation encompassing a wide field of activities, including textiles and some of the most imaginative commercial real estate developments in the UK . . .' There followed details of some of the schemes, with nothing further about the man himself.

It seemed to her, with her limited knowledge of the subject, that the project being presented here had most of the right answers, and this was confirmed by overheard snippets of conversation from the people around her. It didn't surprise her. She had always admired Raj's thoroughness and application as a student, and when she had read about Amin's expulsion of the Indians, she had assumed that he would find his way back to London. She had imagined, though, that he would involve himself in academic or political life rather than commerce.

From time to time, she glanced round the room to watch Raj. Eventually, finding him quite close, she gritted her teeth and approached from behind his right shoulder.

'Mr Kalianji, Diana Quinn, NBC News. I wonder if you could tell me how an Indian businessman from Britain finds himself engaged in real estate in Texas?'

Raj turned sharply, an apprehensive half-smile on his lips. When he saw it really was her, a quick look of mild guilt, as if at the memory of some small social gaffe, passed over his eyes, to be quickly replaced with a look of bland welcome.

'Diana, how extraordinary to see you. How very nice, even if it is in your official capacity.'

'I'm not really in my official capacity. It's not my kind of story – I'm political. But when I saw your press release lying around, I thought I'd better come and check you out.'

'Well I hope you approve.' He waved towards the model of the building.

'Oh, it looks fine; I'm sure it'll be a success. But I'm not interested in that – it's you I came to find out about. I've wondered loads of times what happened to you and all your ideas for Uganda, and how you coped with the Amin situation.'

It was a long time since anyone had expressed this kind of interest in Raj. He found the questions disturbing. Apart from distant childhood memories, he had avoided dwelling on those years in Uganda. And, if he had ever had any real political ambitions, he had long since abandoned them as irrelevant.

He certainly had no wish to talk about them, but Diana was still very beautiful, obviously in command, and making the most of her life and talents. And seeing those candid eyes and curly hair framing her little face, he felt stirring within him emotions he had forgotten.

'I could give you an extended interview over dinner,' he said. His deep brown eyes looked steadily into hers. She started as she felt his hand lightly take her arm. 'Would you like that?' he asked.

His tone was so assured that she couldn't help saying, 'Oh, yes, I would, but . . .' Her voice trailed off.

'But what?' enquired Raj.

'It doesn't matter. I'd love to have dinner. Where shall I meet you?'

'I'm having a few people for drinks in my suite. Why not join us there, then you and I can go on.'

Diana left the reception as if she had taken in a couple of lungfuls of ether. She felt her head floating and knew that she was no longer in control; but she didn't mind. She almost skipped as she went to retrieve her car from the parking lot.

Raj, Disch and Blackwell made an odd team, but this Houston deal had given them each parts to play that created a well-balanced, self-policing interdependence. They had little in common beyond the desire to make money. But this is a desire that can bind together the most disparate of people, more strongly, often, than shared politics, religion or genes.

None of them cared, particularly, that there was no other basis for their relationship. They were, all three, ambitious loners with their own furrows to plough, but they recognised this in each other and so they valued each other's contribution to this project.

The response to their presentation had been perfectly satisfactory. They were confident that within a month they would have tenants for the offices and a buyer for the freehold. Their investments would be repaid, their guarantees released and their profit of a million or so apiece safely in M. Disch's bank.

The conversation turned to other, more personal, matters – and a common enemy.

Ross drew thoughtfully on his cigar. 'When do you think your . . . associate, Mr Freeman, will be ready for plucking?' he asked Raj.

'That fruit will take time to ripen, but it will be worth waiting for, I assure you.'

Disch chuckled. 'I think it's already ripening for me. Mademoiselle Milinaire does not like a man with worries or problems.'

'You're a very fortunate fellow, Michel. Most men spend money in achieving their amorous aims. For you, it's been a very profitable exercise.'

Disch's chubby little head nodded smugly.

At that moment, a knock on the door was followed by the entrance of Diana Quinn and Ross and the banker took their leave. The Texan wanted to catch a plane to Los Angeles, and Michel was anxious to go to bed with Danielle.

'Interesting friends you have now, Raj,' Diana remarked when they had left.

'Not friends, business associates,' he replied.

'What sort of friends do you have, then?'

Raj didn't reply for a moment, then asked, 'Where would you like to have dinner?'

'I don't care. Anywhere, just as long as you're prepared to be communicative. I think you owe me that.'

'Forgive me. I haven't found it necessary to discuss personal matters for a very long time. I am unused to it – and you are a journalist.'

'For God's sake, I'm not here as a reporter. I'm someone who was very close to you, in case you've forgotten.'

'Yes, yes, of course; I think perhaps I'd like to talk. Let's find somewhere to eat.'

They sat at a quiet table in one of Houston's 'international' restaurants, which meant that it served American food with a French accent. By the time they had reached the restaurant, Diana had confirmed her earlier impression that whatever common ground may have existed for them before had now been eroded beyond recognition. Every time he spoke or glanced at her though, she was reminded of the passion he had generated in her and she wanted to spend this evening with him. And if he had changed as much as she suspected, being with him might exorcise from her mind the ghost of what he had once been to her. To begin with, he avoided her questions by asking his own about her.

He listened, it seemed to her, with fascinated approval to the story of her career to date. After a successful period as a junior reporter on the *New York Times*, her looks and televisual spontaneity had brought her to the attention of an East Coast television station, where for a while she had anchored a local current-affairs programme. She had developed an insouciance that disguised an incisive interview technique. She worked hard at political coverage. Her reports on the election of the state senator had attracted very favourable comment and had been nationally networked. And after that, it was inevitable she should move to one of the giant broadcasting companies. Now she was a reporter of considerable stature in the political world, and, because of her face and style of delivery, of great popularity among the public.

She enjoyed telling Raj about it. After all, it was while he had been her lover that she had first recognised her ambitions to enter journalism, and the absence of his response from Uganda had prompted her to go to New York. When she had reached the present in the résumé of her career, she stopped. But Raj wanted more.

'Do you still call yourself Diana Quinn for professional purposes only?'

'Do you mean – am I married?'

He nodded.

'No.' She said it with no particular inflections of regret. 'The job I do is inclined to make one cynical, and cynicism in a woman is something most men, especially Americans, find hard to cope with. What about you?'

'I am married – to the girl my parents arranged back in Africa.'

Diana waited for more detail, but when none was

400

offered, she asked, 'Well, what's she like? How do you find marriage? Have you got any children?'

'I have a son, of one and a half. He is called Paul.'

They were silent for a while. There was no vestige of the contact they once had. Diana felt like crying, as if at the belated news of the death of an old friend. Raj was looking at her now with unmistakable excitement. He put his hand across the table and caressed hers. 'Diana, I should have mentioned it before, but you look as beautiful as ever. I must tell you it took me some time to get you out of my mind.'

'But like most things you've set out to achieve, you managed it in the end.'

'Don't be like that. I knew it was impossible to go on, even then. And when our family was made penniless by Amin, it was completely out of the question.'

'You don't seem too penniless now,' remarked Diana drily. 'And anyway, I wouldn't have given a damn.'

'As you rightly observe, I am not penniless now, and I don't ever intend to be again; but it has required my total dedication.'

'Yes, I can see that. I'm afraid I have to say you have changed completely. Are you aware of that? What the hell has happened to you?'

'Diana, I think you are being a little hard. We all change, we grow older – and, yes, less idealistic. Age breeds wisdom, realism.'

'Yes, and cynical pragmatism. But you've become more than just pragmatic. I can see glimpses of it behind those soft brown eyes. You're as hard as nails now. You're only interested in yourself.'

Raj smiled, unembarrassed.

'Just now,' he said, caressing her bare forearm, 'I'm very interested in you.'

Diana gave him a cynical smile. 'I can see a sort of randy gleam in your eye,' – and in my own, she thought, and felt her body responding explosively at the memory of their love-making. Damn it, his mind may have changed, but his body hasn't. Why the hell shouldn't I?

'Look, Raj, if you want a fuck . . .' she paused, pleased by his apprehension and the power she held over him for that moment, 'I'm on.'

She was rather impressed by his self control. He just nodded, very slightly, and she felt his hand tighten a little on her arm.

Making love with a man without a soul was, Diana imagined, rather like making love to a robot. A skilfully engineered and programmed robot in this case: no shortage in the bodily satisfaction it delivered, no power-cuts to curtail its performance.

And each deep thrust of the well-oiled automaton helped to drive out the memory of the old Raj.

In the morning, as she showered and Raj lay still asleep in bed, she felt very much a woman; a woman in control; a woman freed from a burden she had carried for a very long time.

A little later, Raj shook himself awake and looked around for Diana. She was gone. A strange, inexplicable gloom closed about him. For one crazy moment, he thought of getting up and chasing after her, begging her to return. But he lay back on the pillow with a twisted smile and shook his head. He had chosen his road, and it allowed for no diversions.

# Autumn 1978

Alison sat with her legs up on the sofa. The deep cushions in their unbleached shantung silk coverings gave soft support to her aching limbs.

She had been schooling horses all day, and was now trying to relax in the drawing-room of the sixteenth-century farmhouse, which belonged to the stud. She hadn't been sitting long when, through the window facing down the beech-lined drive, she saw a small red Ferrari slither wildly through the gateposts and shoot up towards the house, kicking up a wake of gravel.

It was not a car she knew, but she was unsurprised to see Leo get out, slam the door and walk quickly towards the front door. She heard him open it, then clatter through to the back of the house.

'Ali – Ali, where the hell are you?'

He appeared in the doorway, clutching a can of beer. 'I'm glad you've got time to relax. Christ, what a week I've had!' He paced around the room, threw another log on the blazing fire, and collapsed in an armchair.

'What's the trouble?' Alison asked coolly. 'You seem even more fraught than usual.'

Leo looked up. His lips twitched impatiently. 'I don't think you'd understand. It's business.'

'Try me. I'm not a financial moron, you know. If I appear ignorant about your business affairs, it's only because you don't ever tell me about them.'

'Well, I don't want you to have to worry. That's my job. And anyway, there's nothing you can do to help.'

Alison got up from the sofa and walked stiffly over to

the drinks table to pour herself a vodka and tonic. 'Leo, you must have learned by now that you're not the only person with all the answers. I'm sure it would be a great help to talk things through with me. I used to ask you all the time, but I'm afraid I gave up a few years ago because you'd never tell me anything. Anyway, things must be bad if you've got rid of the Rolls.'

Leo laughed. 'I got less for it than I had to pay for the Ferrari. I slung the Roller because it's an old fart's car. Driving round these lanes a bit quickly was like trying to take the QE II up the Regents Canal.' His frown returned. 'No, I've got a few problems, but it'll be a while before I'm down to my last Mini.'

'Okay, so break the habit of a lifetime. Tell me.'

She sat in the chair opposite him, her legs curled up beneath her bottom, a curtain of dark hair across her face and the little finger of her left hand tucked into the corner of her mouth.

Leo took a deep breath, and committed himself. 'Right, first the bad news. The factory's in liquidation.'

'What – Raj's?' Alison was incredulous.

'No, no. Mine – in Scotland – you knew we had one there for God's sake?'

'Yes, I did, but I didn't know that it had become particularly important. And I thought it bloody odd you starting it in the first place.'

'Look, if you're simply going to sit there and be wise after the event, then let's not bother to discuss it.'

'Okay, I'm sorry,' Alison said quickly. 'Go on.'

'Well, I tried like hell to make that place work. I mean, we were much too dependent on that bloody Kalianji, but the women there are so slow. We tried everything to get them to go faster, but they just don't seem to be able to. I've pumped a hundred thousand quid into it, and now I've lost the lot. There's only a few grands' worth of assets and no lease.'

'But Rags can absorb a loss like that, surely? It's only a tiny fraction of your turnover.'

'But Rags didn't own the factory. I did, personally.'

'How come? You must be mad!'

'Look,' warned Leo. 'You said you wanted to hear, so listen, and save your comments till later.'

'All right. Go on, but first tell me how you had it in your own name.'

Leo told her all the developments of the past two years.

Raju Kalianji owned the property company which owned the freehold of the Kensington store and was taking a percentage of turnover instead of rent on it. It had also recently emerged that he owned the freehold of at least a dozen other Rags stores, including the one in Paris.

The Rainbow Room Club had folded and Raj had taken it over and turned it into an Indian brasserie.

He also owned the bulk of the stock in the European shops – and was collecting a ten per cent surcharge over the factory price.

The wholesale business had been transferred to West Textiles, and Rags simply received a small royalty on sales.

At the time when the sale-or-return deal had first been done, Leo had been forced to transfer the club, the factory, the US Rags, the studio and the stud into his own holding company, which had been funded only on the strength of his personal guarantees and secured by his holding in Rags. Now the club and factory had gone, along with a quarter of a million pounds of his own money. The shops in America seemed incapable of making a profit, however much they took. He had finally had to accept that they never would without substantial reorganisation. As for the studio, it was still making a small operating profit, but failing to service its capital costs.

It was true that the European retail business was still very strong, but margins had been hammered by Raj's surcharge.

But, unbelievably, the stud seemed to be paying its way.

'I've got to hand you that, Ali, I'd never have thought you could make a place like this profitable, especially in so short a time.'

'Well, Pat the Paddy's been a great help – and so has Simon.'

'Oh, has he? How?' asked Leo sourly.

'Just in helping me to run my books and things. I asked you, but you were always too busy.'

'Well, anyway, at least it's not costing me money to run it, though I may need my capital out of it sometime. Do you think your brother could help you to re-finance it?'

Alison couldn't help feeling excited at this possible turn of events, although she knew how disloyal this was. She had really thrown herself into her horses and she didn't want them to be exposed to the evident precariousness of Leo's position.

'I don't know. I'll ask him. But I'm going to need a large chunk of money in the New Year; I want to buy a new stallion and some brood-mares from Don Luis. I'm beginning to get quite a few customers for my Andalusians.'

Leo shook his head. 'No way. Not at the moment. I've just tried to tell you, I'm up to my eyes right now. But things should improve next spring.'

Alison bit her lip. She had set her heart on the new stallion. Maybe she could find another way. But it seemed unfair of Leo – after all, she had made this place work and if he hadn't been so stubborn and secretive about his own business, he wouldn't be in such a mess now.

'But, Leo,' she coaxed, 'things can't be that bad if Rags is still going strong here, can they?'

'I just told you, margins are tight and I'm personally strapped. All told, I owe the banks a million and a half quid, and the only way I can pay it will be to sell the American operations, or this place, or some of my shares in Rags.'

'Well, don't you dare sell this place,' said Alison, guilty at the harshness of her tone.

Leo scowled at her. 'Thanks for your support. And you wonder why I don't tell you things!'

'Look, Leo, I'm sorry if I don't seem sympathetic. But over the years you have ignored me and abused me. You've tried to flatten me and failed, and that upsets you. You've discovered you're not as wonderful as you thought you were, but you still can't accept it. You had a brilliant entrepreneurial mind. You probably still have, but you've let it get warped and misguided by your own ego. You see everything in terms of yourself and what you imagine to be other people's views of you. You stopped listening to alternative opinions years ago and started making your decisions on the basis of emotion, not logic. These are all things I've told you dozens of times. And now that you're reaping a rotten harvest, don't blame me.'

'My God, Ali, I know you feel sore. I suppose you have a right to, but you don't have to kick me when I'm down. I really did want your support and understanding. I've got no one else to turn to – and things are really beginning to crowd me.' He stopped for a moment. 'And I'll tell you something I haven't told anyone else . . .' he went on. Alison tried to feel some sympathy when she saw dampness and fear in his eyes. 'I think Raj Kalianji is determined to get me, to put me out of my own company, to destroy me. Why?' Leo pleaded. 'Why should he want to do that to me?'

'If you hadn't been so obsessed with trying to beat Raj, you wouldn't be in the mess you're in now. Yes, he's a bastard, but he's only human, and you've consistently laid yourself open to him. He's a greedy businessman. He was bound to take advantage of the chances you offered him. If you think he's beating you, you'd better join him – at least he's one person you know you can't walk over.'

Leo stood up, trembling with fury. He advanced towards her, fist raised. 'You bloody *bitch*. You know I hate his guts. It makes me sick to have to kow-tow to his terms. But he's wormed his way in; he's used everybody he can to get at me – including my own sister.' His face crumpled. His raised hand fell limply by his side.

Alison still sat calmly. 'Well, I'm glad you've decided not to hit me, because that would have been the last straw. When I made my marriage vows to you, I meant them and I intended to keep them. I can't see the point of making a solemn promise if one doesn't keep it – one might just as well save one's breath. And the idea of divorce is absolutely anathema to what religious principles I've still got. But after the way you've treated me, I could just be driven to it, and I can certainly tell you that any fisticuffs from you would tip the balance. I'm sorry you're in a mess, but it's your own fault. And you're quite right: until you learn to listen to reason, there's nothing I can do to help.'

Leo glowered at her, then turned on his heel. 'Well, I'm going to see someone who can do something to help,' he yelled over his shoulder. 'Someone who can at least offer a bit of feminine understanding.'

As he stomped across the hall, Alison called, 'I wouldn't count on it. I don't think that French slag of yours is very strong on understanding. She thinks with her genitals.'

Most of the Friday-evening flights to Paris were full, but Leo used his pushy charm to great effect on the girl at the Air France booking desk, and forty-five minutes after arriving at Heathrow, he was settling into a first-class seat.

He told the frenetic taxi-driver to drop him at the Place Victor Hugo, just around the corner from Danielle's apartment. He wanted to have a quick drink before turning up unannounced. He sat for twenty minutes in the *brasserie* on the Place drinking generous Parisian measures of Scotch and wondering what the hell he was doing there. Of course, Alison was right: Danielle wouldn't understand. He didn't expect her to and he certainly wasn't going to tell her his problems, but at least, on one level and without restraint, she appreciated him.

He had brought no luggage with him and didn't even have a raincoat to protect him from the autumn drizzle as he walked down the quiet, cobbled street to the elegant *fin de siècle* building where Danielle lived.

The *concierge* recognised him and nodded sourly as she opened the front door and watched him bound up the shallow steps to the first floor. She knew he was going to be disappointed and gave a satisfied smirk when, after a few minutes banging and bell-ringing, he came down again.

'Mademoiselle Milinaire?' Leo asked.

The woman answered with a non-committal shrug.

'When come back?' Leo pointed to his watch. Again, no more than a shrug.

He tore a page out of the back of his pocket diary, wrote 'Danny, I'll be back here at 11.00 – L. xx', and handed it, folded, to the unhelpful doorkeeper. She took it and retreated to her little glass-fronted lair from where she pretended not to watch Leo leave the building.

Leo was drunk when he returned at 11.15. The bar had been practically empty and there had been no one to talk to in English, so he had concentrated on his whisky.

As he approached Danielle's apartment building, a chauffeur-driven limousine drew up. He saw her get out. Then, as the chauffeur held the door, she said something, laughed and leaned in – obviously to give and receive a farewell kiss. It was more than a minute before her head emerged once more.

In the scanty street light, Leo could just see the back of a bald head through the rear window of the car as it pulled away.

He leaned against the damp wall of the building, feeling slightly sick. He knew that he would have to give Danielle time to let herself in and read his note before he went up.

For the second time that evening, the *concierge* grumpily admitted him. He staggered up the stairs and rang Danielle's bell. She opened the door looking annoyed and flushed.

'Why don't you tell me you are coming, Leo?' she said sharply. 'Oh, my God – you're drunk already.'

Leo swayed slightly in the doorway, rain dripping from his soaked jacket. 'Oh, well, come in,' she muttered without warmth.

Leo lurched in, then went straight to the bathroom where he was violently sick. He felt weaker but better. He was vaguely aware that the emotional trauma of the day and the unaccustomed measures of Scotch had combined to react so forcefully. He brushed his teeth and tried to dry his hair before going out to confront Danielle.

She was pacing around, looking trapped. 'Look Leo, I am supposed to go out again, to a party. There's someone

409

calling for me in an hour. I was just going to change. Where are you staying? We could meet tomorrow.'

Leo flopped down into a chair and laughed. 'What, is old baldy coming back then? Well, you can tell him it's not his lucky night and he'd better go and find a tart in the *Bois*. Who is he, anyway?'

'You don't have to be so rude. He is an old friend – Michel Disch. I mentioned him to you before, he is a *banquier*, and deliciously powerful.' She delivered the last words with a lasciviousness that Leo ignored.

'Well, do me a favour and get rid of him tonight. Ring him now and tell him you've got a headache. If he turns up here I might give *him* one.'

Danielle laughed cynically. 'You couldn't hurt a fly at the moment. But I don't want a drama; I'll call him.'

She disappeared into the bedroom and shut the door before telephoning. When she came back she snapped, 'Okay – why are you here?'

'Why the hell do you think I'm here? Why do I ever come to see you?'

'No. It's not like normal. There is something wrong. You look sort of . . . desperate.'

'Me – desperate?' Leo barked out an unconvincing laugh. 'Why should I be desperate?'

Danielle shrugged. 'I don't know and don't care, but I don't like it. I think you should go to your hotel and sleep.'

Leo looked at her bleakly. 'Don't, Danny. Don't be difficult now. I haven't booked into a hotel . . . I only arrived in Paris this evening.'

Danielle was astounded. 'What for?'

'Well . . . to see you.'

'Oh God, Leo. There must be something wrong. Well, I don't want to be involved. I heard you have problems and I can't help you.'

'Who said I've got problems? That's balls. Things are going great. You know that. You know how much of your tatty styles we still sell.'

'Ah,' the French woman said coolly, 'but who is "we"? Raj Kalianji is doing the wholesale now, isn't he?'

'Who've you been talking to?'

'I saw Raj quite recently, and before in Houston. He does some deals with Michel.'

'What? Raj and Baldy? Well, there's a coincidence. Why didn't you tell me before?'

She shrugged. 'I thought you knew. Michel said you did.'

'Bloody hell,' said Leo pensively, as if observing a distant natural phenomenon. 'The vultures gather.'

'What are you talking about?' asked Danielle impatiently.

'It doesn't matter. I have got problems, you're right, but don't worry – I'll deal with them.'

He stood up and, steadying himself, crossed over to Danielle and wrapped his arms around her. 'Let's do some aerobics,' he whispered huskily. He fumbled up her skirt and tried to unclip a stocking-top but she drew away. 'No, Leo, I don't want to go to bed with you like this. You're drunk and strange. I don't like it. You sleep there,' she pointed at the sofa. 'I sleep on my own.'

Before he could stop her, she had slipped away from him, closed her bedroom door and shot the bolts.

He banged on the delicately painted door. 'What the hell are you doing?'

'Leo, if you do that I'm calling the *flics*. Shut up and go to sleep.'

Leo was still just rational enough to know she would indeed call the police. He walked around her *salon*, poured a drink, looked at himself in the glass above the fireplace, then sat down and started, as silently as possible, to weep.

He was overwhelmed by waves of self-pity, regret and remorse.

Why, oh, *why* had he been such a fool? Why reject everyone who had ever tried to help him? He glanced at the bedroom door. That bitch didn't give a damn. Leo didn't care. She was just an expensive fucking machine . . .

But Alison? How had he driven her so far from himself? She had really loved him and understood him. Why had he been unable to accept that? He lay on the sofa on his back and stared at the ceiling. A thousand scenes passed through his mind: those army satchels, Tommy and the Tigers, the girl in the Hampstead shop, Sammy, Sarah's first collection, the exquisite excitement of the first Rags shop . . . God, those were good times. And then meeting Alison and their peaceful honeymoon.

How had he let all these things slip away?

But they hadn't slipped away. He had driven them away, deliberately cut them loose so that he could rise and rise.

Eventually he slept, and was woken by an isolated clang of a dustbin lid in the quiet, early Saturday outside. Daylight seeped through low cloud. The rain had stopped and an occasional bird call could be heard above the distant noise of traffic on the great boulevards of the Etoile.

Quietly Leo went to wash, and shaved with a razor that Danielle must have used for her legs. He let himself out and managed to slip past the *concierge* without her seeing him. He didn't want to give her the satisfaction of witnessing his débâcle.

He walked through the just-awakening boulevards, up to the Arc de Triomphe, then turned down the Champs Elysées and, with a brisk wind in his face, headed down to the Place de la Concorde.

The walking helped to clear his head, restored a sense of perspective.

Things weren't that bad. If he took everyone else's advice, sold off his unprofitable companies and joined forces with Raj, he would still have part of a very large and successful business, and no debt. He would change his approach to Alison, start listening to her, appreciating her. He was sure she still loved him. It would make her so happy if he turned over a new leaf.

And as he walked, he saw her long legs, bright, naughty eyes below the raven-hair fringe, her mouth turning up quirkily on one side as she delivered one of her more sardonic observations.

She really was an unusual woman – original, witty, and hard to beat in an argument, completely without fear in

412

her dealings with people – and possessed of so many talents and skills.

What the hell had he been doing, coming over to see Danny? He had never even liked, let alone trusted, her.

Leo crossed the river at Concorde and carried on down the Boulevard St Germain walking contemplatively through the rustling, fallen leaves. This whole event had been, he felt, a major, much-needed, purge. It had forced him to review his emotional circumstances in sharp-focused objectivity. He reached the Deux Magots, ordered espresso and cognac, looked out at the world and began to feel relaxed and confident in his new-found resolve.

One of the critical, and more arbitrary factors in personal relationships, as in so many human events, is timing.

Leo had decided to change, but he had decided too late. Alison had passed the stage where she could accept this new, humble and attentive Leo. She couldn't bring herself to believe in the transformation. She would have liked to do so but she wasn't prepared to expose herself to the humiliating consequences if the change turned out to have been merely a stage-managed illusion.

Leo tried everything he could to convince her that his motives were genuine but, to his mortifying frustration, he failed. And the frustration turned to bitterness – not towards her particularly, but towards all the complicated circumstances of his life. This bitterness destroyed his resolutions, and drove him further into himself. It increased his paranoia and made him more determined than ever to get out from under Raj's oppressive influence.

The banks reluctantly agreed to the re-scheduling of his loans, but warned him this was the last time; he would have to start selling assets if things didn't turn around.

A brief respite in the seemingly relentless downward spiral was provided by the sale of the stud. Alison had formed herself, with Simon's help, into a limited company whose aims were 'to breed, train and trade in livestock'. This company, on the strength of her previous track record, had been able to raise the money to buy the property and all its inmates.

This meant, of course, that Leo was no longer the provider of this important element in his wife's life. Curiously, it led to a slight softening in Alison's attitude to him. They spent the days after Christmas and New Year's Eve at the farmhouse, just the two of them, and for the first time in several years seemed to recapture a few moments of their early intimacy. But the balance had changed. Leo knew that when Alison was good to him it was out of kindness, not love.

He made an effort to interest himself in the horses and even became enthusiastic about her plans for the new stallion for which, mercifully, her bank was providing the funds. But in the New Year, he was confronted once more with his continuing problems. Trade up to Christmas had satisfied expectations, but, when the profit and loss were analysed with all the inevitably rising costs, Raj Kalianji seemed to be the big winner.

While Leo struggled to find a way of redressing this imbalance, he got the news about the studio. Initially, just a telex: '*Studio involved in major fire. Total wipe-out. Will call. Robinson.*'

And then a frantic telephone call and the sting in the tail. Their insurance, which had been due for renewal on the first of the year, had lapsed through non-payment of the premium – an oversight, not lack of funds. The American insurance companies and their brokers were adamant: they were not paying. They had already got the lawyers to say so.

When he put the phone down, Leo was in a cold sweat. He felt as though he had been hammered in the gut and as though his heart had stopped beating. Three quarters of a million dollars written off.

He was, in his own words, absolutely stuffed.

# Spring 1979

There weren't many people on the mid-week flight to Seville. Alison sat by a window in the Iberia 727. The Datchet Reservoir disappeared from view as the plane penetrated the thick, low cloud. She was glad and relieved to be getting away from England, from her obligations to Leo; from Leo.

She felt sad she didn't love him and guilty that now, when he really needed her, she couldn't find a genuine wish to help him. She wanted to admire his determination as brave tenacity, but could only see it as pathetic petulance.

'Please help him, God,' – she had never lost the habit of praying – 'because I can't.'

Now, for ten days or so, she could forget all about this tedious responsibility and throw herself into the business of studying and selecting horse-flesh.

There were few breeders of Iberian horses in England, and most of them had bred from Portuguese Lusitano stock. There were a number of reasons for this. The Portuguese kept a better stud book, their breeders had been far more conscientious and selective, and each time there had been internal upheavals in Spain, most of the Spanish breeding stock had crossed the border. The result was that horses being produced in the traditional Andalusian breeding grounds had lost the more important characteristics for which the old Iberian war horse had, for centuries, been revered.

Carriage horses and flashy riding horses for farmers to take to the *ferias* could still be found, characterised by the circular 'dishing' action of their forelegs. But it was only relatively recently that classically-bred, straight-moving, brave and biddable horses were being produced once more in Spain by traditionalists like Don Luis Rodriguez-Ortega, already famous for his fine fighting bulls.

For several generations, the great mounted bullfighters, the *rejoneadores*, had bought their horses from the famous studs of Portugal. But now they were pleased to find what they wanted in their own country, on Don Luis' Hacienda de San José de Praja.

Alison had discovered Don Luis by chance, when her interest in breeding was first developing. She had been introduced to him by an English friend in Marbella and had spent hours talking to him and learning from him. This had led to a visit to his *hacienda* and the purchase of two mares in foal.

Since then, encouraged by the quality that she was achieving, she had bought several more mares and a young stallion, and her herd in England was growing. Now she needed new blood; an alternative sire.

As they approached to land at Seville, Alison could see the greenness that only touches Andalusia in the spring. A comfortable warmth and the dusty smells of southern Europe greeted her as she stepped out of the plane.

She was excited. She had last been to Don Luis' hacienda a couple of years before with Leo. She knew the old-fashioned Spaniard had not approved of Leo, certainly didn't like him and had only shown them the minimum courtesy that the buyer of six expensive brood-mares could expect. Without Leo she would see and experience a great deal more and the strength of her personality would be warmly appreciated by the Andalusian men.

She was met by a *vaquero* or cowboy, thinly disguised as a chauffeur, who took her bags and put them in the back, of a new, very dusty Mercedes. They drove out of the airport and skirted the northern edge of Seville. The smells there, of low-octane petrol, exhaust fumes and garbage, only increased her pleasurable sense of anticipation.

They left the straggling outskirts of the city and headed out across the plain towards the setting sun. The driver was showing off, blaring his horn, swearing at peasants in old vans and on bicycles. He spoke no English and seemed unimpressed by his passenger's friendly demeanour and striking good looks. Alison asked a few questions in her inadequate Castilian Spanish, but these were barely acknowledged, let alone answered. Don Luis was an old-style, autocratic *hidalgo*, and no doubt his staff, still almost in a feudal relationship with him, were inclined to adopt his attitude to foreign visitors.

About forty minutes out of Seville, they turned left off the road between two great white, peeling gateposts, shaded a little by an isolated group of pines. Beyond, a dusty track led up a slight hill and over the low brow. About a quarter of a mile away, on the far side of the ridge, stretched the *hacienda*.

There was a cluster of large buildings spread around the white and pale yellow house. Beside the big square tower that dominated it stood a large arched gateway with a picture-tile of the *hacienda*'s patron saint embedded in the plaster. Beyond the house, Alison could see the little bullring, with its elegant carved gallery, which was used for training and testing the horses. A group of *vaqueros* were riding in from the bull pastures, shouting and laughing at each other.

The driver took the car under the arch and into the courtyard. As he turned the motor off, the great double oak doors to the house were opened and a servant in an elaborately embroidered waistcoat was followed out by Don Luis himself. The car door was opened for Alison; she climbed out and looked around at the unexpected splashes of vivid, implausibly coloured flowers and shrubs, which contrasted with the grassless dustiness of the paddocks. The driver and the other servant carried her bags into the house and Don Luis descended the few steps from the front door. She remembered the exaggerated ram-rod back, accentuated by his pronounced limp. Tall among his workers and retainers, he had a long, thin face, a large Roman nose and fine silvery hair swept back from an undisguised receding hairline.

He smiled thinly. 'Señora Freeman, I welcome you. It is rare that a beauty such as yours comes here to set off my jacarandas. A rare pleasure, of course.'

My God, thought Alison, he almost sounds pleased to see me.

'Don Luis, how kind. I've been looking forward so much to visiting the *Hacienda de San José* again. I can hardly believe I've arrived, though the scent of these wonderful flowers is beginning to convince me.'

Don Luis took her hand, and led her through the great hallway into a high gloomy room. Huge stuffed heads of black fighting bulls projected from the walls and, between them, mounted ears and tails, trophies of Don Luis' youthful successes in the *rejon*. They passed through into a cool atrium, open to the sky, where a small fountain played into a vivid blue tile-lined pool, which spoke eloquently of the Moorish ancestry of the Andalusian *haciendas*.

They entered the formal dining-room with its heavy oak table and chairs and walked through on to a south-facing veranda. A large porcelain jug on an elaborately carved table contained sangria – cold, sweet, easy to drink.

Much too easy, Alison thought as she sat and felt it relax her limbs and lighten her head. Don Luis himself sipped from a long, thin glass of very pale *fino*, and began to titillate Alison with surprisingly spicy flatteries.

'I thought, after you have spent the day looking at my horses tomorrow, you would like to see some of my other animals in action. Don Mateo Degrando, one of our great *rejoneadores*, fights two of my bulls in Sevilla. In the absence of any royalty, I will have the royal box and there will be a little party for Don Mateo, if he deals well with my bulls.' He paused and eyed her mischievously. 'I think you will enjoy the bullfight – and the bullfighter.'

His attitude towards her had changed greatly from that of her previous visit. He hadn't referred at all to Leo and now, it seemed, he was planning to throw her into the ring with Don Mateo, to be dealt with after Don Luis' bulls.

'I will look forward to it,' she said politely. 'I have never met Mateo Degrando or seen him fight.'

'I know you have not met him. I asked him and he said so. I am sure he would have remembered, even though many beautiful women have passed, if you will forgive the expression, through his hands.'

Then the old Spaniard rose, and abruptly changed the subject. 'How do you think you are going to persuade me to part with my best young stallion?' he asked, walking to the edge of the veranda and looking at the disappearing sun.

'At least your question suggests that perhaps it could be done,' replied Alison, 'but I don't think I'll reveal my tactics just yet, Don Luis. Let me look at him first and decide how hard I'm going to try.'

He turned back to her slowly, put an elegant forefinger to the side of his large nose, and smiled slightly. 'He really is a quite special horse, you know. I don't know why I even indicated to you that I might consider an offer, but you have the most enchanting voice on the telephone and I couldn't stop you coming.'

He looked thoughtfully at a colossal vermillion bloom which hung down from the pantiled roof, then clapped his hands gently for a servant. The summons was answered quickly. He confirmed that dinner would be in an hour, then had Alison shown to her room.

The large bedroom contained an elaborately draped four-poster bed and a massive mahogany wardrobe, into which all Alison's Armani, St Laurent and Zandra Rhodes outfits had already been unpacked. The windows faced south. Alison walked over to one of them and gazed out across the plain which disappeared into a distant pinkish haze. She could see a few men leading in mares with their foals from the paddocks, and some bullocks, peacefully chewing, occasionally making half-hearted lunges at one another. Half a mile away, on rising ground to the west, the fighting bulls grazed. She could recognise in the black shapes the huge shoulders and sharply sloping backs.

She had only once been to a *corrida*, and seen these extraordinary animals in the ring. She remembered how impressed she had been with the first bull. It had seemed to her the embodiment of physical power and ferocity; it was magnificent in its complete assurance that it could deal with all the annoying little men who rushed around it, goading it, teasing it, irritating it. Then there had been confusion when the bull began to feel the pain, and it realised that its mighty strength was ebbing; then the look of proud, puzzled defiance as it faced the arrogant matador for the last time. An unforgettable impression had been left on her by the shapeless black lump which mules had dragged across the blood-stained sand of the ring – the same package of muscle and bone that had trotted into the arena, snorting and looking for a fight, only twenty minutes before.

Alison, Don Luis, his sister and brother-in-law, took their seats in the box at the Plaza de Toros de Sevilla, the premier bullring of Andalusia. It was a mixed programme: four bulls to be killed by a matador, and two, the third and the last, by a *rejoneador*, Don Mateo. The first two were competently but unspectacularly dispatched. The next was the *rejon*, the first that Alison had seen.

This is the old way of fighting bulls, the way the sons of rich men had traditionally fought, from the back of a horse. It is still, by and large, the domain of landed people, not the village boys whose bravery singles them out to fight the bull on foot. The mounted *rejoneador* needs a great deal of skill but less courage than the unmounted matador; he needs skilled, fast and brave horses.

In the *rejon*, the whole fight is conducted by one man. Assistants lurk behind wooden screens, the *burladeros*, around the edge of the ring to draw the bull away should the *rejoneador* be dismounted or his horse wounded. *Banderillas* and *pics* of increasing size and barbed viciousness are applied to the bull's shoulders to weaken his neck muscles and drop his head for the *coup de grâce*.

Using only his legs to command his horse, the *rejoneador* gallops straight at the bull, neatly side-stepping at the last moment and leaning over to place a pair of gaily beribboned *banderillas* behind the bull's neck. And the furious bull will turn to chase the fleeing horse, his deadly sharp horns only inches from its rump.

But the horse is trained to sprint and stop and turn on its quarters, to respond instantly to every subtle message transmitted by its rider's calves and heels.

Alison was appalled at the risks, spellbound at the skill and enthralled at seeing a man put his horse and his judgement to such a test.

When Don Mateo, with an arrogant flourish, finally plunged his short sword between the big black heaving shoulders of his second bull, the crowd stood to acclaim him, shouting and stamping their approval and their demand to the President of the *corrida* that this brave and skilful dispatcher of bulls be awarded an ear of his last victim. The President gave the signal and the crowd cheered wildly as Don Mateo trotted his sweating horse around the ring, acknowledging the applause with an occasional inclination of his head.

Later, no longer wearing the ornate gilt bolero and breeches of the *corrida* and away from the primeval, mystical air that surrounds the melodrama, the ballet and the sport of the ring, Mateo Degrando retained an undeniable presence and the aura that proclaimed his ancient occupation.

At the party that Don Luis held in honour of the *rejoneador*, Alison could see Don Mateo was held in the same awe as a von Karajan, an Ali or a Lennon. In a way, he possessed their attributes and she was struck by an underlying similarity in his demeanour to Wolf Amadeus; both had an inextinguishable confidence and dedication. To those who knew no better, this might have been taken for aloof arrogance, but it was only an uncomplicated acceptance of their own excellence in their fields.

Dinner was held in a private room in Seville's oldest and grandest hotel. There were twenty or so guests, all Spanish, all Andalusians, except Alison. They talked, laughed, sang and drank without inhibition.

Alison was seated on Don Luis' right, almost opposite Mateo, who, so far, had said little and completely ignored the classically dark Spanish beauties who flanked him. She studied the still, dark brown eyes, set below a heavy brow and a mass of thick black curling hair. The mouth, not large but full-lipped, was framed by an uncompromising jaw. His nostrils flared slightly each time he took a long gulp from his mug of Rioja.

Earlier, Don Luis had briefly introduced them, but Mateo spoke no English so no real conversation had followed. Alison sat with her left elbow on the table, her chin in the palm of her hand and her finger in the corner of her mouth, causing her lips to pout a little. She glanced across from time to time at the beautiful man and found him staring at her intently. She lifted her head slightly and looked straight back at him, and suddenly it was as if a great flash of energy was crackling between their eyes.

Alison felt almost weak, stunned by her body's reactions. For a while, with relief, she turned to Don Luis who was asking about her reactions to the day. She hid behind the conversations gathering around her. But she could not avoid, every so often, further startling eye contact with the bullfighter.

When the meal of *dorada en sal* and suckling pig was over, the people on Alison's side of the table turned their chairs around to watch the musicians, dancers and singers who had come into the room to entertain the party. The energy and excitement which these *gitanas* produced seemed more primitive and thrilling than anything Alison had heard before. The raw earthiness of the voices and the rhythms needed no translation. Now a man was singing, punctuating his song with sharp, hard clicks of his high heels on the tiled floor. Sweat poured off him. When he slapped his tight-trousered thigh he left the perfect wet imprint of his hand there. The songs, which had found their way into southern Spain through North Africa, from the bazaars of the Middle East, dealt with the age-old problems of death and unrequited love. The dancers expressed grief and frustration in movements of the body, hands and face, while all the time the rhythm posed questions, then gave answers.

To a great cheer, Mateo stood, bounded over the table and took the floor himself. The gispy women surrounded him, furiously clicking their castanets, weaving around him an undulation of frills, arms and *mantillas*.

Mateo broke through the ring towards Alison. He leaned over and picked her up as if she were a small kitten and whirled her round and round to the clicking and the clapping and the sharply strummed guitars. It was like being on a spinning fairground ride and she thought it would never stop; she didn't really want it to, but all too soon she found herself deposited lightly back on her chair and Mateo was joined on the floor by one of the sloe-eyed señoritas of the party.

The evening went on, in complete abandon. Alison was immersed in the raw heat of the event, joining in the singing, clapping and dancing instinctively. When, maybe hours later, she felt the *rejoneador*'s hard-muscled arm around her and a husky unintelligible whisper in her ear, she was in no condition to seek, or find, reasons for not concurring with the unmistakable message in his eyes.

He took her by the hand and led her from the room. He shut the door behind them and, in the sudden calm, turned his face to hers and kissed her with savage softness.

She felt his hard fingers explore her buttocks, which tightened in response, then her thighs, her breasts and, through the extravagant chiffon folds of her Zandra Rhodes dress, he touched her tingling vagina.

She didn't try to stop him and could not deny her hungry passion.

He lifted her and carried her along the corridor, up a short flight of stairs and through a grandly framed door into the room in which he had donned and later discarded his elaborate ritual fighting clothes. They were still there, hanging in an open wardrobe. On the carved oak bed lay huge bunches of flowers, tributes from admiring aficionados.

As Mateo brushed these on to the floor, Alison's eye was caught by a large crucifix above the bed. She had to look away to dispel a sudden thought of Leo, a sharp pang of guilt.

Then he took her shoulders and kissed her again. His eyes asked her to undress. She did so, slowly. He seemed simply to shake his clothes off to reveal a rock-hard body blemished but somehow enhanced by a wide scar that ran from just below the back of his right shoulder, round his right side and diagonally across his stomach to a point between his navel and the base of his uncompromisingly rigid organ.

He pushed her on to the bed and was on her, kissing, touching, caressing – and then, with gentle power, in her and Alison lost all thoughts of time or place as her body greedily soaked up his passion.

A pale blue sky and a weak, early spring sun lit Chelsea. Leo noisily backed his Ferrari from its garage and burbled through the uncluttered streets to his office in Adam and Eve Mews.

As he drove, he tried to convince himself that his position could be worse. To help himself, he cast his mind back to the early days of carefree, dynamic optimism. Nostalgically he recalled how he had prided himself on finding no problem too great to deal with. But then he had been in control. He had been in charge of every string on every limb of the puppets he operated, and even Alison, whom he had never controlled, had loved him, so that didn't matter.

The thought of the sadness in her eyes when he had seen her off to Spain two days before filled him with a desperate yearning to go back ten years in time, and to rewrite his role.

He parked and walked into the office building in a state of intense depression. It was not lifted by the atmosphere which now prevailed there. The people who worked for him knew. They knew he was losing his grip. They were working more efficiently than before, taking their own initiatives more. No longer did they feel they must constantly refer to Leo. They were aware he had lost the will to fight. And because their jobs depended on the continuing success of Rags, there was a sense of earnest dedication about the place.

Leo hated coming here now. The stores were doing as well as ever but he, personally, was deriving little benefit from them. Raj Kalianji, his West Textiles and his property group were the big winners. And there was nothing that he could do about it. Especially not now.

The American banks had started calling in their loans as soon as the news of the studio fire had become known. They were not interested in how he raised the money. If it meant liquidating Rags's American retailing operation, it was too bad. Simon and his other advisors had indicated that would be the most sensible thing to do. There was enough asset value to cover nearly all the American borrowings and a secret buyer for the whole operation emerged, though offering only a small premium for the Rags name and goodwill.

But Leo was not going to give up this last vestige of his independence from Raj. Especially as – he was certain – it was at last beginning to make money.

It was Raj, of course, who had presented him with a solution. He had offered to buy twenty-five per cent of Leo's eighty per cent holding in the European retail business. From Leo's perspective, this business, in spite of its turnover, was making so little that, owning fifty-five per cent, he was hardly going to be worse off. And Raj had offered a very fair price, subject to his own appointment to the board and a minority shareholder's rights clause being inserted in the company's articles. It was a harmless enough provision, so Leo had taken the money and paid off most of his American debts – and still owned the stores in New York, Dallas and Los Angeles.

The trouble was he felt like an outsider in his own business. Raj's influence was everywhere.

Now a director, Raj had called several meetings among most levels of staff and, short of bursting in and throwing him out, Leo couldn't see how he could stop him.

And most of the staff, with very little reluctance, had seen that Raj's reforms were for the good of the business and themselves.

Sarah's only comment when Leo agreed to sell his shares to Raj had been less than approving: 'Leo, if you regret this later, just remember, it was entirely your decision. Frankly, I think you're mad not to have sold out in America and settled down to consolidate things here. But *nobody*, not even Raj, has put any pressure on you to do this.'

She and Leo had scarcely spoken over the last few weeks, so he was surprised to see her appear unannounced around the door of his office.

'Well I'm honoured. You wish to consult the managing director?' he asked.

'Oh, piss off, Leo. Do you think it's been easy for me with what's been going on around here lately? God knows why I should, but every time I see you, I feel like a traitor. It seems crazy that I should be going along with Raj's ever-rising star at your expense. But selling was your choice, and you left me with none.'

'Look, we've been through this. Raj Kalianji may be sitting on my head, but at least I've still got a few limbs moving freely – and that's more than I'd have if I'd sold out America. Anyway, what do you want?'

There was soft concern in Sarah's brown eyes. 'I didn't come to see you for a fight, Leo. I want to talk to you. We may not have been communicating much, but, though you don't deserve it, I've still got a lot of sisterly affection for you and I know you're bloody miserable.'

Leo looked back at his sister, awash with lonely self-concern. Oh yes, he wanted to talk to someone. If only Alison were with him . . .

Sarah read his thoughts. 'I don't think Alison's going to be a patient listener now Leo, and you can't blame her. Maybe sometime she'll regain some respect for you, but you're going to have to earn it. You may as well talk to

426

me. Come on, let's get out of here. We'll go and walk round the Serpentine and have some coffee in that hideous café.'

They drove in an awkward silence to Hyde Park.

'Why do we have to come here?' Leo grumbled, as they pulled up by the lake.

'Because if you walk, you can talk better.'

They clambered out of the Ferrari. Leo watched a uniformed cavalry officer trot past on his black charger; he wondered if Alison knew the soldier, or the horse. He mentioned this to Sarah. 'She was always trying to make me come out with her on one of those things, but I never did. I couldn't stand the idea of those chinless wonders all showing off and thinking they were living in the last century.'

'Well,' said Sarah, 'maybe you should have come, or at least watched her a couple of times. She's a very independent lady, but even independent ladies need their lover's approval sometimes.'

They walked slowly through the sunshine which glinted off the Serpentine. The squawks of the water birds and the yapping of pursuing dogs diminished the hum of traffic from Park Lane and Bayswater Road. The budding trees did their best to obscure Basil Spence's monolithic barracks. Joggers and well-wrapped ladies with small dogs passed them from both directions. Leo found himself talking.

Of course Sarah understood. It was the first time Leo had spoken to her without restraint since they were children. And now, after years of his egotistical arrogance keeping her at arm's length, she could, and wanted to, help him.

At first, she just let him talk. Only as he became more confident in her and more honest in his articulation of his state of mind could she start, gently, to make suggestions.

By the time they had made a circuit of the lake, she acknowledged that Alison's support was a key factor. If Leo were to calm down and rationalise the position he found himself in, and come to terms with the humiliation he felt Raj had visited upon him, he certainly needed Alison's encouragement and help. At the moment his perspective was so twisted that he was only going to dig himself obstinately into an ever-deepening hole.

Sarah was privately doubtful that Alison possessed the will to help, but she also knew the surprising strength of her sister-in-law's sense of rightness. Perhaps she could be persuaded to give Leo a few more last chances.

'Where did you say she's gone?' asked Sarah.

'To Spain, Seville, to look at some horses she's buying.'

'When did she go?'

'The day before yesterday,' Leo replied.

'And when is she back?'

'In a week or two I suppose. I think she was glad to get away from my hassles.'

'Yes, I'm sure she was. Are you looking forward to seeing her again?'

'God, yes! But she's like you. She can't see why it's so important for me to hang on to my own thing in the States. But I've told her and I've told you: it's not a question of pride, it's a question of money in the long term.'

Sarah made a face that reiterated her earlier arguments against this point of view.

'Well, never mind that. Why don't you forget things here for a bit? It might give you a fresh view if you get away from them. Go and join Alison in Spain; take an interest in what she's doing. But don't go and bog her down with your problems. Just enjoy being an intelligent observer for a change. I'm sure she'd be glad if you turned up.'

'Oh, I don't know. And that snotty old Spaniard she's staying with won't be glad to see me.'

'Bugger him. Just go. Alison's spending money with him. He'll put up with you.'

Leo thought for a moment, and brightened. 'Okay. It's a good idea. I don't seem to have much to do here just now, and I'm not planning on going to the States till next month.' He started walking briskly back to the car. 'Yeah

– I'll drop in and pick up a ticket on the first flight I can get.'

Sarah smiled. It was a long shot, but it might be the first stage in Leo's search for equilibrium.


Alison awoke.

She was alone in a big, carved bed.

The sun threw bright sharp lines between still-closed shutters. The only sign of the bunches of flowers was a single red rose on the pillow beside her. Judging by the lack of warmth in the rest of the bed, Mateo had been gone some time. She sat up and looked around slowly.

She looked up. The crucifix was still there.

Had it really happened?

My God – a real, old-fashioned, one-night stand.

No meaningful relationship, no sympathetic exchange of ideas.

Just a hell of a fuck with a man who killed bulls for a living.

She lay back, closed her eyes and felt her body suffused with the memory of it.

When she opened her eyes, she saw the crucifix again. She winked at it. 'Sorry God.' Then, more thoughtfully 'Sorry, Leo. It was bloody good, but it won't happen again.'

She climbed off the bed and gathered up her elaborate costume of the previous evening. She laughed at the thought of walking out through the hotel lobby dressed like this at nine in the morning. But when she did get down to the hotel's sombre and old-fashioned hall, Don Luis' driver walked towards her with a knowing look on his face.

'*Buenos días, Señora*,' he said, gesturing towards the Mercedes waiting outside the front door.


When Alison arrived back at the hacienda, she bathed, changed into white jeans and a red silk blouse and drank some coffee on the shady veranda. Then she went to look for Don Luis. He hadn't been in when the driver had dropped her back, and he was not, according to the servants, in the house now.

She made her way to the other side of the house and out of the courtyard through the high archway. Opposite was a stone-built shed, about fifty yards long. Its enormous double door stood open. In the gloom within, she knew, Don Luis' horses were installed.

In a pair of individual boxes just inside, two of the best stallions were kept. One, she hoped, was shortly to become hers. She leaned over the door of his box, and studied him acquisitively. He slowly turned his noble grey head on its thick arched neck towards her, and carried on chewing a mouthful of grain. She admired his proud carriage, broad straight shoulders and well-muscled quarters. Beneath a long, white forelock, his dark eyes blinked. Lazily he switched his well-groomed tail.

She was joined in her contemplation by a little toothless groom, who grinned at her and nodded towards the stallion. '*E muy bueno*,' he said and clutched his right arm in a universal symbol of copulation.

Alison raised her eyebrows and tried to look prim but she couldn't help a small smile. It was just what she had been thinking.

She wandered up between the two rows of stalls inspecting all the inmates – carriage mares to the right, working stallions and learning colts to the left.

She looked at them carefully, recognising the brand marks on their quarters which identified their breeders. Many, of course, carried Don Luis' own G in a circle with a star, but there was no shortage of alternative bloodlines, mostly from Portugal, in his breeding stock.

She went right through and out the other end of the barn, where, on a sandy arena, two young horses were being schooled. They were taught all the paces and movements of classical dressage before they were tested for speed, bravery, suppleness and obedience. If they were outstanding in all those things, they would be offered for sale to the *rejoneadores*. It was a long, patient process to train a horse for the *rejon* and Don Luis was one of the great horsemasters, devoting several hours every morning to this vital part of his business.

Sitting on a rough wooden chair, he never took his eyes off the animals in the arena, every so often giving a quiet, firm instruction to one of the riders.

Alison knew better than to disturb him. She leaned against an abandoned cart to watch.

When the session was over, Don Luis turned to her with a smile.

'You look very beautiful this morning, Señora.' His eyes flickered over her, acknowledging her body inside her loose blouse. 'A red rag to a bull, perhaps! I hope it doesn't affect bullfighters in that way – Mateo is coming this evening to try two of my horses.'

Alison gasped, unprepared for her own reaction to this news.

Don Luis noticed, but said nothing and stood up indicating she should precede him into the stable. As they walked, Alison found it hard to concentrate on what the breeder was saying.

She didn't want to see Mateo again. That would spoil the rarity, the innocence of that first, unplanned encounter.

To meet again would involve unspoken collusion. Knowing that he was coming, knowing what would happen – that would be premeditated.

And yet, and yet – she could do nothing to still her excitement.

She felt as if, like Jesus, she were being offered all the kingdoms in the world by Satan. And she knew she was going to take them.

No matter that Leo would never know. *She* would always know, and her knowledge would make her pity him, even despise him more.


In the late afternoon – an afternoon that had felt like a week – she stood on a wall above a narrow, open-topped passage between two corrals.

The *vaqueros* were cutting the black bull calves from their mothers. Mixed in among a herd of wide-horned brown and white domestic cows, the little fighting bulls and their mothers displayed their inbred anger.

Some of the cowhands respectfully stood on walls or behind sturdy stone *burladeros* for protection. They knew about the fighting cow. And the calves, once separated, furiously threw themselves head on at the metal doors and the walls. Centuries of careful breeding had produced these spectacular beasts, selected for their strength, determination and anger.

Alison looked up. She could see the mature bulls, grazing unconcerned, in the distance. No man went near them on foot. They were always herded by mounted *vaqueros* and could be approached in a car, but a pedestrian out there would stand no chance, and he would spoil the bull for the *corrida*. Once a bull has learned to charge the man not the cape, he becomes lethal as soon as he enters the ring.

One of the cows was isolated from the herd and put in a pen alongside the little bullring. Spherical tips were fitted to the tops of her sharp, upturned horns. She was to be used to test the bravery of the horses Don Mateo was going to try.

Seeing her at such close range, Alison was worried what this fighting cow, a quarter of the weight of her male counterparts, might do to Mateo on a young horse.

'Don't worry,' the grooms told her, laughing. 'Don Mateo and the horse both know what they are doing. There is no danger.'

The rest of the cattle were taken off to their respective paddocks. The sun slanted sharply across the ancient buildings. In the quiet, Alison could hear the penned cow snorting angrily from time to time and venting her anger on the gate that opened into the ring. Then a Land Rover, spewing a cloud of dust, dropped down the drive from the brow of the hill towards the hacienda, and before it had pulled up, Don Luis was out through the archway and welcoming Mateo with a long shake of the hand.

Alison saw them disappear into the stable barn and waited impatiently for them to come out. After a quarter of an hour, a horse and rider approached the ring. One of the *vaqueros* opened the main gate to let them in. Mateo didn't look up to where Alison sat, oblivious of what the grime and birdshit were doing to her white jeans, perched on the wall of the bullring.

He made two or three half passes diagonally across the ring, then skipped around the edge in a series of flying leg changes. This was impressive; he could have walked away with all the honours in any dressage contest in England, in spite of the Andalusian horse's inability to extend his stride in the preferred northern European fashion.

Then he slowed to a walk, on a lengthened rein, and relaxed the horse for a couple of circuits. Only once, almost shyly, he threw a dark, concentrated glance at Alison from beneath his heavy brow, a slight smile curling his lips.

When he was on the opposite side of the arena to the exit from the pen, he gave a shout. The cow was let in. She knew immediately what to do and charged directly at Mateo and his horse. He cantered straight towards her, then, a pace away from the careering cow, he touched his mount lightly with his heel, a little behind the girth, and the horse, unflinching, neatly side-stepped and cantered on along a parallel course.

The cow turned. Mateo waited.

She started running towards him. Still he waited. Then, a few yards before she reached him, he bunched his horse back on its quarters, squeezed with his knees and his mount shot forward, leaving the cow furious and bemused.

After a couple more passes, he trotted up to the main gate and called out again. The gate opened and he and his horse slipped out. It swung shut again before the cow had realised what had happened.

Alison watched enthralled as he repeated the performance with a second horse. When at last he left the ring, she made her way round to the back of the stable building and sat on the old cart.

After a while, Mateo emerged into the evening sun. He

stopped when he saw her and nodded. '*Buenas tardes, Señora*. What do you think of these two horses?'

His Spanish was less dialectal than that of the ranch-hands. She had no trouble understanding him.

God! she thought. They had hardly exchanged a word the previous night, yet he had invaded her body as intimately as any man ever had.

'They looked astonishing to me,' she answered, 'but then I'm not used to horses trained to do the job you need them for. Their performances must depend on you, don't they?'

Mateo shrugged slightly. 'Maybe, but I need animals that need the minimum of help from me.'

His eyes wandered up and down her body, resting for a moment on her tightly-clad hips. She couldn't help the increase in her pulse, the warmth that flooded her groin. She tried to look away, but his eyes irresistibly drew hers back.

He stood still. His damp shirt hung open to his stomach, his long scar only partially hidden by black, sweat-beaded curls. Alison had to do something. She shook a finger of hair from her eyes and smiled meekly. Mateo's lips twitched in one corner, and abruptly he turned away.

'I am going to look at Don Luis' bulls.'

'Where – on the pastures?' Alison asked, not wanting him to leave.

He nodded.

'Can I come with you?' she said. 'I'd like to try the stallion I'm buying.'

'No. It is not a good idea. Not for a woman.'

'Why not? It can't be that dangerous. The *vaqueros* do it all the time.'

As she spoke, Don Luis emerged from the stable-block. Mateo turned to him, questioning. 'It's all right, Mateo. She is a good horsewoman. If she decides to buy Cristobal, she should know his temperament. Just take special care in the pastures.'

Mateo looked at Alison for a moment. 'I will take you

434

then. But it is dangerous. You must stay close by me all the time.'

Don Luis instructed the grooms to have the appropriate animals ready in an hour, and Alison strolled back to the house with the two Spaniards.

In the fountain-cooled shade of the atrium, a bottle of *fino* and glasses had been placed on a table. They sat and Don Luis poured. As they sipped the pale, chilled liquid, the two men talked of bulls and horses.

They might have been bankers talking exchange rates or stockbrokers discussing the market. Alison listened and mused on these people whose lives were dedicated to the breeding and dramatic, ritual slaughter of fighting bulls.

The pink sky in the west was reflected by the low hills when Alison and Mateo left the hacienda and set off along a level track towards the sparsely treed pastures where the bulls grazed and built up weight and muscle for their first and last public appearance.

At the end of the track they reached a gate that gave on to a vast expanse of patchy grassland. Mateo leant down expertly from the back of his horse, opened the gate and held it to allow Alison and her horse to pass through. While he fastened it again, Alison's calm compliant stallion stood and waited.

Fifty yards away, unconcerned, a large slope-backed bull glanced up at her. Then he carried on ambling about, looking for tufts of fresh, green grass. Alison and Mateo put their horses into a gentle trot. The great, horned head came up again and gazed round suspiciously, then, reassured, dropped down to concentrate on feeding.

Mateo led them alongside the wire fencing. Ahead, a low ridge grew out of the plain and swung away to the north-east. When they reached it, they followed it round on a level, rising crest. To their left, the escarpment became more pronounced; to their right, down in the sheltered bowl, the bulls were scattered, uninterested.

The ridge was interspersed with random outcrops of rock, no higher than a man, and a few short, thorny trees.

Mateo covered the even ground at a slow rocking canter. Alison followed, thrilled at the undulating motion of her supremely schooled horse, and the closeness of the black fighting bulls.

A quarter of a mile along the ridge, they were preparing to make a detour around a small patch of scrubby bush and a jagged hump of rock. A lone bull appeared from behind it. He bent his head to graze, his solid bulk across their path.

Mateo turned round in his saddle, waved his arm over to the left and dropped down the steep side of the ridge.

The bull looked up. Its nostrils twitched at the unfamiliar scent. Alison felt a rush of adrenaline and excitement.

It was an excitement that quickly turned to panic.

The bull had trotted a few challenging paces forward to greet her cantering horse, and the horse responded with all the experience of his old fighting days – he took hold on the bit and quickened his pace towards the bull.

Desperately, Alison yanked the big grey head to the left. The horse came back on his hocks with a grunt, lost his footing on the loose ground on the edge of the escarpment, and scrabbled to regain it. Rocks rattled down the hill. The grey head reared up again and struck Alison hard on her forehead. She slid back, lost her stirrups, struggled wildly to grasp the horse's neck. For a moment her hand clutched at air, then found a handful of thick curling mane. Still precarious, but relieved, she tried to find her dangling irons. But the elegantly booted feet cast around blindly.

'Mateo?' A breathless whimper, unheard above the sounds of the struggling horse.

A few heaving strides, and they were back on the ridge. Where the bull still waited. Nowhere for the horse to go – no space to side-step or jink as in the ring. With a startled whinny, he reared again, right back on his sturdy hocks. Alison, dazed – head spinning, hands weak – was hurled down over the broad dappled-grey quarters.

Instinctively twisting as she fell, she hit the ground hard with her right shoulder; heard a crack and knew in a lucid split-second that she had snapped her collar-bone. Then she felt the pain, and gasped for the wind that had been pumped from her lungs by the fall.

Her horse disappeared from view down the slope. Hooves and loose stones clattered.

Through the firm ground against her face – another rhythmic thudding of hooves.

She scrabbled on the sharp, stony ground, trying to turn her broken torso. She gasped in pain as she twisted round and lifted her head.

It was the black eyes more than the lowered horns that told her that she was going to die.

In a slow-motion trance, she watched the huge head and its one and a half tons of driving force approach her. The long sharp points of the horns were parallel to the ground and only a few inches above it.

They were aimed straight at her winded, helpless body.

When Mateo had turned round to check that Alison had followed him down, he saw her stallion tossing its head to throw off the bridle.

He couldn't see Alison.

Frantically he turned his horse to scramble back up to the brow of the hill.

When, with one last struggling leap, they reached the ridge, Mateo stopped his horse and froze with horror.

The rear end of the bull showed that it was in an unassailable attacking position. It had just reached Alison; its shoulders heaved from side to side as it buried both horns into its target.

When it lifted its head it was as if the red dye from her silk blouse had run down through the whiteness of Alison's jeans.

The bull, angered by the weight carried on his horns, shook his head and lowered it again. The thin body slid to the ground and the bull backed off a couple of paces to assess the position.

Mateo galvanised his mount into an instant gallop and thundered up alongside the great angry animal.

Knowing that it would do little more than irritate it,

he lashed his long, thin dressage whip across the bull's shoulders. This was enough to make it look up and view Mateo and his horse as a new and greater threat than the small motionless heap in front of it.

Now Mateo had turned and galloped straight towards the bull, with very little margin on the narrow ridge. As he and his horse side-stepped, he felt its breath and its heaving side against his boot.

When he passed, he swivelled in his saddle to see that the great beast had turned towards him and away from Alison. It charged, and he waited until it was within six feet before taking off and leading it a hundred yards along the crest of the hill. Then, very nimbly, before its pursuer could work out what had happened, he turned at a right-angle, almost at full gallop, and carried on straight down the steep scrubby slope.

Gathering up his reins, he rode as fast as this horse had ever run in a large loop around the bull herd, back to the gate through which he and Alison had passed only ten minutes before.

Then he asked his horse to do something it had never done: with scarcely any check, at speed, they flew over the gate and thundered down the track to the hacienda.

Mateo knew he had drawn the bull off Alison. But he couldn't risk going back to her, for it might see her again and continue its attack. So he galloped straight into the courtyard, yelled at two grooms to come, dismounted and leaped into the Land Rover with them.

Don Luis emerged from the house to investigate the commotion. The courtyard was empty, and he walked briskly through the arch to see the vehicle hurtling up the track towards the bull pasture, spewing a wake of dust.

There had been no shortage of taxis at Seville Airport, but Leo took a long time agreeing a price for the trip to the Hacienda de San José de Praja. He felt oddly nervous as he neared the end of his journey. He was approaching Alison on an unfamiliar basis. This encounter was going to be something of a watershed – he would find that either

438

she had reached the point where it was no longer possible for her to reappraise her relationship with him, or she would accept that his need for her, and his humility, were real.

He had, he supposed, always loved her, but now she mattered more than he had ever known.

He remembered the tatty gateway as they turned into the drive and when the taxi started rattling down towards the hacienda, he looked around him with far greater interest than on his previous visit.

He gazed across the shallow green undulations of the estate and his eye was caught by a vehicle careering crazily towards the house from the opposite direction.

Bloody mad dagos, he thought.

His car drove in among the buildings, and stopped. When he got out, he was nearly run down by the Land Rover hurtling into the courtyard.

And then he saw his wife.

The two grooms were lifting a limp, blood-drenched body from the back of the Land Rover. The head hung loosely backwards. The long black hair was rippled by the light breeze.

Leo was paralysed – in his limbs, his lungs and his heart.

He didn't need to see the face.

They were already carrying her through the front door when he reacted.

'Alison!' he screamed, and ran frantically towards the house. 'For Christ's sake, what the hell's happened?' he sobbed. 'What have you done to her?'

They carried her through into a little ante-room off the hall and laid her on a much worn, red velvet chaise longue. They straightened her legs and put a cushion behind her head.

Leo heard a low moan.

'Thank God – she's alive.'

He flung himself down on his knees beside her, trying to avert his eyes from the carnage which extended from her breast to her hips.

'Alison – Angel! My God, what happened?'

439

He leaned his ear close to her mouth; short faint breaths were still coming.

He must do something.

He looked up. For the first time he noticed the other men in the room – three in a line along the back of the chaise longue: the two grooms and, opposite him, above Alison's head, another man, with brown eyes motionless below a thick brow and black curling hair.

Leo stood up. 'For Christ's sake, have you got her a doctor? An ambulance? Whoever the hell you are, have you done *any*thing?'

The dark eyes flickered towards Leo for an instant before returning to Alison.

From behind him, Leo heard a deep Spanish voice.

'There is nothing to do.'

Don Luis came into the room and stood beside Leo. 'I have telephoned to the doctor and the hospital. They will come, but . . .' He shrugged. 'You must know. She will die.'

'What are you talking about?' Leo shouted. 'She's still breathing! Of course they can do something! If they can't, then get the best bloody doctor in Spain here, right now!'

Don Luis shook his head. 'I'm sorry, Mr Freeman. The damage is terrible; I do not know how she still breathes.'

Leo seethed with frustration. 'Christ, you fucking dozy dagos! You can't just stand there doing nothing!' He felt his whole body choking with anguish. 'Please, *please*!' he beseeched all the people in the room. 'She's the most important, most precious thing in the world to me. I can't let her go. I can't watch her die. Please do *something*.'

Don Luis took his arm. 'Would she like a priest?'

Leo turned and stared down at her. 'Yes,' he said. 'Yes. Get her a priest. She's a Catholic – it matters to her.'

'I will send a car to fetch him. He has only a bicycle.'

Leo swung round angrily.

'Oh, God – you people. Tell him to get a move on! And when's this doctor coming?'

'Soon, but he must come from Seville.'

Don Luis motioned the two grooms out and left the room with them. Leo and Mateo were left facing one another across the unstirring, faintly breathing body.

They both looked down at the tattered remains of the silk blouse, the ripped and blood-soaked jeans.

'We must cover her,' said Leo. He looked around for something suitable.

Mateo walked towards a dusty old cape that was displayed across one wall of the room. He tore it down and laid it very gently over Alison, up to her chin.

Leo nodded his thanks, and they stood for several minutes more in silence.

'How did it happen?' Leo asked huskily.

He could see from the blank look in the other man's eyes that he hadn't understood.

And, when the Spaniard looked down again at Alison, the realisation that this other man had loved her too hit Leo like a sledge-hammer. He stared at Mateo. When the other's eyes met his, they both understood.

They continued their vigil until the sound of a car pulling into the courtyard announced the arrival of the priest.

He bustled in wearing his biretta and stole and carrying a little wooden box. This he placed on the floor and unlocked. He took out two small bottles and put them on a side table near Alison's head.

Then, almost under his breath, he started a Latin monologue to the accompaniment of several signs of the cross, on himself and over Alison. Then he leaned towards her and whispered in her ear in Spanish.

There was no response. He continued and gave her absolution, blessed her with holy water and, dipping his thumb into the holy oil in the other bottle, he made the sign of the cross with it on her forehead.

Then he knelt beside her, took her arms from beneath the musty cape and laid them across her breast. Once again he made the sign of the cross in oil on the backs of both her hands. He prayed quietly beside her for a few more minutes then stood, bowed slightly in offering his condolences, and left.

The two men stayed where they were and continued their helpless watching.

Then Alison gave a small sigh. The hand on her breast moved slightly. Leo dropped to his knees again. She was still breathing.

Quite suddenly, her eyelids flickered up. Her eyes moved between the two faces above her. Slowly she lifted her hand to her forehead where the oil was beginning to run down to her temple.

She touched the oil and smiled very slightly.

She looked again at both men then spoke in a faint, breathless voice, 'Has a priest been? Has God forgiven me?' She saw two dark-eyed heads nod slowly together. She turned her head to look only at Leo. 'And will you forgive me, Leo?' she whispered.

He said no words, but she felt his answer as he leaned over her and his warm tears fell on her cheek.

Leo gazed at the purple-draped coffin resting on trestles in the centre of the Little Oratory in Knightsbridge. It was piled high with wreaths and all around the altar were large white and yellow arrangements of fresh spring flowers.

He hardly noticed the black-clothed people crowding into the inward-facing pews. Alison's parents sat beside him, her father stifling his grief, her mother unashamedly weeping.

Without really seeing, Leo looked around at the other mourners; he didn't know who most of them were – so many friends and relations of Alison's that he had never known, never wanted to know – but he could tell that they had loved her. Their grief was patently genuine.

Behind him, his mother sat still and white-faced. Beside her was Simon, solemn and tragic with a glistening of unshed tears in his eyes. He had, at Leo's request, made all the arrangements for the requiem mass, booked the choir, chosen the readings, decided on the music and invited a gentle, unworldly priest to officiate.

Leo had felt unexpectedly grateful to his brother-in-law.

Their shared misery at Alison's horrible death had evoked a hitherto unlikely mutual warmth.

Opposite sat Raju Kalianji with his back upright against the wall, staring expressionlessly at the altar. Reena was beside him, looking sadly around the crowded chapel. Leo knew Raj seemed upset in a confused and nebulous way, but he seethed with anger that he should have come. It was true that the Indian had made all the appropriate noises of condolence, but Leo had sensed a sort of triumphant gleam behind the inscrutable face.

The mass was a very moving ceremony. Even the most confirmed atheists in the congregation believed that this was the proper way to celebrate the life and death of someone as thoughtful and beautiful as Alison.

At the end, after the choir had sung Franck's *Panis Angelicus* and the coffin had been carried to the hearse outside, there was an almost happy peacefulness to the event.

But gazing at the coffin from the graveside, as the first token spadefuls of earth drummed on to the light, polished oak, Leo was more unbearably desolate than he would have believed possible: the finality of knowing he would never see those mischievous blue eyes and that gleaming black hair, or hear again the clever, confident laughter; that he would never hold the slender body; that the only person who had ever really known him, really loved him, was gone.

For several days, Leo stayed at home.

He went through Alison's belongings. Each one evoked a memory or a surprise. He found little sketches she had made, snippets of her written thoughts on people and events, copiously annotated catalogues of picture exhibitions and concert programmes. Looking at her clothes, he found himself transported back to the last occasion on which she had worn each of them. His only companion was the permanently tearful Filipino, who padded around wordlessly, getting on with running the house without any instructions from Leo.

Then he drove down to Goring. The sadness of the people there was real, though underscored by uncertainty about the future of the stud. Leo was in no frame of mind to make any decisions. Ironically, as Alison's next of kin, the whole set-up was now his, but he felt it would be quite wrong of him to go on operating it – even if he had known how.

And anyway, walking round the yard, looking at the big Roman-nosed heads protruding from the boxes, he blamed these horses for Alison's death.

Once again, he was surrounded by a thousand re-minders, a thousand causes for remorse. He remembered the row that had, just a few months before, sent him banging his way out of the house to go and see Danielle. He remembered how he had laughed at what he had considered Alison's optimistic naïvety in starting the stud. The trophies on the mantelpiece reminded him how wrong he had been.

He couldn't stand the thought of spending a night there and drove slowly down the avenue to the main gates for the last time. He never wanted to see the place again.

The rest of that summer Leo lived in a miasmic haze.

He went to America and visited his three shops, but couldn't find the energy to put into action the changes that he knew were essential if his business was to have any real chance of survival.

The people who worked for him there were frustrated by his lack of response and Leo was sickened by the unmistakable insincerity of their sympathy. His bankers once again advised him to cut his losses and sell, but he refused. At least, over here he was in charge. He wasn't ready to give that up.

In England, he found himself with less and less to do. Raj had been very successful in introducing an eager middle-management of professional retailers. Most of Leo's suggestions were reasonably but firmly rejected. When he blustered furiously that he was the majority shareholder, his attention was politely drawn to the minority shareholders' clause, which stopped him from implementing any decisions without their consent.

He began to find going to his office humiliating and irksome. Often he didn't get there until midday, sometimes not at all. He started drinking a great deal more, and when this depressed him, he would supplement it with increasing quantities of cocaine.

He had no wish, nor inclination, to spend time with women – comparisons with Alison precluded this and were sharply painful to him. When his physical urges needed satisfying, he would ring up Dawn, who ran the house near Montpelier Street, and have her send round the best available. Always, afterwards, he felt nauseous and miserable and after a few months, he stopped even doing that. As a substitute, he started to gamble. He found that he could anaesthetise himself by sitting for hours, half-drunk, at a black-jack table, playing sometimes for thousands of pounds a hand and, on the whole, playing well and not losing much. He found it was the only way now of getting adrenaline into his system and he was becoming addicted to his own chemistry.

No one seemed to care, or tried to stop him. He became very unsociable and the few friends he still had gave up trying to raise his spirits or to divert his attention in more constructive directions.

Sarah, of course, did care, but she knew he tended to think of her as a traitor because she had continued to work with Raj and had become more important in Rags than Leo was. And it was she who had urged him off to Spain to witness his wife's death, to become aware of her infidelity. For, though he had forgiven Alison and hadn't found it hard to do so, the knowledge that she had slept with another man the night before she died had magnified his misery.

Sarah had tried many times to talk to Leo, to show him she cared and that she loved him, but he had refused. The fleeting revival of their childhood closeness just before he went to meet Alison in Spain had, apparently, withered and gone for good. She, too, was surviving only by having

445

built and maintained an emotional cocoon around herself. She therefore understood the reluctance to have this penetrated. So, frustrated but sympathetic, she had eventually ceased her approaches to Leo.

Simon contacted Sarah that autumn. She had seen nothing of him since the funeral and she was glad to accept his invitation to lunch at the House of Commons. On her way there in a taxi she wondered how he was settling in to parliamentary life. She knew that at the beginning of the new session he had been appointed Parliamentary Private Secretary to the Home Secretary, and that, in a few months of the newly elected Tory Government's existence, he was already making a name for himself.

They had a drink in one of the bars before lunch and it was clear Simon was enjoying his new position of influence.

She liked and admired Simon, in spite of her general disapproval of his type, and when they sat down in the noisy restaurant, she congratulated him enthusiastically and genuinely on his successes.

But it was Leo Simon wished to discuss. 'I've tried to get in touch with him dozens of times. On the odd occasions I have got through to him, he's been very reluctant to talk. I've asked him to lunch and dinner several times, but he won't come. It's very odd. At the funeral, I got the impression we were communicating better than we had ever done before. I know he was absolutely shattered by Ali's death – and I respected him more for the depth of his grief.'

Sarah nodded. 'What made it worse for him was that he went out to Spain to show her he was prepared to be interested in her on her own terms,' she said. 'It was the first expression of remotely considerate thinking I'd heard him make for about twenty years.' She paused. 'Admittedly, it had taken a series of absurd, unnecessary crises to get him to that point, but it seemed as if he had learned something from them, about himself.'

'Yes.' Simon nodded thoughtfully. 'And he's learned something from losing Ali. But from what I hear, he simply can't cope with it. How have you found him?'

'Same as you. He won't talk. Now that Raj has more or less taken over the admin at Rags – well, not taken over, but put in his systems and his eager young beavers in blazers – Leo feels he's been usurped. I suppose he has really, but there's still a lot he could do if only he'd swallow his pride. But he's very unhappy at the office and, of course, everyone knows it and knows why – which doesn't help.'

'Just what is his position now?' asked Simon.

'He still owns fifty-five per cent of the Rags stores in England and Europe, but when Raj bought in, he effectively shortened our margins to a point where they do little more than cover costs. There's nothing I can do about it. I just take the long view that the capital value of the company is increasing all the time; I still own twenty per cent of it; I draw a fat salary and a design royalty on all garments Raj manufactures for wholesale. It's not the best of deals, but it's good enough for me. The way we were heading before, we were almost certain to go under. The trouble is, there is a hard core of borrowings that we just haven't been able to get rid of. We're really only servicing the loans. Raj has offered to buy more equity, but of course Leo's having none of that.'

'What about America?'

'Oh, well – Leo's being bloody-minded. He's hocked up to the eye-balls. He'll never make any money there. He's got no choice but to buy his stock from Raj, who's let him have more and more on tick. But I've got a feeling that Raj is just waiting for the right moment to pull the line in again. Leo still has the stud, though God knows why – Alison's Irishman is running it for him – and he's got the house in Chelsea Square, which must be worth three or four hundred thousand. As a matter of fact, if he got his act together and consolidated he'd be fine, but he won't. And he won't listen – like he's never listened. The only difference now is that he doesn't shout back. He just ignores you.' She looked at Simon hopefully. 'Do you think there's *anything* you can do?'

'Frankly, not much. I told you, I've tried. But the main

problem is that he's the object of a well-orchestrated plan to undermine his position, or so it seems to me. I'm not going to mention names, but what's being done is perfectly legal. It simply depends on the persistence of Leo's vanity – and that's a pretty safe bet, I'm afraid.'

# 1980

The following spring, a year after Alison's death, Simon and Claire Riley were asked to dinner at Raju Kalianji's new house in Winnington Road, Hampstead.

'Why has he invited us?' Claire asked on the way. 'After all, you've not seen much of him over the last few years, and I'm afraid I never made much effort to disguise the fact that I found him pretty unsympatico.'

Simon laughed. 'I shouldn't think that worried him much. But he's become a fairly major wheeler-dealer and he wants friends who walk in the corridors of power. I suppose he thinks I come into that category, and I've known him a long time.'

'I guess you're right. He certainly seems to be making contacts all over the place. I've read bits in gossip columns about him at parties in Switzerland, yacht trips from Monte Carlo and film premières in Paris. You wouldn't have thought he was interested in that kind of thing.'

'Yes, he does seem to be emerging as something of a dark horse.'

When they arrived at the large white gateposts of the rambling, neo-Georgian house, they drove up a short, pristine tarmac drive to the large sweep in front of the pillared portico. As they climbed from the car, the front door was opened by a white-coated English manservant. They were shown into a drawing-room furnished in the impeccable manner of an English country house, but with large Mogul paintings on the walls.

The other guests, drinking champagne cocktails, were impressive: the Indian High Commissioner; a senior civil servant from the Treasury; the chairman of a small but respected merchant bank; a female Home Office minister and their respective spouses.

Raj Kalianji saw the Rileys enter and came over to welcome them.

'How very good to see you, Simon, Claire.' He shook hands with them both. 'I'm sorry it's been so long. The last time we met must have been at that very beautiful ceremony for your sister's funeral – about a year ago, I think.'

'Yes,' said Simon, 'it was. And we were very grateful for all those magnificent flowers you had put in the church. We're all human, and these things, like the singing and the incense, all encourage the right frame of mind on those occasions.'

'Believe me, I'm sure they weren't necessary to accentuate people's grief – that was genuine enough. Reena and I sent those flowers out of our regard for a strong, intelligent and beautiful woman who must have been a great loss to Leo – and the rest of her family, of course.'

Simon acknowledged these sentiments with a nod. He still missed her a lot, but he didn't want to talk about her in these platitudinous terms. He changed the subject. 'And is there any particular significance to this evening's gathering?'

'No, not really, though I am celebrating my acquisition of a small bank,' Raj said.

Simon raised an impressed eyebrow. 'Are you, indeed? What is it?' He mentioned the name of the bank whose chairman stood nearby.

'Good heavens, no. Nothing so grand. I have simply resuscitated a dormant but licensed deposit-taker called the Anglo-Assam Bank – a vestige and victim of your empire's decline and fall.'

'Well, I'm sure you're capable of administering the kiss of life to an ailing bank. What are you going to do with it?'

'We shall be offering a range of financial services, with affiliates in Geneva and New York,' said Raj vaguely, 'but this isn't meant to be a promotional affair, just a quiet dinner among people who know what's going on.' He turned to Claire, 'Are you as interested in paintings as you used to be? I thought you might like to see my newest acquisitions from India – let me show you.'

And he led her over to the largest of the Mogul paintings in which a fat, turbaned and bejewelled Nawab was perched in a gilt howdah on top of an elephant. The Nawab was firing a very long flint-lock gun, rather unsportingly, at a tiger that cringed implausibly a few yards in front of his elephant's tusks.

Simon turned to the Treasury mandarin whom he knew slightly and, prompted by the paintings, started talking about the performance of the England cricket team currently touring India; he had already learned the technique of discussing Government policy with civil servants.

Over dinner, he found himself next to the mandarin's wife, who turned out to be a knowledgeable and enthusiastic gossip.

Early in the meal she was leaning towards him, almost covering her mouth with one hand as she confided, 'Of course, our host is really a glorified gambler. He's been making a killing, an absolute killing, on the coffee and silver markets – all off-shore, of course, but he wants to get respectable.'

Simon tried to look surprised. 'But I thought he was in textiles and property,' he said.

'Oh, yes, of course he is, among other things. But now he wants to establish himself as a financial mogul, like his ancestors on the wall.' She nodded at a stylised courtly scene hanging opposite them.

'Those aren't his ancestors – wrong religion,' said Simon. 'But I do agree that his ambitions seem to be keeping one step ahead of him.'

As Reena Kalianji was on his other side, he felt it injudicious, not to say plain rude, to carry on this conversation and indicated this by turning to her and engaging her in a conversation about her new home.

Reena was a very impressive woman now. Always possessed of considerable potential, Raj's assiduous training and money appeared to have fully realised it. Simon thought she looked like, and seemed to have modelled herself on, Ayesha, the widowed Maharani of Jaipur and daughter of a maharajah of Cooch-Behar. She was very sophisticated and very beautiful by any standards, without in any way compromising her Indianness. It was remarkable that inside half a dozen years she had been able to carry off a social occasion like this with complete equanimity, as if she had never known any other lifestyle. She was also, Simon discovered, a useful PR tool for her husband. After discussing the house and its characteristics for a while, she turned to other evidently more important matters.

'Raj is a little disappointed that he's had no real help or encouragement in setting up his centre for Hindu studies. He did think your boss might have shown more interest, if not money. After all, wasn't a regard for minority cultures implied in your manifesto?'

Simon smiled. 'Ah, I see I'm here to be lobbied. To be honest with you, I know nothing about it. Has he been in touch with the Home Office about it?'

'Oh, yes, of course, though it seems to me they are quite selective on what they pass on to their ministers. Perhaps you could find out for us?' She smiled with a charm that could not be denied.

Simon agreed to do what he could and asked with real interest what the project was all about. It surprised him initially that Raj should have got involved. His interest in religion had not previously been all that noticeable. But then, Simon supposed, he must be making a play for some position of influence among the Indian community – hence the High Commissioner. It was certainly true that, commercially, the Asians were becoming a force to be reckoned with and would, no doubt, provide a few clients for his bank. Anyway, Simon listened, impressed, to Reena's genuine enthusiasm for the scheme, and then he turned the conversation in another direction.

'How do Leo and Raj get on now?'

Reena looked down at her plate for a moment. 'Raj hasn't told me, but I think there are difficulties. Of course, Raj isn't at the Rags office so much now – with the new bank and everything – but it seems a pity that two men should be partners but not friends. All the family said he was wrong to involve himself with an Englishman, but of course, as I'm sure you must know, he makes his own mind up about those sort of things.'

'About most sort of things I should have thought,' said Simon.

'Well, yes, that is true,' replied Reena, and Simon perceived a broad and vulnerable crack in her sophisticated exterior.

Over the next twelve months, painful anniversaries exacerbated Leo's morbid existence. He pondered, with indelible guilt, his behaviour towards Alison when she had been alive. When he gazed in the mirror, the irrepressible jauntiness was gone; the arrogance had turned to dogged stubbornness. He accepted the haggard, pasty face and uncertain eyes that stared back at him as a penance for his treatment of Alison.

He attributed the relentless deterioration in his emotional and financial state to an erstwhile envious world taking its revenge. Nothing occurred to encourage him to shake off his sense of being trapped and victimised. He simply couldn't stand far enough away from his problems to see what was happening to him.

He had increased both the amount he drank and the sums he was prepared to lose in the casinos. He had become a member of the regiment of taciturn men who sought to test their courage by seeing how much they were prepared to risk on the turn of a card. His was now a regular face to be seen in Crockfords and the Clermont.

The only reason his drinking stayed in control at all was that the gaming laws forbad the consumption of alcohol at the casino tables, and being at the tables was what mattered most.

He had tried, without much optimism, to take out a few

girls, but he found they bored or persecuted him. He had become paranoid about women's motives. He thought they believed either that he still had a lot of money, which was all they were interested in, or that he had lost it and they were sorry for him. Whichever, they kept him from the casinos, where there was no ambiguity about the numbers on the cards, and where excitement was guaranteed.

His attempt to run the stud at long distance had been a predictable failure. His only compensation was that a fast-rising market secured him a spectacular price for it when he finally decided to sell. This was particularly fortuitous, as increasing interest rates were making the necessity of a fresh injection of capital into Rags look inevitable. Raj was ready to stump up, but unless Leo could match further investment pro rata his holding, he would be forced to cede more of the company. On top of this, his gambling was now making significant inroads into his remaining personal assets – principally his house.

Despite all overtures from Sarah and Simon, he had remained introspective and uncommunicative. The past few years' experience had made him grudgingly uncertain of his own judgements, and so many of his previous pronouncements seemed to have turned out to be wrong that he was reluctant to make any definite statements about anything. He remained obsessive, however, about his instinctive approach to retailing and had taken to prowling round the stores, castigating department managers and sales staff for any shortcomings, however trivial. The window-dressing and display teams were subject to constant vilification for their efforts, but, surprisingly, they didn't resent it. Leo still had the gift of making his point, illustrating it with vivid metaphor and past experience.

He was helped in the gradual re-establishment of his influence in Rags by Raj's absence from the office. Raj still appeared regularly, but usually for short visits. He was in the process of drawing all his activities into one corporate holding company, which he was intending eventually to float on the Stock Market as a public company.

Along with his textile, property, commodity and banking

interests, he had acquired several small but profitably active international companies: this package was likely to be of interest to all but the most cautious of fund managers. Raj's skill at spotting unlikely acquisitions and gearing them up was already being widely talked and written about. This was, the pundits thought, the right attitude for the eighties; a very different proposition from the asset-stripping whizz-kids of the early seventies.

As it transpired, Raj short-cut the business of going for a Stock Exchange flotation by finding and buying control of an ancient and moribund publicly-quoted company called the Calcutta Trading Company, whose shares were traded in pennies, and whose only asset appeared to be a small dockside warehouse on the Isle of Dogs. He sought, and was granted, planning permission to convert this building into a block of unusually spacious studio apartments and, in the deliberately low-key publicity that this generated, he renamed the company Calco and backed all his other onshore activities into it, including his twenty-five per cent holding in Rags. He then went to market with a series of rights issues, which would increase the capital base ten-fold. Most of his own holdings were disguised in offshore nominee companies, which engaged in judicious leap-frogging between each issue.

Leo suffered real humiliation when articles began to appear in the financial pages, pointing out that although Calco's holding in Rags retail contributed very little to group profits, it provided a substantial and profitable outlet for the manufacturing company and, because of its concessionary rental arrangement, a very large income for the property company that owned the Kensington freehold.

Simon, failing to persuade Leo to come and meet him, had written to him as soon as Raj's plans became clear, suggesting that Leo raise all he could to buy into Calco.

Even if he had been able to raise the kind of money that would have made this worth doing, Leo refused, dismissing the whole scheme as an elaborate con-trick.

Raj's attitude to him, though, remained polite. Leo assumed that this was because any bad publicity for Rags would rock the corporate boat. So it was with a re-awakened sense of purpose that he left for the States again to continue his struggle for profitability and independence there.

In New York – at last – gross profits were outstripping running costs. Michael Rappaciolo, who had run the store since it opened in 1973, was a determined and ambitious fighter – and he was on Leo's side. After eight years of skilful and aggressive retailing, they were making real money there. Of course, New York was better placed than other American cities to take advantage of Rags's very solid success in Europe. People there, if they weren't travelling across the Atlantic regularly, were at least prepared to look across it.

But this hard-won success on the East Coast was offset by the gloom that greeted Leo in Texas and California. In both places the losses were large and inexplicable. Leo was certain that he was being robbed, but he couldn't see where. Furthermore, the fakes had made a reappearance in Los Angeles.

To compound all this, his American banks now dug their heels in. It was only by impassioned and ultimately convincing argument that Leo extracted an agreement that they would hold off for a further twelve months to see if the western branches could catch up with New York. If not they would all have to go.

Leo knew this was a hollow victory, and that with the counterfeit stock – which he had omitted to mention to the bankers – undermining his margins, the chances of recovery were slim. This time he would have been prepared to cut his losses and close down the two loss-makers, but that wouldn't come near to squaring his position, and he would lose New York as well. His only chance was to raise about a million dollars, interest free, without giving any equity away. The quickest way to do that would be to sell more of his holdings in Rags's European retail – to Raj. That was out of the question. He was, he conceded to himself, unlikely to make it playing black-jack or chemmy, and he didn't know anything about robbing banks.

456

He returned to the Bel Air, where, as usual, he was staying. He couldn't face going out to any of the clubs or restaurants, and instead, he sat in the bar scowling at anyone who came in and pouring Jack Daniels down his throat.

Suddenly he thought that he was experiencing *déjà vu*.

'How y'all doin', Leo?'

Ross Blackwell stood beside him, beaming broadly, eyes gleaming with goodwill.

'How the hell do you always turn up when I'm here?' asked Leo, pleased, despite himself, to see any familiar face.

'Maybe I'm your guardian angel,' Ross boomed, and slapped Leo on the back. 'I heard you were in town; I called this place yesterday and they said you were in. Easy.'

'Well, if you want to do me a favour, come out and get ratted with me. I don't want to have to do it alone.'

'Right on! Of course I'll get drunk with you – that's what guardian angels are for, ain't it?'

Christmas 1981 was hell.

Leo drove to his mother's house, picked her up with Sarah, and carried on to his uncle's where they were joining a dozen more relations. He wondered how he had let himself get talked into going. He had managed to avoid this kind of family gathering since his father had died. As soon as he arrived, he knew how right he had been to do so.

All of the men had been charting his career for years, monitoring the press, analysing it and prognosticating about it with each other, and now they had an opportunity to give him the benefit of their considered opinion, they weren't going to waste it. They clamoured around him, advising, pontificating, commiserating – and that was what stung most.

The last thing he wanted from these people was their sympathy: for Christ's sake, he may have been going through a bad patch, but he was still worth twenty times more than any of them.

He had to tolerate four hours of this torture before he could get away and then only in the face of his mother's tears and Sarah's anger.

'You're still a selfish bastard, Leo,' she hissed. 'I did hope after everything that's happened to you, you might have climbed down a bit, but, oh no, not the great Leo Freeman. No one can tell him what to do, or that he might be wrong – just once in a blue moon.'

Driving back to Chelsea on his own, Leo smarted from this onslaught.

He knew exactly how wrong he had been and what mistakes he had made – far better than anyone else. He was the expert on his own shortcomings. He didn't need to be told about them by anyone else. Couldn't Sarah see that? He had always assumed, in spite of the lack of their communication now, that she still understood that.

The bastards, he thought. When I've got all this mess sorted out, I'll show them; I'll be Mr Nice Guy; I've just got to be Mr Copper-bottomed Rich Guy first.

He thought venomously about his relations and their relish at his demise; how they were rubbing their hands with glee at the mighty fallen.

Then he thought of Christmas three years before, when Alison had persuaded him to drive up to London with her to go to midnight mass at the Oratory – an ornate cavern filled with people, music and incense-smoke. And although he had known that she was finding it difficult to love him then, she had tried, she had tried bloody hard. Hers had been a big heart, beating in the body of a real woman. If anyone was in heaven now with the angels, she was.

A few days after Christmas, Leo's self-appointed guardian angel got in touch by phone.

When Leo had gone out with Ross that evening in LA, he had been determined to isolate himself from reality by getting blind drunk, and he had succeeded. But in the process, as if in the confessional or on a psychiatrist's couch, he had poured out his troubles and fears. Ross had been a good listener.

Leo couldn't remember now how much he had told him, and now he was alarmed to hear him ask: 'Do you still need a few billion bucks in a hurry?'

Leo blustered, 'Yeah, of course, don't we all?'

Ross cut across his laughter. 'Right. I've got a plan. Meet me at the Carlton Tower in an hour.'

When Leo reached Cadogan Place, Ross was outside the hotel, pacing up and down, looking like a caricature of a Texan soap hero. He strode over to Leo's car, opened the passenger door, and got in.

'It's too goddamn quiet in that place. Let's go to some noisy bar where we can talk without a lot of flapping ears around.'

Leo nodded. 'Okay.' He headed towards an habitually crowded wine bar in Draycott Avenue.

They found a table and bought a bottle of champagne. They could hardly hear each other above the braying and hooting of young stockbrokers and their Sloane Rangers.

'This is just fine,' Ross approved.

'Good. Now what's your plan?' asked Leo.

'First of all, you're gonna need two million pounds, in cash, for about four days. Can you get that?'

Leo was suspicious. 'Yeah – I guess so. It depends what for.'

'I'll tell you what for, but there's no point unless you're sure you can get your hands on two million.'

'Okay. I can. Go on.'

'Right. Do you know the size of the coke market in LA?'

'No. But it must be bloody huge – the way everyone gets through it out there. Are you in that business?'

'Well, let's say that with your money, you could be too.'

'Is this your plan for making a few million bucks?' asked Leo, incredulous, doubtful, excited.

'Not just a few million bucks,' Ross paused, looking hard at Leo. 'Ten million pounds, in five days; half for you, half for me.'

'But for Christ's sake, you're crazy! That business is all run by the mob.'

'Uh-huh,' Ross shook his head. 'Last year the street value of the coke sold in the Hollywood area alone was one and a quarter *billion* dollars. That's one thousand, two hundred and fifty million dollars. We're talking here about forty million dollars-worth. That's peanuts; there's room for a lot of operators in a market that size. And you're in for one hit, and one hit only.'

'Hang on, I'm not in for any hits. That's too heavy. I don't know anything about the business, and what do you want me in for anyway?'

'Not knowing anything about the business didn't stop you investing before,' Ross said coldly. 'How much did you lose over that studio?'

'Yeah, but that was legitimate.'

'And that makes it okay to lose money?' Ross laughed. 'Listen, you don't have to know about this business, because I do. I know the guys in Colombia. I've eaten my share of cazuela at José O'Campo's joint in Medellin; I know the guys in the aviation business in Ventura County and I know the big buyers. And I ain't askin' you to join me because I'm soft. I'm already committed to four shipments, but I can always use another five million pounds, if you can come up with the stake money.'

'No way,' Leo said firmly. 'That's out of my league. I need the money, but not that badly. I'm not interested in spending my old age locked up with a bunch of gay coons in San Quentin.'

'Leo, Leo,' said Ross, 'you've been watching too much TV. The only straight cops in LA are doing traffic duty. And the others are very fair; you only have to pay 'em if they catch you.' He stopped and looked at Leo as he took a long swig of his champagne and lit a cigar. 'Think about it. You find two million, you put it down, you pick up seven. Simple as that. But you don't have to make up your mind right now. I'm over here for three more days, and then I go to Amsterdam. If you want, I'll call by again on my way back.'

But Leo was shaking his head. 'Leave me out of it, Ross. I'm not interested. I'm not bloody desperate enough for that.'

For an instant Ross's eyes glazed over. He looked very angry. With a visible effort, he controlled himself. 'Well, my friend, the offer's there. Any time you feel you want it bad enough, there's a pile of money waitin' for you.' He stood up and stamped his narrow trouser legs down over his boots. 'I've gotta be going. You call me, d'you hear?' He winked his left eye, and held out his large right hand.

Leo shook it. 'I don't think so, Ross, but see you, anyway.'

He watched the broad back barge its way out through closely packed champagne-quaffing toffs. At least none of them could have overheard us, he thought, and none of them look like plain-clothes fuzz.

He sat and finished his bottle, trying to damp down the excitement caused by even this ridiculous prospect for solving all his problems. With five million he would spring right out of the shit in the States, and he would be able to exercise his option agreement with Raj to buy back all of the UK retail company.

It was a very tempting notion, but impossible – and anyway, how the hell did he know that Ross knew what he was doing?

There was another consideration too.

Though Leo had used coke – sometimes a lot – from time to time, he disapproved of the people who made money out of dealing it because they didn't normally restrict their activities to cocaine. In Britain, heroin presented a far bigger market and most of the coke was brought in by established heroin dealers. Leo despised the people whose trade depended on the slow and painful deaths of their customers. And he surprised himself by the vehemence of his reaction to becoming one of them – if only by association.

He made up his mind that he would push the idea right out of his head and, pleased at his decision, got up and left the bar.

'Mr Kalianji, there's a Mr Blackwell on the phone. He insists that I interrupt your meeting so that he can talk to you. Shall I put him through?'

Raj listened as his secretary's voice rang round the room from the intercom. A quick grimace of angry irritation passed over his normally immobile features. 'In future, please contact me with these interruptions over the telephone. I have guests in my office. Now, put him through.'

'Hello, Raj.' There was some tension behind the easy drawl. 'You were wrong. Our fat plum is not ripe for picking yet.'

Raj's mouth twitched on one side. It was a moment before he spoke again. 'How have you left things?'

'I told him to call me in Amsterdam if he changes his mind.'

'Stay in Amsterdam then. He will call you quite soon, I'm sure.'

Two days later, Leo received the worst blow yet administered to his ego.

At the monthly board meeting of the retailing company, Raj proposed that Leo resign as managing director. He proposed it very reasonably.

'After all, Leo, your time is very well spent going round keeping them on their toes on the sales floors. Nobody would deny your skill and experience there. But the administration, you know, the boring day-to-day stuff – I think that should be handled by a person, or people, close to the administrative centre and the products. Let's face it, you haven't shown much real interest in that side of things for some time now.'

Leo stared round the table at his fellow directors, then let his gaze rest on Raj.

'You must be bloody mad. I'm managing director of this company, and I will be until they carry me off in a brass-handled box. Anyway, you're not going to get any support for a fucking silly idea like that from the rest of the board.' He glanced round confidently. 'But, as a matter of curiosity, who were you going to propose to replace me?'

'Two people actually, as joint MDS – Sarah, and Mike Morris.'

Leo turned to the proposees. 'Did you know about this?' he asked quietly.

Sarah looked down at the pad in front of her, then up again at Leo. 'Yes,' she gulped.

Mike Morris mumbled, acutely embarrassed, 'Well, we've discussed the possibility, of course.'

'You mean "yes",' said Leo. 'I see. Well – it seems a waste of time, but we might as well go through the formality of rejecting your proposal, Raj; so would you like to let us have the precise wording, for the minutes?'

Raj nodded to the company secretary, who handed round a prepared written proposal.

'Okay – gentlemen and ladies. There it is. Who's in favour?'

All six raised their hands.

Leo was dumbfounded. He felt as if he'd been hit in the solar plexus by a battering ram. He had expected Raj's two nominees to the board, and Raj of course, to vote – but not Mike, Sarah and Min. He had assumed he would carry it, four to three.

He gaped at Sarah, shaking his head in bewilderment.

Then the company secretary broke the silence. 'Shall I minute the motion as carried then?'

Leo turned on him. 'Don't waste your bloody time. I'm still the majority shareholder round here, and I'm calling an Extraordinary General Meeting to take a vote on this.' He stabbed a forefinger at Raj. 'And don't think your minority clause can help you, because I've also got the right to veto your proposals. This is your motion, and I'm going to veto it.'

He glared around the table triumphantly.

Mike Morris cleared his throat loudly. 'I'm afraid you're wrong there, Leo. It's your motion. You are proposing to the shareholders that a majority board decision be overturned – and Raj's veto clause can block that.'

463

Leo stared at him. 'Do you mean that though I'm managing director and I own fifty-five per cent of this company, I can't make *any* bloody decisions?'

'Oh, yes – of course you can,' said Mike hurriedly, 'if enough of the board or shareholders agree with you.'

Leo stood up and smashed his fist down on the table. 'You fucking bastards! You Judases! After all I've done to create this company! I've employed you, made you a lot of money. And now you just sit there and watch this brown bastard stab me in the back. Why not bloody well hold me down so he can't miss? You'll regret this, you ungrateful little *shits*!'

He turned, kicking over his chair. The room shook as he slammed the door behind him.

Leo got through to Ross in Amsterdam.

'Hi, Leo. I'm glad you called. D'you want to meet?'

'Yeah, I'm on. Ring me when you get back to London.'

Two days later they were sitting in a busy, anonymous pub in Mayfair.

'Can you get the money – in cash?' asked Ross.

'Yeah, but it's going to take some time. Did you know sharks came in double-breasted, pin-striped suits? When's the latest you can use it?'

'Well, it's nearly too late already for the next shipment, so I'll have to fix you up in a couple of months. Is that gonna be okay?'

Leo nodded. 'Yes, in two months I can get the cash, but I've got to tell you – it's about all I can get and if this goes wrong, I'm wiped out.'

'What's changed so much from last week? You were very squeamish then.'

'Never mind,' said Leo. 'Personal reasons. I've got some scores to settle and I need a lot of bread to do it. But, I've got some provisos. First, I bring the money and hand it over myself when I've seen the goods, and then I stay with the goods until the money is handed over to us – okay?'

Ross shrugged, wide-eyed. 'What? Don't you trust me, Leo?'

'I wouldn't trust my mother with seven million quid – so don't get sensitive.'

'Listen, you can come along if you like, but if it gets hard, you've got to look after yourself.'

'That's all right.' Leo expressed a confidence that he did not feel.

But now he was committed.

The manager of the tiny, one-branch bank, the seventh Leo had visited, offered a pudgy wet hand as Leo was shown into a barely furnished office. The bland, brown face wore an ugly mechanical smile below dark, hooded eyes. For Leo, the pleasing irony of borrowing money from one Indian in order to out-manoeuvre another did not outweigh the humiliation of having to come out to a West London suburb to find someone prepared to loan him money against the security of his shares in Rags. None of the big banks had wanted to know. His shares in a private company with an unimpressive profit record were, they said, virtually unmarketable, and therefore valueless as security.

'But look at the bloody balance sheet,' Leo had pleaded. 'At worst, in a break-up situation there are net assets of seven or eight million, and I own fifty-five per cent of them.'

'Then liquidate the company and claim your share. It'd be far more valuable to you than what you've got now.'

As each bank turned him down, his desperation and determination to get the money and do the deal had increased.

And now he found himself sitting in front of this fat loan shark. He was sweating slightly and trying to smile nonchalantly as the bank manager inspected the share certificates and company accounts. Eventually the Indian looked up. 'Lending against this kind of security is very risky, and troublesome if anything goes wrong.'

'I've told you, it's only a bridging loan for a property

deal I'm doing in California – here are the details.' Leo pushed over a folder of fictional material, provided mainly by Ross. 'I'll only need the money for a few days, a week at the outside. It's really a back-to-back deal.'

The banker hardly glanced at the folder. 'If we are to do business, Mr Freeman, we shall need more security. Are you prepared to lodge the deeds of your house with us, and give us a charge on all your personal possessions?'

'For Christ's sake,' Leo said loudly. 'What else do you want? – A couple of pints of my blood and a pair of testicles?'

The Indian attempted another smile. 'Oh, no, Mr Freeman, I don't think they would realise much in the event of a default.'

'Yeah, all right, all right – as it's only for a few days.'

'Of course, the interest we charge is commensurate with the size of risk we are taking. We shall have to charge you one and a half per cent for every seven days or part thereof that the loan is outstanding.'

'What! That's seventy-five per cent – thirty grand for a week's loan. That's usury!'

'It's business, Mr Freeman. And anyway, this project of yours you say will net half a million, so there will be plenty left for you, won't there?'

'Well, I'm not paying that rate,' said Leo adamantly.

'Then I'm sorry. We can't do business,' said the Indian, without any expression of regret.

'Come on,' said Leo, but he had forgotten how to wheedle.

He left the scruffy building with an understanding that once the appropriate searches had been made, and he had signed and lodged the necessary documents, the loan would be available on the terms originally stipulated. Interest would start to accrue from the moment the money was transferred to a Californian bank.

This time, Leo didn't stay at the Bel Air. The anonymity of the Sheraton Plaza was more suitable. Ross came up to his room soon after he had arrived. The meeting was brief.

466

Leo was to rent a car and pick up the cash, as discreetly as possible, in hundred dollar bills and have them packed in two Samsonite suitcases, around two million dollars in each.

He should make his way north-west out of Los Angeles, towards Ventura. Just past Oxnard, between the highway and the railroad, he would meet Ross at a small airfield belonging to Evans Aviation.

As he pulled away from the bank, Leo wondered what the hell he was doing.

It had occurred to him, among the many other hitches and potential disasters which had happened to him, that the bank simply may not have had it all in readies and the whole operation would get out of sync before it had started, but in this west Hollywood shopping mall the bank clerk had shown no surprise at Leo's request to have the whole amount in his account handed over in cash.

And now, driving down the Santa Monica freeway in a slow, relentless stream of traffic and an everyday Chevrolet, he wondered for the hundredth time if he should turn round and pull out of this crazy scheme, but the thought of the lost pride and the freedom this could recover for him kept him going.

Eventually he saw the airfield: a small hangar with a Cessna Citation, and two Piper Commanches in orange and lime green livery standing outside. As soon as Leo had parked beside the small control tower, he saw Ross walking towards him.

'Morning, Mr Freeman,' said Ross in a loud voice. 'I'm Ross Blackwell and I'm your pilot for today. D'you have any bags?'

'Yeah – in the boot, the, er, trunk, that is.'

Ross walked round to the back of the car and lifted out the two heavy cases. He carried them towards one of the Commanches and nodded at Leo to follow. They stepped in over the wing, heaved the money in and stowed it on the back row of seats, then installed themselves in front.

Ross put on a headset and muttered into the mike, then

467

switched it off, started the engines and turned, grinning, to Leo. 'Well, here we go. When today's over, you can call yourself a man – a rich man!'

They taxied and took off northwards into the wind, then swung east-north-east over Ventura County, and the St Gabrielle mountains.

Leo didn't talk. There was nothing to say. He had made Ross run through the plans a dozen times, and now his only thought was to get the whole thing over and done. He wasn't excited at the prospect – just terrified.

Beyond the mountains, the naked red-brown earth and rock of the Mojave Desert stretched away to the eastern horizon. The overhead sun was beating down hard, glinting on the railroad tracks that ran from north to south below them, then picking up the remains of winter water which still lay in the central marshes.

Just beyond these, Ross started to take the plane down, and as the little town of Kramer came into sight, about ten miles to the north-east, he circled and landed on a small, dried mudflat.

He taxied up beside a protrusion of jagged, reddish rocks and switched the engines off.

The silence was overwhelming and eerie.

'I still don't see why the hell we have to do the swap-over in this God-forsaken place,' said Leo.

Ross waved his arm around at the emptiness, lifeless but for a single soaring buzzard. 'Look, no witnesses, no nothing – and an easy place to land.' He looked at his watch. 'We've got maybe twenty minutes to wait, and then the Colombians arrive. D'you want a beer?' He reached behind him and took two cans of Coors from a flying bag. He handed one to Leo.

Leo reluctantly pulled the ring and poured the fluid down his throat into an unreceptive stomach. 'I think I need a piss – I'm going to get out and stretch my legs.'

'Suit yourself,' shrugged Ross.

Leo clambered down and walked over to where the rocks had speared their tips up through the cracking mud. He tried to urinate, but nothing came, so he pulled his zip up and started pacing up and down, wishing that he could pass out and wake up when it was all over.

He heard the throbbing from the west before he saw the other plane, then it flew into view, circled, landed and drew up about fifty yards away.

Ross called to him from their plane: 'Here – take this money!' He swung the black suitcases out of the door. Leo went over and lifted them down, placed them beside him.

'No,' said Ross. 'Carry them over beside that rock.'

Leo did so. The Texan jumped down and joined him.

They looked over at the other plane, from which two men descended, with two red suitcases.

'Okay, I'll go and check the merchandise and one of them will come and check the money. When we're all happy, he'll take the money and I'll bring back the merchandise. You don't have to do nothin' or say nothin'.'

An Hispanic voice floated across the flat, dry ground between the two groups. 'Are you guys ready?'

Ross yelled back. 'Sure – let's get started!' He began to walk towards the South Americans; one of them started towards the rocks where Leo waited. When he reached him, he grinned and indicated that Leo should open one of the cases. He knelt down and expertly started counting notes and bundles. While he did this, Leo looked across and saw Ross bending over the suitcases by the second plane.

The Colombian repeated his counting with the contents of the other suitcase, then stood up and shouted across to his compatriot. '*Bueno!*'

Ross also turned round and shouted, 'Okay!'

Both men picked up their respective burdens and walked towards each other. They crossed and arrived at their original starting points.

Just as Ross put down the two red cases, a third man jumped down from the Colombians' plane, holding a Kalashnikov. Before the firing had even started, Leo, petrified, flung himself at the ground. He felt a searing pain as his elbow, with all his weight behind it, hit an upturned, jagged rock. He rolled over in agony behind it, out of sight of the gunman.

Bullets ricocheted all round him and then he heard Ross yell as he too fell to the ground.

'You goddamn dago bastard.'

Then the fuel tank of the Piper was hit and Leo felt a blast of heat as it exploded into a ball of fire. Bits of the plane dropped all around him. After a moment he heard a juddering sound as the other plane started up. He tentatively raised his head to look over his protecting rock.

And for the first time he noticed that the other plane was identical to their own – a Commanche in orange and lime green livery – like the second one parked at Evans Aviation.

He shook his head. A coincidence. Maybe Evans had hundreds of them, like black cabs in London. And then he heard Ross groaning a few yards away. He turned to him and saw him clutching a blood-stained thigh.

'Are you all right Ross?'

'Yeah, sure. Just keep down, they haven't gone yet.'

But Leo saw the Commanche taxi away and turn into the wind. 'It's okay – they're going. What the hell was that for? They've got the money and we've got the coke – haven't we?'

He looked around, panic-stricken, and felt a surge of relief. The two red suitcases were still standing where Ross had put them down.

The pain in Leo's arm had relented a little. He staggered to his feet. 'Christ, I think I've broken my fucking arm! What's happened to you?'

'The dumb bastard shot me, that's what.' Ross gritted his teeth as he dragged himself backwards to lean against a rock. 'But it's no big deal – straight in and out the flesh – ain't touched the bone. Here, just help me wrap somethin' around it.'

With his good arm, Leo tore the Texan's trouser leg, made a tourniquet with some of the cloth and tried to clean up the wound with the rest.

When Ross seemed comfortable, Leo lit a cigar for him

and tried to assess his own damage. He couldn't move his left arm without an unbearable, piercing pain. He pulled his shirt off, and, with Ross's help, made a sling, which at least prevented excessive movement. 'Okay – now you tell me how a couple of cripples are going to walk a hundred miles back to LA carrying two suitcases full of coke?'

'You'll have to walk into Kramer and pick up a car, and some dressings for this leg – and some new pants.'

Leo shook his head. 'My jacket, my bread, all my plastic was in there.' He nodded at the still burning remains of their Commanche.

'S'okay, I got some.' Ross painfully pulled a bunch of hundred dollar bills from his undamaged trouser pocket.

'Great. Well, at least we've got the coke. Let's have a look at it.'

'Hey, man, we got plenty of time to do that later. Let's get the hell out of here first,' Ross said quickly.

'Yeah, okay. Sorry, you must be hurting like hell.' Leo took the money from Ross. 'Okay, which way?'

'Head due east. About four miles. There's the highway up from Summit and San Bernadino. A truck'll give you a ride, but keep down if you see a highway patrol.'

Leo nodded, and in spite of the pain and the predicament, he strode off buoyantly.

Dishevelled and bare-chested, he stood beside the empty road. He was beginning to get angry – five or six vehicles had passed him going north and ignored him – and puzzled by what had happened. There didn't seem to be any point in the suppliers shooting them and destroying their plane. And Ross's reactions had been odd. Still, they were alive and they had the stuff.

Then a pick-up slowed and stopped beside him. 'You wanna go to Kramer?'

'Yeah, thanks.'

'Okay. Get in.'

The man was evidently some kind of small farmer. He didn't look as though he did too well out of it, but he was cheerful enough. His speech, which emanated through a gap in his teeth at the side of his mouth, was almost incomprehensible. In twenty minutes they reached the uninspiring little town, and Leo got out with relief.

He found a petrol station that would rent him an old pick-up, but he would have to bring it back. He asked them what they would sell it for, and gave them the first price that they asked without arguing.

He bought some jeans for Ross, a shirt for himself, some bandages and iodine. He drove back down the road, found the point where he had joined it, and bumped off through the boulders and scrub until he reached the far side of the rocks where he had left Ross.

The big Texan seemed half-pleased to see him.

'You gotta do somethin' about this leg. It's beginning to hurt like shit.'

He hissed as Leo dabbed on iodine and tried to clear away the mess around the entry and exit holes. After that, Leo bandaged tightly right around Ross's thigh. 'Okay. Now try to stand.'

Ross pulled himself up, stood for a minute, then managed a few limping paces. 'Okay – give me them pants.'

They pulled the jeans onto him and managed to get them up and closed in spite of the layers of bandages. Ross looked around warily. 'We've got to get the hell out of here before someone spots this wreck from the air and calls out the cops.'

'Right. Can you carry one of the cases? At least you've got two good arms.'

'Sure.'

Leo picked up one and staggered up and over the rocks to the car. Ross was taking a lot longer. Once Leo had his case in the back of the pick-up, he couldn't resist opening it to have a look at his new stock.

He unclipped it and lifted the lid.

There were rows of hundreds of neat little polythene packets, each one containing half a pound of fine, white powder. On the top, in the middle, one of the packets had been opened – presumably when Ross was checking it. Leo picked it out, licked his finger, and dipped it in. He took a tentative tongue to the powder.

472

He was no connoisseur, but it seemed like A1 coke to him. Nothing like dealing in good quality merchandise. He picked out another of the packets at random and opened that. Once again he dipped his finger and licked.

He froze.

It was fine, powdery, sweet-tasting. It was icing-sugar.

With frantic, fumbling hands, he tore open another packet, and another, and another – all sugar.

For a few moments he stood staring at the suitcase full of worthless powder.

They had been tucked up! Conned, robbed – of two million quid!

Ross had just come over the top of the rocks and was struggling painfully down. When he saw Leo's face and the open suitcase, he stopped.

Leo advanced on him, screaming. 'You brainless, fucking cowboy jerk! You've just lost me *two million quid*! You dumb fucking arsehole! What have you bloody done to me? You said you knew the business – you knew the guys! You didn't know fucking nothing! We've been conned like a couple of school-kids.'

Ross was scrambling down now. He threw his case to the ground near Leo, who pounced on it and tore it open.

Once again, one packet was open and contained high quality cocaine. The rest were sugar.

'Christ – they really saw you coming, didn't they? You had to open the only two good bags in the whole bloody delivery.'

Ross was beside him now. 'What the fuck are you talking about? I picked any old bag from each case and they were grade A stuff. You just don't know what this stuff should taste like. I mean, some might be a little less pure, but it still gets the same money . . .'

'Don't be a dumb cunt. I can tell the difference between coke and fucking icing-sugar.' He grabbed a bag and poured some of the contents into the palm of his hand. 'Here. Snort some of that and see what it does for you.'

'Hey – no – I never touch it.'

'So it bloody seems!' Leo tossed the handful of powder

into the air, where it disappeared with the warm breeze.

He gazed desolately around him – at the silent desert and the lengthening shadows, then at the two suitcases for which he had paid a million pounds each.

'I'm stuffed,' he said quietly, 'totally and utterly stuffed. I've got a pound of coke that won't even pay a week's interest on the loan I got, about fifty bucks' worth of sugar and two battered suitcases.' He turned on Ross and shrieked, 'And it's all your fucking fault!'

'Look Leo . . . Don't get so mad . . . They won't get away with it . . . I'll get your bread back, or I'll kill the bastards.'

'You,' Leo laughed bitterly. 'You're all mouth. You can't do fuck-all except talk. I always thought you were full of bullshit. Your ranch and your planes and your cowboy army – it's all *bullshit!*'

'Look,' growled Ross, 'my leg's gonna turn bad if we don't get out of here and find someone to mend it. Put the cases in the back and we'll go through the whole lot when we find somewhere less exposed. And don't worry. If it's all wrong, I'll get your money, or more stock, so help me.'

He clambered into the pick-up and Leo squeezed behind the wheel. He started the clapped-out motor and drove furiously across the desert to the highway, wishing that the Colombians had shot him, and shot him good.

They headed south towards San Bernadino, Leo's arm throbbing with continuous pain now. He and Ross didn't speak until they saw a motel just south of Summit, where they agreed to pull in. They booked into a cabin and lugged in the cases.

Ross nodded painfully at them. 'You check through all the merchandise. I'll go find a medico greedy enough to keep his mouth shut.'

He hobbled out and Leo picked up the phone to order a bottle of whisky to drown the pain. He put the cases in a cupboard, and when the bottle arrived, propped himself up on his bed and poured half a tumbler full.

474

He must have moved in his sleep.

The sharp, stabbing pain woke him, and there was a feeble light outside, competing with the single naked bulb in the room.

He looked at his watch. It was six – must be morning.

He looked at the other bed. It was empty. His head throbbed almost as much as his arm. The near-empty whisky bottle told him why. He groaned and tried to sleep again.

When at last he rolled painfully out of bed and lurched to the window, he saw that the pick-up had gone. Where the hell was Ross? The bloody fool was probably locked in a cell already.

He was going to have to get out before someone came looking for *him*.

Slowly he went through every bag of powder, pouring the contents of each one down the lavatory. He was left with the two original bags of coke. That was it – one pound – twenty, thirty thousand pounds if he was lucky.

He tried to flush away the little polythene bags, but they choked in the U-bend, and he had to prod them round with a wire coat-hanger.

He left the empty red cases in the cupboard, stuffed the two bags of cocaine into his trousers pockets and went to pay his bill with Ross's bundle of hundreds. A few enquiries found him a taxi that would take him back to LA, and, with relief, he collapsed in the back seat, wishing he would never have to face reality again.

'Why, hello, Leo! It's good to hear from you,' Robinson sounded doubtful. Leo smiled to himself and wished that he could see the other's face. Their last meeting had not been friendly. It was entirely due to Robinson's oversight and inefficiency that they had been uninsured when the studio had burnt down. At the time, Leo had mounted one of his more spectacular displays of wrath – and had meant it. Now, it didn't matter a damn. He was wiped out anyway, and Robinson was the only person he could think of who might know where to get rid of the cocaine at a tolerable price.

'Robinson, I've got a small favour I want to ask you. I've got a problem and you might be able to help.'

'Sure, Leo, sure. Tell me. I'll see what I can do.'

'Can you come round to the Chateau Marmont? I'll tell you here.'

'Right on – I'll see you in a half hour.'

Robinson was struck by Leo's relaxed amiability. 'What's happened to you, man? You're cool! And your arm's busted. Maybe sufferin's good for you.'

'Yeah, well, maybe it is. I've suffered, that's for sure. But don't concern yourself with that.' He produced the two packets of cocaine from his trousers pockets. 'You'd be going a long way to making up for past events if you could dispose of this for me, at the right price.'

Robinson opened one packet and tasted the contents. 'No problem, man – it's not something I can do myself, but I'll bring you a friend who can, and he's straight. Well, he's gay and he's a crook, but otherwise he's straight. If I ask him, he'll give you the right money.'

'Great. Get onto it. I'm not used to this kind of excitement – I want to get rid of the stuff.'

Robinson left, assuring Leo that he would be back with his buyer before the end of the day.

Then Leo got on the phone to each of the three managers of his American stores.

'We're closing down in four weeks. Put the whole store on sale and keep the prices dropping until there's no stock left. And don't accept any more deliveries coming in from England. Then start selling the fittings.'

He apologised and offered each of them a substantial bonus in lieu of notice.

He rang real estate people in the three locations and instructed them to dispose of the properties. With luck, when this was done, he would be clear of his American borrowings.

He took a cab down to the store in Rodeo where the manager greeted him gloomily. Leo went into the office with him, his good arm around his shoulder.

'Look, I'm sorry, but I'm giving up. I admit defeat, to

476

the fakers, the banks and the great American competition. Do me a favour though: don't tuck me up now. I'm trusting you. I've got to get the banks paid off and I'll make sure you get some of what's left – okay?'

The manager nodded. He had been ready for a fight but, strangely, this Leo was harder to resist that the old one.

Leo went back into the store and sorted himself out a few shirts, trousers and jackets, then told the manager, 'Okay, do your best. I'll see you in four weeks.'

He went round to the local American Express office and arranged to replace his lost card. Then he went to the car rental people where he had hired the Chevrolet two days before, told them where it was and rented another.

He drove down to Venice, sat by the beach and watched the endless parade as he lunched. He felt a great weight lifting off his shoulders.

Robinson arrived with his dealer friend, who had brought the money – the right money – with him. It was a leisurely transaction and they even had a drink in the bar afterwards: Leo with his wad of five-hundred-dollar bills in his pocket, the dealer with the coke in his.

When they had left, Leo had an appointment with an osteopath whom the house doctor had recommended. His elbow had been slightly chipped, not broken, and had been severely dislocated. It was back in place now, but still very sore.

After half an hour of gentle manipulation it was improving and Leo went back to his hotel room relaxed, clear-headed and ready for a long sleep.

He checked out of the hotel and set off early next day in the anonymous Chevrolet. He was going to do something that, at the back of his mind, he had always wanted to do – drive unhurriedly through the southern Rockies and Albuquerque to Texas.

He wanted to think, to observe, to take stock. Rumbling along Route 66, tuned to a country-and-western station, uncommitted to a schedule, he was happy to be there in an unpredatory role. Nothing was expected of him and he expected nothing. As he drove he thought of Alison, of his father, of the early days in the Hampstead flat, of Sammy and Sarah coming round from college, of the promise of success twenty years before. He had found the crock of gold at the end of his rainbow – and he had stubbed his toe on it.

The foothills of the New Mexico Rockies were a revelation to him, the peaceful rolling pasture and forest giving way to mind-stretching tracts of rugged scrubland and desert.

At Albuquerque he took a detour up to Santa Fé, where the really big mountains began.

At a tumbledown diner, fifty miles out of town, where he had stopped for a late breakfast, he asked casually about a beautiful ranch set in the shallow valley four or five miles back.

'That belongs to a big singer – sorta country-pop – called Wolf Amadeus.'

Leo's mind was tugged back with a jerk to the time when he was certain that Alison had had an affair with Wolf. Nobody had ever confirmed it, but over a long period of time, coincidental circumstances, odd remarks and attitudes, had left him fairly sure that Alison had at least spent some time with him when she had walked out for that month five or six years before.

But he felt no resentment towards the singer or towards the memory of Alison. Maybe the guy had loved her for the same reasons that he had. It would be good to talk to someone who had shared that experience.

He got up from the rickety little table and into his car, then headed back the way he had just come.

He found the entrance to the estate, low-key but very well kept, and drove down the long lane to the spreading Spanish-American house. There were a number of cars and farm vehicles parked around and noises of activity from the adjacent stable.

Anticipating with pleasure a meeting with this man, he

478

walked up and rang a clanging bell by the front door. A little Mexican maid opened it.

'Is Mr Amadeus at home?'

'Sorry, Sir. Mr Wolf no come back for two weeks.'

Leo felt very let down. He suddenly, desperately, wanted to talk to someone about Alison, someone who had known her well. And he was convinced that Wolf had.

'Could I come in and write a message for him?'

'Oh, sure, Sir.' She opened the door wide to let him through.

From his hotel in Dallas Leo rang the number of Ross Blackwell's ranch in Denton. When he asked for Ross he was told icily, 'Mr Blackwell sold up and moved out of this place eight years ago – and if you see him, you can tell him we're still getting plenty of nasty looking mail for him.'

Leo was not now all that surprised. He rang the Dallas Country Club where, as he had expected, he got a similar reception.

He flew to New York and spent a single night there, among the relaxed and tatty charm of the Chelsea Hotel.

Michael Rappacioli was devastated but sympathetic. Leo had a suggestion for him. 'With the sales record of this place, you should be able to raise the finance to buy it yourself. I can make it easy for you on supplies of merchandise and the use of the name. It would be a hell of a shame to waste all the effort you've put into it. If you can pull it off, best of luck to you. But take my advice – don't start thinking too big. That way you'll stay happy.'

Leo had been away thirteen days when he walked back into the Indian bank in Southall.

The manager showed no particular pleasure at seeing him. Leo started the conversation. 'I haven't got the money. Not the principal, nor the interest. You'll have to realise the securities I gave you and give me the change.'

'Oh my goodness,' said the Indian, but he didn't appear to be put out.

Leo, as chairman, called a meeting of the shareholders of Rags to announce his resignation and his wish to sell his shareholding. Raj and Sarah had first rights, pro rata their holdings, to buy his. Neither of them had seen Leo since his return to England and Sarah was completely bewildered by his announcement, and the relaxed way in which he delivered it.

Raj, too, was puzzled and annoyed. He disguised this well, however.

'I'm very sorry to hear this, Leo,' he said. 'What on earth has made you decide to do it?'

Leo turned to him. 'Raj, I know and you know that you're not the slightest bit sorry, and the reasons for my decision are my business – all right? Now, first of all, I want to point out to Sarah, in case she is unaware, that she'll only have the protection of the minority share-holders' clause if she ups her holding to twenty-five per cent.' He turned to her. 'I suggest you organise that.'

Sarah, still astonished, nodded vaguely.

Leo went on, to Raj. 'You've been paid for all stock that's been shipped and received by the stores in the States, but you'll find the last few consignments have not been accepted, and the open revolving letter of credit has not been triggered. I suggest you leave the stock there in bond. Michael Rappacioli is buying the New York store and is making provision for necessary credit. I'm aware I can't put any pressure on you to go on supplying him, but as he'll be a substantial customer, I don't think it likely you'll refuse to sell to him.'

'So you've sold out in America as well, Leo? This is amazing news.'

'Is it?' asked Leo cynically. 'Well, just remember, I still own the name there, so if you've got any ideas about moving in – forget 'em.'

Sarah waited in Simon Riley's office in the House of Commons. She had arranged to meet him there before going on to Raj's office in the City. Simon was the only person she could think of whom she trusted enough and who was knowledgeable enough to help her. He came striding into the room with his customary energy and *bonhomie*.

'Sorry you should have been kept waiting by affairs of state,' he said. 'Well, a rather minor in-house power struggle, really.'

Sarah laughed. 'You – struggling for power?'

'Heavens, no. It never does to be seen to struggle, on the basis that if it costs you an effort to get there, you don't deserve to be there. Anyway, I've been through all this stuff of yours and, broadly speaking, Leo's right about your need to acquire an extra five per cent. Trouble is, the retail company is so much at the mercy of Raj's manufacturing company that, in the end, it won't make a great deal of practical difference. On balance though, I would say it was worth your while to pay a hundred and fifty thousand pounds to secure those minority rights.'

'So you're saying I should do it?' Sarah asked.

'Yes, I am.' He sat down behind his desk and was silent for a moment. 'Look,' he said. 'I don't know how else to put this, so you'll have to excuse my bluntness. Is there still anything, as it were, active between you and Raj?'

Sarah laughed. 'God no! There hasn't been for years – though he has made the odd suggestion from time to time and I know you well enough to tell you that sometimes it was bloody hard to turn him down. But there is, as they say, another man in my life now – has been for a while.'

Simon looked relieved. 'Oh, good. Who is he?'

'James Gladstone, on the foreign desk at *The Sunday Times*. Very tall, very clever and very thoughtful, and he's away a lot – which keeps me interested.'

'I know what you mean. Thing is, I don't know how much Raj has got to do with the whole of Leo's débâcle, but I'm pretty certain he's involved.'

'He seemed almost as surprised as me when Leo announced he was selling.'

'Was he surprised at the announcement, or the calmness of Leo's capitulation?'

'Oh – I don't know. You know Raj. He doesn't give

much away. But I don't see how he could have known in advance what Leo was going to do. It came right out of the blue after he came back from one of his American trips.'

'I know,' said Simon, 'and I know he's selling up there, too. It's absolutely the opposite of what I would have expected him to do, which is why I feel there must have been some coercion. Still, you say he seems happier, or at least calmer. That must be good. But watch out for Raj, now you're on your own with him.'

Sarah smiled cynically. 'Raj will be as good as gold – as long as I'm producing winning collections. I'm not saying he'd actually kiss my arse if I said I was quitting, but I think he'd start licking his lips and bending over.'

Simon winced and grinned. 'You've got a nasty turn of phrase. Still I daresay you can look after yourself.'

Simon used Vishnu Kalianji's death as an excuse to write to Raj.

Having offered his condolences, he gave three optional dates for a meeting over lunch. Raj got in touch to confirm the earliest of them.

When he arrived, Simon sympathised with the loss and asked after the rest of the Kalianji family.

'My mother is very lonely now,' Raj said. 'Reena has asked her to come and live with us in Hampstead. I'm afraid she won't enjoy it much. As you know, we run a pretty much western household. But these women are hard to fight once they're united.'

The preliminaries over, they discussed generalities and one or two of Raj's specific projects over lunch. When they were drinking coffee and armagnac, Simon spoke without any obvious significance, 'You do realise that if there was any kind of scandal or suggestion of commercial misconduct in any of your companies, your banking licence could be rescinded?'

Raj was quite still for a second, then smiled easily. 'Of course I know that – and of course it's purely academic. All my businesses have, at one time or another, been subjected to the most thorough of scrutinies by various government agencies. It is very reassuring for me to know that, right down the line, no irregularities have ever been found, especially these days when so much delegation is necessary.'

'Yes,' said Simon. 'Yes, of course. It's just that, because of your involvement in banking, the slightest whiff of suspicion would affect the whole group. I wanted you, for your own sake, to be thoroughly aware of that.'

'My dear Simon, if there's anything you think I ought to know . . .'

'No. Nothing at all. Just a general, non-specific, observation.'

In the Chateau Marmont in LA, Leo was luxuriating in an unhurried bath and the first taste of real freedom he had ever enjoyed.

He had always imagined before that his success had brought him freedom, but now he knew he had been a bondsman to his banks, his staff, his suppliers, his creditors, his landlords, and, indeed, his own image of himself.

Now he owed nothing – no money, no allegiance, no responsibility – to anyone.

He didn't own much, either.

The sale of his shares in Rags, the unmortgaged balance of the sale proceeds of his house and a hurried sale of all his personal possessions had left him with no debts in the UK and about seventy thousand pounds, which, along with the money for the packets of powder, was sitting in a deposit account in the Wells Fargo Bank.

And tomorrow he would know what the final balance was from the disposal of his three American shops. They looked like providing a small surplus, most of which he would use for paying off his longest-serving staff.

And then . . .

And then he could go wherever the hell he wanted; not first class, not a VIP, but his own man.

He had heard nothing more of Ross. He hadn't even tried very hard to find him. He didn't care – was almost grateful, indeed, to the oafish Texan for getting him off the hook.

Leo wanted to get to know himself; to try to find out how he had managed to get so hung up on such a naïve perception of his own importance.

He supposed that, right from his earliest days of hustling – maybe before that – he had been trying to prove himself to other people, trying to deflect the jibes that he knew, and sometimes imagined, they directed at him.

He turned off the hot water tap with his foot, poured the remains of a can of beer into a glass and lay back in the frothy warm water.

The phone rang while he was drying himself. Without any of the forebodings that had previously accompanied the answering of telephones, he picked it up.

'Hi, Leo.' A deep, quiet Californian voice. 'It's Wolf Amadeus.'

'Well, what a surprise! You got my message?'

'Yeah, I did. But it's been a hassle trying to find you – Robinson told me to try you at the Marmont.'

'Well, I'm glad you did find me. Can we meet?'

'Yeah, sure. Do you wanna come out to Laurel Canyon this evening?'

'Not a party, I hope? I couldn't stand a party.'

'Nope. Just you and me and some booze.'

'Great.'

'I'll send a car.'

'Don't bother, I've got a rented rust bucket.'

'Okay – fine. I'll see you 'bout eight.'

They lounged in deck chairs, a bottle of wine between them, on a terrace looking down the canyon to where the sun had been.

'Ross Blackwell,' drawled Wolf, 'is a big-time nobody. He's all front, and everyone else's sidekick. He puts it about that he's into everything, but he knows nothing about the dope business. A bit of real estate maybe. A few wet-backs, probably – a bit of running around for the big guys – but that's all. When he makes a bit of bread, he

spends it five times, then moves on when it gets too hot.'
Wolf stopped talking and looked at Leo thoughtfully, then
decided to go on. 'He had a reputation for being a real
Jew-hater but it seems like he did you a favour.'

Leo nodded at the irony, and they sat silently for a while
listening to the night sounds.

'I know,' Leo said eventually, 'you had some kind of
scene with Alison but – and this is strange – I don't mind.
I suppose I'd have minded like hell if I'd known at the
time, but I think I've changed; and she's dead. But I'm
pretty sure you must have seen the same things in her that
I did.'

'I did,' agreed Wolf. 'She was the most exceptional lady.
She had her short scene with me, that's true.' He smiled
honestly. 'But it was never consummated. Before it
peaked, before it got complicated, she wanted to be back
with you. She knew she had to be. I was real unhappy
about it – but I understood, and I envied you.'

'Like Joni Mitchell says: "You don't know what you've
got till it's gone"; I didn't really. But somehow, Ali's still
around. I've learned more from her since she's died than
I did when she was alive.'

They lapsed into a comfortable silence again, until Wolf
spoke.

'Look, man, if you'd like it, there's a guest house up at
my ranch. If you wanna stay there for a while – as long as
you like – and, relax, get your head together, you're very
welcome.'

Leo turned to him and smiled, slowly nodding his head.
'That,' he said, 'would be perfect.'

# 1983

After the General Election in the spring of 1983, Simon Riley was given a junior ministerial job in the new Parliament. He had been clearly identified as a rising star, and was regularly lobbied by leading City figures and industrialists who recognised his potential.

At one of the many functions he had attended in this capacity, he had met Sir John 'Beefy' Balfour. Sir John was a very short, wiry Scot who looked like Willie Carson with white hair and a good tailor. He possessed a legendary energy and astuteness. He was Chairman of Bridelta, one of Britain's largest multinational companies, and had built it up over thirty years from a small moribund East African mining company into an organisation which encompassed mineral extraction and trading, oil exploration, physical trading in soft commodities, property, retailing and newspaper publishing.

Beefy Balfour had been impressed by Simon's lack of obsequiousness and obvious grasp of international business and he had taken to asking him, and often his wife, to regular informal dinners. It was on one of these occasions that Sir John, very casually, raised the subject of Raj. 'You know Kalianji of Calco, don't you, Simon?'

'Yes, quite well. Or at least as far as he lets anyone know him.'

'Yes, they're an inscrutable lot, these Indians. Just when you think you've got 'em, they'll pull another rabbit out of the hat and bugger you.'

'Raj is more inscrutable than most. He's very single-minded and, as far as I know, he makes very few mistakes.'

'And what's his Achilles heel?'

Simon pondered a moment. 'I think, probably, vanity. But he's got it well under control. And of course, he's very greedy, but then that's a common failing of all successful entrepreneurs.' He laughed.

Sir John laughed with him. 'You know, that's not necessarily true. After a time, for a lot of us, additional personal gain becomes irrelevant; running the business becomes a competitive game, and making money is how you keep the score. But I take your point. What about women?'

'Who – Raj? I think he has the odd adventure. I dare say he's as interested in all that as anyone else, but he wouldn't have an affair that would jeopardise his family or his business. There was almost a fracas years ago over Sarah Freeman, Leo's sister – she's managing director of Calco's Rags subsidiary now – so I guess that's under control. And I think he's occasionally seen around with rich, randy women of independent inclinations, but there's not much risk with them. No, on the whole, I'd say he keeps his nose pretty clean. Why the interest?'

'Oh, just keeping up to date, you know,' Sir John said vaguely.

Betty and Connie were as long-legged, firm-fleshed and long-blonde-haired as any glossy cover girl; both very pretty and very healthy.

But they weren't models, they were grooms. And they were sitting on the low wall that made the fourth side of a U-shaped block of white, rough-rendered stables on Wolf Amadeus' estate.

They wore tight, stretchy jeans and scuffed workaday cowgirl boots. They were having a short break, smoking and gossiping before doing evening stables.

'No, he's not a fag,' said Connie. 'You can tell that from the way he sometimes looks at you through them sexy dark eyes, and he ain't shy. But in a year, I ain't seen him with no girls.' She giggled. 'The other mornin', he was up on Blondy and I asked him if he wanted me to shorten his leathers, and when I did, I sort of ran my hand up the inside of his thigh, and he looks down and says, "Hey, take it easy girl, or my jeans'll burst."'

'I wish the hell he'd show that much interest in me,' complained Betty. 'Sure would make a change from the ignorant, dumb cowboys round here.'

'Hey, maybe we should sort of seduce him. We could go on up to the little house and get him drunk one night.'

'Nope. He'll come across when he's ready. You'll see.'

Betty turned to look in the direction of the sound of an all-terrain vehicle bouncing up the valley from the river. 'This is him coming now. Must have been fishing with that injun.'

A very dusty, dented Chevy Blazer rumbled into view and drew up in front of the main house.

Leo jumped down. So did a fit-looking young Navajo from the reservation called Johnny Big Claw. They pulled rods and tackle from the back of the truck and went into the house.

Johnny had been teaching Leo how to catch fish with no more than a long knife and much patience. In return Leo had tried to demonstrate the satisfaction to be derived from making and casting a feather fly.

When Wolf was away, Leo had the run of the house, and they clomped through into the huge kitchen, sat down, put their feet on the table and opened a couple of beer cans.

Leo got on well with the Indians in the reservation. He had spent a lot of time up there helping them with the merchandising and marketing of their craft products. He had had them send off samples or photographs of their silver and turquoise jewellery to stores all over the world instead of relying on the casual wheeler-dealers with whom they usually did business. And he suggested that they should concentrate on those products and styles that were obviously more popular than others.

But he didn't get involved in the money. He didn't want to and didn't need to. He was quite happy to give them the benefit of his experience, and they were happy to take it.

They were, on the whole, easy going and unambitious. Generations of reservation living had bred the spirit out of them and Leo felt concern for them. Lost in a time-warp, they had become a purposeless people, with no future, no direction: just waiting for extinction.

Some of them, of course, got out of it; the ones who had been reached by education.

But Johnny Big Claw was an exception. He was educated, even sophisticated, but he didn't want to get out. He wanted to get some purpose back into the life of his people – and that was a daunting, unrewarding mission.

In Leo he recognised a sympathy for his aspirations, and a thorough understanding of the ways of the modern world. They had become good friends and spent a lot of time together. Leo was in no doubt that he had gained more from the relationship than had the Indian, but he did his best to tell Johnny the things he wanted to know as dispassionately and objectively as he could.

The year or so during which he had lived on the ranch had been a revelation to Leo. He had read, thought, listened, talked in ways and on matters he hadn't even considered before. He had lost none of his energy, instinct or powers of observation, but he channelled them into his quest for self-knowledge and peace of mind. He would never have believed, a few years before, that he was capable of sitting by a stream for hours on end, silently, patiently, waiting for a single fish.

He had taken to riding into the mountains or along the valleys most days, and had grown to love it. It had brought him closer to the memory of Alison.

He had noticed the girls, of course, and felt a twitch in his groin at the sight of the slender healthy limbs, bouncing breasts, and candid, inviting blue eyes. He would have liked to see those bodies naked, felt them alongside his, either of them, both of them . . . oh, yes, he would have enjoyed making love to them. But that wasn't enough of a reason any more. He knew the offer was there, and that pleased him, but he didn't accept.

Maybe sometime, with a woman who could give as much

with her mind as with her body, but not just for the sake of a grapple and an orgasm.

He chatted with Johnny for a while. Then, when the Indian had left, he walked thoughtfully up the hill to his cabin.

Leo was happy here and could have gone on enjoying this existence for a long time yet, but at the back of his mind he knew he would eventually have to take himself, altered, overhauled and renewed as he was, back into the real world. He told himself, however, that when the time was ripe, it would be obvious. He had just started to kick off his boots when the telephone tinkled. It was the maid down at the main house. 'Mr Leo, there's a lady here, an Indian lady, come here to see you – will you come down?'

'Yeah, sure.' Leo was surprised. It was odd for one of them to come down from the reservation to find him. It must be something serious – something wrong.

He pulled his boots on again hurriedly and ran back down the hill. When he reached the front hall, which was almost in darkness, he didn't see anyone at first. Then he heard a soft voice.

'Leo – is that you?'

He turned sharply, puzzled by the English accent. He discerned a slim, fashionably and expensively clad body. His gaze slid up to be met by grinning, wide eyes set in a high-boned, stunning brown face. His mind travelled back through eight years to a scene sufficiently distasteful to make him wince at the memory of the part he had played.

'Gita?' he asked tentatively. 'Are you Gita?'

She nodded and the smile widened. 'Well done Leo!'

'What on earth are you doing out here?'

'I've come to see you – Reena asked me to.'

Beefy Balfour asked Simon Riley if he could get away for an early evening drink and a chat. Simon looked at the schedule of likely divisions and said he could.

'Good. Would you mind coming to my office? I'm rather stuck here at the moment.'

'No, that's fine.'

A couple of hours later he and Balfour were sitting in armchairs in the chairman of Bridelta's City office.

'I want to talk about Calco,' Sir John started. 'Do you know how much is held by Kalianji?'

'I could make a well-informed guess, the same as you. There are those shares that are openly in his name, about thirty-eight per cent, and I would think nearly all the nominee and off-shore shareholdings are his in one way or another, say, another fifteen per cent. If you're asking does he have outright control, I would say undoubtedly yes.'

'Hmmm – you're probably right; this is what we've assumed. That gives us two problems. First, finding enough shares to buy. Second, getting the price down. We're holding twelve per cent at the moment, and have declared this, though, of course, as you might have read, we categorically denied any bid intentions. Needless to say this hasn't stopped the price rocketing.'

'And needless to say, your denial does not precisely reflect the facts,' added Simon.

'You mean it's a lie? Well, not quite; we certainly aren't buying any more at the current price. There's already been a thirty per cent uplift since we started buying, and the shares were really a little over-valued then. But we are very interested in Calco. Kalianji's put together a portfolio of activities that would fit very neatly into us. There's no dead wood, and there's a very good spread.'

'Yes, I can see how it might suit you – but why did you want to see me?'

'I have a hunch that somewhere there is a cupboard, and in that cupboard there is a skeleton with its bony finger pointing straight at Mr Kalianji. I've no proof, I've no theories, but I can't believe his growth, particularly his early growth, could have been achieved without some skulduggery. You know Kalianji, and from what I can gather you are not all that enamoured of him. Well, we would be grateful, very grateful, if you were able, very subtly, to indicate to him your awareness of the skeleton, and your inclination to do something about it if he doesn't yield up control.'

'Nobody could accuse you of being mealy-mouthed, could they, John? Effectively, you want me to blackmail him on your behalf. Me – a minister – albeit a junior one – of the Crown.'

'Let me put it another way,' said Sir John. 'Calco owns a bank – not a big bank it's true, but it has a high profile. It would suit neither the government, nor the nation, if this bank were seen to be in the control of a man of questionable business practices. I would say that it was your duty to do all you can to bring the group that owns it, and therefore runs it, under the control of one of the country's largest and most unimpeachable conglomerates before there's a scandal and a subsequent loss of faith in all the other small banks.'

Simon smiled. 'Duty to one's nation, and profit to one's friends. Worthy and practical – very Scottish. It's a pity my over-developed social conscience won't allow me to make a penny out of it. However, I am, I'm happy to say, in a position to help you.'

Beefy Balfour smiled. 'I thought you might be. You're not fond of Kalianji, are you?'

'No, I'm not,' Simon agreed. 'I have, as I may have told you, reasons for believing that Raj was behind Leo's downfall.' He paced round the large office. 'I'm not certain why. But I can tell you that when Raj arrived in England he appeared to be determined, but honourable. He had been to England before that, you know. He did a year at LSE in '68. I don't know what his outlook was then, but when I first met him, straight off the plane from Entebbe, he seemed a wholesome, ethical capitalist. He had a little money, and wanted to rebuild his family's fortunes through hard work, good planning and intelligent foresight.

'He came into contact with Leo quite early on, and I know there was instant antagonism between them. This coincided with the period when Raj was really getting his business off the ground. He was absolutely committed to succeeding, and I had the impression that ethics had become less important to him by then. Later, the affair he had with Sarah Freeman went wrong – though God knows, there could have been uglier scenes. At the time I rather admired Raj for his sang-froid, because, in an oriental sort of way, he did love her. That's the curious thing about him. You'd have thought that he was quite incapable of loving – but I can tell you, he really dotes on his son Paul. He spends a lot of time with him, and he's infinitely patient in teaching the boy about anything which he shows an interest in.' Simon stopped and glanced at Sir John. 'I'm sorry, I'm rather getting off the point.'

'Oh, no,' the Scot shook his head. 'This is all relevant.'

'I suppose what I'm trying to say is that Raj started his career with some kind of principles, but his encounters with racism in general, and Leo's aggression in particular, made him obsessed with proving that he could beat all comers. Also, in commercial fairness to him, once he'd got a stake in Rags, he recognised that Leo was becoming something of a liability, though that was only an incidental motive for squeezing him out. He had detested him for a long time.' Simon paused. 'Since our last chat about him, I've been doing some research and I've also developed one or two pretty alarming theories. They are only theories now, so I won't expand on them. But if I'm right, and I can give him the impression that I can prove it, then I think Mr Kalianji will cease to pose an obstruction to your acquisitive purposes.'

As it happened, Raj was in touch before Simon had made his opening move.

Pleased with the advantage that this gave him, Simon willingly and promptly presented himself at Calco's brand new head office on the South Bank, with its views across the river to St Paul's and the City, where rents were three times higher. He was asked to go straight into Raj's bland, impersonal office.

The Chairman of Calco greeted Simon with slightly overstated politeness and, more unusually, a suspicion of anxiety. 'Simon, I hope you'll forgive me for asking you to come over here at such short notice, but I may have a battle on my hands and I need all the help and information I can get. Please sit down. Drink?'

Simon accepted a whisky and Raj poured one for himself.

'You must know that Bridelta have been making a play for us?'

Simon nodded and Raj went on: 'Of course, they've issued a denial of bid intentions, but it's clear to the most unsubtle observers that they're after us – and with very good reason. Calco would fit very comfortably into their existing operations. Everyone knows that, and everyone knows how aggressively acquisitive Sir John Balfour can be.'

'Yes, he usually gets what he wants, but in this case he's got a problem. You must control more than fifty per cent of the stock.'

Raj didn't answer for a moment, then spoke guardedly. 'Effectively, yes, in that I have some influence with some of the foreign shareholders. But frankly, I am reluctant to have that influence exposed, and in an all-out battle, there is a strong risk that it would be.'

Simon took his cue. 'There's also a risk that other aspects of your business could be exposed.'

'What on earth do you mean?' asked Raj sharply.

'Well, let's start with aspects which are legal and, taken independently, fairly innocuous, but which, cumulatively, are fairly damning and at least indicative of a personal ruthlessness which would find few admirers among the British public or the Establishment.'

'Simon, I didn't ask you here to insult me. We are, after all, old friends. Would you kindly explain what you are referring to, so that I can clear up any misapprehension under which you find yourself?'

'I'm talking about the systematic undermining and ultimate destruction of Leo Freeman's position in the company which he created and built up over twenty years.'

'My dear fellow, what on earth are you talking about? Nobody was more sad than I when he sold out last year.

494

I've no idea why he did. I think he must have got involved in some kind of foolhardy speculation, and had no choice – but that was hardly my doing.'

'Look, Raj, if anyone were to sit down and chart your business relationship and dealings with Leo since they started in 1973, it would rapidly become very clear that you conducted a campaign to reduce his control, to humiliate him and ultimately to extract a forced sale of his shares at less than half their value. As I say, none of these things is illegal. But if, carefully documented, they were published as a business story or perhaps a human interest story in one of the Sundays, you would not be being libelled, and the public could draw the obvious conclusions.'

'Really I don't think any serious businessmen are going to be impressed with that kind of gutter journalism – and how dare you threaten me? I'm sorry, I'm going to have to ask you to leave. It's clear that for years I have misjudged you.'

'It's clear that for years you've used me whenever it suited you,' replied Simon, relaxed, and took another sip from his glass.

'Would you kindly get out!'

Simon had never seen Raj lose his temper. He was enjoying it. He stood and walked over to the window to look across at the bowler hat of St Paul's among the encroaching office blocks.

'There are, of course, other aspects of your business which rely less on circumstantial analysis for their significance. They could, of course, be coincidental, but no doubt a deeper scrutiny would establish that.' Simon paused and, without seeing Raj, could feel the tension in the room increase.

'I hope you will be very careful of what you say,' the Indian almost whispered.

Simon turned back to face him. 'Shipments of clothing from a factory in Hong Kong arriving in San Francisco. Coincidentally, a flood of cheap, counterfeit copies of Rags's clothing. Coincidentally, you never bought into the Rags operation in the US.'

'This is evidence of nothing! This is not proof – it is a flight of fancy.'

Simon raised both eyebrows and indulged in a small smile. 'You are seen with an American, a Texan of doubtful reputation, called Ross Blackwell. Mr Blackwell has been known to ring you at your office. He is also known to have a fervent dislike of Leo Freeman. Would your relationship with this acknowledged, if unconvicted, conman bear scrutiny?' Raj showed signs of being about to interrupt, but Simon increased the pitch and speed of his voice. 'A credit arrives in a private account at a bank in Geneva from Los Angeles. It is for two million pounds, give or take a few pounds on the exchange. A few days later, Leo Freeman, just returned from a trip in America, is apparently forced to sell his holdings, for two million pounds. Could there be a connection? Who knows? Would this bear scrutiny?'

'I don't know what you're talking about – and you've gone far enough, more than far enough. Now leave.'

'Yes I'll leave, and I'll leave you with a last thought. If there is no take-over battle, there will probably be no scrutiny. If I were in your position, I would release five per cent of my holding in Calco each week until it was all disposed of – at whatever price – then quietly walk away.'

Sarah showed little surprise at Simon's hypothesis.

She was, she said, prepared to believe that Raj would go to any lengths he considered he could get away with.

'Yes, well, I'm afraid that this time his judgement is faulty,' said Simon. 'That's the trouble with arrogance – it leads to underestimation of other people's abilities.'

'But he must be mad to get involved in those kinds of deals, with those kinds of people. If you tuck them up, they don't hang about waiting for solicitors to issue a High Court summons on their behalf.'

'No. Well, we shall see. Meanwhile, I suggest you buy Calco shares. Wait until you see them start dropping, then carry on until I tell you to stop – and be discreet. I didn't tell you – all right? At least that will be some vindication for Leo. How is he, by the way? Have you heard?'

'Quite recently.' She smiled. 'It's extraordinary, really – he's written a few times and I can only believe that he wrote the letters because I know his writing so well. He seems to have utterly changed. He's living out in the middle of nowhere and loving it. He's just as enthusiastic as he ever was, but now it's for fishing and spotting eagles, and Navajo crafts. I've no idea what he's living on, or what his plans are, but I hope I'm going to be able to see him in the States this spring. My young man might have an assignment in LA and he wants me along to keep his bed warm.'

The view of Raju Kalianji's front door was slightly obscured by two thickly leaved rhododendron branches. Otherwise, the fifty yards between the gunman and the spot where his target would emerge were uninterrupted. The smoothly mown lawns and the flower-beds, neat to the point of blandness, glittered with the evidence of an early morning shower. A lone thrush hopped across the grass, stopping from time to time to stab at his breakfast. The man stood waiting in the bushes. He had barely moved since he had arrived in darkness two hours before. He glanced at his watch – 7.55 – and his pulse quickened a little as he crouched to check his weapon. The movement caused a stir in the enveloping shrubs. The gunman swore softly as a blackbird fled, panicking and loudly squawking. He picked up his rifle, an M-16 American assault weapon, light and very accurate. Gingerly, to avoid any click, he inserted the magazine. The .223 softnose bullets had a concavity in the copper heads so that, when they made high-velocity contact with a fleshy target, they would flatten and produce a cone-shaped area of destruction.

Raju Kalianji habitually emerged from his house at eight o'clock. On most days, he drove himself to work, and a pale cream Rolls-Royce Silver Spirit was parked six yards from the front door. A man in a white jacket, presumably some kind of servant, appeared from around the side of the house. He walked over to the car, climbed in and started the engine, then re-emerged with a chamois cloth and wiped the rain from all the windows.

The man in the bushes, not for the first time, knelt on one knee on the damp, leafy ground. On the other, he rested his left elbow, and raised his rifle. He put his eye to the telescopic sight and focused on one of the neo-Georgian pillars that framed the entrance to the house.

The manservant had disappeared. The gunman didn't move. He had waited a long time for this, and a few more minutes of immobility were quite bearable.

He was completely prepared when the front door suddenly opened.

Raju Kalianji took two steps out and paused momentarily to sniff the air and look at the sky.

Before his brain had an opportunity to register the sharp crack, it was leaving the back of his shattered skull. The assassin saw a small red circle in his victim's forehead, above wide-open, unmoving, eyes.

The body inside the finely cut, impeccably pressed suit seemed to deflate. It crumbled slowly to the ground.

A thin, satisfied smile spread across the face of the man in the rhododendrons. Quickly but calmly he picked among the dead leaves for the spent shell, found it, put it in his pocket, stood and scuffled a booted foot over the patch of ground where he had crouched. He retrieved a large Burberry trenchcoat from a branch where he had hung it earlier. He tucked the rifle by his side and put on the coat. Then he slipped with unobtrusive rustling to the garden gate through which he had passed a couple of hours before. Out on the wide empty pavement of Winnington Road, he walked briskly north, down to the A1 at Lyttleton Road, which was thick with traffic heading for the City. He crossed over at the bottom of Bishops Avenue, and joined a small queue of people waiting for a bus. It was seven minutes since he had pulled the trigger of the weapon whose butt still nestled in his armpit.

Simon heard the news an hour later on his car radio. He drove straight to Winnington Road.

Reena and her parents sat in baffled silence in the elegant drawing-room. Detectives, police photographers and ballistics experts swarmed around the house and grounds.

Raj's body still lay where it had fallen, a patch of congealed blood round his head. On the white door pillar, there was a large messy hole, circled with a pattern of more splattered blood.

Paul sat upstairs, holding his grandmother's hand. She was rigid with grief.

The chief inspector was surprised at a Home Office minister taking such a personal interest, but he gave him all the information he could. Simon tried to console the family. They silently nodded their gratitude, and he used his influence to have the corpse removed and cleared up as soon and as thoroughly as possible.

He was just climbing into his car to leave when Sarah arrived. He stopped her from going into the house. 'There's nothing you can do, believe me, and it's very nasty. Reena's shattered, of course, but her parents are there. Leave her for a couple of days.'

Sarah frowned and glanced towards the house, then shrugged. 'Okay. If you say so.'

'I do, but as you're here, can we go somewhere and talk?'

Sarah followed him up the drive in her car, and down to Hampstead, where Simon pulled up beside one of the quieter pubs.

When they were sitting with a couple of large drinks, Simon spoke first. 'Though it's a horrible and messy way to die, I'm afraid I can't find it in me to feel any regret; there is a sort of justice to it.'

'Do you have any idea who did it?'

'I have a few theories, but as yet they're far too vague to bother the police with them.'

'What about Reena? I mean, you must feel sorry for her. She's a good woman.'

'Yes, she is. Of course I do. She never had anything to do with Raj's skulduggery. She had no influence in his business affairs, and when it comes down to it, she didn't have any say in choosing him as a husband. I think she had a notion of some of the things he was up to and I'm sure she didn't approve, especially of what he did to Leo.'

Sarah leaned forward, suddenly excited.

'Do you think this situation might give Leo a chance to recoup some of his losses?'

'If I can persuade Reena – yes. As a matter of fact, I've already laid the foundations of a come-back. Before Leo went away, he gave me his power of attorney – really to deal with any family matters or any residual affairs of Alison's. Using that power of attorney, I instructed his stockbrokers to start buying modest parcels of Calco stock. I only hope that he's got the money to pay for them. You see, for very different reasons than today's events, I thought Raj's days at Calco were numbered. Of course, as of now there is still a substantial amount of stock in Raj's name, and I'm pretty certain that Reena will now control it. If I can persuade her she owes it to Leo to bring him back, and that anyway it's the only way of protecting Calco from being gobbled up on the cheap by Bridelta, then I think we might expect Leo to be back and filling his rightful role before too long. The only question is, would he want to come back? Is he ready for it?'

'I don't know – I honestly haven't a clue. Like I told you last week, he seems very content and completely together. I guess it depends on how it's put to him. He certainly won't be interested in charitable gestures.' She thought for a minute. 'Maybe if it was put to him on the basis that Reena needed his help – and isn't that the truth, after all?'

Leo shook his head with amazement. Then, smiling at Gita, he held open the door of the large, rustic sitting-room, and beckoned her through it. 'You'd better come in and sit down and tell me all about it.' He put a light to the log fire. It quickly blazed up and served to dispel the evening chill of the early spring.

Leo was still grappling with the incongruity of this intrusion by his other life into the secluded peace of the mountains. He asked Gita if she wanted a drink, and called the maid to bring some tea for her.

'What's happened, Gita? It must be something cataclysmic to get you out here.'

Silently, Gita opened her bag and handed Leo a small bundle of press-cuttings. He unfolded the first, the front page of a tabloid daily a few days old.

Next to the headline 'INDIAN TYCOON SHOT BY HIT MAN', there was a head and shoulders photograph of Raj, looking thoughtful, prudent, trustworthy. There followed a speculative, scantily informed report of the assassination, and a simplified, inaccurate charting of Raj's commercial career. The wealth and glamorous lifestyle of the victim was stressed; testimonies to the soundness of his character and the correctness of his activities had been elicited from plausibly authoritative sources.

Leo was dumbfounded, unable and unwilling to accept the varied emotions which the news evoked in him. He sat down and read carefully through all the other newspaper reports, but they told him nothing more than the first had done.

For several minutes he didn't speak. He stared at the flames jumping from the logs. Gita sat back on the deep sofa, relaxed, with her legs stretched out and an expectant smile on her lips.

Eventually, Leo turned to her. 'I'm very sorry for Reena. Why has she sent you here?'

Gita's smile widened. 'You know why, don't you? By asking me to come, she's shown that she trusts you. Do you remember the last time we met?'

Leo turned his eyes back towards the fire. 'I'm not proud of a lot of things I've done, and that incident sparked off a long sequence of events, even the reason for my being in this place now.' He waved an arm round the room. 'Still, I guess it provided a valuable part of your education

501

'– you look pretty much in control of your own life now.'

'You may think that's a good thing,' she replied, 'but my parents don't. And if you don't mind my saying so, Leo, you look as if you have learned a few lessons.'

Leo grinned. 'No, I don't mind you saying so. But now, tell me how Reena is.'

Gita became serious. 'When the man died who had been the focal point of her life since she was a young teenage girl, it was impossible for her not to be sad, whatever kind of man he was. But Leo, we don't expect you to be sad – we know what he did to you.' She paused. 'In a way, you helped him though, didn't you?'

Leo nodded reflectively. 'You mean by being arrogant as a pig and stubborn as a mule? Yes – I made it easy for him.' For a while there was only the sound of the thick pine logs crackling and spitting in the fire. 'Why have you come to see me?'

'To ask you to help in protecting Reena's financial position . . . and to give you justice.' Gita looked at Leo from under long lashes, and a grin spread across her face. 'It's funny isn't it? – me being here to tell you. You know, after that time you took me to the Rainbow Room, my family was furious; they kept me up for hours interrogating me, trying to find out what I'd been doing. They just wouldn't believe that I'd only got a bit drunk. Anyway, they kept me under lock and key, practically, after that – and you became my sort of fantasy hero. The odd thing is, I didn't really like you.' She became more serious. 'But you've changed. Sarah said you had, and I can see it. Don't you think you are wasting yourself hidden away out here?'

'Let me assure you,' said Leo slowly, 'I haven't been wasting my time out here.'

He studied Gita for a while, then walked over to look out at the clear-skied dusk, the gently moving trees on the mountainside, the young moon just appearing over the black peaks to the east.

'Okay – I'll come back. We'll leave tomorrow.'

502

Leo did not go to India for the funeral. He had seen the mourning party aboard their plane and had driven back to his new office overlooking the Thames at Bankside.

He shook off the gloom that the scene at the airport had engendered and got down to the business of getting to know all Calco's activities and personnel. He was impressed. It was the most formidable set-up, and Raj had only employed Grade A people to run it.

Leo had been inviting the directors and managers of various subsidiaries and departments to lunch with him each day in the board dining-room. They had all left these lunches unanimous in their view that the alarming reputation which had preceded their new chief executive was ill-founded.

Leo glanced at his diary to see who he was having lunch with that day: Laura Mansell-Evans, director of Group PR.

He was wondering what this person did and how well she did it when she arrived.

And Leo was thrown momentarily off balance.

Long, dark-stockinged legs emanated from a skirt just above her knees, a black skirt, not too tight and with a full, beige silk blouse tucked into it. Above this, a long neck, a face of classic features and a strong chin. A crop of short black hair added to the impression of alertness and knowingness in her clear blue eyes.

'Ms Mansell-Evans, I presume.'

'Good morning, Mr Freeman.'

'Leo, please,' said Leo.

'Laura, please,' said Laura.

He couldn't remember when he had last enjoyed a meal so much. Whichever way he looked at her, Laura was impressive. She was very good company, and quite masterly at her job. This was, Leo thought, because she liked and understood people, had a broad mind and a sense of humour.

Early on, Leo asked her what immediate results she was getting. She produced a folder and took out a cutting from that morning's *Times* Business News.

'The money scribblers are still trying to decide whether

you're the death-knell or the new Messiah for Calco. The improved share price and the retreat of the Bridelta raiding party seem to be tipping the balance in favour of the new Messiah theory. We've been very careful not to push too hard; these chaps like to think they've reached their own conclusions.'

Leo grinned. He had enjoyed the press's reaction to his reappearance. In the old days he would probably have been issuing writs. Laura had arranged for him to meet two journalists who should dispel most lingering doubts in their columns the following Sunday and Leo appreciated the choice she had made.

He could hardly believe they had been in the dining-room for an hour and a half when Laura excused herself for another meeting. He felt a distinct disappointment when she had gone.

A week after the funeral party returned from Delhi, there was an Extraordinary General Meeting of the shareholders of Calco. Leo's appointment as group chief executive was ratified. He was also proposed and accepted as chairman of the Group's main board.

Afterwards, there was an informal board meeting to which Simon Riley, though not a board member, was invited. He announced that he had it from the horse's mouth that Beefy Balfour had retired licking his wounds, and counting a small profit from his foray.

He had, Simon said, taken it with remarkable good nature. 'But don't be lulled into a sense of false security. He'll be back.'

When the meeting broke up, Leo and Simon sat on in the boardroom.

'Would you consider me extravagant,' asked Simon, 'if I suggested that today's events merited the opening of a bottle of Krug?'

'It'd be a shame to break with tradition completely, wouldn't it?' replied Leo, smiling slowly as he reached for the telephone. 'Could you have a bottle of Krug brought up to the boardroom,' he asked his secretary, 'and find Ms

504

Mansell-Evans and ask her if she'd be good enough to come to my office at about six. Thanks.'

'Working late tonight, Leo?' asked Simon.

'Not if I can help it.'

Simon laughed. Then Leo became more serious. 'You've still not really told me your theories about Raj's murder. I've thought of a lot of possibilities, but none of them very plausible.'

'Well, my theories are based on my own observations over the last few years and on information I've been able to obtain in my official capacity in the Home Office. It would be quite improper for me to divulge it to anyone, but there is one lead that whittles it down to maybe half a million suspects. They found a footprint in a flower-bed, which indicates that the gunman was wearing a size ten western boot, with a riding heel, made by Justin Boots of El Paso. Do you think you can whittle down the list of suspects still further?'

Leo was astonished. 'Ross? Why the hell should Ross want to kill Raj? I didn't even know they knew each other.' He stared at Simon in bewilderment, then had a sudden thought. 'Or is it just a crazy coincidence – someone wanted Raj shot, and hired Ross?' Then he shook his head. 'No. Ross may not have been all he pretended to be, but I don't think he would sink so low as to offer his services as a gunman . . . or wasn't it Ross?'

'Oh, yes,' said Simon. '*I* don't think there's any doubt it was Ross, and he certainly knew Raj. One of your weak points is, or at least was, the capacity to ignore things happening under your own nose, to imagine you were immune from becoming one of the world's mugs. But you did. You were well and truly conned, and that's why Raj is dead. That and his own greed. After his men flew away with your two million quid . . .'

'What? The Colombians?'

'They weren't Colombians,' Simon laughed. 'Anyway, Ross never got his half of the proceeds. Extraordinarily enough, Raj must have thought he could get away with it. I suppose he had never seen a cowboy movie, and didn't

505

anticipate Ross's reactions to a deeply wounded sense of honour – not to mention an unpaid million quid. So, Raj got his comeuppance, and you've got your business back. A magnificent irony, wouldn't you say, particularly when you consider the quality of his caretaker management?'

He looked quizzically at Leo, whose smile widened, and broke into incredulous laughter. Simon joined him. Their mirth built to a crescendo, as the sheer absurdity of the situation overwhelmed them.

Eventually, Leo wiped a tear from his eye. He picked up the champagne bottle and refilled their glasses. 'I give you a toast,' he announced, still laughing. 'To Ross Blackwell!'

Leo's secretary had left at six sharp, so his concentration on the market reports in front of him was interrupted by a knock on the office door.

He looked up and felt his body tense in anticipation. 'Come in,' he called huskily.

'Good evening, Leo.' Laura strode into his office and stood in front of his desk. 'You wanted to see me?'

'Oh yes.' Leo feigned vagueness. 'There was something I wanted to ask you – something rather important.'

'Yes?'

'Yes. Will you have dinner with me tonight?'

'Work?'

'No.'

'Then, yes. I'd be delighted.'

'Great, I'll pick you up at eight.'

'I'll be ready and waiting,' she said, and swung out of the office.

He watched the buttocks at the top of her long legs sway rhythmically beneath the loosely clinging skirt. He smiled and did not try to stop the adrenaline surging around his system.

And from somewhere up above, he heard Alison. 'Go to it, Leo – you've earned it!'